MURDER ON CUE

STAGE, SCREEN, AND RADIO FAVORITES

MURDER ON CUE

STAGE, SCREEN, AND RADIO FAVORITES

Stories from *Ellery Queen's Mystery Magazine*
Edited by Eleanor Sullivan

WALKER AND COMPANY
NEW YORK

Originally published as *Ellery Queen's Media Favorites.*

All the characters and events portrayed in this story are fictitious.

First published in hardcover in the United States of America in 1989
by Walker Publishing Company, Inc.

Published simultaneously in Canada by Thomas Allen & Son
Canada, Limited, Markham, Ontario

Library of Congress Cataloging-in-Publication Data

Murder on cue : stage, screen, and radio favorites / edited by Eleanor Sullivan.
p. cm.—(Stories from Ellery Queen mystery magazine)
ISBN 0-8027-5731-6
1. Detective and mystery stories. American. 2. Detective and mystery stories, English. I. Sullivan, Eleanor. II. Series.
PS648.D4M875 1989 88-31185
813'.0872'08—dc19 CIP

Printed in the United States of America

10 9 8 7 6 5 4 3 2 1

Acknowledgments

Grateful acknowledgment is hereby made for permission to include the following:

What You Been Up To Lately? by George Baxt, copyright © 1980 by Davis Publications, Inc., reprinted by permission of the author.

Nothing Short of Highway Robbery by Lawrence Block, copyright © 1977 by Davis Publications, Inc., reprinted by permission of the author.

Backward, Turn Backward by Dorothy Salisbury Davis, copyright 1954, renewed © 1982 by Dorothy Salisbury Davis, reprinted by permission of McIntosh & Otis, Inc.

Watch for It by Joe Gores, copyright © 1973 by Mystery Writers of America, reprinted by permission of the author.

Sauce for the Goose by Patricia Highsmith, copyright © 1972 by Patricia Highsmith, reprinted by permission of the author.

The Theft from the Onyx Pool by Edward D. Hoch, copyright © 1967 by Edward D. Hoch, reprinted by permission of the author.

One Way Out by Clark Howard, copyright © 1965 by Davis Publications, Inc., reprinted by permission of the author.

A Man with a Fortune by Peter Lovesey, copyright © 1980 by Peter Lovesey, reprinted by permission of John Farquharson, Ltd.

The Letter by W. Somerset Maugham, copyright © 1924 by W. Somerset Maugham, renewed, reprinted by permission of A. P. Watt, Ltd.

CONTENTS

INTRODUCTION ix
Eleanor Sullivan

THE LETTER 1
W. Somerset Maugham

WATCH FOR IT 35
Joe Gores

A PRESENT FOR PATRICIA 45
Ruth Rendell

NABOTH'S VINEYARD 55
Melville Davisson Post

THE BOILER 69
Julian Symons

ANGEL FACE 81
Cornell Woolrich

NOTHING SHORT OF HIGHWAY ROBBERY 107
Lawrence Block

A MAN WITH A FORTUNE 119
Peter Lovesey

THE THEFT FROM THE ONYX POOL 133
Edward D. Hoch

SAUCE FOR THE GOOSE 145
Patricia Highsmith

THE ADVENTURE OF THE GOOD SAMARITAN 159
Ellery Queen

BACKWARD, TURN BACKWARD 175
Dorothy Salisbury Davis

THE MEMORY EXPERT 201
Henry Slesar

THE RED-HEADED LEAGUE 213
Sir Arthur Conan Doyle

WHAT YOU BEEN UP TO LATELY? 237
George Baxt

THE GHOST OF JOHN HOLLING 245
Edgar Wallace

ONE WAY OUT 257
Clark Howard

OWEN WINGRAVE 273
Henry James

THE WISDOM OF EVE 309
Mary Orr

INTRODUCTION

In the movie *All About Eve,* Margo Channing (Bette Davis) watches her nemesis, Eve Harrington (Anne Baxter), as she leaves the Cub Room of the Stork Club and she says, "There goes Eve. Eve evil, little Miss Evil."

With the exception of an original radio play by Ellery Queen written for the popular nineteen-forties' radio series *The Adventures of Ellery Queen,* this new Ellery Queen anthology consists of short stories that were later adapted for other media. The history of "The Wisdom of Eve" by Mary Orr is both typical and atypical. The story first appeared in the May 1946 issue of *Cosmopolitan* and was then adapted for radio. Three years later, James Fisher, then head of Twentieth Century-Fox's story department, sent copies to the studio's various contracted producers, writers, and directors. It attracted the attention of Joseph L. Mankiewicz, who began writing his famous screenplay, using the working title *Best Performance,* in the fall of 1949. He would later direct the movie as well.

The greatest deviation Mankiewicz made from Miss Orr's story was in the character of the older actress, not simply in changing her name from Margola Cranston but in altering her happily married state to that of unhappily unmarried. Well past forty and happily married were exactly what he did *not* want the actress to be: "I complicated and compounded her problem by having her—at age forty—in love with Bill, her director. Another curve I threw the poor woman was to make Bill eight years younger than she."

It is interesting to see what does, and does not, happen to fiction in its transition to stage, radio, cinema, and/or television. When Lawrence Block's "Nothing Short of Highway Robbery" was adapted by Luther Murdoch for the Anglia Television series *Tales of the Unexpected,* the two brothers, Vernon and Newt, became a young married couple. Perhaps when an author adapts his or her own work, such changes are less likely to occur. When Henry James made a play of "Owen Wingrave," Bernard Shaw tried unsuccessfully to convince him he should change the ending, but in his introduction to *The Henry James Reader* (Scribners), Leon Edel explains why James thought Shaw's suggested ending was too far removed from the basic intention of the story—indeed too far removed from the name he'd given his central character—and so it remained intact.

Some of the stories in this collection have been much adapted. Arthur Conan Doyle's "The Red-Headed League," for example, has been, among other things, a 1932 movie with Clive Brook and Reginald Owen, a Sherlock Holmes *Mystery!* episode with Jeremy Brett and Roger Hammond, and (as of this writing) a musical playing at New York's Theaterworks/U.S.A., with book by John Forster, Greer Woodward, and Rick Cummins.

Others of these stories were adapted for radio—in America, England, France, and South Africa—and more than half have been produced on TV, most notably on *Tales of the Unexpected* and on the various Alfred Hitchcock television presentations. Melville Davisson Post's "Naboth's Vineyard" played on Broadway under the title *Signature* in 1945—twenty-seven years after its first publication as a short story. Five stories were made into feature films—"The Letter" (which was also an extremely successful play) twice, first in 1929 with Jeanne Eagels as Mrs. Crosbie and Herbert Marshall as Hammond, then in 1940 (directed by William Wyler) with Bette Davis playing Mrs. Crosbie and Herbert Marshall this time cast as Crosbie.

And so we have both Bette Davis and Jeanne Eagels bringing W. Somerset Maugham's haunted woman to life in performances eleven years apart—and then another character Bette Davis was to portray ten years later saying, in "The Wisdom of Eve": "Clem insisted that I come down to the theater and give Eve some suggestions. By this time I was so curious to see this future Jeanne Eagels that I consented."

Both Edgar Wallace and Cornell Woolrich contributed greatly to the movies of the thirties and forties. They are represented here by Wallace's "The Ghost of John Holling"—which became the 1934 film, *Mystery Liner* (Monogram), with Noah Beery and Astrid Allwyn—and Woolrich's "Angel Face" (published also under the titles "Face Work" and "One's Night in New York"), which was released by Columbia under the title *Convicted* and starred Rita Hayworth, Charles Quigley, and Marc Lawrence. (The special contribution of Cornell Woolrich's short fiction to radio and television is described in meticulous detail in Francis M. Nevins's collection of Woolrich stores, *Nightwebs.* And there was, incidentally, a 1952 Otto Preminger movie titled *Angel Face,* starring Jean Simmons and Robert Mitchum, but it wasn't based on the Woolrich story.)

It is interesting to note in any anthology of stories selected from different decades of publication how each one, recent or not so recent, reflects the flavor, mores, fashions, economics, and biases of the time in which it was set or written. Depending on the story's point of view—or POV, as film writers shorthand it—the reader is reminded of how much better the world has become in some ways, and how much worse in others.

Professional writers recognize the integral collaboration of their readers. With the growth of the performing arts, especially on film, they increasingly recognize the further collaboration with other artists their work may enjoy after initial publication. Later this year there will be a sequel to this Ellery Queen anthology in which we will again celebrate the long life of the short story—and the interesting process of art imitating art.

E.S.

W. SOMERSET MAUGHAM

THE LETTER

Outside on the quay the sun beat fiercely. A stream of motors, lorries, and buses, private cars and hirelings, sped up and down the crowded thoroughfare, and every chauffeur blew his horn. Rickshaws threaded their nimble path amid the throng, and the panting coolies found breath to yell at one another; coolies, carrying heavy bales, sidled along with their quick jog-trot and shouted to the passersby to make way. Itinerant vendors proclaimed their wares.

Singapore is the meeting-place of a hundred peoples, and men of all colors—black Tamils, yellow Chinks, brown Malays, Armenians, Jews, and Bengalis—called to one another in raucous tones. But inside the office of Messrs. Ripley, Joyce & Naylor it was pleasantly cool; it was dark after the dusty glitter of the street and agreeably quiet after its unceasing din. Mr. Joyce sat in his private room, at the table, with an electric fan turned full on him. He was leaning back, his elbows on the arms of the chair, with the tips of the outstretched fingers of one hand resting neatly against the tips of the outstretched fingers of the other. His gaze rested on the battered volumes of the Law Reports which stood on a long shelf in front of him. On the top of a cupboard were square boxes of japanned tin on which were painted the names of various clients.

There was a knock at the door.

"Come in."

A Chinese clerk, very neat in his white ducks, opened it.

"Mr. Crosbie is here, sir."

He spoke beautiful English, accenting each word with precision, and Mr. Joyce had often wondered at the extent of his vocabulary. Ong Chi Seng was a Cantonese, and he had studied law at Gray's Inn. He was spending a year or two with Messrs. Ripley, Joyce & Naylor in order to prepare himself for practice on his own account. He was industrious, obliging, and of exemplary character.

"Show him in," said Mr. Joyce.

He rose to shake hands with his visitor and asked him to sit down. The light fell on him as he did so. The face of Mr. Joyce remained in shadow. He was by nature a silent man, and now he looked at Robert Crosbie for quite a minute without speaking. Crosbie was a big fellow, well over six feet high, with broad shoulders, and muscular. He was a rubber-planter, hard with the constant exercise of walking over the estate and with the tennis which was his relaxation when the day's work was over. He was deeply sunburned. His hairy hands, his feet in clumsy boots, were enormous, and Mr. Joyce found himself thinking that a blow of that great fist would easily kill the fragile Tamil. But there was no fierceness in his blue eyes. They were confiding and gentle, and his face, with its big, undistinguished features, was open and frank, and honest. But at this moment it bore a look of deep distress. It was drawn and haggard.

"You look as though you hadn't had much sleep the last night or two," said Mr. Joyce.

"I haven't."

Mr. Joyce noticed now the old felt hat, with its broad double brim, which Crosbie had placed on the table, and then his eyes traveled to the khaki shorts he wore, showing his red, hairy thighs, the tennis shirt open at the neck, without a tie, and the dirty khaki jacket with the ends of the sleeves turned up. He looked as though he had just come in from a long tramp among the rubber trees. Mr. Joyce gave a slight frown.

"You must pull yourself together, you know. You must keep your head."

"Oh, I'm all right."

"Have you seen your wife today?"

"No, I'm to see her this afternoon. You know, it's a damned shame that they have arrested her."

"I think they had to do that," Mr. Joyce answered in his level, soft tone.

"I should have thought they'd have let her out on bail."

"It's a very serious charge."

"It is damnable. She did what any decent woman would do in her place. Only nine women out of ten wouldn't have the pluck. Leslie's the best woman in the world. She wouldn't hurt a fly.

Why, hang it all, man, I've been married to her for twelve years—do you think I don't know her? God, if I'd got hold of the man I'd have wrung his neck. I'd have killed him without a moment's hesitation. So would you."

"My dear fellow, everybody's on your side. No one has a good word to say for Hammond. We're going to get her off. I don't suppose either the assessors or the judge will go into court without having already made up their minds to bring in a verdict of Not Guilty."

"The whole thing's a farce!" said Crosbie violently. "She ought never to have been arrested in the first place. It's terrible, after all the poor girl's gone through, to subject her to the ordeal of a trial. There's not a soul I've met since I've been in Singapore, man or woman, who hasn't told me that Leslie was absolutely justified. I think it's awful to keep her in prison all these weeks."

"The law is the law. After all, she confesses that she killed the man. It is terrible, and I'm dreadfully sorry both for you and for her."

"I don't matter a hang," interrupted Crosbie.

"But the fact remains that murder has been committed, and in a civilized community a trial is inevitable."

"Is it murder to exterminate noxious vermin? She shot him as she would have shot a mad dog."

Mr. Joyce leaned back again in his chair and once more placed the tips of his ten fingers together. The little construction he formed looked like the skeleton of a roof. He was silent for a moment. "I should be wanting in my duty as your legal adviser," he said at last, in an even voice, looking at his client with his cool brown eyes, "if I did not tell you that there is one point which causes me just a little anxiety. If your wife had only shot Hammond once, the whole thing would be absolutely plain sailing. Unfortunately, she fired six times."

"Her explanation is perfectly simple. In the circumstances, anyone would have done the same."

"I daresay," said Mr. Joyce, "and of course I think the explanation is very reasonable. But it's no good closing our eyes to the facts. It's always a good plan to put yourself in another man's place, and I can't deny that if I were prosecuting for the Crown that's the point on which I could center my inquiry."

"My dear fellow, that's perfectly idiotic."

Mr. Joyce shot a sharp glance at Robert Crosbie. The shadow of a smile hovered over his shapely lips. Crosbie was a good fellow, but he could hardly be described as intelligent.

"I daresay it's of no importance," answered the lawyer. "I just thought it was a point worth mentioning. You haven't got very long to wait now, and when it's all over I recommend you go off somewhere with your wife on a trip and forget all about it. Even though we are almost dead certain to get an acquittal, a trial of that sort is anxious work and you'll both want a rest."

For the first time, Crosbie smiled, and his smile strangely changed his face. You forgot the uncouthness and saw only the goodness of his soul.

"I think I shall want it more than Leslie. She's borne up wonderfully. By God, there's a plucky little woman for you."

"Yes, I've been very much struck by her self-control," said the lawyer. "I should never have guessed that she was capable of such determination."

His duties as her counsel had made it necessary for him to have a good many interviews with Mrs. Crosbie since her arrest. Though things had been made as easy as could be for her, the fact remained that she was in jail, awaiting her trial for murder, and it would not have been surprising if her nerves had failed her. She appeared to bear her ordeal with composure. She read a great deal, took such exercise as was possible, and by favor of the authorities worked at the pillow lace which had always formed the entertainment of her long hours of leisure.

When Mr. Joyce saw her, she was neatly dressed in cool, fresh, simple frocks, her hair was carefully arranged, and her nails were manicured. Her manner was collected. She was able even to jest upon the little inconveniences of her position. There was something casual about the way in which she spoke of the tragedy which suggested to Mr. Joyce that only her good breeding prevented her from finding something a trifle ludicrous in a situation which was eminently serious. It surprised him, for he had never thought that she had a sense of humor.

He had known her off and on for a good many years. When

she paid visits to Singapore, she generally came to dine with his wife and himself, and once or twice she had passed a weekend with them at their bungalow by the sea. His wife had spent a fortnight with her on the estate and had met Geoffrey Hammond several times. The two couples had been on friendly, if not on intimate, terms, and it was on this account that Robert Crosbie had rushed over to Singapore immediately after the catastrophe and begged Mr. Joyce to take charge of his unhappy wife's defense.

The story she told him the first time he saw her she had never varied in the smallest detail. She told it as coolly then, a few hours after the tragedy, as she told it now. She told it connectedly, in a level, even voice, and her only sign of confusion was when a slight color came into her cheeks as she described one or two of its incidents.

She was the last woman to whom one would have expected such a thing to happen. She was in the early thirties, a fragile creature, neither short nor tall, and graceful rather than pretty. Her wrists and ankles were very delicate, but she was extremely thin and you could see the bones of her hands through the white skin, and the veins were large and blue. Her face was colorless, slightly sallow, and her lips were pale. You didn't notice the color of her eyes. She had a great deal of light-brown hair and it had a slight, natural wave. It was the sort of hair that with a little touching-up would have been very pretty, but you couldn't imagine that Mrs. Crosbie would think of resorting to any such device. She was a quiet, pleasant, unassuming woman. Her manner was engaging, and if she was not very popular it was because she suffered from a certain shyness. This was comprehensible enough, for the planter's life is lonely, and in her own house, with people she knew, she was in her quiet way charming. Mrs. Joyce, after her fortnight's stay, had told her husband that Leslie was a very agreeable hostess. There was more in her, she said, than people thought, and when you came to know her you were surprised how much she had read and how entertaining she could be.

She was the last woman in the world to commit murder.

* * *

Mr. Joyce dismissed Robert Crosbie with such reassuring words as he could find and, once more alone in his office, turned over the pages of the brief. But it was a mechanical action, for all its details were familiar to him. The case was the sensation of the day, and it was discussed in all the clubs, at all the dinner tables up and down the peninsula from Singapore to Penang.

The facts that Mrs. Crosbie gave were simple. Her husband had gone to Singapore on business and she was alone for the night. She dined by herself, late, at a quarter to nine, and after dinner sat in the sitting room, working at her lace. It opened onto the verandah. There was no one in the bungalow, for the servants had retired to their own quarters at the back of the compound. She was surprised to hear a step on the gravel path in the garden, a booted step which suggested a white man rather than a native, for she had not heard a motor drive up and she could not imagine who could be coming to see her at that time of night. Someone ascended the few stairs that led up to the bungalow, walked across the verandah, and appeared at the door of the room in which she sat. At the first moment, she did not recognize the visitor. She sat with a shaded lamp and he stood with his back to the darkness.

"May I come in?" he said.

She did not recognize the voice.

"Who is it?" she asked. She worked with spectacles, and she took them off as she spoke.

"Geoff Hammond."

"Of course. Come in and have a drink."

She rose and shook hands with him cordially. She was a little surprised to see him, for though he was a neighbor neither she nor Robert had been lately on very intimate terms with him, and she had not seen him for some weeks. He was the manager of a rubber estate nearly eight miles from theirs and she wondered why he had chosen this late hour to come and see them.

"Robert's away," she said. "He had to go to Singapore for the night."

Perhaps he thought his visit called for some explanation, for he said: "I'm sorry. I felt rather lonely tonight, so I thought I'd come along and see how you were getting on."

"How on earth did you come? I never heard a car."

"I left it down the road. I thought you might both be in bed and asleep."

This was natural enough. The planter gets up at dawn in order to take the roll call of the workers, and soon after dinner he is glad to go to bed. Hammond's car was in point of fact found next day a quarter of a mile from the bungalow.

Since Robert was away, there was no whisky and soda in the room. Leslie didn't call the boy, since he was probably asleep, but fetched it herself. Her guest mixed himself a drink and filled his pipe.

Geoff Hammond had a host of friends in the colony. He was at this time in the late thirties, but he had come out as a lad. He had been one of the first to volunteer on the outbreak of war and had done very well. A wound in the knee caused him to be invalided out of the Army after two years, but he returned to the Federated Malay States with a D.S.O. and an M.C. He was one of the best billiard players in the colony. He had been a beautiful dancer and a fine tennis player, but, though able no longer to dance, and his tennis, with a stiff knee, was not so good as it had been, he had the gift of popularity and was universally liked. He was a tall, good-looking fellow, with attractive blue eyes and a fine head of black, curling hair. Old stagers said his only fault was that he was too fond of the girls, and after the catastrophe they shook their heads and vowed that they had always known this would get him into trouble.

He began now to talk to Leslie about the local affairs, the forthcoming races in Singapore, the price of rubber, and his chances of killing a tiger which had been lately seen in the neighborhood. She was anxious to finish by a certain date the piece of lace on which she was working, for she wanted to send it home for her mother's birthday, and so put on her spectacles again and drew toward her chair the little table on which stood the pillow.

"I wish you wouldn't wear those great horn-spectacles," he said. "I don't know why a pretty woman should do her best to look plain."

She was a trifle taken aback at this remark. He had never used that tone with her before. She thought the best thing was to make light of it.

"I have no pretensions to being a raving beauty, you know, and, if you ask me point-blank, I'm bound to tell you that I don't care two pins if you think me plain or not."

"I don't think you're plain. I think you're awfully pretty."

"Sweet of you," she answered ironically. "But in that case, I can only think you half-witted."

He chuckled. But he rose from his chair and sat down in another by her side. "You're not going to have the face to deny that you have the prettiest hands in the world," he said. He made a gesture as though to take one of them.

She gave him a little tap. "Don't be an idiot. Sit down where you were before and talk sensibly or I shall send you home."

He did not move. "Don't you know I'm awfully in love with you?" he said.

She remained quite cool. "I don't. I don't believe it for a minute, and even if it were true I don't want you to say it."

She was the more surprised at what he was saying, since during the seven years she had known him, he had never paid her any particular attention. When he came back from the war, they had seen a good deal of one another, and once when he was ill Robert had gone over and brought him back to their bungalow in his car. He had stayed with them then for a fortnight. But their interests were dissimilar and the acquaintance had never ripened into friendship. For the last two or three years, they had seen little of him. Now and then he came over to play tennis, now and then they met him at some planter's who was giving a party, but it often happened that they didn't set eyes on him for a month at a time.

Now he took another whisky and soda. Leslie wondered if he had been drinking before. There was something odd about him, and it made her a trifle uneasy. She watched him help himself with disapproval.

"I wouldn't drink any more if I were you," she said, good-humoredly still.

He emptied his glass and put it down. "Do you think I'm talking to you like this because I'm drunk?" he asked abruptly.

"That's the most obvious explanation, isn't it?"

"Well, it's a lie. I've loved you ever since I first knew you. I've held my tongue as long as I could, and now it's got to come out. I love you, I love you, I love you."

She rose and carefully put aside the pillow. "Goodnight," she said.

"I'm not going now."

At last she began to lose her temper. "But, you poor fool, don't you know I've never loved anyone but Robert, and if I didn't love Robert you're the last man I should care for."

"What do I care? Robert's away."

"If you don't go away this minute I shall call the boys and have you thrown out."

"They're out of earshot."

She was very angry now. She made a movement as though to go onto the verandah, from which the houseboy would certainly hear her, but he seized her arm.

"Let me go!" she cried furiously.

"Not much. I've got you now."

She opened her mouth and called, "Boy! Boy!" but with a quick gesture he put his hand over it. Then, before she knew what he was about, he had taken her in his arms and was kissing her passionately. She struggled, turning her lips away from his burning mouth. "No, no, no!" she cried. "Leave me alone! I won't!"

She grew confused about what happened then. All that had been said before she remembered accurately, but now his words assailed her ears through a mist of horror and fear. He seemed to plead for her love. He broke into violent protestations of passion. And all the time he held her in his tempestuous embrace. She was helpless, for he was a strong, powerful man and her arms were pinioned to her sides. Her struggles were unavailing and she felt herself growing weaker—she was afraid she would faint, and his hot breath on her face made her feel desperately sick. He kissed her mouth, her eyes, her cheeks, her hair. The pressure of his arms was killing her. He lifted her off her feet. She tried to kick him, but he only held her more closely. He was carrying her now. He wasn't speaking any more, but his face was pale and his eyes hot with desire. He was taking her into the bedroom. He was no longer a civilized man, but a savage. And as he ran, he stumbled against a table that was in the way. His stiff knee made him a little awkward on his feet, and with the burden of the woman in his arms he fell.

In a moment, she had snatched herself away from him and ran round the sofa. He was up in a flash and flung himself toward her. There was a revolver on the desk. She was not a nervous woman, but Robert was to be away for the night and she had meant to take it into her room when she went to bed. That was why it happened to be there. She was frantic with terror now. She didn't know what she was doing. She heard a report. She saw Hammond stagger. He gave a cry. He said something, she didn't know what. He lurched out of the room onto the verandah. She was in a frenzy now, she was beside herself. She followed him out, yes, that was it, she must have followed him out, though she remembered nothing of it, she followed, firing automatically shot after shot till the six chambers were empty. Hammond fell down on the floor of the verandah. He crumpled up into a bloody heap.

When the boys, startled by the reports, rushed up, they found her standing over Hammond with the revolver still in her hand, and Hammond lifeless. She looked at them for a moment without speaking. They stood in a frightened, huddled bunch. She let the revolver fall from her hand and without a word turned and went into the sitting room. They watched her go into her bedroom and turn the key in the lock. They dared not touch the dead body, but looked at it with terrified eyes, talking excitedly to one another in undertones. Then the head-boy collected himself—he had been with them for many years, he was Chinese and a level-headed fellow. Robert had gone into Singapore on his motorcycle and the car stood in the garage. He told the seis to get it out—they must go at once to the Assistant District Officer and tell him what had happened. He picked up the revolver and put it in his pocket.

The A.D.O., a man called Withers, lived on the outskirts of the nearest town, which was about thirty-five miles away. It took them an hour and a half to reach him. Everyone was asleep and they had to rouse the boys. Presently Withers came out and they told him their errand. The head-boy showed him the revolver in proof of what he said. The A.D.O. went into his room to dress, sent for his car, and in a little while was following them back along the deserted road.

The dawn was just breaking as he reached the Crosbies' bungalow. He ran up the steps of the verandah, and stopped short as he saw Hammond's body lying where he fell. He touched the face. It was quite cold.

"Where's mem?" he asked the house-boy.

The Chinese pointed to the bedroom. Withers went to the door and knocked. There was no answer. He knocked again. "Mrs. Crosbie!" he called.

"Who is it?"

"Withers."

There was another pause. Then the door was unlocked and slowly opened. Leslie stood before him. She had not been to bed and wore the tea-gown in which she had dined. She stood and looked silently at the A.D.O.

"Your house-boy fetched me," he said. "Hammond. What have you done?"

"He tried to rape me and I shot him."

"My God! I say, you'd better come out here. You must tell me exactly what happened."

"Not now. I can't. You must give me time. Send for my husband."

Withers was a young man, and he did not know exactly what to do in an emergency which was so out of the run of his duties. Leslie refused to say anything till at last Robert arrived. Then she told the two men the story, from which since then, though she had repeated it over and over again, she had never in the slightest degree diverged.

The point to which Mr. Joyce recurred was the shooting. As a lawyer, he was bothered that Leslie had fired not once but six times, and the examination of the dead man showed that four of the shots had been fired close to the body. One might almost have thought that when the man fell, she stood over him and emptied the contents of the revolver into him. She confessed that her memory, so accurate for all that had preceded, failed her here. Her mind was blank. It pointed to an uncontrollable fury, but uncontrollable fury was the last thing you would have expected from this quiet and demure woman. Mr. Joyce had known her a good many years and had always thought her an unemotional person. During the weeks that had passed since the tragedy, her composure had been amazing.

Mr. Joyce shrugged his shoulders. "The fact is, I suppose," he reflected, "that you can never tell what hidden possibilities of savagery there are in the most respectable of women." There was a knock at the door. "Come in."

The Chinese clerk entered and closed the door behind him. He closed it gently, with deliberation but decidedly, and advanced to the table at which Mr. Joyce was sitting.

"May I trouble you, sir, for a few words' private conversation?" he said.

The elaborate accuracy with which the clerk expressed himself always faintly amused Mr. Joyce, and now he smiled. "It's no trouble, Chi Seng," he replied.

"The matter on which I desire to speak to you, sir, is delicate and confidential."

"Fire away."

Mr. Joyce met his clerk's shrewd eyes. As usual, Ong Chi Seng was dressed in the height of local fashion. He wore very shiny patent-leather shoes and gay silk socks. In his black tie was a pearl-and-ruby pin, and on the fourth finger of his left hand a diamond ring. From the pocket of his neat white coat protruded a gold fountain pen and a gold pencil. He wore a gold wristwatch, and on the bridge of his nose invisible pince-nez. He gave a little cough.

"The matter has to do with the case R. v. Crosbie, sir."

"Yes?"

"A circumstance has come to my knowledge, sir, which seems to me to put a different complexion on it."

"What circumstance?"

"It has come to my knowledge, sir, that there is a letter in existence from the defendant to the unfortunate victim of the tragedy."

"I shouldn't be at all surprised. In the course of the last seven years, I have no doubt that Mrs. Crosbie often had occasion to write to Mr. Hammond." Mr. Joyce had a high opinion of his clerk's intelligence and his words were designed to conceal his thoughts.

"That is very probable, sir. Mrs. Crosbie must have communicated with the deceased frequently, to invite him to dine with her, for example, or to propose a tennis game. That was my first thought when the matter was brought to my notice. This letter, however, was written on the day of the late Mr. Hammond's death."

Mr. Joyce did not flicker an eyelash. He continued to look at Ong Chi Seng with the smile of faint amusement with which he generally talked to him. "Who has told you this?"

"The circumstances were brought to my knowledge, sir, by a fliend of mine."

Mr. Joyce knew better than to insist.

"You will no doubt recall, sir, that Mrs. Crosbie has stated that until the fatal night she had had no communication with the deceased for several weeks."

"Have you got the letter?"

"No, sir."

"What are its contents?"

"My fliend gave me a copy. Would you like to peruse it, sir?"

"I should."

Ong Chi Seng took from an inside pocket a bulky wallet. It was filled with papers, Singapore dollar notes, and cigarette cards. From the confusion he presently extracted a half sheet of thin notepaper and placed it before Mr. Joyce. The letter read as follows:

> "R. will be away for the night. I absolutely must see you. I shall expect you at eleven. I am desperate and if you don't come I won't answer for the consequences. Don't drive up.
>
> —L."

It was written in the flowing hand which the Chinese were taught at the foreign schools. The writing, so lacking in character, was oddly incongruous with the ominous words.

"What makes you think this note was written by Mrs. Crosbie?"

"I have every confidence in the veracity of my informant, sir," replied Ong Chi Seng. "And the matter can very easily be put to the proof. Mrs. Crosbie will no doubt be able to tell you at once whether she wrote such a letter or not."

Since the beginning of the conversation, Mr. Joyce hadn't taken his eyes off the respectful countenance of his clerk. He wondered now if he discerned in it a faint expression of mockery. "It is inconceivable that Mrs. Crosbie should have written such a letter," said Mr. Joyce.

"If that is your opinion, sir, the matter is of course ended. My fliend spoke to me on the subject only because he thought, as I was in your office, you might like to know of the existence of this letter before a communication was made to the Deputy Public Prosecutor."

"Who has the original?" asked Mr. Joyce sharply.

Ong Chi Seng made no sign that he perceived in this question and its manner a change of attitude. "You will remember, sir, no doubt, that after the death of Mr. Hammond it was discovered that he had had relations with a Chinese woman. The letter is at present in her possession."

That was one of the things which had turned public opinion most vehemently against Hammond. It came to be known that for several months he had had a Chinese woman living in his house.

For a moment, neither of them spoke. Indeed everything had been said and each understood the other perfectly.

"I'm obliged to you, Chi Seng. I will give the matter my consideration."

"Very good, sir. Do you wish me to make a communication to that effect to my fliend?"

"I daresay it would be as well if you kept in touch with him," Joyce answered with gravity.

"Yes, sir."

The clerk noiselessly left the room, shutting the door again with deliberation, and left Mr. Joyce to his reflections. He stared at the copy, in its neat, impersonal writing, of Leslie's letter. Vague suspicions troubled him. They were so disconcerting that he made an effort to put them out of his mind. There must be a simple explanation of the letter, and Leslie without doubt could give it at once, but, by heaven, an explanation was needed. He rose from his chair, put the letter in his pocket, and took his topee.

When he went out, Ong Chi Seng was busily writing at his desk. "I'm going out for a few minutes, Chi Seng," he said.

"Mr. George Reed is coming by appointment at twelve o'clock, sir. Where shall I say you've gone?"

Mr. Joyce gave him a thin smile. "You can say that you haven't the least idea."

But he knew perfectly well that Ong Chi Seng was aware that he was going to the jail. Though the crime had been committed in Belanda and the trial was to take place at Belanda Bharu, since there was in the jail there no convenience for the detention of a white woman Mrs. Crosbie had been brought to Singapore.

When she was led into the room in which he waited, she held out her thin, distinguished hand and gave him a pleasant smile. She was as ever neatly and simply dressed and her abundant, pale hair was arranged with care. "I wasn't expecting to see you this morning," she said graciously.

She might have been in her own house, and Mr. Joyce almost expected to hear her call the boy and tell him to bring the visitor a gin pahit.

"How are you?" he asked.

"I'm in the best of health, thank you." A flicker of amusement flashed across her eyes. "This is a wonderful place for a rest cure."

The attendant withdrew and they were left alone.

"Do sit down," said Leslie.

He took a chair. He didn't quite know how to begin. She was so cool that it seemed almost impossible to say to her that thing he had come to say. Though she was not pretty, there was something agreeable in her appearance. She had elegance, but it was the elegance of good breeding in which there was nothing of the artifice of society. You had only to look at her to know what sort of people she had and what kind of surroundings she had lived in. Her fragility gave her a singular refinement. It was impossible to associate her with the vaguest idea of grossness.

"I'm looking forward to seeing Robert this afternoon," she said in her good-humored, easy voice. It was a pleasure to hear her speak, her voice and her accent were so distinctive of her class. "Poor dear, it's been a great trial to his nerves. I'm thankful it'll all be over in a few days."

"It's only five days now."

"I know. Each morning when I awake I say to myself, 'one less.' " She smiled. "Just as I used to do at school and the holidays were coming."

"By the way, am I right in thinking that you had no communication whatever with Hammond for several weeks before the catastrophe?"

"I'm quite positive of that. The last time we met was at a tennis-party at the MacFarrens'. I don't think I said more than two words to him. They have the two courts, and we didn't happen to be in the same sets."

"And you hadn't written to him?"

"Oh, no."

"Are you quite sure of that?"

"Oh, quite," she answered with a little smile. "There was nothing I should write to him for except to ask him to dine or to play tennis, and I hadn't done either for months."

"At one time you'd been on fairly intimate terms with him. How did it happen that you'd stopped asking him to anything?"

Mrs. Crosbie shrugged her thin shoulders. "One gets tired of people. We hadn't anything very much in common. Of course, when he was ill, Robert and I did everything we could for him, but the last year or two he's been quite well and he was very popular. He had a good many calls on his time and there didn't seem to be any need to shower invitations upon him."

"Are you quite certain that was all?"

Mrs. Crosbie hesitated for a moment. "Well, I may just as well tell you. It had come to our ears that he was living with a Chinese woman, and Robert said he wouldn't have him in the house. I had seen her myself."

Mr. Joyce was sitting in a straight-backed armchair, resting his chin on his hand, and his eyes were fixed on Leslie. Was it his fancy that as she made this remark her black pupils were filled, for the fraction of a second, with a dull red light? The effect was startling. Mr. Joyce shifted in his chair. He placed the tips of his ten fingers together. He spoke very slowly, choosing his words.

"I think I should tell you that there is in existence a letter in your handwriting to Geoff Hammond."

He watched her closely. She made no movement, nor did her face change color, but she took a noticeable time to reply.

"In the past I've often sent him little notes to ask him to something or other, or to get me something when I knew he was going to Singapore."

"This letter asks him to come and see you because Robert was going to Singapore."

"That's impossible. I never did anything of the kind."

"You'd better read it for yourself."

He took it out of his pocket and handed it to her. She gave it a glance and with a smile of scorn handed it back to him. "That's not my handwriting."

"It's said to be an exact copy of the original."

She took it back and read the words now, and as she read a horrible change came over her. Her colorless face grew dreadful to look at. It turned green. The flesh seemed to fall away and her skin was tightly stretched over the bones. Her lips receded, showing her teeth, so that she had the appearance of making a grimace. She stared at Joyce with eyes that started from their sockets. He was looking now at a gibbering death's head.

"What does it mean?" she whispered. Her mouth was so dry that she could utter no more than a hoarse sound. It was no longer a human voice.

"That is for you to say," he answered.

"I didn't write it. I swear I didn't write it."

"Be very careful what you say. If the original is in your handwriting, it would be useless to deny it."

"It would be a forgery."

"It would be difficult to prove that. It would be easy to prove it was genuine."

A shiver passed through her lean body, but great beads of sweat stood on her forehead. She took a handkerchief from her bag and wiped the palms of her hands. She glanced at the letter again and gave Mr. Joyce a sidelong look. "It's not dated. If I had written it and forgotten all about it, it might have been written years ago. If you'll give me time, I'll try and remember the circumstances."

"I noticed there was no date. If this letter were in the hands of the prosecution, they would cross-examine the boys. They would soon find out whether someone took a letter to Hammond on the day of his death."

Mrs. Crosbie clasped her hands violently and swayed in her chair so that he thought she would faint. "I swear to you that I didn't write that letter."

Mr. Joyce was silent for a little while. He took his eyes from her distraught face and looked down on the floor, reflecting. "In these circumstances, we need not go into the matter further," he said slowly, at last breaking the silence. "If the possessor of this letter sees fit to place it in the hands of the prosecution you will be prepared."

His words suggested that he had nothing more to say to her, but he made no movement of departure. He waited. To himself he seemed to wait a very long time. He did not look at Leslie, but he was conscious that she sat very still. She made no sound.

At last it was he who spoke. "If you have nothing more to say to me, I think I'll be getting back to my office."

"What would anyone who read the letter be inclined to think that it meant?" she asked.

"He'd know that you had told a deliberate lie," answered Mr. Joyce sharply.

"When?"

"You have stated definitely that you had had no communication with Hammond for at least three months."

"The whole thing has been a terrible shock to me. The events of that dreadful night have been a nightmare. It's not very strange if one detail has escaped my memory."

"It would be very unfortunate, when your memory has reproduced so exactly every particular of your interview with Hammond, that you should have forgotten so important a point as that he came to see you in the bungalow on the night of his death at your express desire."

"I hadn't forgotten. After what happened, I was afraid to mention it. I thought none of you would believe my story if I admitted he'd come at my invitation. I daresay it was stupid of me, but I lost my head—and after I'd said once that I'd had no communication with Hammond, I was obliged to stick to it." By now, Leslie had recovered her admirable composure and she met Mr. Joyce's appraising glance with candor. Her gentleness was very disarming.

"You'll be required to explain, then, *why* you asked Hammond to come and see you when Robert was away for the night."

She turned her eyes full on the lawyer. He had been mistaken in thinking them insignificant. They were rather fine eyes, and unless he was mistaken they were bright now with tears. Her voice had a little break in it.

"It was a surprise I was preparing for Robert. His birthday is next month. I knew he wanted a new gun and you know I'm dreadfully stupid about sporting things. I wanted to talk to Geoff about it. I thought I'd get him to order it for me."

"Perhaps the terms of the letter are not very clear to your recollection. Will you have another look at it?"

"No, I don't want to," she said quickly.

"Does it seem to you the sort of letter a woman would write to a somewhat distant acquaintance because she wanted to consult him about buying a gun?"

"I daresay it's rather extravagant and emotional. I do express myself like that, you know. I'm quite prepared to admit it's very silly." She smiled. "And, after all, Geoff Hammond wasn't quite a distant acquaintance. When he was ill, I'd nursed him like a mother. I asked him to come when Robert was away because Robert wouldn't have him in the house."

Mr. Joyce was tired of sitting so long in the same position. He rose and walked once or twice up and down the room, choosing the words he proposed to say, then he leaned over the back of the chair in which he had been sitting. He spoke slowly in a tone of deep gravity. "Mrs. Crosbie, I want to talk to you very, very seriously. This case was comparatively plain sailing. There was only one point which seemed to me to require explanation. As far as I could judge, you had fired no less than four shots into Hammond when he was lying on the ground. It was hard to accept the possibility that a delicate, frightened, and habitually self-controlled woman, of gentle nurture and refined instincts, should have surrendered to an absolutely uncontrolled frenzy. But of course it was admissible. Although Geoffrey Hammond was much liked and on the whole thought highly of, I was prepared to prove that he was the sort of man who might be guilty of the crime which in justification of your act you accused him of. The fact, which was discovered after his death, that he had been living with a Chinese woman gave us something very definite to go on. That robbed him of any sympathy which might have been felt for him. We made up our minds to make use of the odium which such a connection cast upon him in the minds of all respectable people. I told your husband this morning that I was certain of an acquittal, and I wasn't just telling him that to give him heart. I do not believe the assessors would have left the court."

They looked into one another's eyes. Mrs. Crosbie was strangely still. She was like a little bird paralyzed by the fascination of a snake. He went on in the same quiet tones. "But this letter has thrown an entirely different complexion on the case. I am your legal adviser, I shall represent you in court. I take your story as you tell it to me, and I shall conduct your defense according to its terms. It may be that I believe your statements, and it may be that I doubt them. The duty of counsel is to persuade the court that the evidence placed before it is not such as to justify it in bringing in a verdict of Guilty, and any private opinion he may have of the guilt or innocence of his client is entirely beside the point."

He was astonished to see in Leslie's eyes the flicker of a smile. Piqued, he went on somewhat drily, "You're not going to deny that Hammond came to your house at your urgent, and I may even say, hysterical invitation?"

Mrs. Crosbie, hesitating for an instant, seemed to consider. "They can prove that the letter was taken to his bungalow by one of the house-boys. He rode over on his bicycle."

"You mustn't expect other people to be more stupid than you. The letter will put them on the track of suspicions which have entered nobody's head. I will not tell you what I personally thought when I saw the copy. I do not wish you to tell me anything but what is needed to save your neck."

Mrs. Crosbie gave a shrill cry. She sprang to her feet, white with terror. "You don't think they'd hang me?"

"If they came to the conclusion that you hadn't killed Hammond in self-defense, it would be the duty of the assessors to bring in a verdict of Guilty. The charge is murder. It would be the duty of the judge to sentence you to death."

"But what can they prove?" she gasped.

"I don't know what they can prove. I don't want to know. But if their suspicions are aroused, if they begin to make inquiries, if the natives are questioned—what is it that can be discovered?" She crumpled up suddenly. She fell on the floor before he could catch her. She had fainted.

He looked round the room for water, but there was none there, and he did not want to be disturbed. He stretched her out on the floor and kneeling beside her, waited for her to recover. When she opened her eyes, he was disconcerted by the ghastly fear that he saw in them. "Keep quite still," he said. "You'll be better in a moment."

"You won't let them hang me," she whispered. She began to cry hysterically, while in undertones he sought to quieten her.

"For goodness' sake, pull yourself together," he said.

"Give me a minute."

Her courage was amazing. He could see the effort she made to regain her self-control, and soon she was once more calm. "Let me get up now."

He gave her his hand and helped her to her feet. Taking her arm, he led her to the chair. She sat down wearily. "Don't talk to me for a minute or two," she said.

"Very well."

When at last she spoke, it was to say something he didn't expect. She gave a little sigh. "I'm afraid I've made rather a mess of things," she said.

He didn't answer, and once more there was a silence.

"Isn't it possible to get hold of the letter?" she said at last.

"I don't think anything would have been said to me about it if the person in whose possession it is was not prepared to sell it."

"Who's got it?"

"The Chinese woman who was living in Hammond's house."

A spot of color flickered for an instant on Leslie's cheekbones. "Does she want a lot for it?"

"I imagine she has a very shrewd idea of its value. I doubt if it would be possible to get hold of it except for a very large sum."

"Are you going to let me be hanged?"

"Do you think it's so simple as all that to secure possession of an unwelcome piece of evidence? It's no different from suborning a witness. You have no right to make any such suggestion to me."

"Then what is going to happen to me?"

"Justice must take its course."

She grew very pale. A little shudder passed through her body. "I put myself in your hands. Of course, I have no right to ask you to do anything that isn't proper."

Mr. Joyce had not bargained for the little break in her voice which her habitual self-restraint made quite intolerably moving. She looked at him with humble eyes and he thought that if he rejected their appeal they would haunt him for the rest of his life. After all, nothing could bring poor Hammond back to life again. He wondered what really was the explanation of that letter. It wasn't fair to conclude from it that she had killed Hammond without provocation. He had lived in the East a long time and his sense of professional honor wasn't perhaps so acute as it had been twenty years before.

He stared at the floor. He made up his mind to do something which he knew was unjustifiable, but it stuck in his throat and he felt dully resentful toward Leslie. It embarrassed him a little to speak. "I don't know exactly what your husband's circumstances are."

Flushing a rosy red, she shot a swift glance at him. "He has a good many tin shares and a small share in two or three rubber estates. I suppose he could raise money."

"He would have to be told what it was for."

She was silent for a moment. She seemed to think.

"He's in love with me still. He would make any sacrifice to save me. Is there any need for him to see the letter?"

Mr. Joyce frowned a little, and, quick to notice, she went on. "Robert is an old friend of yours. I'm not asking you to do anything for me, I'm asking you to save a rather simple, kind man who never did you any harm from all the pain that's possible."

Mr. Joyce did not reply. He rose to go and Mrs. Crosbie, with the grace that was natural to her, held out her hand. She was shaken by the scene, and her look was haggard, but she made a brave attempt to speed him with courtesy. "It's so good of you to take all this trouble for me. I can't begin to tell you how grateful I am."

Mr. Joyce returned to his office. He sat in his own room, quite still, attempting to do no work, and pondered. His imagination brought him many strange ideas. He shuddered a little. At last there was the discreet knock on the door which he was expecting. Ong Chi Seng came in.

"I was just going out to have my tiffin, sir," he said.

"All right."

"I didn't know if there was anything you wanted before I went."

"I don't think so. Did you make another appointment for Mr. Reed?"

"Yes, sir. He will come at three o'clock."

"Good."

Ong Chi Seng turned away, walked to the door, and put his long, slim fingers on the handle. Then, as though on an afterthought, he turned back. "Is there anything you wish me to say to my fliend, sir?" Although Ong Chi Seng spoke English so admirably, he had still a difficulty with the letter *r*.

"What friend?"

"About the letter Mrs. Crosbie wrote to Hammond deceased, sir."

"Oh! I'd forgotten about that. I mentioned it to Mrs. Crosbie and she denies having written anything of the sort. It's evidently a forgery." Joyce took the copy from his pocket and handed it to Ong Chi Seng. Ong Chi Seng ignored the gesture.

"In that case, sir, I suppose there would be no objection if my fliend delivered the letter to the Deputy Public Prosecutor."

"None. But I don't quite see what good that would do your friend."

"My fliend, sir, thought it was his duty in the interests of justice."

"I am the last man in the world to interfere with anyone who wishes to do his duty, Chi Seng."

The eyes of the lawyer and of the Chinese clerk met. Not the shadow of a smile hovered on the lips of either, but they understood each other perfectly.

"I quite understand, sir," said Ong Chi Seng, "but from my study of the case R. v. Crosbie I am of the opinion that the production of such a letter would be damaging to our client."

"I have always had a very high opinion of your legal acumen, Chi Seng."

"It has occurred to me, sir, that if I could persuade my fliend to induce the Chinese woman who has the letter to deliver it into our hands it would save a great deal of trouble."

Mr. Joyce idly drew faces on his blotting-paper. "I suppose your friend is a businessman. In what circumstances do you think he would be induced to part with the letter?"

"He has not got the letter. The Chinese woman has the letter. He is only a relation of the Chinese woman. She is an ignorant woman—she did not know the value of the letter till my fliend told her."

"What value did he put on it?"

"Ten thousand dollars, sir."

"Good God! Where on earth do you suppose Mrs. Crosbie can get ten thousand dollars! I tell you, the letter's a forgery!"

He looked up at Ong Chi Seng as he spoke. The clerk was unmoved by the outburst. He stood at the side of the desk, civil, cool, and observant. "Mr. Crosbie owns an eighth share of the Betong Rubber Estate and a sixth share of the Selantan River Rubber Estate. I have a fliend who will lend him the money on the security of his properties."

"You have a large circle of acquaintance, Chi Seng."

"Yes, sir."

"Well, you can tell them to go to hell. I would never advise Mr. Crosbie to give a penny more than five thousand for a letter that can be very easily explained."

"The Chinese woman does not want to sell the letter, sir. My fliend took a long time to persuade her. It is useless to offer her less than the sum mentioned."

Mr. Joyce looked at Ong Chi Seng for at least three minutes. The clerk bore the searching scrutiny without embarrassment. He stood in a respectful attitude with downcast eyes. Mr. Joyce knew his man. Clever fellow, Chi Seng, he thought, I wonder how much he's going to get out of it.

"Ten thousand dollars is a very large sum."

"Mr. Crosbie will certainly pay it rather than see his wife hanged, sir."

Again Mr. Joyce paused. What more did Chi Seng know than he had said? He must be pretty sure of his ground if he was obviously so unwilling to bargain. That sum had been fixed because whoever it was that was managing the affair knew it was the largest amount Robert Crosbie could raise.

"Where is the Chinese woman now?" asked Mr. Joyce.

"She is staying at the house of my fliend, sir."

"Will she come here?"

"I think it more better if you go to her, sir. I can take you to the house tonight and she will give you the letter. She is a very ignorant woman, sir, and she does not understand checks."

"I wasn't thinking of giving her a check. I will bring banknotes with me."

"It would only be waste of valuable time to bring less than ten thousand dollars, sir."

"I quite understand."

"I will go and tell my fliend after I have had my tiffin, sir."

"Very good. You'd better meet me outside the club at ten o'clock tonight."

"With pleasure, sir," said Ong Chi Seng.

He gave Mr. Joyce a little bow and left the room. Joyce went out to have luncheon, too. He went to the club, and here, as he had expected, he saw Robert Crosbie. He was sitting at a crowded table, and as he passed him, looking for a place, Mr. Joyce touched him on the shoulder. "I'd like a word or two with you before you go," he said.

"Right you are. Let me know when you're ready."

* * *

Mr. Joyce had made up his mind how to tackle him. He played a rubber of bridge after luncheon in order to allow time for the club to empty itself. He didn't want on this particular matter to see Crosbie in his office. Presently Crosbie came into the card-room and looked on till the game was finished. The other players went on their various affairs, and the two were left alone.

"A rather unfortunate thing has happened, old man," said Joyce, in a tone which he sought to render as casual as possible. "It appears that your wife sent a letter to Hammond asking him to come to the bungalow on the night he was killed."

"But that's impossible," cried Crosbie. "She's always stated that she had had no communication with Hammond. I know from my own knowledge that she hadn't set eyes on him for a couple of months."

"The fact remains that the letter exists. It's in the possession of the Chinese woman Hammond was living with. Your wife meant to give you a present on your birthday, and she wanted Hammond to help her to get it. In the emotional excitement that she suffered from after the tragedy, she forgot all about it, and having once denied having any communication with Hammond she was afraid to say she'd made a mistake. It was of course very unfortunate, but I daresay it wasn't unnatural."

Crosbie didn't speak. His large red face bore an expression of complete bewilderment, and Mr. Joyce was at once relieved and exasperated by his lack of comprehension. He was a stupid man, and Joyce had no patience with stupidity. But his distress since the catastrophe had touched a soft spot in the lawyer's heart and Mrs. Crosbie had struck the right note when she asked him to help her, not for her sake but for her husband's.

"I need not tell you that it would be very awkward if this letter found its way into the hands of the prosecution. Your wife has lied, and she would be asked to explain the lie. It alters things a little if Hammond did not intrude, an unwanted guest, but came to your house by invitation. It would be easy to arouse in the assessors a certain indecision of mind."

Mr. Joyce hesitated. He was face to face now with his decision. If it had been a time for humor, he could have smiled at the reflection that he was taking so grave a step and that the man for whom he was taking it had not the smallest conception of its gravity. If he gave the matter a thought, he probably imagined that what Mr. Joyce was doing was what any lawyer did in the ordinary run of business.

"My dear Robert, you are not only my client but my friend. I think we must get hold of that letter. It'll cost a good deal of money. Except for that, I should have preferred to say nothing to you about it."

"How much?"

"Ten thousand dollars."

"That's a devil of a lot. With the slump and one thing and another, it'll take just about all I've got."

"Can you get it at once?"

"I suppose so. Old Charlie Meadows will let me have it on my tin shares and on those two estates I'm interested in."

"Then will you?"

"Is it absolutely necessary?"

"If you want your wife to be acquitted."

Crosbie grew very red. His mouth sagged strangely. "But—" He couldn't find words, his face now was purple. "But I don't understand. She can explain. You don't mean to say they'd find her guilty? They couldn't hang her for putting a noxious vermin out of the way!"

"Of course they wouldn't hang her. They might only find her guilty of manslaughter. She'd probably get off with two or three years."

Crosbie started to his feet and his red face was distraught with horror. "Three years!"

Then something seemed to dawn in that slow intelligence of his. His mind was darkness across which shot suddenly a flash of lightning, and though the succeeding darkness was as profound there remained the memory of something not seen but perhaps just descried. Mr. Joyce saw that Crosbie's big red hands, coarse and hard with all the odd jobs he had set them to, trembled.

"What was the present she wanted to make me?"

"She says she wanted to give you a new gun."

Once more that great red face flushed a deeper red. "When have you got to have the money ready?" There was something odd in his voice now. It sounded as though he spoke with invisible hands clutching at his throat.

"At ten o'clock tonight. I thought you could bring it to my office at about six."

"Is the woman coming to you?"

"No, I'm going to her."

"I'll bring the money. I'll come with you."

Mr. Joyce looked at him sharply. "Do you think there's any need for you to do that? I think it would be better if you left me to deal with this matter by myself."

"It's my money, isn't it? I'm going to come."

Mr. Joyce shrugged his shoulders. They rose and shook hands. Mr. Joyce looked at him curiously.

At ten o'clock they met in the empty club.

"Everything all right?" asked Mr. Joyce.

"Yes. I've got the money in my pocket."

"Let's go, then."

They walked down the steps. Mr. Joyce's car was waiting for them in the square, silent at that hour, and as they came to it, Ong Chi Seng stepped out of the shadow of a house. He took his seat beside the driver and gave him a direction. They drove past the Hotel de l'Europe and turned up by Sailors' Home to get into Victoria Street. Here the Chinese shops were open still, idlers lounged about, and in the roadway rickshaws and motor-cars and gharries gave a busy air to the scene.

Suddenly their car stopped and Chi Seng turned round. "I think it more better if we walk here, sir." he said. They got out and he went on. They followed a step or two behind. Then he asked them to stop. "You wait here, sir. I go in and speak to my fliend."

He went into a shop, open to the street, where three or four Chinese were standing behind the counter. It was one of those strange shops where nothing was on view and you wondered what it was they sold there. They saw him address a stout man in a duck suit with a large gold chain across his breast and the man shot a quick glance out into the night. He gave Chi Seng a key and Chi Seng came out. He beckoned to the two men waiting and slid into a doorway at the side of the shop. They followed him and found themselves at the foot of a flight of stairs.

"If you wait a minute, I will light a match," he said, always resourceful. "You come upstairs, please."

He held a Japanese match in front of them, but it scarcely dispelled the darkness and they groped their way up behind him. On the first floor, he unlocked a door and, going in, lit a gas-jet. "Come in, please," he said.

It was a small, square room with one window, and the only furniture consisted of two low Chinese beds covered with matting. In one corner was a large chest with an elaborate lock, and on this stood a shabby tray with an opium pipe on it and a lamp. There was in the room the faint, acrid scent of the drug.

They sat down and Ong Chi Seng offered them cigarettes. In a moment, the door was opened by the fat Chinaman they'd seen behind the counter. He bade them good evening in very good English and sat down by the side of his fellow countryman.

"The woman is just coming," said Chi Seng.

A boy from the shop brought in a tray with a teapot and cups and the Chinaman offered them a cup of tea. Crosbie refused. The Chinese talked to one another in undertones, but Crosbie and Mr. Joyce were silent.

At last there was the sound of a voice outside—someone was calling in a low tone—and the Chinaman went to the door. He opened it, spoke a few words, and ushered a woman in. Mr. Joyce looked at her. He had heard much about her since Hammond's death, but he had never seen her. She was a stoutish person, not very young, with a broad, phlegmatic face. She was powdered and rouged and her eyebrows were thin black lines, but she gave the impression of a woman of character. She wore a pale-blue jacket and a white skirt. Her costume was not quite European nor quite Chinese, but on her feet were little Chinese silk slippers. She wore heavy gold chains round her neck, gold bangles on her wrists, gold earrings, and elaborate gold pins in her black hair. She walked in slowly, with the air of a woman sure of herself, but with a certain heaviness of tread, and sat down on the bed beside Ong Chi Seng. He said something to her and, nodding, she gave an incurious glance at the two white men.

"Has she got the letter?" asked Mr. Joyce.

"Yes, sir."

Crosbie said nothing, but produced a roll of five-hundred-dollar notes. He counted out twenty and handed them to Chi Seng. "Will you see if that is correct?"

The clerk counted them and gave them to the fat Chinaman. "Quite correct, sir."

The Chinaman counted them once more and put them in his pocket. He spoke again to the woman and she drew from her bosom a letter. She gave it to Chi Seng, who cast his eyes over it. "This is the right document, sir," he said, and was about to give it to Mr. Joyce when Crosbie took it from him.

"Let me look at it," he said.

Mr. Joyce watched him read and then held out his hand for it. "You'd better let me have it."

Crosbie folded it up deliberately and put it in his pocket. "No, I'm going to keep it myself. It's cost me enough money."

Mr. Joyce made no rejoinder. The three Chinese watched the little passage, but what they thought about it, or whether they thought, was impossible to tell from their impassive countenances. Mr. Joyce rose to his feet. "Do you want me any more tonight, sir?" said Ong Chi Seng.

"No." Joyce knew the clerk wished to stay behind in order to get his agreed share of the money and he turned to Crosbie. "Are you ready?"

Crosbie did not answer, but stood up. The Chinaman went to the door and opened it for them. Chi Seng found a bit of candle and lit it in order to light them down, and the two Chinese accompanied them to the street. They left the woman sitting quietly on the bed, smoking. When they reached the street, the Chinese left them and went once more upstairs.

"What are you going to do with that letter?" asked Mr. Joyce.

"Keep it."

They walked to where the car was waiting for them and here Mr. Joyce offered his friend a lift. Crosbie shook his head. "I'm going to walk." He hesitated a little and shuffled his feet. "I went to Singapore on the night of Hammond's death partly to buy a new gun that a man I knew wanted to dispose of. Goodnight."

He disappeared quickly into the darkness . . .

Mr. Joyce was quite right about the trial. The assessors went into court fully determined to acquit Mrs. Crosbie. She gave evidence on her own behalf. She told her story simply and with straightforwardness. The D.P.P. was a kindly man and it was plain that he took no great pleasure in his task. He asked the necessary questions in a deprecating manner. His speech for the prosecution might really have been a speech for the defense, and the assessors took less than five minutes to consider their popular verdict. It was impossible to prevent the great outburst of applause with which it was received by the crowd that packed the courthouse. The judge congratulated Mrs. Crosbie and she was a free woman.

No one had expressed a more violent disapprobation of Hammond's behavior than Mrs. Joyce. She was a woman loyal to her friends and she had insisted on the Crosbies staying with her after the trial—for she, in common with everyone else, had no doubt of the result—till they could make arrangements to go away. It was out of the question for poor, dear, brave Leslie to return to the bungalow at which the horrible catastrophe had taken place.

The trial was over by half past twelve, and when they reached the Joyces' house a grand luncheon was awaiting them. Cocktails were ready—Mrs. Joyce's million-dollar cocktail was celebrated through all the Malay states—and Mrs. Joyce drank Leslie's health. She was a talkative, vivacious woman, and now she was in the highest spirits. It was fortunate, for the rest of them were silent. She did not wonder, her husband never had much to say, and the other two were naturally exhausted from the long strain to which they had been subjected. During luncheon, she carried on a bright and spirited monologue. Then coffee was served.

"Now children," she said in her gay, bustling fashion, "you must have a rest, and after tea I shall take you both for a drive to the sea."

Mr. Joyce, who lunched at home only by exception, had of course to go back to his office.

"I'm afraid I can't do that, Mrs. Joyce," said Crosbie. "I've got to get back to the estate at once."

"Not today?" she cried.

"Yes, now. I've neglected it for too long and I have urgent business. But I shall be very grateful if you will keep Leslie until we've decided what to do."

Mrs. Joyce was about to expostulate, but her husband prevented her. "If he must go, he must, and there's an end of it." There was something in the lawyer's tone which made her look at him quickly. She held her tongue and there was a moment's silence. Then Crosbie spoke again.

"If you'll forgive me, I'll start at once so that I can get there before dark." He rose from the table. "Will you come and see me off, Leslie?"

"Of course."

They went out of the dining room together.

"I think that's rather inconsiderate of him," said Mrs. Joyce. "He must know that Leslie wants to be with him just now."

"I'm sure he wouldn't go if it wasn't absolutely necessary."

"Well, I'll just see that Leslie's room is ready for her. She wants a complete rest, of course, and then amusement."

Mrs. Joyce left the room and Joyce sat down again. In a short time, he heard Crosbie start the engine of his motorcycle and then noisily scrunch over the gravel of the garden path. He got up and went into the drawing room. Mrs. Crosbie was standing in the middle of it, looking into space, and in her hand was an open letter. He recognized it. She gave him a glance as he came in and he saw that she was deathly pale.

"He knows," she whispered.

Mr. Joyce went up to her and took the letter from her hand. He lit a match and set the paper afire. She watched it burn. When he could hold it no longer, he dropped it on the tiled floor and they both looked at the paper curl and blacken. Then he trod it into ashes with his foot.

"What does he know?"

She gave him a long, long stare and into her eyes came a strange look. Was it contempt or despair? Mr. Joyce could not tell. "He knows that Geoff was my lover."

Mr. Joyce made no movement and uttered no sound.

"He'd been my lover for years. He became my lover almost immediately after he came back from the war. We knew how careful we must be. When we became lovers, I pretended I was tired of him and he seldom came to the house when Robert was there. I used to drive out to a place we knew and he met me, two or three times a week, and when Robert went to Singapore he used to come to the bungalow late, when the boys had gone for the night. We saw one another constantly, all the time, and not a soul had the smallest suspicion of it. And then lately, a year ago, he began to change. I didn't know what was the matter. I couldn't believe he didn't care for me any more. He always denied it. I was frantic. I made scenes. Sometimes I thought he hated me. Oh, if you knew what agonies I endured! I passed through hell! I knew he didn't want me any more and I wouldn't let him go! Misery! Misery! I loved him. I'd given him everything, he was my life!

"And then I heard he was living with a Chinese woman. I couldn't believe it. I wouldn't believe it. At last I saw her, I saw her with my own eyes, walking in the village, with her gold bracelets and her necklaces, an old fat Chinese woman. She was older than I was. Horrible! They all knew in the kampong that she was his mistress. And when I passed her, she looked at me and I knew that she knew I was his mistress, too. I sent for him—I told him I must see him. You've read the letter. I was mad to write it. I didn't know what I was doing. I didn't care. I hadn't seen him for ten days. It was a lifetime. And when last we'd parted he took me in his arms and kissed me and told me not to worry. And he went straight from my arms to hers."

She had been speaking in a low voice, vehemently, and now she stopped and wrung her hands.

"That damned letter. We'd always been so careful. He always tore up any word I wrote to him the moment he'd read it. How was I to know he'd leave that one? He came and I told him I knew about the Chinawoman. He denied it. He said it was only scandal. I was beside myself. I don't know what I said to him. Oh, I hated him then. I tore him limb from limb. I said everything I could to wound him. I insulted him. I could have spat in his face. And at last he turned on me. He told me he was sick and tired of me and never wanted to see me again. He said I bored him to death. And then he acknowledged that it was true about the woman. He said he'd known her for years, before the war, and she was the only woman who really meant anything to him, and the rest was just pastime. And he said he was glad I knew, and now at last I'd leave him alone. And then I don't know what happened, I was beside myself. I seized the revolver and I fired. He gave a cry and I saw I'd hit him. He staggered and rushed for the verandah. I ran after him and fired again. He fell, and then I stood over him and I fired and fired till the revolver went click, click, and I knew there were no more cartridges."

At last she stopped, panting. Her face was no longer human—it was distorted with cruelty, and rage and pain. You would never have thought that this quiet, refined woman was capable of such a fiendish passion. Mr. Joyce took a step backward. He was absolutely aghast at the sight of her. It was not a face, it was a gibbering, hideous mask. Then they heard a voice calling from another room, a loud, friendly, cheerful voice. It was Mrs. Joyce.

"Come along, Leslie darling, your room's ready. You must be dropping with sleep."

Mrs. Crosbie's features gradually composed themselves. Those passions, so clearly delineated, were smoothed away as with your hand you would smooth a crumpled paper, and in a minute the face was cool and calm and unlined. She was a trifle pale, but her lips broke into a pleasant, affable smile. She was once more the well-bred and even distinguished woman.

"I'm coming, Dorothy dear. I'm sorry to give you so much trouble," she called.

JOE GORES

WATCH FOR IT

Eric's first one. The very first.

And it went up early.

If I'd been in my apartment on Durant, with the window open, I probably would have heard it. And probably, at 4:30 in the morning, would have thought like any straight that it had been a truck backfire. But I'd spent the night balling Elizabeth over in San Francisco while Eric was placing the bomb in Berkeley. With her every minute, I'd made sure, because whatever else you can say about the Federal pigs, they're thorough. I'd known that if anything went wrong, they'd be around looking.

Liz and I heard it together on the noon news when we were having breakfast before her afternoon classes. She teaches freshman English at SF State.

"Eric Whitlach, outspoken student radical on the Berkeley campus, was injured early this morning when a bomb he allegedly was placing under a table in the Student Union detonated prematurely. Police said the explosive device was fastened to a clock mechanism set for 9:30, when the area would have been packed with students. The extent of the young activist's injuries is not known, but—"

"God, that's terrible," Liz said with a shudder. She'd been in a number of upper-level courses with both Eric and me. "What could have happened to him, Ross, to make him do something like that?"

"I guess—well, I haven't seen much of him since graduation last June." I gestured above the remains of our eggs and bacon. "Student revolutionary—it's hard to think of Eric that way." Then I came up with a nice touch. "Maybe he shouldn't have gone beyond his M.A. Maybe he should have stopped when we did—before he lost touch."

When I'd recruited Eric without appearing to, it had seemed

a very heavy idea. I mean, nobody actually expects his vocal, kinky, Rubin-type radical to go out and set bombs. Because they don't. We usually avoid Eric's sort ourselves—they have no sense of history, no discipline. They're as bad as the Communists on the other side of the street, with their excessive regimentation, their endless orders from somewhere else.

I stood up. "Well, baby, I'd better get back across the Bay."

"Ross, aren't you—I mean, can't you—"

She stopped there, coloring, still a lot of that corrupting Middle America in her. She was ready to try anything at all in bed, but to say right out in daylight that she wanted me to ball her again after class—that still sort of blew her mind.

"I can't, Liz," I said, all aw-shucksy, laughing down inside at how *straight* she was. "I *was* his roommate until four months ago, and the police or somebody might want to ask me questions about him."

I actually thought that they might, and nothing brings out pig paranoia quicker than somebody not available for harassment when they want him.

But nobody showed up. I guess they knew that as long as they had Eric, they could get whatever they wanted out of him just by shooting electricity into his balls or something, like the French pigs in Algeria. I know how the Fascists operate.

Beyond possible questions by the pigs, however, I knew there'd be a strategy session that night in Berkeley. After dark at Zeta Books, on Telegraph south of the campus, is the usual time and place for a meet. Armand Marsh let me in and locked the door behind me. He runs the store for the Student Socialist Alliance as a cover. He's a long skinny, redheaded cat with ascetic features and quick, nervous mannerisms, and is cell-leader for our three-man focal.

I saw that Danzer was in the mailing room when I got there, as was Benny. I didn't like Danzer being there. Sure, he acted as liaison with other Bay Area focals, but he never went out on operations and so he was an outsider. No outsider can be trusted.

"Benny," said Armand, "how badly is Whitlach really hurt?"

Benny Leland is night administrator for Alta Monte Hospital.

With his close-trimmed hair and conservative clothes, he looks like the ultimate straight.

"He took a big splinter off the table right through his shoulder. Damned lucky that he'd already set it and was on his way out when it blew. Otherwise they'd have just found a few teeth and toes."

"So he'd be able to move around?"

"Oh, sure. The injury caused severe shock, but he's out of that now, and the wound itself is not critical." He paused to look pointedly at me. "What I don't understand is how the damned thing went off prematurely."

Meaning I was somehow to blame, since I had supplied Eric with the material for the bomb. Armand looked over at me, too.

"Ross? What sort of device was it?"

"Standard," I said. "Two sticks of dynamite liberated from that P.G. and E. site four months ago. An electric blasting-cap with a small battery to detonate it. Alarm-clock timer. He was going to carry the whole thing in a gift-wrapped shoebox to make it less conspicuous. There are several ways that detonation could—"

"None of that is pertinent now," interrupted Danzer. His voice was cold and heavy, like his face. He even looked like a younger Raymond Burr. "Our first concern is: will the focal be compromised if they break him down and he starts talking?"

"Eric was my best friend before I joined the focal," I said, "and he was my roommate for four years. But once we'd determined it was better to use someone still a student than to set this one ourselves, I observed the standard security procedures in recruiting him. He believes the bombing was totally his own idea."

"He isn't even aware of the *existence* of the focal, let alone who's in it," Armand explained. "There's no way he could hurt us."

Danzer's face was still cold when he looked over at me, but I had realized he *always* looked cold. "Then it seems that Ross is the one to go in after him."

"If there's any need to go in at all," said Benny quickly. I knew what he was thinking. Any operation would entail the hospital, which meant he would be involved. He didn't like that. "After all, if he can't hurt us, why not just—" He shrugged.

"Just leave him there? Mmmph." Danzer publishes a couple of underground radical newspapers even though he's only twenty-seven, and also uses his presses to run off porn novels for some outfit in L.A. I think he nets some heavy bread. "I believe I can convince you of the desirability of going in after him. If Ross is willing."

"Absolutely." I kept the excitement from my voice. Cold. Controlled. That's the image I like to project. A desperate man, reckless, careless of self. "If anyone else came through that door, Eric would be convinced he was an undercover pig. As soon as he sees me, he'll know that I've come to get him away."

"Why couldn't Ross just walk in off the street as a normal visitor?" asked Danzer.

"There's a twenty-four-hour police guard on Whitlach's door." Benny was still fighting the idea of a rescue operation. "Only the doctors and one authorized nurse per shift get in."

"All right. And Ross *must not* be compromised. If he is, the whole attempt would be negated, worse than useless." Which at the moment I didn't understand. "Now let's get down to it."

As Danzer talked, I began to comprehend why he'd been chosen to coordinate the activities of the focals. His mind was cold and logical and precise, as was his plan. What bothered me was my role in that plan. But I soon saw the error in my objections. I was Eric's friend, the only one he knew he could trust—and I had brought him into it in the first place. There was danger, of course, but that only made me feel better the more I thought of it. You have to take risks if you're to destroy a corrupt society—because like a snake with a broken back, it still has venom on its fangs.

It took three hours to work out the operational scheme.

Alta Monte Hospital is set in the center of a quiet residential area off Ashby Avenue. It used to be easy to approach after dark—just walk to the side entrance across the broad blacktop parking lot. But so many doctors going out to their cars have been mugged by heads looking for narcotics that the lot is patrolled now.

I parked on Benvenue, got the hypo kit and the cherry bombs from the glove box, and slid them into my pocket. The thin, strong nylon rope was wound around my waist under my dark-blue windbreaker. My breath went up in grey wisps on the chilly, wet night air. After I'd locked the car, I held out my hand to look at it by the pale illumination of the nearest streetlamp. No tremors. The nerves were cool, man. *I* was cool.

3:23 A.M. my watch.

In seven minutes, Benny Leland would unlock the small access door on the kitchen loading dock. He would relock it three minutes later, while going back to the staff coffee room from the men's lavatory. I had to get inside during those three minutes or not at all.

3:27.

I hunkered down in the thick hedge rimming the lot. My palms were getting sweaty. Everything hinged on a nurse who came off work in midshift because her old man worked screwy hours and she had to be home to babysit her kid. If she was late—

The guard's voice carried clearly on black misty air. "All finished, Mrs. Adamson?"

"Thank God, Danny. It's been a rough night. We lost one in post-op that I was sure would make it."

"Too bad. See you tomorrow, Mrs. Adamson."

I had a cherry bomb in my rubber-gloved hand now. I couldn't hear her soft-soled nurse's shoes on the blacktop, but I could see her long, thin shadow coming bouncing up the side of her car ten yards away. I came erect, threw, stepped back into shadow.

It was beautiful, man—like a sawed-off shotgun in the silent lot. She gave a wonderful scream, full-throated, and the guard yelled. I could hear his heavy feet thudding to her aid as he ran past my section of hedge.

I was sprinting across the blacktop behind his back on silent garage-attendant's shoes, hunched as low as possible between the parked cars in case anyone had been brought to a window by the commotion. Without checking my pace, I ran down the kitchen delivery ramp to crouch in the deep shadow under the edge of the loading platform.

Nothing. No pursuit. My breath was ragged in my chest, more from excitement than my dash. The watch said 3:31. Beautiful.

I threw a leg up and rolled onto my belly on the platform. Across to the access port in the big overhead accordion steel loading door. It opened easily under my careful fingertips. Benny was being cool, too, producing on schedule for a change. I don't entirely trust Benny.

Hallway deserted, as per the plan. That unmistakable hospital smell. Across the hall, one of those wheeled carts holding empty food trays ready for the morning's breakfasts. Right where it was supposed to be. I put the two cherry bombs on the front left corner of the second tray down, turned, and went nine quick paces to the firedoor.

My shoes made slight scuffing noises on the metal runners. By law, hospital firedoors cannot be locked. I checked my watch. In nineteen seconds, Benny Leland would emerge from the men's room and, as he walked back to the staff coffee room, would relock the access door and casually hook the cherry bombs from the tray. I then would have three minutes to be in position.

It had been 150 seconds when I pulled the third-floor firedoor a quarter inch ajar. No need to risk looking out—I could visualize everything from Benny's briefing earlier.

"Whitlach's room is the last one on the corridor, right next to the fire stairs," he'd said. "I arranged that as part of my administrative duties—actually, of course, in case we *would* want to get to him. The floor desk with the night-duty nurse is around an ell and at the far end of the corridor. She's well out of the way. The policeman will be sitting beside Whitlach's door on a metal folding chair. He'll be alone in the hall at that time of night."

Ten seconds. I held out my hand. No discernible tremor.

Benny Leland, riding alone in the elevator from the basement to the fourth-floor administrative offices, would just be stopping here at the third floor. As the doors opened, he would punch *four* again. As they started to close, he would hurl his two cherry bombs down the main stairwell, and within seconds would be off the elevator and into his office on the floor above. The pig could only think it had been someone on the stairs.

Whoomp! Whump!

Fantastic, man! Muffled so the duty nurse far down the corridor and around a corner wouldn't even hear them, but loud enough so the pig, mildly alert for a possible attempt to free Whitlach, would have to check.

I counted ten, pulled open the firedoor, went the six paces to Eric's now unguarded door. Thirty feet away, the pig's beefy blue-clad back was just going through the access doors to the elevator shaft and the main stairwell.

A moment of absolute panic when Eric's door stuck. Then it pulled free and I was inside. Sweat on my hands under the thin rubber gloves. Cool it now, baby.

I could see the pale blue of Eric's face as he started up from his medicated doze. His little nightlight cast harsh, antiseptic shadows across his lean face. Narrow, stubborn jaw, very bright blue eyes, short nose, wiry, tight-curled brown hair. I felt a tug of compassion—he was very pale and drawn.

But then a broad grin lit up his features. *"Ross!"* he whispered. "How in the hell—"

"No time, baby." My own voice was low, too. I already had the syringe out, was stabbing it into the rubber top of the little phial. "The pig will be back from checking out my diversion in just a minute. We have to be ready for him. Can you move?"

"Sure. What do you want me to—"

"Gimme your arm, baby." I jammed the needle into his flesh, depressed the plunger as I talked. "Pain-killer. In case we bump that shoulder getting you out of here, you won't feel anything."

Eric squeezed my arm with his left hand. There were tears in his eyes. How scared that poor cat must have been when he woke up in the hands of the fascist pigs!

"Christ, Ross, I can't believe—" He shook his head. "Oh, Jesus, right out from under their snouts! You're beautiful, man!"

I got an arm around his shoulders, as the little clock in my mind ticked off the seconds, weighing, measuring the pig's native stupidity against his duty at the door. They have that sense of duty, all right, the pigs, but no smarts. We had them by the shorts now.

"Gotta get you to the window, cat," I breathed. Eric obediently swung his legs over the edge of the bed.

"Why—window—" His head was lolling.

I unzipped my jacket to show him the rope wound around my waist. "I'm lowering you down to the ground. Help will be waiting there."

I slid up the aluminum sash, let in the night through the screen. Groovy. Like velvet. No noise.

"Perch there, baby," I whispered. "I want the pig to come in and see you silhouetted so I can take him from behind, dig?"

He nodded slowly. The injection was starting to take effect. It was my turn to squeeze his arm.

"Hang in there, baby."

I'd just gotten the night light switched off, had gotten behind the door, when I heard the pig's belatedly hurrying steps coming up the hall. Too late, you stupid Fascist bastard, much too late.

A narrow blade of light stabbed at the room, and widened to a rectangle. He didn't even come in fast, gun in hand, moving down and to the side as he should have. Just trotted in, a fat old porker to the slaughter. I heard his sharp intake of breath as he saw Eric.

"Hey! You! Get away from—"

I was on him from behind. Right arm around the throat, forearm grip, pull back hard while the left pushes on the back of the head.

They got out easily with that grip, any of them. Good for disarming a sentry without using a knife, I had been taught. I hadn't wasted my Cuban sojourn chopping sugar cane like those student straights on the junkets from Canada. I feel nothing but contempt for *those* cats—they have not yet realized that destroying the fabric of society is the only thing left for us.

I dragged the unconscious pig quickly out the door, lowered his fat butt into his chair, and stretched his legs out convincingly. Steady pulse. He'd come around in a few minutes. Meanwhile, it actually would have been possible to just walk Eric down the fire stairs and out of the building.

For a moment I was tempted—but doing it that way wasn't

in the plan. The plan called for the maximum effect possible, and merely walking Eric out would minimize it. Danzer's plan was everything.

Eric was slumped sideways against the window frame, mumbling sleepily. I pulled him forward, letting his head loll on my shoulder while I unhooked the screen and sent it sailing down into the darkness of the bushes flanking the concrete walk below. I could feel the coils of thin nylon around my waist, strong enough in their synthetic strength to lower him safely to the ground.

Jesus, he was one sweet guy. I paused momentarily to run my hand through his coarse, curly hair. There was sweat on his forehead. Last year he took my French exam for me so I could get my graduate degree. We'd met in old Prof Cecil's Western Civ course our junior year, and had been roomies until the end of grad school.

"I'm sorry, baby," I told his semiconscious, sweat-dampened face.

Then I let go and nudged so his limp form flopped backward through the open window and he was gone—gone instantly, just like that. Three stories, head-first, to the concrete sidewalk. He hit with a sound like an egg dropped on the kitchen floor. A bad sound, man. One I won't soon forget.

The hall was dark and deserted as I stepped over the pig's outstretched legs. He'd be raising the alarm soon, but nobody except the other pigs would believe him. Not after the autopsy.

The first sound of sirens came just after I had stuffed the thin surgical gloves down a sewer and was back in my car, pulling decorously away from the curb. The nylon ropes, taken along only to convince Eric that I meant to lower him from the window, had been slashed into useless lengths and deposited in a curbside trash barrel awaiting early-morning collection.

On University Avenue, I turned toward an all-night hamburger joint that had a pay phone in the parking lot. I was, can you believe it, ravenous. But more than that, I was horny. I thought about that for a second, knowing I should feel sort of sick and ashamed at having a sexual reaction to the execution. But instead I felt—*transfigured.* Eric had been a political prisoner, anyway. The pigs would have made sure he wouldn't have lived to come to trial. By his necessary death, *I* would be changing the entire history of human existence. *Me.* Alone.

And there was Liz over in the city, always eager, a receptacle in which I could spend my sexual excitement before she went off to teach. But first, Armand. So he could tell Danzer it was all right to print what we had discussed the night before.

Just thinking of that made me feel elated, because the autopsy would reveal the presence of that massive dose of truth serum I had needled into Eric before his death. And the Establishment news media would do the rest, hinting and probing and suggesting before our underground weeklies even hit the street with our charge against the Fascists.

Waiting for Armand to pick up his phone, I composed our headline in my mind:

PIGS PUMP REVOLUTIONARY HERO FULL
OF SCOPOLAMINE—HE DIVES FROM WINDOW
RATHER THAN FINK ON THE MOVEMENT

Oh, yes, man. Beautiful, just beautiful. Watch for it.

RUTH RENDELL

A PRESENT FOR PATRICIA

"Six should be enough," he said. "We'll say six tea chests, then, and one trunk. If you'll deliver them tomorrow, I'll get the stuff all packed and maybe your people could pick them up Wednesday." He made a note on a bit of paper. "Fine," he said. "Round about lunchtime tomorrow."

She hadn't moved. She was still sitting in the big oak-armed chair at the far end of the room. He made himself look at her and he managed a kind of grin, pretending all was well.

"No trouble," he said. "They're very efficient."

"I couldn't believe," she said, "that you'd really do it. Not until I heard you on the phone. I wouldn't have thought it possible. You'll really pack up all those things and have them sent off to her."

They were going to have to go over it all again. Of course they were. It wouldn't stop until he'd got the things out and himself out, away from London and her for good. And he wasn't going to argue or make long defensive speeches. He lit a cigarette and waited for her to begin, thinking that the pubs would be opening in an hour's time and he could go out then and get a drink.

"I don't understand why you came here at all," she said.

He didn't answer. He was still holding the cigarette box, and now he closed its lid, feeling the coolness of the onyx on his fingertips.

She had gone white. "Just to get your things? Maurice, did you come back just for *that?*"

"They are my things," he said evenly.

"You could have sent someone else. Even if you'd written to me and asked me to do it—"

"I never write letters," he said.

She moved then. She made a little fluttering movement with her hand in front of her mouth. "As if I didn't know!" she gasped, and making a great effort she steadied her voice. "You were in Australia for a year, a whole year, and you never wrote to me once."

"I phoned."

"Yes, twice. The first time to say you loved me and missed me and were longing to come back to me and would I wait for you, and there wasn't anyone else, was there? And the second time, a week ago, to say you'd be here by Saturday and could I—could I *put you up*. My God, I'd lived with you for two years, we were practically married, and then you phone and ask if I could put you up!"

"Words," he said. "How would you have put it?"

"For one thing, I'd have mentioned Patricia. Oh, yes, I'd have mentioned her. I'd have had the decency, the common humanity, for that. D'you know what I thought when you said you were coming? I ought to know by now how peculiar he is, I thought, how detached, no writing or phoning or anything. But that's Maurice, that's the man I love, and he's coming back to me and we'll get married and I'm so happy!"

"I did tell you about Patricia."

"Not until after you'd made love to me first."

He winced. It had been a mistake, that. Of course he hadn't meant to touch her beyond the requisite greeting kiss. But she was very attractive and he was used to her and she seemed to expect it—and, oh, what the hell. Women never could understand about men and sex. And there was only one bed, wasn't there? A hell of a scene there'd have been that first night if he'd suggested sleeping on the sofa in here.

"You made love to me," she said. "You were so passionate, it was just like it used to be, and then the next morning you told me. You'd got a resident's permit to stay in Australia, you'd got a job all fixed up, you'd met a girl you wanted to marry. Just like that you told me, over breakfast. Have you ever been smashed in the face, Maurice? Have you ever had your dreams trodden on?"

"Would you rather I'd waited longer? As for being smashed in the face—" he rubbed his cheekbone "—that's quite a punch you pack."

She shuddered. She got up and began slowly and stiffly to

pace the room. "I hardly touched you. I wish I'd killed you!" By a small .table she stopped. There was a china figurine on it, a bronze paperknife, an onyx pen jar that matched the ashtray. "All those things," she said. "I looked after them for you. I treasured them. And now you're going to have them all shipped out to her. The things we lived with. I used to look at them and think, Maurice loves that, Maurice liked that placed just here, Maurice bought that when we went to—oh, God, I can't believe it. Sent to *her!*"

He nodded, staring at her. "You can keep the big stuff," he said. "You're specially welcome to the sofa. I've tried sleeping on it for two nights and I never want to see the bloody thing again."

She picked up the china figurine and hurled it at him. It didn't hit him because he ducked and let it smash against the wall, just missing a framed drawing. "Mind the Lowry," he said laconically. "I paid a lot of money for that."

She flung herself onto the sofa and burst into sobs. She thrashed about, hammering the cushions with her fists. He wasn't going to be moved by that—he wasn't going to be moved at all. Once he'd packed those things, he'd be off to spend the next three months touring Europe. A free man, free for the sights and the fun and the girls, for a last fling of wild oats. After that, back to Patricia and a home and a job and responsibility. It was a glowing future which this hysterical woman wasn't going to mess up.

"Shut up, Betsy, for God's sake," he said. He shook her roughly by the shoulder, and then he went out because it was now eleven and he could get a drink.

Betsy made herself some coffee and washed her swollen eyes. She walked about, looking at the ornaments and the books, the glasses and vases and lamps, which he would take from her tomorrow. It wasn't that she much minded losing them, the things themselves, but the barrenness which would be left, and the knowing that they would all be Patricia's.

In the night she had got up, found his wallet, taken out the photographs of Patricia, and torn them up. But she remembered the face, pretty and hard and greedy, and she thought of those bright eyes widening as Patricia unpacked the tea chests, the predatory hands scrabbling for more treasures in the trunk. Doing it all perhaps before Maurice himself got there, arranging the lamps and the glasses and the ornaments in *their* home for his delight when at last he came.

He would marry her, of course. I suppose she thinks he's faithful to her, Betsy thought, the way I once thought he was faithful to me. I know better now. Poor stupid fool, she doesn't know what he did the first moment he was alone with me, or what he might get in France and Italy. That would be a nice wedding present to give her, wouldn't it, along with all the pretty bric-a-brac in the trunk?

Well, why not? Why not rock their marriage before it had even begun? A letter. A letter to be concealed in, say, that blue-and-white ginger jar. She sat down to write. Dear Patricia—what a stupid way to begin, the way you had to begin a letter even to your enemy.

> Dear Patricia: I don't know what Maurice has told you about me, but we have been living here as lovers ever since he arrived. To be more explicit, I mean we have made love, have slept together. Maurice is incapable of being faithful to anyone. If you don't believe me, ask yourself why, if he didn't want me, he didn't stay in a hotel. That's all. Yours—

And she signed her name and felt a little better—well enough and steady enough to take a bath and get herself some lunch.

Six tea chests and a trunk arrived on the following day. The chests smelled of tea and had drifts of tea leaves lying in the bottom of them. The trunk was made of silver-colored metal and it had clasps of gold-colored metal. It was rather a beautiful object, five feet long, three feet high, two feet wide, and the lid fitted so securely that it seemed a hermetic sealing.

Maurice began to pack at two o'clock.

He used tissue paper and newspapers. He filled the tea chests with kitchen equipment and cups and plates and cutlery, with books, with those clothes of his he had left behind him a year before. Studiously, and with a certain grim pleasure, he avoided everything Betsy might have insisted was hers—the poor, cheap things, the stainless-steel spoons and forks, the Woolworth pottery, the awful-colored sheets, red and orange and olive, that he had always loathed. He and Patricia would always sleep on white sheets.

Betsy didn't help him. She watched, chain-smoking. He nailed the lids on the chests, and on each lid he wrote in white paint his address in Australia. But he didn't paint the letters of his own name. He painted Patricia's. This wasn't done to needle Betsy, but he was glad to see it was needling her.

He hadn't come back to the flat till one that morning, and of course he didn't have a key. Betsy had refused to let him in, had left him down there in the street, and he had to sit in the car he'd hired till seven. She looked as if she hadn't slept either.

Miss Patricia Gordon, he wrote, painting fast and skillfully.

"Don't forget your ginger jar," said Betsy. "I don't want it."

"That's for the trunk." *Miss Patricia Gordon, 23 Burwood Park Avenue, Kew, Victoria, Australia 3101.* "All the pretty things are going in the trunk. I intend it as a special present for Patricia."

The Lowry came down and was carefully padded and wrapped. He wrapped the onyx ashtray and the pen jar, the alabaster bowl, the bronze paperknife, the tiny Chinese cups, the tall hock glasses. The china figurine, alas—

He opened the lid of the trunk.

"I hope the Customs open it!" Betsy shouted at him. "I hope they confiscate things and break things! I'll pray every night for it to go to the bottom of the sea before it gets there!"

"The sea," he said, "is a risk I must take. As for the Customs—" He smiled. "Patricia works for them, she's a Customs officer, didn't I tell you? I very much doubt if they'll even glance inside." He wrote a label and pasted it on the side of the trunk. *Miss Patricia Gordon, 23 Burwood Park Avenue, Kew.* "And now I'll have to go out and get a padlock. Keys, please. If you try to keep me out this time, I'll call the police. I'm still the legal tenant of this flat, remember."

She gave him the keys. When he had gone she put her letter in the ginger jar. She hoped he would close the trunk at once, but he didn't. He left it open, the lid thrown back, the new padlock dangling from the gold-colored clasp.

"Is there anything to eat?" he said.

"Go and find your own bloody food! Go and find some other woman to feed you!"

He liked her to be angry and fierce; it was her love he feared. He came back at midnight to find the flat in darkness, and he lay down on the sofa with the tea chests standing about him like defenses, like barricades, the white paint showing faintly in the dark. *Miss Patricia Gordon . . .*

Presently Betsy came in. She didn't put on the light. She wound her way between the chests, carrying a candle in a saucer which she set down on the trunk. In the candlelight, wearing a long white nightgown, she looked like a ghost, like some wandering madwoman, a Mrs. Rochester, a Woman in White.

"Maurice."

"Go away, Betsy, I'm tired."

"Maurice, *please.* I'm sorry I said all those things. I'm sorry I locked you out."

"Okay. I'm sorry, too. It's a mess, and maybe I shouldn't have done it the way I did. But the best way is for me just to go and my things to go and make a clean split. Right? And now will you please be a good girl and go away and let me get some sleep?"

What happened next he hadn't bargained for. It hadn't crossed his mind. Men don't understand about women and sex. She threw herself on him, clumsily, hungrily. She pulled his shirt open and began kissing his neck and chest, holding his head, crushing her mouth to his mouth, lying on top of him and gripping his legs with her knees.

He gave her a savage push. He kicked her away, and she fell and struck her head on the side of the trunk. The candle fell off, flared, and died in a pool of wax. In the darkness he cursed floridly. He put on the light and she got up, holding her head where there was a little blood.

"Oh, get out, for God's sake," he said, and he manhandled her out of the room, slamming the door after her.

* * *

In the morning, when she came into the room, a blue bruise on her forehead, he was asleep, fully clothed, spreadeagled on his back. She shuddered at the sight of him. She began to get breakfast, but she couldn't eat anything. The coffee made her gag and a great nauseous shiver went through her. When she went back to him he was sitting up on the sofa, looking at his plane ticket to Paris.

"The men are coming for the stuff at ten," he said as if nothing had happened, "and they'd better not be late. I have to be at the airport at noon."

She shrugged. She had been to the depths and she thought he couldn't hurt her any more.

"You'd better close the trunk," she said absent-mindedly.

"All in good time." His eyes gleamed. "I've got a letter to put in yet."

Her head bowed—the place where it was bruised was sore and swollen—she looked loweringly at him. "You never write letters."

"Just a note. One can't send a present without a note to accompany it, can one?" He pulled the ginger jar out of the trunk, screwed up her letter without even glancing at it, and threw it on the floor. Rapidly, yet ostentatiously, and making sure that Betsy could see, he scrawled across a sheet of notepaper: *All this is for you, darling Patricia, forever and ever.*

"How I hate you," she said.

"You could have fooled me." He took a large angle lamp out of the trunk and set it on the floor. He slipped his note into the ginger jar, rewrapped it, tucked the jar in between the towels and cushions padding the fragile objects. "Hatred isn't the word I'd use to describe the way you came after me last night."

She made no answer. Perhaps he should have put a heavy object like that lamp in one of the chests, perhaps he should open up one of the chests now. He turned round for the lamp. It wasn't there. She was holding it in both hands.

"I want that, please."

"Have you ever been smashed in the face, Maurice?" she said breathlessly, and she raised the lamp and struck him with it full on the forehead. He staggered and she struck him again, and again and again like a madwoman, raining blows on his face, his head. He screamed. He sagged, covering his face with bloody hands. Then, with all her strength, she gave him a great swinging blow, and he fell to his knees, rolled over, and at last was stilled and silenced.

There was quite a lot of blood, though it quickly stopped flowing. She stood there looking at him, and she was sobbing. Had she been sobbing all the time? She was covered with blood. She tore off her clothes and dropped them in a heap around her. For a moment she knelt beside him, naked and weeping, rocking backward and forward, speaking his name, biting her fingers that were all sticky with his blood.

But self-preservation is the primal instinct. It is more powerful than love or sorrow, hatred or regret. The time was nine o'clock, and in an hour those men would come. Betsy fetched water in a bucket, detergent, cloths, and a sponge. The hard work, the great cleansing, stopped her tears, quieted her heart, and dulled her thoughts. She thought of nothing, working frenziedly, her mind a blank.

When bucket after bucket of reddish water had been poured down the sink, and the carpet was soaked but clean, the lamp washed and dried and polished, she threw her clothes into the hamper in the bathroom and took a bath. She dressed carefully and brushed her hair. Eight minutes to ten. Everything was clean and she had opened the window, but the dead thing still lay there on a pile of reddened newspapers.

"I loved him," she said aloud, and she clenched her fists. "I hated him."

The men were punctual. They came at ten sharp. They carried the six tea chests and the silver-colored trunk with the gold-colored clasps downstairs.

When they had gone and their van had driven away, Betsy sat down on the sofa. She looked at the angle lamp, the onyx pen jar and ashtray, the ginger jar, the alabaster bowls, the hock glasses, the bronze paperknife, the little Chinese cups, and the Lowry that was back on the wall. She was quite calm now, and she didn't really need the brandy she had poured for herself.

Of the past she thought not at all, and the present seemed to exist only as a palpable nothingness, a thick silence that lay around her. She thought of the future, of three months hence, and into the silence she let forth a steady, rather toneless peal of laughter.

Miss Patricia Gordon, 23 Burwood Park Avenue, Kew, Victoria, Australia 3101. The pretty, greedy, hard face, the hands so eager to undo the padlock and prize open those golden clasps to find the treasure within.

And how interesting that treasure would be in three months' time—like nothing Miss Patricia Gordon had seen in all her life! It was as well, so that she would recognize it, that it carried on top of it a note in a familiar hand:

All this is for you, darling Patricia, forever and ever.

MELVILLE DAVISSON POST

NABOTH'S VINEYARD

One hears a good deal about the sovereignty of the people in this republic; and many persons imagine it a sort of fiction, and wonder where it lies, who are the guardians of it, and how they would exercise it if the forms and agents of the law were removed. I am not one of those who speculate upon this mystery, for I have seen this primal ultimate authority naked at its work. And, having seen it, I know how mighty and how dread a thing it is. And I know where it lies, and who are the guardians of it, and how they exercise it when the need arises.

There was a great crowd, for the whole country was in the courtroom. It was a notorious trial.

Elihu Marsh had been shot down in his house. He had been found lying in a room, with a hole through his body that one could put his thumb in. He was an irascible old man, the last of his family, and so lived alone. He had rich lands, but only a life estate in them, the remainder was to some foreign heirs. A girl from a neighboring farm came now and then to bake and put his house in order, and he kept a farmhand about the premises.

Nothing had been disturbed in the house when the neighbors found Marsh; no robbery had been attempted, for the man's money, a considerable sum, remained on his body.

There was not much mystery about the thing, because the farmhand had disappeared. This man was a stranger in the hills. He had come from over the mountains some months before, and gone to work for Marsh. He was a big blond man, young and good-looking; of better blood, one would say, than the average laborer. He gave his name as Taylor, but he was not communicative, and little else about him was known.

The country was raised, and this man was overtaken in the foothills of the mountains. He had his clothes tied into a bundle and a long-barreled fowling-piece on his shoulder. The story he told was that he and Marsh had settled that morning and he had left the house at noon, but that he had forgotten his gun and had gone back for it, had reached the house about four o'clock, gone into the kitchen, got his gun down from the dogwood forks over the chimney, and at once left the house. He had not seen Marsh and did not know where he was.

He admitted that this gun had been loaded with a single huge lead bullet. He had so loaded it to kill a dog that sometimes approached the house, but not close enough to be reached with a load of shot. He affected surprise when it was pointed out that the gun had been discharged. He said that he had not fired it, and had not until then noticed that it was empty. When asked why he had so suddenly determined to leave the country, he was silent.

He was carried back and confined in the county jail, and now he was on trial at the September term of the circuit court.

The court sat early. Although the judge, Simon Kilrail, was a landowner and lived on his estate in the country some half dozen miles away, he rode to the courthouse in the morning, and home at night, with his legal papers in his saddle-pockets. It was only when the court sat that he was a lawyer. At other times he harvested his hay and grazed his cattle and tried to add to his lands like any other man in the hills, and he was as hard in a trade and as hungry for an acre as any.

It was the sign and insignia of distinction in Virginia to own land. Mr. Jefferson had annulled the titles that George III had granted, and the land alone remained as a patent of nobility. The judge wished to be one of these landed gentry, and he had gone a good way to accomplish it. But when the court convened he became a lawyer and sat upon the bench with no heart in him, and a cruel tongue like the English judges.

I think everybody was at this trial. My Uncle Abner and the strange old doctor, Storm, sat on a bench near the center aisle of the courtroom, and I sat behind them, for I was a half-grown lad and permitted to witness the terrors and severities of the law.

The prisoner was the center of interest. He sat with a stolid countenance, like a man careless of the issues of life. But not everybody was concerned with him, for my Uncle Abner and

Storm watched the girl who had been accustomed to bake for Marsh and red up his house.

She was a beauty of her type, dark-haired and dark-eyed like a gypsy, and with an April nature of storm and sun. She sat among the witnesses with a little handkerchief clutched in her hands. She was nervous to the point of hysteria, and I thought that was the reason the old doctor watched her. She would be taken with a gust of tears, and then throw up her head with a fine defiance, and she kneaded and knotted and worked the handkerchief in her fingers. It was a time of stress and many witnesses were unnerved, and I think I should not have noticed this girl but for the whispering of Storm and my Uncle Abner.

The trial went forward, and it became certain that the prisoner would hang. His stubborn refusal to give any reason for his hurried departure had but one meaning, and the circumstantial evidence was conclusive. The motive, only, remained in doubt, and the judge had charged on this with so many cases in point and with so heavy a hand that any virtue in it was removed. The judge was hard against this man, and indeed there was little sympathy anywhere, for it was a foul killing—the victim an old man and no hot blood to excuse it.

In all trials of great public interest, where the evidences of guilt overwhelmingly assemble against a prisoner, there comes a moment when all the people in the courtroom, as one man and without a sign of the common purpose, agree upon a verdict; there is no outward or visible evidence of this decision, but one feels it, and it is a moment of the tensest stress.

The trial of Taylor had reached this point, and there lay a moment of deep silence, when this girl sitting among the witnesses suddenly burst into a very hysteria of tears. She stood up, shaking with sobs, her voice choking in her throat and the tears gushing through her fingers.

What she said was not heard at the time by the audience in the courtroom, but it brought the judge to his feet and the jury crowding about her, and it broke down the silence of the prisoner and threw him into a perfect fury of denials. We could hear his voice rise above the confusion, and we could see him struggling to get to the girl and stop her. But what she said was presently known to everybody, for it was taken down and signed; and it put the case against Taylor, to use a lawyer's term, out of court.

The girl had killed Marsh herself. And this was the manner and the reason for it: she and Taylor were sweethearts and were to be married. But they had quarreled the night before Marsh's death and the following morning Taylor had left the country. The point of the quarrel was some remark that Marsh had made to Taylor touching the girl's reputation. She had come to the house in the afternoon and, finding her lover gone and maddened at the sight of the one who had robbed her of him, had taken the gun down from the chimney and killed Marsh. She had then put the gun back into its place and left the house. This was about two o'clock in the afternoon and about an hour before Taylor returned for his gun.

There was a great veer of public feeling with a profound sense of having come at last upon the truth, for the story not only fitted to the circumstantial evidence against Taylor but it fitted also to his story and it disclosed the motive for the killing. It explained, too, why he had refused to give the reason for his disappearance. That Taylor denied what the girl said and tried to stop her in her declaration meant nothing except that the prisoner was a man and would not have the woman he loved make such a sacrifice for him.

I cannot give all the forms of legal procedure with which the closing hours of the court were taken up, but nothing happened to shake the girl's confession. Whatever the law required was speedily got ready, and she was remanded to the care of the sheriff in order that she might come before the court in the morning.

Taylor was not released, but was also held in custody, although the case against him seemed utterly broken down. The judge refused to permit the prisoner's counsel to take a verdict. He said that he would withdraw a juror and continue the case. But he seemed unwilling to release any clutch of the law until someone was punished for this crime.

It was on our way, and we rode out with the judge that night. He talked with Abner and Storm about the pastures and the pride of cattle, but not about the trial as I hoped he would do, except once only and then it was to inquire why the prosecuting attorney had not called either of them as witnesses, since they were the first to find Marsh, and Storm had been among the doctors who examined him. And Storm had explained how he had mortally offended the prosecutor in his canvass by his remark that only a gentleman should hold office. He did but quote Mr. Hamilton, Storm said, but the man had received it as a deadly insult, and thereby proved the truth of Mr. Hamilton's expression. And Abner said that as no circumstance about Marsh's death was questioned, and others arriving about the same time had been called, the prosecutor doubtless considered further testimony unnecessary.

The judge nodded and the conversation turned to other questions. At the gate, after the common formal courtesy of the country, the judge asked us to ride in, and to my astonishment Abner and Storm accepted his invitation. I could see that the man was surprised, and I thought annoyed, but he took us into his library.

I could not understand why Abner and Storm had stopped here, until I remembered how from the first they had been considering the girl, and it occurred to me that they thus sought the judge in the hope of getting some word to him in her favor. A great sentiment had leaped up for this girl. She had made a staggering sacrifice, and with a headlong courage, and it was like these men to help her if they could.

And it *was* to speak of the woman that they came, but not in her favor. And while Simon Kilrail listened, they told this extraordinary story.

They had been of the opinion that Taylor was not guilty when the trial began, but they had suffered it to proceed in order to see what might develop. The reason was that there were certain circumstantial evidences, overlooked by the prosecutor, indicating the guilt of the woman and the innocence of Taylor. When Storm examined the body of Marsh, he discovered that the man had been killed by poison and was dead when the bullet was fired into his body. This meant that the shooting was a fabricated evidence to direct suspicion against Taylor. The woman had baked for Marsh on this morning, and the poison was in the bread which he had eaten at noon.

Abner was going on to explain something further when a servant entered and asked the judge what time it was. The man had been greatly impressed, and he now sat in a profound reflection. He took his watch out of his pocket and held it in his hand, then he seemed to realize the question and replied that his watch had run down. Abner gave the hour and said that perhaps his key would wind the watch. The judge gave it to him and he wound it and laid it on the table. Storm observed my uncle with what I thought a curious interest, but the judge paid no attention. He was deep in his reflection and oblivious to everything. Finally he roused himself and made his comment.

"This clears the matter up," he said. "The woman killed Marsh from the motive which she gave in her confession and she created this false evidence against Taylor because he had abandoned her. She thereby avenged herself desperately in two directions. It would be like a woman to do this, and then regret it and confess."

He then asked my uncle if he had anything further to tell him, and although I was sure that Abner was going to say something further when the servant entered, he replied now that he had not, and asked for the horses.

The judge went out to have the horses brought and we remained in silence. My uncle was calm, as with some consuming idea, but Storm was as nervous as a cat. He was out of his chair when the door was closed and hopping about the room looking at the law books standing on the shelves in their leather covers. Suddenly he stopped and plucked out a little volume. He whipped through it with his forefinger, smothered a great oath, and shot it into his pocket; then he crooked his finger to my uncle and they talked together in a recess of the window until the judge returned.

We rode away. I was sure that they intended to say something to the judge in the woman's favor, for, guilty or not, it was a fine thing she had done to stand up and confess. But something in the interview had changed their purpose. Perhaps when they heard the judge's comment they saw it would be of no use. They talked closely together as they rode, but they kept before me and I could not hear. It was of the woman they spoke, however, for I caught a bit.

"But where is the motive?" said Storm.

And my uncle answered, "In the twenty-first chapter of the Book of Kings."

We were early at the county seat, and it was a good thing for us, because the courtroom was crowded to the doors. My uncle had got a big record book out of the county clerk's office as he came in, and I was glad of it, for he gave it to me to sit on and it raised me up so I could see. Storm was there, too, and, in fact, every man of any standing in the county.

The sheriff opened the court, the prisoners were brought in, and the judge took his seat on the bench. He looked haggard, like a man who had not slept, as, in fact, one could hardly have done who had so cruel a duty before him. Here was every human feeling pressing to save a woman, and the law to hang her. But for all his hag-ridden face, when he came to act, the man was adamant.

He ordered the confession read and directed the girl to stand up. Taylor tried again to protest, but he was forced down into his chair. The girl stood up bravely, but she was white as plaster and her eyes dilated. She was asked if she still adhered to the confession and understood the consequences of it, and, although she trembled from head to toe, she spoke out distinctly. There was a moment of silence, and the judge was about to speak, when another voice filled the courtroom. I turned about on my book to find my head against my Uncle Abner's legs.

"I challenge the confession!" he said.

The whole courtroom moved. Every eye was on the two tragic figures standing up: the slim, pale girl and the big, somber figure of my uncle. The judge was astounded.

"On what ground?" he said.

"On the ground," replied my uncle, "that the confession is a lie!"

One could have heard a pin fall anywhere in the whole room. The girl caught her breath in a little gasp, and the prisoner, Taylor, half rose and then sat down as though his knees were too weak to bear him. The judge's mouth opened, but for a moment or two he did not speak, and I could understand his amazement. Here was Abner assailing a confession which he himself had supported before the judge, and speaking for the innocence of a woman whom he himself had shown to be guilty, taking one position privately and another publicly. What did the man mean? And I was not surprised that the judge's voice was stern when he spoke.

"This is irregular," he said. "It may be that this woman killed Marsh, or it may be that Taylor killed him, and there is some collusion between these persons, as you appear to suggest. And you may know something to throw light on the matter, or you may not. However that may be, this is not the time for me to hear you. You will have ample opportunity to speak when I come to try the case."

"But you will never try the case!" said Abner.

I cannot undertake to describe the desperate interest that lay on the people in the courtroom. They were breathlessly silent; one could hear the voices from the village outside and the sounds of men and horses that came up through the open windows. No one knew what hidden thing Abner drove at. But he was a man who meant what he said, and the people knew it.

The judge turned on him with a terrible face.

"What do you mean?" he said.

"I mean," replied Abner, and it was in his deep, hard voice, "that you must come down from the Bench."

The judge was in a heat of fury.

"You are in contempt!" he roared. "I order your arrest. Sheriff!"

But Abner did not move. He looked the man calmly in the face.

"You threaten me," he said, "but God Almighty threatens you." And he turned about to the audience. "The authority of the law," he said, "is in the hands of the electors of this county. Will they stand up?"

I shall never forget what happened then, for I have never in my life seen anything so deliberate and impressive. Slowly, in silence, and without passion, as though they were in a church of God, men began to get up in the courtroom.

Randolph was the first. He was a justice of the peace, vain and pompous, proud of the abilities of an ancestry that he did not inherit. And his superficialities were the annoyance of my

Uncle Abner's life. But whatever I may have to say of him hereafter I want to say this thing of him here, that his bigotry and his vanities were builded on the foundations of a man. He stood up as though he stood alone, with no glance about him to see what other men would do, and he faced the judge calmly above his great black stock. And I learned then that a man may be a blusterer and a lion.

Hiram and Arnold got up, and Rockford, and Armstrong, and Alkire, and Coopman, and Monroe, and Elnathan Stone, and my father, Lewis, and Dayton and Ward, and Madison from beyond the mountains. And it seemed to me that the very hills and valleys were standing up.

It was a strange and instructive thing to see. The loud-mouthed and the reckless were in that courtroom, men who would have shouted in a political convention, or run howling with a mob, but they were not the persons who stood up when Abner called upon the authority of the people to appear. Men rose whom one would not have looked to see—the blacksmith, the saddler, and old Asa Divers. And I saw that law and order and all the structure that civilization had builded up rested on the sense of justice that certain men carried in their breasts, and that those who possessed it not, in the crisis of necessity, did not count.

Father Donovan stood up; he had a little flock beyond the valley river, and he was as poor and almost as humble as his Master, but he was not afraid—and Bronson, who preached Calvin, and Adam Rider, who traveled a Methodist circuit. No one of them believed in what the other taught, but they all believed in justice, and when the line was drawn there was but one side of them all.

The last man up was Nathaniel Davisson, but the reason was that he was very old, and he had to wait for his sons to help him. He had been time and again in the Assembly of Virginia, at a time when only a gentleman and landowner could sit there. He was a just man, and honorable and unafraid.

The judge, his face purple, made a desperate effort to enforce his authority. He pounded on his desk and ordered the sheriff to clear the courtroom. But the sheriff remained standing apart. He did not lack for courage, and I think he would have faced the people if his duty had been that way. His attitude was firm, and no one could mark uncertainty upon him, but he took no step to obey what the judge commanded.

The judge cried out at him in a terrible voice, "I am the representative of the law here! Go on!"

The sheriff was a plain man and unacquainted with the nice expressions of Mr. Jefferson, but his answer could not have been better if that gentleman had written it out for him.

"I would obey the representative of the law," he said, "if I were not in the presence of the law itself!"

The judge rose. "This is revolution," he said. "I will send to the Governor for the militia."

It was Nathaniel Davisson who spoke then. He was very old and the tremors of dissolution were on him, but his voice was steady.

"Sit down, Your Honor," he said, "there is no revolution here, and you do not require troops to support your authority. We are here to support it if it ought to be lawfully enforced. But the people have elevated you to the Bench because they believed in your integrity, and if they have been mistaken they would know it."

He paused as though to collect his strength and then went on. "The presumptions of right are all with Your Honor. You administer the law upon our authority and we stand behind you. Be assured that we will not suffer our authority to be insulted in your person." His voice grew deep and resolute. "It is a grave thing to call us up against you, and not lightly, nor for a trivial reason shall any man dare to do it." Then he turned about. "Now, Abner," he said, "what is this thing?"

Young as I was, I felt that the old man spoke for the people standing in the courtroom, with their voice and their authority, and I began to fear that the measure which my uncle had taken was high-handed. But he stood there like the shadow of a great rock.

"I charge him," he said, "with the murder of Elihu Marsh! And I call upon him to vacate the Bench."

When I think about this extraordinary event now, I wonder at the calmness with which Simon Kilrail met this blow, until I reflect that he had seen it on its way and had got ready to meet it. But even with that preparation, it took a man of iron nerve to face an assault like that and keep every muscle in its place. He had tried violence and had failed with it, and he had recourse now to the attitudes and mannerisms of a judicial dignity. He sat with his elbows on the table and his clenched fingers propping up his jaw. He looked coldly at Abner, but he did not speak, and there was silence until Nathaniel Davisson spoke for him. His face and his voice were like iron.

"No, Abner," he said, "he shall not vacate the Bench for that, nor upon the accusation of any man. We will have your proofs, if you please."

The judge turned his cold face from Abner to Nathaniel Davisson, and then he looked over the men standing in the courtroom.

"I am not going to remain here," he said, "to be tried by a mob, upon the *viva voce* indictment of a bystander. You may nullify your court, if you like, and suspend the forms of law for yourselves, but you cannot nullify the constitution of Virginia, nor suspend my right as a citizen of the commonwealth.

"And now," he said, rising, "if you will kindly make way, I will vacate this courtroom, which your violence has converted into a chamber of sedition."

The man spoke in a cold, even voice, and I thought he had presented a difficulty that could not be met. How could these men before him undertake to keep the peace of this frontier, and force its lawless elements to submit to the forms of law for trial, and deny any letter of those formalities to this man? Was the grand jury, and the formal indictment, and all the right and privilege of an orderly procedure for one and not for another?

It was Nathaniel Davisson who met this dangerous problem.

"We are not concerned," he said, "at this moment with your rights as a citizen; the rights of private citizenship are inviolate, and they remain to you when you return to it. But you are not a private citizen. You are our agent. We have selected you to administer the law for us, and your right to act has been challenged. As the authority behind you, we appear and would know the reason."

The judge retained his imperturbable calm.

"Do you hold me a prisoner here?" he said.

"We hold you an official in your office," replied Davisson. "Not only do we refuse to permit you to leave the courtroom, but we refuse to permit you to leave the Bench. This court shall remain as we have set it up until it is our will to readjust it. And it shall not be changed at the pleasure or demand of any man but by us only, and for a sufficient cause shown to us."

And again I was anxious for my uncle, for I saw how grave a thing it was to interfere with the authority of the people as manifested in the forms and agencies of the law. Abner must be very sure of the ground under him.

And he was sure. He spoke now, with no introductory expressions, but directly and in the simplest words.

"These two persons," he said, indicating Taylor and the girl, "have each been willing to die in order to save the other. Neither is guilty of this crime. Taylor has kept silent, and the girl has lied, to the same end. This is the truth: there was a lovers' quarrel and Taylor left the country precisely as he told us, except the motive, which he would not tell lest the girl be involved. And the woman, to save him, confesses to a crime that she did not commit.

"Who did commit it?" He paused and included Storm with a gesture. "We suspected this woman because Marsh had been killed by poison in his bread, and afterwards mutilated with a shot. Yesterday we rode out with the judge to put those facts before him." Again he paused. "An incident occurring in that interview indicated that we were wrong; a second incident assured us, and still later a third convinced us. These incidents were, first, that the judge's watch had run down; second, that we found in his library a book with all the leaves in it uncut except at one certain page; and, third, that we found in the county clerk's office an unindexed record in an old deed book.

"In addition to the theory of Taylor's guilt or this woman's, there was still a third, but it had only a single incident to support it and we feared to suggest it until the others had been explained. This theory was that someone, to benefit by Marsh's death, had planned to kill him in such a manner as to throw suspicion on this woman who baked his bread, and finding Taylor gone, and the gun above the mantel, yielded to an afterthought to create a further false evidence. It was overdone!

"The trigger guard of the gun in the recoil caught in the chain of the assassin's watch and jerked it out of his pocket. He replaced the watch, but not the key, which fell to the floor and which I picked up beside the body of the dead man."

Abner turned toward the judge.

"And so," he said, "I charge Simon Kilrail with this murder because the key winds his watch, because the record in the old deed book is a conveyance by the heirs of Marsh's lands to him at the life tenant's death, and because the book we found in his library is a book on poisons with the leaves uncut except at the very page describing that identical poison with which Elihu Marsh was murdered."

The strained silence that followed Abner's words was broken by a voice that thundered in the courtroom. It was Randolph's.

"Come down!" he said.

And this time Nathaniel Davisson was silent.

The judge got slowly on his feet. A resolution was forming in his face, and it advanced swiftly.

"I will give you my answer in a moment," he said.

Then he turned about and went into his room behind the Bench. There was but one door, and that opening into the court, and the people waited.

The windows were open and we could see the green fields, and the sun, and the far-off mountains, and the peace and quiet and serenity of autumn entered. The judge did not appear. Presently there was the sound of a shot from behind the closed door. The sheriff threw it open, and upon the floor, sprawling in a smear of blood, lay Simon Kilrail, with a dueling pistol in his hand.

JULIAN SYMONS

THE BOILER

Harold Boyle was on his way out to lunch when the encounter took place that changed his life. He was bound for a vegetarian restaurant, deliberately chosen because to reach it he had to walk across the park. A walk during the day did you good, just as eating a nut, raisin, and cheese salad was better for you than consuming chunks of meat that lay like lead in the stomach. He always returned feeling positively healthier, ready and even eager for the columns of figures that awaited him.

On this day he was walking along by the pond, stepping it out to reach the restaurant, when a man coming toward him said,"Hallo." Harold gave a half smile, half grimace, intended as acknowledgment while suggesting that in fact they didn't know each other. The man stopped. He was a fleshy fellow, with a large aggressive face. When he smiled, as he did now, he revealed a mouthful of beautiful white teeth. His appearance struck some disagreeable chord in Harold's memory. Then the man spoke, and the past came back.

"If it isn't the boiler," the man said. "Jack Cutler, remember me?"

Harold's smallish white hand was gripped in a large red one.

From that moment onward things seemed to happen of their own volition. He was carried along on the tide of Cutler's boundless energy. The feeble suggestion that he already had a lunch engagement was swept aside, they were in a taxi and then at Cutler's club, and he was having a drink at the bar although he never took liquor at lunchtime.

Then lunch, and it turned out that Cutler had ordered already, great steaks that must have cost a fortune, and a bottle of wine. During the meal Cutler talked about the firm of building contractors he ran and of its success, the way business was waiting for you if you had the nerve to go out and get it. While he talked, the large teeth bit into the steak as though they were shears. Then his plate was empty.

"Talking about myself too much, always do when I eat. Can't tell you how good it is to see you, my old boiler. What are you doing with yourself?"

"I am a contract estimator for a firm of paint manufacturers."

"Work out price details, keep an eye open to make sure nobody's cheating? Everybody cheats nowadays, you know that. I reckon some of my boys are robbing me blind, fiddling estimates, taking a cut themselves. You reckon something can be done about that sort of thing?"

"If the estimates are properly checked in advance, certainly."

Cutler chewed a toothpick. "What do they pay you at the paint shop?"

It was at this point, he knew afterward, that he should have said no, he was not interested, he would be late back at the office. Perhaps he should even have been bold enough to tell the truth, and say that he did not want to see Cutler again. Instead he meekly gave the figure.

"Skinflints, aren't they? Come and work for me and I'll double it."

Again he knew he should have said no, I don't want to work for you. Instead, he murmured something about thinking it over.

"That's my good old careful boiler," Cutler said, and laughed.

"I must get back to the office. Thank you for lunch."

"You'll be in touch?"

Harold said yes, intending to write a note turning down the offer. When he got home, however, he was foolish enough to mention the offer to his wife, in response to a question about what kind of day he had had. He could have bitten out his tongue the moment after. Of course, she immediately said that he must take it.

"But Phyl, I can't. I don't like Cutler."

"He seems to like you, taking you to lunch and making this offer. Where did you know him?"

"We were at school together. He likes power over people, that's all he thinks of. He was an awful bully. When we were at school he called me a boiler."

"A *what?* Oh, I see, a joke on your name. I don't see there's much harm in that."

"It wasn't a joke. It was to show his—his contempt. He made other people be contemptuous, too. And he still says it—when we met he said it's the boiler."

"It sounds a bit childish to me. You're not a child now, Harold."

"You don't understand," he cried out in despair. "You just don't understand."

"I'll tell you what I do understand," she said. Her small pretty face was distorted with anger. "We've been married eight years, and you've been in the same firm all the time. Same firm, same job, no promotion. Now you're offered double the money. Do you know what that would mean? I could get some new clothes, we could have a washing machine, we might even be able to move out of this neighborhood to somewhere really nice. And you just say no to it, like that. If you want me to stay you'd better change your mind."

She went out, slamming the door. When he went upstairs later, he found the bedroom door locked. He slept in the spare room.

Or at least he lay in bed there. He thought about Cutler, who had been a senior when he was a junior. Cutler was the leader of a group who called themselves The Razors, and one day Harold found himself surrounded by them while on his way home. They pushed and pulled him along to the house of one boy whose parents were away. In the garden shed there, they held a kind of trial in which they accused him of having squealed on a gang member who had asked Harold for the answers to some exam questions. Harold had given the answers, some of them had been wrong, and the master had spotted these identical wrong answers. Under questioning, Harold told the master what had happened.

He tried to explain that this was not squealing, but the gang remained unimpressed. Suggestions about what should be done to him varied from cutting off all his hair to holding him face down in a lavatory bowl. Somebody said that Boyle should be put in a big saucepan and boiled, which raised a laugh. Then Cutler intervened. He was big even then, a big red-faced boy, very sarcastic.

"We don't want to *do* anything. He'll only go sniveling back to teacher. Let's call him something. Call him the boiler."

Silence. Somebody said, "Don't see he'll mind."

"Oh, yes, he will." Cutler came close to Harold, his big face sneering. "Because I'll tell him what it means, and then he'll remember every time he hears it. Now, you just repeat this after me, boiler." Then Cutler recited the ritual of the boiler and Harold, after his hair had been pulled and his arm twisted until he thought it would break, repeated it.

He remembered the ritual. It began: *I am a boiler. A boiler is a mean little sneak. He can't tie his own shoelaces. A boiler fails in everything he tries. A boiler stinks. I am a boiler.*

Then they let him go, and he ran home. But that was the beginning of it, not the end. Cutler and his gang never called him anything else. They clamped their fingers to their noses when he drew near and said, "Watch out, here's the boiler, pooh, what a stink."

Other boys caught on and did the same. He became a joke, an outcast. His work suffered, he got a bad end-of-term report. His father had died when he was five, so it was his beloved mother who asked him whether something was wrong. He burst into tears. She said that he must try harder next term, and he shook his head.

"It's no good, I can't. I can't do it, I'm a boiler."

"A boiler? What do you mean?"

"A boiler—it means I'm no good, can't do anything right. It's what they call me."

"Who calls you that?"

He told her. She insisted on going up to school and seeing the headmaster, although he implored her not to, and afterward of course things were worse than ever. The head had said that he would see what could be done, but that boys would be boys and Harold was perhaps oversensitive. Now the gang pretended to burst into tears whenever they saw him, and said poor little boiler should run home to mummy.

And he often did run home from school to mummy. He was not ashamed to remember that he had loved his mother more than anybody else in the world, and that his love had been returned. She was a highly emotional woman, and so nervous that she kept a tiny pearl-handled revolver beside her bed. Harold had lived with her until she died. She left him all she had, which was a little money in gilt-edged stocks, some old-fashioned jewelry, and the revolver. He sold the stocks and the jewelry, and kept the revolver in a bureau which he used as a writing desk.

It was more than twenty years ago that Cutler had christened him boiler, but the memory remained painful. And now Phyllis wanted him to work with the man. Of course, she couldn't know what the word meant, how could anybody know? He saw that in a way Phyllis was right. She had been only twenty-two, ten years younger than Harold, when they married after his mother's death. It was true that he had expected promotion, he should have changed jobs, it would be wonderful to have more money. You mustn't be a boiler all your life, he said to himself. Cutler was being friendly when he offered him the job.

And he couldn't bear to be on bad terms with Phyl, or to think that she might leave him. There had been an awful time, four years ago, when he had discovered that she was carrying on an affair with another man, some salesman who had called at the door to sell a line of household brooms and brushes. He had come home early one day and found them together. Phyl was shamefaced but defiant, saying that if he only took her out a bit more it wouldn't have happened. Was it the fact that the salesman was a man of her own age, he asked. She shook her head, but said that it might help if Harold didn't behave like an old man of sixty.

In the morning he told Phyl that he had thought it over and changed his mind. She said that he would have been crazy not to take the job. Later that day he telephoned Cutler.

To his surprise, he did not find the new job disagreeable. It was more varied than his old work, and more interesting. He checked everything carefully, as he had always done, and soon unearthed evidence showing that one of the foremen was working with a sales manager to inflate the cost of jobs by putting in false invoices billed to a nonexistent firm. Both men were sacked immediately.

He saw Cutler on most days. Harold's office overlooked the

entrance courtyard, so that if he looked out of the window he could see Cutler's distinctive gold-and-silver-colored Rolls-Royce draw up. A smart young chauffeur opened the door and the great man stepped out, often with a cigar in his mouth, and nodded to the chauffeur, who then took the car round to the parking lot. Cutler came in around ten-thirty, and often invaded Harold's office after lunch, smelling of drink, his face very red. He was delighted by the discovery of the invoice fraud and clapped Harold on the back.

"Well done, my old boiler. It was a stroke of inspiration asking you to come here. Hasn't worked out too badly for you, either, has it?" Harold agreed. He talked as little as possible to his employer. One day Cutler complained of this.

"Damn it, man, anybody would think we didn't know each other. Just because I use a Rolls and have young Billy Meech drive me in here every morning doesn't mean I'm standoffish. You know why I do it? The Rolls is good publicity, the best you can have, and I get driven in every morning because it saves time. I work in the car dictating letters and so forth. I drive myself most of the time, though—Meech has got a cushy job and he knows it. But don't think I forget old friends. I tell you what—you and your wife must come out and have dinner one night. And we'll use the Rolls."

Harold protested, but a few days later a letter came, signed "Blanche Cutler," saying that Jack was delighted that an old friendship had been renewed and suggesting a dinner date. Phyllis could hardly contain her pleasure and was both astonished and furious when Harold said they shouldn't go, they would be like poor relations.

"What are you talking about? He's your old friend, isn't he? And he's been decent to you, giving you a job. If *he's* not snobby, I don't see why you should be."

"I told you I don't like him. We're not friends."

She glared at him. "You're jealous, that's all. You're a failure yourself, and you can't bear anybody else to be a success."

In the end, of course, they went.

Cutler and Harold left the office in the Rolls, driven by Meech, who was in his middle twenties, and they collected Phyllis on the way. She had bought a dress for the occasion, and Harold could see that she was taking everything in greedily—the way Meech sprang out to open the door, the luxurious interior of the Rolls, the cocktail cabinet from which Cutler poured drinks, the silent smoothness with which they traveled. Cutler paid what Harold thought were ridiculous compliments on Phyllis's dress and appearance, saying that Harold had kept his beautiful young wife a secret.

"You're a lucky man, my old boiler."

"Harold said that was what you called him. It seems a silly name."

"Just a reminder of schooldays," Cutler said easily, and Harold hated him.

The Cutlers lived in a big red-brick house in the outer suburbs, with a garden of more than an acre and a swimming pool. Blanche was a fine, imposing woman, with a nose that seemed permanently raised in the air. Another couple came to dinner, the man big and loud-voiced like Cutler, his wife a small woman loaded down with what were presumably real pearls and diamonds. The man was some sort of stockbroker, and there was a good deal of conversation about the state of the market.

Dinner was served by a maid in cap and apron, and was full of foods covered with rich sauces Harold knew would play havoc with his digestion. There was a lot of wine, and he saw with dismay that Phyllis's glass was being refilled frequently.

"You and Jack were great friends at school, he tells me," Blanche Cutler said, nose in air. What could Harold do but agree? "He says that now you are his right-hand man. I do think it is so nice when old friendships are continued in later life."

He muttered something, and then was horrified to hear the word *boiler* spoken by Phyllis.

"What's that?" the stockbroker asked, cupping hand to ear. Phyllis giggled. She was a little drunk.

"Do you know what they used to call Harold at school? A boiler. What does it mean, Jack, you must tell us what it means."

"It was just a nickname." Cutler seemed embarrassed. "Because his name was Boyle, you see."

"I know you're hiding something from me." Phyllis tapped

Cutler flirtatiously on the arm. "Was it because he looks like a tough old boiling fowl, very tasteless? Because he does. I think it's a very good name for him, a boiler."

Blanche elevated her nose a little higher and said that they would have coffee in the drawing room.

Meech drove them home in the Rolls and gave Phyllis his arm when they got out. She clung to it, swaying a little as they moved toward the front door. Indoors, she collapsed on the sofa and said, "What a lovely, lovely evening."

"I'm glad you enjoyed it."

"I liked Jack. Your friend Jack. He's such good company. *Such* good company."

"He's not my friend, he's my employer."

"Such an attractive man, very sexy."

He remembered the salesman. "I thought you only liked younger men. Cutler's older than I am."

She looked at him with a slightly glazed eye. "Dance with me."

"We haven't got any music."

"Come *on,* doesn't matter." She pulled him to his feet and they stumbled through a few steps.

"You're drunk." He half pushed her away and she fell to the floor. She lay there staring up at him.

"You damn—you pushed me over."

"I'm sorry, Phyl. Come to bed."

"You know what you are? You're a boiler. It's a good name for you."

"Phyl. Please."

"I married a boiler," she said, and passed out. He had to carry her up to bed.

In the morning she did not get up as usual to make his breakfast. In the evening she said sullenly that there was no point in talking any more. Harold was just a clerk and would never be anything else, didn't want to be anything else.

After lunch on the next day, Cutler came into Harold's office and said he hoped they had enjoyed the evening. For once he was not at ease, and at last came out with what seemed to be on his mind. "I'm glad we got together again, for old times' sake. But look here, I'm afraid Phyl got hold of the wrong end of the stick. About that nickname."

"Boiler."

"Yes. Of course, it was only meant affectionately. Just a play on your name." Did Cutler really believe that, could he possibly believe it? His red shining face looked earnest enough. "But people can get the wrong impression, as Phyl did. Better drop it. So no more boiler. From now on it's Jack and Harold, agreed?"

He said that he agreed. Cutler clapped him on the shoulder and said that he was late for an appointment on the golf course. He winked as he said that you could do a lot of business between the first and the eighteenth holes. Five minutes later, Harold saw him driving away at the wheel of the Rolls-Royce, a big cigar in his mouth.

In the next days, Cutler was away from the office a good deal, and came into Harold's room rarely. At home Phyllis spoke to him only when she could not avoid it. At night they lay like statues side by side. He reflected that, although they had more money, it had not made them happier.

Ten days after the dinner party it happened.

Harold went that day to the vegetarian restaurant across the park. Something in his nut steak must have disagreed with him, however, because by midafternoon he was racked by violent stomach pains. He bore them for half an hour and then decided that he must go home.

The bus took him to the High Road, near his street. He turned the corner into it, walked a few steps, and then stopped, unbelieving.

His house was a hundred yards down the street. And there, drawn up outside it, was Cutler's gold-and-silver Rolls.

He could not have said how long he stood there staring, as though by looking he might make a car disappear. Then he turned away, walked to the post office in the High Road, entered a telephone box, and dialed his own number.

The telephone rang and rang. On the wooden framework of the box somebody had written "Peter loves Vi." He rubbed a finger over the words, trying to erase them.

At last Phyllis answered. She sounded breathless.

"You've been a long time."

"I was in the garden hanging out washing—didn't hear you. You sound funny. What's the matter?"

He said that he felt ill and was coming home, was leaving the office now. She said sharply, "But you're in a call box, I distinctly heard the pips."

He explained that he had suddenly felt faint and had been near a pay telephone in the entrance hall.

"So you'll be back in half an hour." He detected relief in her voice.

During that half hour he walked about—he could not afterward have said in what streets, except that he could not bear to approach his own. He could not have borne to see Cutler driving away, a satisfied leer on his face at having once again shown the boiler who was master. Through his head there rang, over and over, Phyllis's words, "Such an attractive man, very sexy," words that now seemed repeated in the sound of his own footsteps.

When he got home Phyllis exclaimed at the sight of him, and said that he did look ill. She asked what he had eaten at lunch, and said that he had better lie down.

In the bedroom, he caught the lingering aroma of cigar smoke, even though the window was open. He threw up in the lavatory and then said to Phyllis that he would stay in the spare room. She made no objection. During the evening she was unusually solicitous, coming up three times to ask whether there was something he would like, taking his temperature, and putting a hand on his forehead. The touch was loathsome to him.

He stayed in the spare room. In the morning he dressed and shaved, but ate no breakfast. She expressed concern.

"You look pale. If you feel ill, come home—but don't forget to call first just in case I might be out."

So, he thought, Cutler was coming again that day. The pearl-handled revolver, small as a toy, nestled in his pocket when he left. He had never fired it.

He spent the morning looking out of his window, but Cutler did not appear. He arrived soon after lunch, brought by Meech. He did not come to Harold's office.

Half an hour passed. Harold took out the revolver and balanced it in his hand. Would it fire properly, would he be able to shoot straight? He felt calm, but his hand trembled.

He took the lift up to the top floor and opened the door of Cutler's office without knocking. Cutler was talking to a recording machine, which he switched off.

"Why the hell don't you knock?" Then he said more genially, "Oh, it's you, my old—Harold. What can I do for you?"

Harold took out the little revolver. Cutler looked astonished, but not frightened. He asked what Harold thought he was doing.

Harold did not reply. Across the desk the boiler faced the man who had ruined his life. The revolver went *crack crack.* Blue smoke curled up from it. Cutler continued to stare at him in astonishment, and Harold thought that he had failed in this as he had failed in so many things, that even from a few feet he had missed. Then he saw the red spot in the middle of Cutler's forehead, and the big man collapsed face down on his desk.

Harold walked out of the room, took the lift, and left the building. He did not reply to the doorman, who asked whether he was feeling all right, he looked rather queer. He was going to give himself up to the police, but before doing so he must speak to Phyllis. He did not know just what he wanted to say, but it was necessary to show her that he was not a boiler, that Cutler had not triumphed in the end.

The bus dropped him in the High Road. He reached the corner of his street. The Rolls was there, standing in front of his house.

He walked down the street toward it, feeling the terror of a man in a nightmare. Was Cutler immortal, that he should be able to get up from the desk and drive down here? Had he imagined the red spot, had his shots gone astray? He knew only that he must find out the truth.

When he reached the car, it was locked and empty. He opened his front door. The house was silent.

The house was silent, and he was silent as he moved up the stairs delicately on tiptoe. He opened the door of the bedroom.

Phyllis was in bed. With her was the young chauffeur, Meech. A cigar, one of his master's cigars, was stubbed out in an ashtray.

Harold stared at them for a long moment of agony. Then, as

they started up, he said words incomprehensible to them, words from the ritual of school. "A boiler fails in everything he tries. I am a boiler."

He shut the door, went into the bathroom, took out the revolver, and placed the tiny muzzle in his mouth. Then he pulled the trigger.

In this final action the boiler succeeded at last.

CORNELL WOOLRICH

ANGEL FACE

I had on my best hat and my warpaint when I dug into her bell. You've heard makeup called that a thousand times, but this is one time it rated it; it was just that—warpaint.

I caught Ruby Rose Reading at breakfasttime—hers, not mine. Quarter to three in the afternoon. Breakfast was a pink soda-fountain mess, a tomato-and-lettuce—both untouched—and an empty glass of Bromo Seltzer, which had evidently had first claim on her. There were a pair of swell ski slides under her eyes—she was reading Gladys Glad's beauty column to try to figure out how to get rid of them before she went out that night and got a couple more. A maid had opened the door and given me a yellowed optic. "Yes, ma'am, who do you wish to see?"

"I see her already," I said, "so skip the Morse code." I went in up to Ruby Rose's ten-yard line. "Wheeler's the name," I said. "Does it mean anything to you?"

"Should it?" She was dark and Salome-ish. She was mean. She was bad medicine. I could see his finish right there, in her eyes. And it hadn't been any fun to dance at Texas Guinan's or Larry Fay's when I was sixteen, to keep him out of the orphan asylum or the reformatory. I hadn't spent most of my young girlhood in a tinseled G-string to have her take apart what I'd built up just to see what made him tick.

I said, "I don't mind coming right out with it in front of your maid—if you don't."

But evidently she did.

She hit her with the tomato-and-lettuce in the left eye as preamble to the request: "Whaddo I pay you for, anyway? Take Foo-Too around the block a couple of times."

"I took him once already, and he was a good boy" was the weather report she got on this.

"Well, take him again. Maybe you can kid him it's tomorrow already."

The maid fastened something that looked like the business end of a floor mop to a leash and went out shaking her head. "You sure didn't enjoy yourself last night. That Stork Club never agrees with you."

As soon as the gallery was out of the way I said, "You lay off my brother!"

She lit a cigarette and nosed the smoke at me. "Well, Gracie Allen, you've come to the wrong place looking for your brother. And, just for the record, what am I supposed to have done to him, cured him of wiping his nose on his sleeve or something?"

"He's been spending dough like wild, dough that doesn't come out of his salary."

"Then where does it come from?" she asked.

"I haven't found out. I hope his firm never does, either." I shifted gears, went into low—like when I used to sing "Poor Butterfly" for the customers—but money couldn't have dragged this performance out of me, it came from the heart, without pay.

"There's a little girl on our street—oh, not much to look at, thinks twelve o'clock's the middle of the night and storks leave babies, but she's ready to take up where I leave off, pinch pennies and squeeze nickels along with him, build him into something, get him somewhere, not spread him all over the landscape. He's just a man who doesn't know what's good for him, doesn't know his bass from his oboe. I can't stand by and watch her chew her heart up. Give her a break, *and* him, *and* me. Pick on someone your own size, someone who can take it. Have your fun and more power to you—but not with all *I've* got!"

She banged her cigarette to death against a tray. "Okay, is the screen test about over? Now, will you get out of here, you ham actress, and lemme get my massage?"

She went over and got the door ready for me. Gave a traffic-cop signal over her shoulder with one thumb. "I've heard of wives pulling this act, and even mothers, and in a pitcher I saw only lately—*Camilly,* it was called—it was the old man. Now it's a sister!" She gave the ceiling the once-over. "What'll they think of next? Send grandma around tomorow—next week *East Lynne.* Come on, make it snappy!" she invited, and hitched her elbow at me. If she'd touched me, I think I'd have murdered her.

"If you feel I'm poison, why don't you put it up to your brother?" she signed off. And very low, just before she walloped the door after me: "And see how far you get!"

She was right.

I said, "Chick, you're not going to chuck your job, you're not going to Chicago with that dame, are you?"

He looked at me funny and he said, "How did you know?"

"I saw your valise all packed when I wanted to send one of your suits to the cleaners."

"You ought to be a detective," he said, and he wasn't pally. "Okay, now that you mention it," and he went in and he got it to show me the back of it going out the door.

But I got over to the door before he did and pulled a Custer's Last Stand. I skipped the verse and went into the patter chorus. And, boy, did I sell it, without a spot and without a muted trumpet solo, either! At the El-Fay in the old days they would have been crying into their gin and wiring home to mother.

"I'm not asking anything for myself. I'm older than you, Chick, and when a girl says that you've got her down to bedrock. I've been around plenty, and 'around' wasn't pretty. Maybe you think it was fun wrestling my way home each morning at five, and no holds barred, just so—so— Oh, I didn't know why myself sometimes—just so you wouldn't turn out to be another corner lizard, a sharp-shooter, a bum like the rest of them. Chick, you're just a punk of twenty-four, but as far as I'm concerned the sun rises and sets across your shoulders. Me and little Mary Allen, we've been rooting for you all along. What's the matter with her, Chick? Just because her face don't come out of boxes and she doesn't know the right grips, don't pass her by for something that ought to be shampooed out of your hair with gasoline."

But he didn't have an ear for music. The siren song had got to him like Ulysses. And once they hear that—

"Get away from the door," he said, way down low. "I never raised a hand to you in my life, I don't want to now."

The last I saw of him he was passing the back of his hand

slowly up and down his side, like he was ashamed of it. The valise was in the other one. I picked myself up from the opposite side of the foyer where he'd sent me, the place all buckling around me like seen through a sheet of water. I called out after him through the open door: "Don't go, Chick! You're heading straight for the eight-ball! *Don't go to her,* Chick!" The acoustics were swell—every door in the hall opened to get an earful.

He stood there a split-second without looking back at me, yellow light gushing out at him through the porthole of the elevator. He straightened his hat, which my chin against his duke had dislodged—and no more Chick.

At about four that morning, I was still sniveling into the gin he'd left behind him and talking to him across the table from me—without getting any answer—when the doorbell rang. I thought it was him for a minute, but it was two other guys. They didn't ask if they could come in, they just went way around to the other side of me and showed me a couple of tin-heeled palms. So I did the coming in after them. I lived there, after all.

They looked the place over like they were prospective tenants being shown an apartment. I didn't go for that; detectives belong in the books you read in bed, not in your apartment at four bells, big as life. "Three closets," I mentioned, "and you get a month's concession. I'm not keeping you gentlemen up, am I?"

One of them was kind of posh-looking. I mean, he'd washed his face lately, and if he'd been the last man in the world, well, all right, maybe I could have overlooked the fact he was a bloodhound on two legs. The other one had a face like one of those cobblestones they dug up off Eighth Avenue when they removed the trolley tracks.

"You're Jerry Wheeler, aren't you?" the first one told me.

"I've known that for twenty-seven years," I said. "What brought the subject up?"

Cobblestone-face said, "Chick Wheeler's sister, that right?"

"I've got a brother and I call him Chick," I consented. "Any ordinance against that?"

The younger one said, "Don't be so hard to handle. You're

going to talk to us and like it." He sat down in a chair and cushioned his hands behind his dome. "What time did he leave here this evening?"

Something warned me, Don't answer that. I said, "I really couldn't say. I'm not a train-dispatcher."

"He was going to Chicago with a dame named Ruby Rose Reading—you knew that, didn't you?"

I thought, I hit the nail on the head—he *did* help himself to his firm's money. Wonder how much he took? Well, I guess I'll have to go back to work again at one of the hot spots. Maybe I can square it for him, pay back a little each week. I kept my face steady.

I said, "Now, why would he go *anywhere* with anyone with a name like that? It sounds like it came off a bottle of nailpolish. Come to the point, gentlemen—yes, I mean you two. What's he supposed to have done?"

"There's no supposition about what he's done. He went to the Alcazar Arms at eight-fifteen tonight and throttled Ruby Rose Reading to death, Angel Face."

And that was the first time I heard myself called that. I also heard the good-looking one remonstrate: "Aw, don't give it to her that sudden, Coley—she's a girl, after all," but it came from way far away. I was down around their feet somewhere sniffling into the carpet.

The good-looking one picked me up and straightened me out in a chair. Cobblestone said, "Don't let her fool you, Burnsie, they all pull that collapsible-concertina act when they wanna get out of answering questions." He went into the bedroom and I could hear him pulling out bureau drawers and rummaging around.

I got up on one elbow. I said, "Burns, he didn't do it! *Please*—he didn't do it! All right, I did know about her. He was sold on her. That's why he couldn't have done it. You don't kill someone you love!"

He just kind of looked at me. He said, "I've been on the squad eight years now. We never in all that time caught a guy as dead to rights as your brother. He showed up with his valise in the foyer of the Alcazar at exactly twelve minutes past eight tonight. He said to the doorman, 'What time is it? Did Miss Reading send her baggage down yet? We've got to make a train.' Well, she had sent her baggage down, and then she'd changed her mind, she'd had it all taken back upstairs again. There's your motive right there. The doorman rang her apartment and said through the announcer, 'Mr. Wheeler's here.' And she gave a dirty laugh and sang out, 'I can hardly wait.'

"So at thirteen past eight she was still alive. He went up, and he'd no sooner got there than her apartment began to signal the doorman frantically. No one answered his hail over the announcer, so he chased up and he found your brother crouched over her, shaking her, and she was dead. At fifteen minutes past eight o'clock. Is that a case or is that a case?"

I said, "How do you know somebody else wasn't in that apartment and strangled her just before Chick showed up? It's got to be that!"

He said, "What d'you suppose they're paying that doorman seventy-five a month for? The only other caller she had that whole day was you yourself, at three that afternoon, five full hours before. And she'd only been dead fifteen to twenty minutes by the time the assistant medical examiner got to her."

I said, "Does Chick say he did it?"

"When you've been in this business as long as I have, you'd have their heads examined if any of them ever admitted doing anything. Oh, no-o, of course he didn't do it. He says he was crouched over her, shaking her, trying to *restore* her."

I took a deep breath. I said, "Gimme a swallow of that gin."

He did. "Thanks." I put the tumbler down again. I looked him right in the eye. "All right, *I* did it! Now how d'you like that? I begged him not to throw his life away on her. Anyway, when he walked out, I beat him to her place in a taxi, got there first, and gave her one last chance to lay off him. She wouldn't take it. She was all soft and squashy and I just took a grip and pushed hard."

"And the doorman?" he said with a smile.

"His back was turned. He was out at the curb seeing some people into a cab. When I left, I took the stairs down. When Chick signaled from her apartment and the doorman left his post, I just walked out. It was a pushover."

His smile was a grin. "Well, if you killed her, you killed her."

He called in to the other room, "Hey, Coley, she says *she* killed her!"

Coley came back, flapped his hand at me disgustedly, and said, "Come on, let's get out of here, there's nothing doing around here."

He opened the door and went out into the hall. I said, "Well, aren't you going to take me with you? Aren't you going to let him go and hold me instead?"

"Who the hell wants you?" came back through the open door.

Burns, as he got up to follow him, said offhandedly, "And what was she wearing when you killed her?" But he kept walking toward the door without waiting for the answer. I swallowed hard. "I—I was too steamed up to notice colors or anything, but she had on her coat and hat, ready to leave."

He turned around at the door and looked at me. His grin was sort of sympathetic, understanding. "Sure," he said softly. "I guess she took 'em off, though, after she found out she was dead and wasn't going anywhere, after all. We found her in pajamas. Write us a nice long letter about it tomorrow, Angel Face. We'll see you at the trial, no doubt."

There was a glass cigarette-box at my elbow. I grabbed it and heaved, berserk. "You rotten, lowdown—*detective,* you! Going around snooping, framing innocent people to death! Get out of here—I hope I never see your face again!"

It missed his head, crashed and tinkled against the door-frame to one side of him. He didn't cringe—he just gave a long drawn-out whistle. "Maybe you did do it at that," he said, "maybe I'm underestimating you," and he touched his hatbrim and closed the door after him.

The courtroom was unnaturally still. A big blue fly was buzzing on the inside of the window-pane nearest me, trying to find its way out. The jurists came filing in like ghosts and slowly filled the double row of chairs in the box. All you could hear was a slight rustle of clothing as they seated themselves. I kept thinking of the Inquisition and wondered why they didn't have black hoods over their heads.

"Will the foreman of the jury please stand?"

I spaded both my hands down past my hips and grabbed the edges of my seat. My handkerchief fell on the floor and the man next to me picked it up and handed it back to me. I tried to thank him but my jaws wouldn't unlock.

"Gentlemen of the jury, have you reached a verdict?"

"We have, Your Honor."

"Gentlemen of the jury, what is your verdict?"

My heart stopped banging. Even the fly stopped buzzing. The whole works stood still.

"We find the defendant guilty of murder in the first degree."

Some woman screamed out "No!" at the top of her lungs. They were all turning their heads to look around at me. The next thing I knew I was outside in the corridor and a lot of people were standing around me. Everything looked blurred. Someone said, "Give her air, stand back." Another voice said, "His sister. She was on the stand earlier in the week." Ammonia fumes kept tickling the membranes of my nostrils. The first voice said, "Take her home. Where does she live? Anybody know where she lives?"

"I know where she lives. I'll take care of her."

Somebody put an arm around my waist and walked me to the creaky courthouse elevator, led me out to the street, got in a taxi after me. I looked, and it was that dick, Burns. I climbed to the corner of the cab, put my feet on the seat, and shuffled them at him. "Get away from me, you devil! You railroaded him, you butcher!"

"Attagirl," he said gently. He gave the old address, where Chick and I had lived. The cab started and I felt too low even to fight any more.

"Not there," I said sullenly. "I'm holed up in a furnished room off Second Avenue now. I've hocked everything I own, down to my vaccination mark. How d'you suppose I got that lawyer Schlesinger for him? And a lot of good it did him. What a washout he turned out to be."

"Don't blame him," he said. "He couldn't buck that case we turned over to the State—Darrow himself couldn't have. What he *should* have done was let him plead guilty to second-degree then he wouldn't be in line for short-circuiting. That was his big mistake."

"No! He wanted to do that, but Chick and I wouldn't hear of it! Why should he plead guilty to anything, when he's innocent? That's a guilty man's dodge, not an innocent man's. He hasn't got half an hour's detention rightfully coming to him—why should he lie down and accept twenty years? He didn't lay a hand on Ruby Reading."

"Eleven million people and the mighty State of New York say he did."

When the cab drew to the curb, I got out and went in the grubby entrance between a delicatessen and a Chinese laundry. "Don't come in with me, I don't want to see any more of you!" I said over my shoulder to Burns. "If I was a man I'd knock you down and beat the living hell out of you!"

He came in, though—and upstairs he closed the door behind him, pushing me out of the way to get in. He said, "You need help, Angel Face, and I'm crying to give it to you."

"Oh, biting the hand that feeds you, turning into a double-crosser—"

"No," he said, "no," and sort of held out his hands as if asking me for something. "Sell me, won't you?" he almost pleaded. "Sell me that he's innocent and I'll work my fingers raw to back you up. I didn't frame your brother, I only did my job. I was sent there by my superiors in answer to the patrolman's call that night, questioned Chick, put him under arrest. You heard me answering their questions on the stand. Did I distort the facts any? All I told them was what I saw with my own eyes, what I found when I got to Reading's apartment. Don't hold that against me, Angel Face. Sell me—convince me he didn't do it and I'm with you up to the hilt."

"Why?" I said cynically. "Why this sudden yearning to undo the damage you've already done?"

He opened the door to go. "Look in the mirror sometime and find out. You can reach me at Centre Street—Nick Burns." He held out his hand uncertainly, probably expecting me to slap it aside.

I took it instead. "Okay, Flatfoot." I sighed wearily. "No use holding it against you that you're a detective, you probably don't know any better. Before you go, gimme the address of that maid of hers, Mandy Leroy. I've got an idea she didn't tell all she knew."

"She went home at five that day. How can *she* help you?"

"I bet she was greased plenty to softpedal the one right name that belongs in this case. She may not have been there, but she knew who to expect around. She may even have tipped him off that Ruby Rose was throwing him over. It takes a woman to see through a woman."

"Better watch yourself going up there alone," he warned me. He took out a notebook. "Here it is, One-eighteenth, just off Lenox." I jotted it down. "If she was paid off like you think, how are you going to restore her memory? It'll take heavy sugar." He fumbled in his pocket, looked at me like he was a little scared of me, then finally took out something and shoved it out of sight on the bureau. "Try your luck with that," he said. "Use it where it'll do the most good. Try a little intimidation with it, it may work."

I grabbed it up and he ducked out in a hurry, the big coward. A hundred and fifty bucks! I ran out to the stairs after him. "Hey," I yelled, "aren't you married or anything?"

"Naw," he called back. "I can always get it back anyway, if it does the trick." And then he added, "I always did want to have something on you, Angel Face."

I went back into my cubbyhole again. I hadn't cried in court when Chick got the ax, just yelled out. But now my eyes got all wet.

"Mandy don't live here no more," the janitor of the 118th Street tenement told me.

"Where'd she go? And don't tell me you don't know, because it won't work."

"She moved to a mighty presumptuous neighborhood all of a sudden. To Edgecomb Ave."

Edgecomb Avenue is nothing to be ashamed of in any man's town. Every one of the trim modern apartment buildings had a glossy private car or two parked in front of the door. I went to the address the janitor had given me and thought they were having a house-warming at first. They were singing inside and it sounded like a revival meeting.

A fat old lady came to the door in a black silk dress, tears streaming down her cheeks. "I'm her mother, honey," she said softly in answer to what I told her, "and you done come at an evil hour. My lamb was run over on the street, right outside this building, only yesterday, first day we moved here. She's in there dead now, honey. The Lawd give and the Lawd has took away again."

I did a little thinking. Why her, when she held the key to the Reading murder? "How did it happen to her, did they tell you?"

"Two white men in a car," she mourned. "Appeared almost like they run her down purposely. She was walking along the sidewalk, folks tell me, nowhere near the gutter, and it swung right up on the sidewalk after her, went over her, then looped out in the middle again and light away without never stopping!"

I went away saying to myself, That girl was murdered as sure as I'm born, to shut her mouth. First she was bribed, then when the trial was safely over she was put out of the way for good!

Somebody big was behind all this. And what did I have to fight that somebody with? A borrowed hundred and fifty bucks, an offer of cooperation from a susceptible detective, and a face.

I went around to the building Ruby Rose had lived in and struck the wrong shift. "Charlie Baker doesn't come on until six, eh?" I asked the doorman. "Where does he live? I want to talk to him."

"He don't come on at all any more. He quit his job, as soon as that"—he tilted his head to the ceiling—"mess we had upstairs was over with and he didn't have to appear in court no more."

"Well, where's he working now?"

"He ain't working at all, lady. He don't have to any more. I understand a relative of his died in the old country, left him quite a bit, and him and his wife and three kids have gone back to England to live."

So he'd been paid off heavily, too. It looked like I was up against Wall Street itself. No wonder everything had gone so smoothly. No wonder even a man like Schlesinger hadn't been able to make a dent in the case.

But I'm not licked yet, I said to myself, back in my room. I've still got this face. It ought to be good for something. If I only knew where to push it, who to flash it on.

Burns showed up that night, to find out how I was making out. "Here's your hundred and fifty back," I told him bitterly. "I'm up against a stone wall every way I turn. But is it a coincidence that the minute the case is in the bag, their two chief witnesses are permanently disposed of, one by exportation, the other by hit-and-run? They're not taking any chances on anything backfiring later."

He said, "You're beginning to sell me. It smells like rain."

I sat down on the floor (there was only one chair in the dump) and took a dejected half-Nelson around my own ankles. "Look, it goes like this. Some guy did it. Some guy that was sold on her. Plenty of names were spilled by Mandy and Baker, but not the right one. The ones that were brought out didn't lead anywhere, you saw that yourself. The mechanics of the thing don't trouble me a bit, the how and why could be cleared up easy enough—even by you."

"Thanks," he said.

"It's the *who* that has me buffaloed. There's a gap there I can't jump across to the other side. From there on, I could handle it beautifully. But I've got to close that gap, that *who,* or I might as well put in the order for Chick's headstone right now."

He took out a folded newspaper and whacked himself disgustedly across the shins with it. "Tough going, kid," he agreed.

"I'll make it," I said. "You can't keep a good girl down. The right guy is in this town. And so am I in this town. I'll connect with him yet, if I've got to use a ouija board!"

He said, "You haven't got all winter. He comes up for sentence Wednesday." He opened the door. "I'm on your side," he let me know in that quiet way of his.

He left the paper behind him on the chair. I sat down and opened it. I wasn't going to do any reading, but I wanted to think behind it. And then I saw her name. The papers had been full of her name for weeks, but this was different; this was just a little boxed ad off at the side.

AUCTION SALE
Jewelry, personal effects, and
furniture belonging to the late
Ruby Rose Reading
Monarch Galleries Saturday A.M.

I dove at the window, rammed it up, leaned halfway out. I caught him just coming out of the door. "Burns!" I screeched at the top of my voice. "Hey, Burns! Bring that hundred and fifty back up here! I've changed my mind!"

The place was jammed to the gills with curiosity-mongers and bargain-hunters—and probably professional dealers, too, although they were supposed to be excluded. There were about two dozen of those 100-watt blue-white bulbs in the ceiling that auction rooms go in for and the bleach of light was intolerable, worse than on a sunny beach at high noon.

I was down front, in the second row on the aisle. I'd gotten there early. I wasn't interested in her diamonds or her furs or her thissas or her thattas. I was hoping something would come up that would give me some kind of a clue, but what I expected it to be I didn't know myself. An inscription on a cigarette case maybe. I knew how little chance there was of anything like that. The D.A.'s office had sifted through her things pretty thoroughly before Chick's trial, and what they'd turned up hadn't amounted to a row of pins. She'd been pretty cagey that way, hadn't left much around. All bills had been addressed to her personally, just like she'd paid her rent with her own personal checks and fed the account herself. Where the funds originated in the first place was never explained. I suppose she took in washing.

They started off with minor articles first, to warm the customers up. A cocktail shaker that played a tune, a makeup mirror with a light behind it, a ship's model, things like that. They got around to her clothes next, and the women customers started ohing and ahing and foaming at the mouth. By the looks of most of them, that was probably the closest they'd ever get to real sin, bidding for its hand-me-downs.

The furniture came next, and they started to talk real money now. This out of the way, her ice came on. Brother, she'd made them say it with diamonds, and they'd all spoken above a whisper, too! When the last of it went, that washed up the sale—there was nothing else left to dispose of but the little rosewood jewel case she'd kept them in. About ten by twelve by ten inches deep, with a little gilt key and lock. Not worth a damn, but there it was. However, if you think an auctioneer passes up anything, you don't know your auctioneers.

"What am I offered for this?" he said almost apologetically. "Lovely little trinket box—give it to your best girl or your wife or your mother to keep her ornaments or old love letters in." He knocked the veneer with his knuckles, held it outward to show us the satin lining. Nothing in it, like in a vaudeville magician's act. "Do I hear fifty cents, just to clear the stand?"

Most of them were getting up and going already. An overdressed guy in my same row across the aisle spoke up. "You hear a buck."

I took a look at him and I took a look at the box. If you want it, I want it, too, I decided suddenly. A guy splurged up like that don't hand a plain wooden box like that to any woman he knows. I opened my mouth for the first time since I'd come in. "You hear a dollar and a quarter."

"Dollar-fifty."

"Two dollars."

"Five." The way he snapped it out, he meant business.

I'd never had such a strong hunch in my life before, but now I wanted that box, had to have it. I felt it would do me some good. Maybe this overdressed monkey had given it to her, maybe Burns could trace where it had been bought.

"Seven-fifty."

"Ten."

"Twelve."

The auctioneer was in seventh heaven. You're giving yourself away, brother, you're giving yourself away! I warned my competitor silently.

We leaned forward out of our seats and sized each other up. If he was giving himself away, I suppose I was, too. I could see a sort of shrewd speculation in his snaky eyes. They screwed up into slits, seeming to say, What's your racket? Something cold went down my back, hot as it was under all those mazdas.

"Twenty-five dollars," he said inexorably.

I thought, I'm going to get that thing if I spend every cent of the money Burns loaned me!'

"Thirty," I said.

With that, to my surprise, he stood up, flopped his hand at it disgustedly, and walked out.

When I came out five minutes later with the box wrapped up under my arm, I saw him sitting in a young dreadnaught with another man a few yards down the street.

So I'm going to be followed home, I said to myself, to find out who I am. That didn't worry me any. I'd rented the room under my old stage name of Honey Sebastian (my idea of a classy tag at sixteen) to escape the notoriety attendant on Chick's trial. I turned up the other way and hopped down into the subway, which is about the best bet when the following is to be done from a car. As far as I could make out, no one came after me.

I watched the street from a corner of the window after I got home, and no one going by stopped or looked at the house or did anything but mind his own business. And if it had been that flashy guy on my tail, you could have heard him coming from a block away. I turned to the wrapped box and broke the string.

Burns's knock at my door at five that afternoon was a tattoo of anxious impatience. "God, you took long to get here!" I blurted out. "I phoned you three times since noon."

"Lady," he protested, "I've been busy, I was out on something else. I only just got back to Headquarters ten minutes ago. Boy, you threw a fright into me."

I didn't stoop to asking him why he should be so worried something had happened to me—he might have given me the right answer. "Well," I said, "I've got him." And I passed him the rosewood jewel case.

"Got who?"

"The guy that Chick's been made a patsy for."

He opened it, looked in, looked under it. "What's this?"

"Hers. I had a hunch, and I bought it. He must have had a

hunch, too, only his agent—and it must have been his agent, he wouldn't show up himself—didn't follow it through, wasn't sure enough. Stick your thumb under the little lock—not over it, down below it—and press hard on the wood."

He did, and something clicked—and the satin bottom flapped up, like it had with me.

"Fake bottom, eh?" he said.

"Read that top letter out loud. That was the last one she got, the very day it happened."

" 'You know, baby,' " Burns read, " 'I think too much of you to ever let you go. And if you ever tired of me and tried to leave me, I'd kill you first, and then you could go wherever you want. They tell me you've been seen going around a lot lately with some young punk. Now, baby, I hope for his sake—and yours, too—that when I come back day after tomorrow I find it isn't so, just some more of my boys' lies. They like to rib me sometimes, see if I can take it or not.' "

"He gave her a bum steer there on purpose," I pointed out. "He came back 'tomorrow' and not the 'day after,' and caught her with the goods."

" 'Milt,' " Burns read from the bottom of the page. And then he looked at me, and didn't see me for once.

"Militis, of course," I said, "the Greek nightclub king. Milton, as he calls himself. Everyone on Broadway knows him. And yet, do you notice how that name stayed out of the trial? Not a whisper from beginning to end. That's the missing name, all right!"

"It reads that way, I know," he said undecidedly, "but she knew her traffic signals. Why would she chuck away the banana and hang onto the skin? In other words, Milton spells real dough, your brother wasn't even carfare."

"But Militis had her branded—"

"Sure, but—"

"No. I'm not talking slang now. I mean actually, physically. It's mentioned in one of these letters. The autopsy report had it, too, remember? Only they mistook it for an operation scar or scald. Well, when a guy does that, anyone would have looked good to her, and Chick was probably a godsend. The branding was probably not the half of it, either. It's fairly well known that Milton likes to play rough with his women."

"All right, kid," he said, "but I've got bad news for you. This evidence isn't strong enough to have the verdict set aside and a new trial called. A clever mouthpiece could blow this whole pack of letters out the window with one breath. Ardent Greek temperament and that kind of thing, you know. You remember how Schlesinger dragged it out of Mandy that she'd overheard more than one guy make the same kind of jealous threats. Did it do any good?"

"This is the McCoy, though. He came through, *this* one, *Militis.*"

"But, baby, you're telling it to me, and I convince easy from you. You're not telling it to the grand jury."

I shoved the letters at him. "Just the same, have 'em photostatted, every last one of them, and put 'em in a cool, dry place. I'm going to dig up something a little more convincing to go with them, if that's what's needed. What clubs does he own?"

"What clubs doesn't he? There's Hell's Bells—" He stopped short, looked at me. "You stay out of there."

"One word from you—" I purred, and closed the door after him.

"A little higher," the manager said. "Don't be afraid, we've seen it all before."

I took another hitch in my hoisted skirt and gave him a look. "If it's my appendix you want to size up, say so. It's easier to uncover the other way around, from up to down. I just sing and dance—I don't bathe for the customers."

"I like 'em like that." He nodded approvingly to his yes-man. "Give her a chord, Mike," he said to his pianist.

" 'The Man I Love,' " I said. "I do dusties, not new ones."

After a few bars, "Good tonsils," he said. "Give her a dance chorus, Mike."

Mike said disgustedly, "Why d'ya wanna waste your time? Even if she was paralyzed from the waist down and had a voice like a frog, ain't you got eyes? Get a load of her face, will you?"

"You're in," the manager said. "Thirty-five, and buy yourself some up-to-date lyrics. Come around at eight and get fitted for some duds. What's your name?"

"Bill me as Angel Face," I said, "and have your electrician give me an amber spot. They take the padlocks off their wallets when I come out in an amber spot."

He shook his head almost sorrowfully. "Hang onto that face, girlie. It ain't gonna happen again in a long time."

Burns was holding up my locked door with one shoulder when I got back. "Here's your letters back. I've got the photostats tucked away in a safe place. Where'd you disappear to?"

"I've landed a job at Hell's Bells. I'm going to get that guy and get him good. If that's the way I've got to get the evidence, that's the way. After all, if he was sold on her *I'll* have him cutting out paper dolls before two weeks are out. What'd she have that I haven't got? Now, you stay out of there. Somebody might know your face and you'll only queer everything."

"Watch yourself, will you, Angel Face? You're playing a dangerous game. That Milton is nobody's fool. If you need me in a hurry, you know where to reach me. I'm right at your shoulder, all the way through."

I went in and stuck the letters back in the fake bottom of the case. I had an idea I was going to have a visitor fairly soon, and wasn't going to tip my hand. I stood it on the dresser top and threw in a few pins and glass beads for luck.

The timing was eerie. The knock came inside of ten minutes. I'd known it was due, but not that quick. It was my competitor from the auction room, flashy as ever—he'd changed flowers, that was all.

"Miss Sebastian," he said, "isn't it? I'd like very much to buy that jewel case you got."

"I noticed that this morning."

He went over and squinted into it.

"That all you wanted it for, just to keep junk like that in it?"

"What'd you expect to find, the Hope diamond?"

"You seemed willing to pay a good deal."

"I lose my head easy in auction rooms. But, for that matter, you seemed to be willing to go pretty high yourself."

"I still am," he said. He turned it over, emptied my stuff out, tucked it under his arm, put something down on the dresser. "There's a hundred dollars. Buy yourself a real good one."

Through the window, I watched the dreadnaught drift away again. Just a little bit too late in getting here, I smiled after it. The cat's out of the bag now and a bulldog will probably chase it.

The silver dress fit me like a wet compress. It was one of those things that break up homes. The manager flagged me in the passageway leading back.

"Did you notice that man all by himself at a ringside table? You know who he is, don't you?"

If I hadn't, why had I bothered turning on all my current his way? "No," I said, round-eyed, "who?"

"Milton. He owns the works. The reason I'm telling you is that you've got a date with a bottle of champagne at his table, starting in right now. Get on in there."

We walked on back.

"Mr. Milton, this is Angel Face," the manager said. "She won't give us her right name—just walked in off Fifty-second Street last Tuesday."

"And I waited until tonight to drop around here!" he laughed. "What you paying her, Berger?" Then, before the other guy could get a word out, "Triple it! And now get out of here."

The night ticked on. He'd look at me, then he'd suddenly throw up his hands as though to ward off a dazzling glare. "Turn it off, it hurts my eyes."

I smiled a little and took out my mirror. I saw my eyes in it, and in each iris there was a little electric chair with Chick sitting strapped in it. Three weeks from now, sometime during that week. Boy, how they were rushing him! It made it a lot easier to go ahead.

I went back to what we'd been talking about—and what are any two people talking about, more or less, in a nightclub at four in the morning? "Maybe," I said, "who can tell? Some night I might just feel like changing the scenery around me, but I couldn't tell you about it, I'm not that kind."

"You wouldn't have to," he said. He fooled with something below table level, then passed his hand to me. I took it and knotted my handkerchief around the latch-key he'd left in it. Burns had been right, it was a dangerous game, and bridges were blazing and collapsing behind me . . .

The doorman covered a yawn with a white kid glove, said, "Who shall I announce?"

"That's all been taken care of," I said, "so you can go back to your beauty sleep."

He caught on, said insinuatingly, "It's Mr. Milton, isn't it? He's out of town tonight."

You're telling me, I thought. I'd sent him the wire that fixed that, signed the name of the manager of his Philly club. "You've been reading my mail," I said, and closed the elevator in his face.

The key worked, and the light-switch worked, and his Filipino had the night off, so the rest was up to me. The clock in his two-story living room said four-fifteen. I went to the second floor of the penthouse and started in on the bedroom. He was using Ruby Rose Reading's jewel case to hold his collar buttons in, hadn't thrown it out. I opened the fake bottom to see if he'd found what he was after, and the letters were gone—probably burned.

I located his wall safe but couldn't crack it. While I was still working at it, the phone downstairs started to ring. I jumped as though a pin had been stuck into me, and started shaking like I was still doing one of my routines at the club. He had two phones, one downstairs, and one in the bedroom, which was an unlisted number. I snapped out the lights, ran downstairs, and picked it up. I didn't answer, just held it.

Burns's voice said, "Angel Face?"

I exhaled. "You sure frightened me!"

"Better get out of there. He just came back—must have tumbled to the wire. A spotter at Hell's Bells tipped me off he was just there asking for you."

"I can't *now,"* I wailed. "I woke his damn doorman up getting in just now and I'm in that silver dress I do my numbers in! He'll tell him I was here. I'll have to play it dumb."

"Did you get anything?"

"Nothing, only that jewel case. I couldn't get the safe open, but he's probably burned everything connecting him to her long ago."

"Please get out of there, kid," he pleaded. "You don't know that guy. He's going to pin you down on the mat if he finds you there."

"I'm staying," I said. "I've got to break him down tonight, it's my last chance. Chick eats chickens and ice cream tomorrow night at six. Oh, Burns, pray for me, will you?"

"I'm going to do more than that," he growled. "I'm going to give a wrong-number call there in half an hour. It's four-thirty now. Five that'll be. If you're doing all right, I'll lie low. If not, I'm not going to wait. I'll break in with some of the guys and we'll use the little we have—the photostats of the letters and the jewel case. I think Schlesinger can at least get Chick a reprieve on them, if not a new trial. If we can't get Milton, we can't get him, that's all."

"We've *got* to get him," I said, "and we're going to! He's even been close to breaking down and admitting it to me, at times, when we're alone together. Then at the last minute he gets leery. I'm convinced he's guilty. So help me, if I lose Chick tomorrow night, I'm going to shoot Milton with my own hands!"

"Remember, half an hour. If everything's under control, cough. If you can get anywhere near the phone, *cough!* If I don't hear you cough, I'm pulling the place."

I hung up and ran up the stairs tearing at the silver cloth. I jerked open a closet door, found the cobwebby negligee he'd always told me was waiting for me there whenever I felt like breaking it in, and chased back downstairs again in it, more like Godiva than anyone else, grabbed up a cigarette, flopped back full length on the handiest divan, and did a Cleopatra just as the outside door opened and he and two other guys came in.

Milton had a face full of stormclouds—until he saw me. Then it cleared, the sun came up in it. "Finally!" he crooned. "Finally you wanted a change of scenery! And just tonight somebody had to play a practical joke on me, start me on a fool's errand to Philly! Have you been here long?"

I was still trying to get my breath back after the quick-change act, but I managed a vampish smile.

He turned to the two guys. "Get out, you two. Can't you see I have company?"

I'd recognized the one who'd contacted me for the jewel case and knew what was coming.

"Why, that's the dame I told you about, Milt," he said, "that walked off with that little box the other day!"

"Oh, hello," I sang out innocently. "I didn't know you knew Mr. Milton."

Milton flared, "You, Rocco! Don't call my lady friends dames! Now scram! You think we need four for bridge?"

"All right, boss, all right," he said soothingly. But he went over to a framed still of me that Milton had brought home from Hell's Bells and stood thoughtfully in front of it for a minute. Then he and the other guy left. It was only after the elevator light had flashed out that I looked over and saw the frame was empty.

"Hey!" I complained. "Your friend Rocco swiped my picture, right under your nose!"

All he saw was a bowl of cream in front of him. "Who can blame him? You're so lovely to look at."

He spent some time working on the theory that I'd finally found him irresistible. After what seemed years of that, I got off the divan just in time.

He was good and peeved. "Are you giving me the runaround? What did you come here, for, anyway?"

"Because she's double-crossing you!" a voice said from the foyer. "Because she came here to frame you, chief!"

The other two had come back. Rocco pulled my picture out of his pocket. "I traced that dummy wire you got, sending you to Philly. The clerk at the telegraph office identified her as the sender from this picture. Ask her why she wanted to get you out of town and come up here and case your layout! Ask her why she was willing to pay thirty bucks for a little wood box when she was living in a seven-buck furnished room! Ask her *who she is!* You weren't at the Reading trial, were you? Well, I was! You're riding for a fall, chief, she's a stoolie!"

Milton turned on me. "Who are you? What does he mean?"

What was the good of answering? It was five to five on the clock. I needed Burns bad.

The other one snarled, "She's Chick Wheeler's sister. I saw her on the stand with my own eyes."

Milton's face screwed up into a sort of despairing agony—I'd never seen anything like it before. He whimpered, "You're so beautiful to have to be killed."

I hugged the negligee around me and looked down at the floor. "Then don't have me killed," I said softly. It was two to five now.

He said with comic sadness, "I got to if you're that guy's sister."

"I say I'm nobody's sister, just Angel Face that dances at your club. I say I only came here because—I like soft carpets."

"Why did you send that telegram to get me out of town?"

He had me there. I thought fast. "If I'm a stoolie I get killed, right? But what happens if I'm the other kind of a double-crosser—a two-timer? Do I still get killed?"

"No," he said. "Your option hadn't been taken up yet."

"That's the answer, then, I was going to use your place to meet my steady—that's why I sent the fake wire."

Rocco's voice was as cracked as a megaphone after a football rally. "She's Wheeler's *sister,* chief. Don't let her ki—"

"Shut up!" Milton said.

Rocco shrugged, lit a cigarette. "You'll find out."

The phone rang. "Get that," Milton ordered. "That's her guy now. Keep him on the wire." He turned and went running up the stairs to the other phone.

Rocco took out a gun, fanned it vaguely in my direction, and sauntered over. "Don't try nothing while that line's open. You may be fooling Milton, you're not fooling us any. He was always a sucker for a twist."

Rocco's buddy said, "Hello?"

Rocco, still holding the gun on me, took a lopsided drag on his cigarette with his left hand and blew smoke vertically. Some of it caught in his throat and he started to cough like a seal. You could hear it all over the place.

I could feel all the blood draining out of my face.

The third guy was purring, "No, you tell me what number you want first, then I'll tell you what number this is. That's the way it's done, pal." He turned a blank face. "Hung up on me!"

Rocco was still hacking away. I felt sick all over. Sold out by Burns's own signal that everything was under control!

There was a sound like dry leaves on the stairs and Milton came whisking down again. "Some guy wanted an all-night delicatess—" the spokesman started to say.

Milton cut his hand at him viciously. "That was Centre Street—police headquarters. I had it traced! Put some clothes on her, she's going to her funeral!"

They forced me back into the silver dress and Milton came over with a flagon of brandy and dashed it all over me. "If she lets out a peep, she's fighting drunk."

They had to hold me up between them to get me to move. Rocco had his gun buried in the silver folds of my dress. The other had a big handkerchief under my face, as though I were nauseated—but really to squelch any scream.

Milton followed behind us. "You shouldn't mix your drinks," he was saying, "and you shouldn't help yourself to my private stock without permission."

The doorman was asleep again on his bench, like when I'd come in. This time he didn't wake up. His eyelids just flickered a little as the four of us went by.

They saw to it that I got in the car first, like a lady should. The ride was one of those things you take to your grave with you. My whole past life flashed before me. I didn't mind dying so terribly much, but I hated to go without being able to do anything for Chick. But it was the way the cards had fallen, that was all.

The house was on the Sound. By the looks of it, Milton lived in it quite a bit. His houseboy let us in.

"Build a fire, Juan, it's chilly," he grinned. And to me, "Sit down, Angel Face, and let me look at you before you go." The other two threw me into a corner of a big sofa, and I just stayed that way, limp like a rag doll. He just stared and stared.

Rocco said, "What're we waiting for? It's broad daylight already."

Milton was idly holding something into the fire, a long poker of some kind. "She's going," he said, "but she's going out as my property. Show the other angels this when you get up there so they'll know who you belong to." He came over to me with the end of the thing glowing dull red. It was flattened into some kind of an ornamental design or cipher. "Knock her out," he said. "I'm not that much of a brute."

Something exploded off the side of my head and I lost my senses. Then he was wiping my mouth with a handkerchief soaked in whiskey, and my side burned just above the hip, where they'd found that mark on Ruby Rose Reading.

"All right, Rocco," Milton said.

Rocco took out his gun again, but he shoved it at the third guy, who held it level at me and took the safety off. His face was sort of green and wet with sweat. I looked him straight in the eyes.

The gun went down like a drooping lily. "I can't, boss," he groaned. "She's got the face of an angel. How can you expect me to shoot her?"

Milton pulled it away from him. "She double-crossed me! Any dame that double-crosses me gets what I gave Reading!"

A voice said softly, "That's all I wanted to know."

The gun went off, and I wondered why I didn't feel anything. Then I saw that the smoke was coming from the doorway and not from Milton's gun at all. He went down at my feet, like he wanted to apologize for what he'd done to me, but he didn't say anything and he didn't get up. There was blood running down the part in his hair in back.

Burns was in the room, with more guys in uniform than I'd ever seen outside of a police parade. One of them was the doorman from Milton's place, or at least the dick that Burns had substituted for him to keep an eye on me while I was up there. Burns told me about that later and about how they followed Milt's little party but hadn't been able to get in in time to keep me from getting branded.

I sat holding my side and sucking in my breath. "It was a swell finish," I panted to Burns, "but what'd you drill him for? Now we'll never get the proof that'll save Chick."

He was at the phone asking to be put through to Schlesinger in the city. "We've got it already, Angel Face," he said ruefully.

"It's right on you, where you're holding your side. Just where it was on Reading. We all heard what he said before he nose-dived. I only wish I hadn't shot him," he glowered, "then I'd have the pleasure of doing it all over again."

LAWRENCE BLOCK

NOTHING SHORT OF HIGHWAY ROBBERY

I eased up on the gas pedal a few hundred yards ahead of the service station. I was putting the brakes on when my brother Newton opened his eyes and straightened up in his seat.

"We haven't got but a gallon of gas left if we got that much," I told him. "And there's nothing out ahead of us but a hundred miles of sand and a whole lot of cactus, and I already seen enough cactus to last me a spell."

He smothered a yawn with the back of his hand. "Guess I went and fell asleep," he said.

"Guess you did."

He yawned again while a fellow a few years older'n us came off of the front porch of the house and walked our way, moving slow, taking his time. He was wearing a broad-brimmed white hat against the sun and a pair of bib overalls. The house wasn't much, a one-story clapboard structure with a flat roof. The garage alongside it must have been built at the same time and designed by the same man.

He came around to my side and I told him to fill the tank. "Regular," I said.

He shook his head. "High-test is all I got," he said. "That be all right?"

I nodded and he went around the car and commenced unscrewing the gas cap. "Only carries high-test," I said, not wildly happy about it.

"It'll burn as good as the regular, Vern."

"I guess I know that. I guess I know it's another five cents a gallon or another dollar bill on a tankful of gas, and don't you just bet that's why he does it that way? Because what the hell can you do if you want regular? This bird's the only game in town."

"Well, I don't guess a dollar'll break us, Vern."

I said I guessed not and I took a look around. The pump wasn't so far to the rear that I couldn't get a look at it, and when I did I saw the price per gallon, and it wasn't just an extra nickel that old boy was taking from us. His high-test was priced a good twelve cents a gallon over everybody else's high-test.

I pointed this out to my brother and did some quick sums in my head. Twelve cents plus a nickel times say twenty gallons was three dollars and forty cents. I said, "Damn, Newton, you know how I hate being played for a fool."

"Well, maybe he's got his higher costs and all—being out in the middle of nowhere and all, little town like this."

"Town? Where's the town at? Where we are ain't nothing but a wide place in the road."

And that was really all it was. Not even a crossroads, just the frame house and the garage alongside it, and on the other side of the road a cafe with a sign advertising home-cooked food and package goods. A couple of cars over by the garage, two of them with their hoods up and various parts missing from them. Another car parked over by the cafe.

"Newt," I said, "you ever see a softer place'n this?"

"Don't even think about it."

"Not thinking about a thing. Just mentioning."

"We don't bother with nickels and dimes no more, Vernon. We agreed on that. By tonight we'll be in Silver City. Johnny Mack Lee's already there and first thing in the morning we'll be taking that bank off slicker'n a bald tire. You know all that."

"I know."

"So don't be exercising your mind over nickels and dimes."

"Oh, I know it," I said. "Only we could use some kind of money pretty soon. What have we got left? Hundred dollars?"

"Little better'n that."

"Not much better, though."

"Well, tomorrow's payday," Newt said.

I knew he was right but it's a habit a man gets into, looking at a place and figuring how he would go about taking it off. Me and Newt, we always had a feeling for places like filling stations and liquor stores, 7-11 stores and like that. You just take 'em off nice and easy, you get in and get out, and a man can make a living that way. Like the saying goes, it don't pay much but it's regular.

But then the time came that we did a one-to-five over to the state pen and it was an education. We both of us came out of there knowing the right people and the right way to operate. One thing we swore was to swear off nickels and dimes. The man who pulls quick-dollar stickups like that, he works ten times as often and takes twenty times the risks of the man who takes his time setting up a big job and scoring it. I remember Johnny Mack Lee saying it takes no more work to knock over a bank than a bakery and the difference is dollars to doughnuts.

I looked up and saw the dude with the hat poking around under the hood. "What's he doing now, Newt? Prospecting for more gold?"

"Checking the oil, I guess."

"Hope we don't need none," I said. " 'Cause you just know he's gotta be charging two dollars a quart for it."

He did a good job of checking under there, topping up the battery terminals and all, then he came around and leaned against the car door. "Oil's okay," he said. "You sure took a long drink of gas. Good you had enough to get here. And this here's the last station for a whole lot of highway."

"Well," I said, "How much do we owe you?"

He named a figure. High as it was, it came as no surprise to me since I'd already turned and read it off of the pump. Then as I was reaching in my pocket he said, "I guess you know about that fan clutch, don't you?"

"Fan clutch?"

He gave a long slow nod. "I suppose you got a few miles left in it," he said. "Thing is, it could go any minute. You want to step out of the car for a moment I can show you what I'm talking about?"

Well, I got out, and Newt got out his side, and we went and joined this bird and peeked under the hood. He reached behind the radiator and took ahold of some damned thing or other and showed us how it was wobbling. "The fan clutch," he said. "You ever replace this here since you owned the car?"

Newt looked at me and I looked back at him. All either of us ever knew about a car is starting it and stopping it and the like.

As a boy, Newt was awful good at starting them without keys. You know how kids are.

"Now if this goes," he went on, "then there goes your water pump. Probably do a good job on your radiator at the same time. You might want to wait and have your own mechanic take care of it for you. The way it is, though, I wouldn't want to be driving too fast or too far with it. Course if you hold it down to forty miles an hour and stop from time to time so's the heat won't build up—"

Me and Newt looked at each other again. Newt asked some more about the fan clutch and the dude wobbled it again and told us more about what it did, which we pretended to pay attention to and nodded like it made sense to us.

"This fan clutch," Newt said. "What's it run to replace it?"

"Around thirty, thirty-five dollars. Depends on the model and who does the work for you, things like that."

"Take very long?"

"Maybe twenty minutes."

"Could you do it for us?"

The dude considered, cleared his throat, spat in the dirt. "Could," he allowed. "*If* I got the part. Let me just go and check."

When he walked off I said, "Brother, what's the odds that he's got that part?"

"No bet a-tall. You figure there's something wrong with our fan clutch?"

"Who knows?"

"Yeah," Newt said. "Can't figure on him being a crook and just spending his life out here in the middle of nowhere. But then you got to consider the price he gets for the gas and all. He hasn't had a customer since we pulled in, you know. Maybe he gets one car a day and tries to make a living off it."

"So tell him what to do with his fan clutch."

"Then again, Vern, maybe all he is in the world is a good mechanic trying to do us a service. Suppose we cut out of here and fifty miles down the road our fan clutch up and kicks our water pump through our radiator or whatever the hell it is? By God, Vernon, if we don't get to Silver City tonight Johnny Mack Lee's going to be vexed with us."

"That's a fact. But thirty-five dollars for a fan clutch sure eats a hole in our capital, and suppose we finally get to Silver City and find out Johnny Mack Lee got out the wrong side of bed and slipped on a banana peel or something? Meaning if we get there and there's no job, then what do we do?"

"Well, I guess it's better'n being stuck in the desert."

"I guess."

Of course, he had just the part we needed. You had to wonder how a little gas station like that would happen to carry a full line of fan clutches, which I never even heard of that particular part before, but when I said as much to Newt he shrugged and said maybe an out-of-the-way place like that was likely to carry a big stock because he was too far from civilization to order parts when the need for them arose.

"The thing is," he said, "all up and down the line you can read all of this either way. Either we're being taken or we're being done a favor for, and there's no way to know for sure."

While he set about doing whatever he had to do with the fan clutch, we took his advice and went across the street for some coffee. "Woman who runs the place is a pretty fair cook," he said. "I take all my meals there my own self."

"Takes all his meals here," I said to Newt. "Hell, she's got him where he's got us. He don't want to eat here he can walk sixty miles to a place more to his liking."

The car that had been parked at the cafe was gone now and we were the only customers. The woman in charge was too thin and rawboned to serve as an advertisement for her own cooking. She had her faded blonde hair tied up in a red kerchief and she was perched on a stool smoking a cigarette and studying a *True Confessions* magazine. We each of us ordered apple pie at a dollar a wedge and coffee at thirty-five cents a cup. When we were eating, a car pulled up and a man wearing a suit and tie bought a pack of cigarettes from her. He put down a dollar bill and didn't get back but two dimes' change.

"I think I know why that old boy across the street charges so much," Newt said softly. "He needs to get top dollar if he's gonna pay for his meals here."

"She does charge the earth."

"You happen to note the liquor prices? She gets seven dollars for a bottle of Ancient Age bourbon. And that's not for a quart either. That's for a fifth."

I nodded. "I just wonder where they keep all that money."

"Brother, we don't even want to think on that."

"Never hurt a man to think."

"These days it's all credit cards, anyways. The tourist trade is nothing but credit cards and his regular customers most likely run a monthly tab and give him a check for it."

"We'll be paying cash."

"Well, it's a bit hard to establish credit in our line of work."

"Must be other people pays him cash. And the food and liquor over here, that's gotta be all cash, or most all cash."

"And how much does it generally come to in a day? Be sensible. As little business as they're doing—"

"I already thought of that. Same time, though, look how far they are from wherever they do their banking."

"So?"

"So they wouldn't be banking the day's receipts every night. More likely they drive in and make their deposits once a week, maybe even once every two weeks."

Newt thought about that. "Likely you're right," he allowed. "Still, we're just talking small change."

"Oh, I know."

But when we paid for our pie and coffee, Newton gave the old girl a smile and told her how we sure had enjoyed the pie, which we hadn't all that much, and how her husband was doing a real good job on our car over across the street.

"Oh, he does real good work," she said.

"What he's doing for us," Newt said, "he's replacing our fan clutch. I guess you probably get a lot of people here needing new fan clutches."

"I wouldn't know about that," she said. "Thing is I don't know much about cars. He's the mechanic and I'm the cook is how we divvy things up."

"Sounds like a good system," Newt told her.

On the way across the street, Newt separated two twenties from our bankroll and tucked them into his shirt pocket. Then

I reminded him about the gas and he added a third twenty. He gave the rest of our stake a quick count and shook his head. "We're getting pretty close to the bone," he said. "Johnny better be where he's supposed to be."

"He's always been reliable."

"That's God's truth. And the bank, it better be the piece of cake he says it is."

"I just hope."

"Twenty thousand a man is how he has it figured. Plus he says it could run three times that. I sure wouldn't complain if it did, brother."

I said I wouldn't, either. "It does make it silly to even think about nickels and dimes," I said.

"Just what I was telling you."

"I was never thinking about it, really. Not in the sense of doing it. Just mental exercise—keeps the brain in order." He gave me a brotherly punch in the shoulder and we laughed together some. Then we went on to where the dude in the big hat was playing with our car. He gave us a large smile and held out a piece of metal for us to admire. "Your old fan clutch," he said, which I had more or less figured. "Take hold of this part. That's it, right there. Now try to turn it."

I tried to turn it and it was hard to turn. He had Newt do the same thing. "Tight," Newt said.

"Lucky you got this far with it," he said, and clucked his tongue and heaved the old fan clutch onto a heap of old metallic junk.

I stood there wondering if a fan clutch was supposed to turn hard or easy or not at all, and if that was our original fan clutch or a piece of junk kept around for this particular purpose, and I knew Newton was wondering the same thing. I wished they could have taught us something useful in the state pen, something that might have come in handy in later life, something like your basic auto-mechanics course. But they had me melting my flesh off my bones in the prison laundry, and they had Newt stamping out license plates, which there isn't much call for in civilian life, being the state penal system has an official monopoly on the business.

Meanwhile, Newt had the three twenties out of his shirt

pocket and was standing there straightening them out and lining up their edges. "Let's see now," he said. "That's sixteen and change for the gas, and you said thirty to thirty-five for the fan clutch. What's that all come to?"

It turned out that it came to just under eighty-five dollars.

The fan clutch, it seemed, had run higher than he'd thought it would. Forty-two fifty was what it came to, and that was for the part exclusive of labor. Labor tacked another twelve dollars onto our tab. And while he'd been working there under the hood, our friend had found a few things that simply needed attending to. Our fan belt, for example, was clearly on its last legs and ready to pop any minute. He showed it to us and you could see how worn it was, all frayed and just a thread or two away from popping.

So he had replaced it, and he'd replaced our radiator hoses at the same time. He fished around in his junkpile and came up with a pair of radiator hoses he said had come off our car. The rubber was old and stiff with little cracks in the surface, and it sure smelled like something awful.

I studied the hoses and agreed they were in terrible shape. "So you just went ahead and replaced them on your own," I said.

"Well," he said, "I didn't want to bother you while you were eating."

"That was considerate," Newt said.

"I figured you fellows would want it seen to. You blow a fan belt or a hose out there, well, it's a long walk back, you know. Course I realize you didn't authorize me to do the work, so if you actually want me to take the new ones off and put the old ones back on—"

Of course, there was no question of doing that. Newt looked at me for a minute and I looked back at him and he took out our roll, which I don't guess you could call a roll any more from the size of it, and he peeled off another twenty and a ten and added them to the three twenties from his shirt pocket. He held the money in his hand and looked at it and then at the dude, then back at the money, then back at the dude again. You could see he was doing heavy thinking, and I had an idea where his thoughts were leading.

Finally he took in a whole lot of air and let it out in a rush and said, "Well, hell, I guess it's worth it if it leaves us with a car in good condition. Last thing either of us wants is any damn trouble with the damn car. This fixes us up, right? Now we're in good shape with nothing to worry about, right?"

"Well," the dude said.

We looked at him.

"There *is* a thing I noticed."

"Oh?"

"If you'll just look right here," he said. "See how the rubber grommet's gone on the top of your shock-absorber mounting—that's what called it to my attention. Now you see your car's right above the hydraulic lift, that's 'cause I had it up before to take a look at your shocks. Let me just raise it up again and I can point out what's wrong."

Well, he pressed a switch and some such to send the car up off the ground, and pointed here and there underneath it to show us where the shocks were shot and something was cutting into something else and about to commence bending the frame. "If you got the time you ought to let me take care of that for you," he said, "because if you don't get it seen to, you wind up with frame damage and your whole front end goes on you, and then where are you?"

He let us take a long look at the underside of the car. There was no question that something was pressing on something and cutting into it. What the hell it all added up to was beyond me.

"Just let me talk to my brother a minute," Newt said to him, and he took hold of my arm and we walked around the side.

"Well," he said, "what do you think? It looks like this old boy here is sticking it in pretty deep."

"It does at that. But that fan belt was shot and those hoses was the next thing to petrified."

"True."

"If they *was* our fan belt and hoses in the first place and not some junk he had around."

"I had that very thought, Vern."

"Now as for the shock absorbers—"

"Something sure don't look altogether perfect underneath that car. Something's sure cutting into something."

"I know it. But maybe he just went and got a file or some such thing and did some cutting himself."

"In other words, either he's a con man or he's a saint."

"Except we know he ain't a saint, not at the price he gets for gasoline, and not telling us how he eats all his meals across the road and all the time his own wife's running it."

"So what do we do? You want to go on to Silver City on those shocks? I don't even know if we got enough money to cover putting shocks on, far as that goes."

We walked around to the front and asked the price of the shocks. He worked it all out with pencil and paper and came up with a figure of forty-five dollars, including the parts and the labor and the tax and all. Newt and I went into another huddle and he counted his money and I went through my own pockets and came up with a couple of dollars, and it worked out that we could pay what we owed and get the shocks and come up with three dollars to bless ourselves with.

So I looked at Newt and he gave a great shrug of his shoulders. Close as we are, we can say a lot without speaking.

We told the dude to go ahead and do the work.

While he installed the shocks, me and Newt went across the street and had us a couple of chicken-fried steaks. They wasn't bad at all even if the price was on the high side. We washed them down with a beer apiece and then each of us had a cup of that coffee. I guess there's been times I had better coffee.

"I'd say you fellows sure were lucky you stopped here," the woman said.

"It's our lucky day, all right," Newt said. When he paid her, I looked over the paperback books and magazines. Some of them looked to be old and secondhand but they weren't none of them reduced in price on account of it, and this didn't surprise me much.

What also didn't surprise me was when we got back to find the shocks installed and our friend with his big hat off and scratching his mop of hair and telling us how the rear shocks was in even worse shape than the front ones. He went and ran the car up in the air again to show us more things that didn't mean much to us.

Newton said, "Well, sir, my brother and I, we talked it over. We figure we been neglecting this here automobile and we really ought to do right by it. If those rear shocks is bad, well, let's just get 'em the hell off of there and new ones on. And while we're here, I'm just about positive we're due for an oil change."

"And I'll replace the oil filter while I'm at it."

"You do that," Newt told him. "And I guess you'll find other things that can do with a bit of fixing. Now we haven't got all the time in the world and all the money in the world, either, but I guess we got us a pair of hours to spare, and we consider ourselves lucky having the good fortune to run up against a mechanic who knows which end of a wrench is which. So what we'll do, we'll just find us a patch of shade to set in and you check that car over and find things to do to her. Only things that need doing, but I guess you'd be the best judge of that."

Well, I'll tell you, he found things to fix. Now and then a car would roll on in and he'd have to go and sell somebody a tank of gas, but we sure got the lion's share of his time. He replaced the air filter, he cleaned the carburetor, he changed the oil and replaced the oil filter, he tuned the engine and drained and flushed the radiator and filled her with fresh coolant. He gave us new plugs and points, he did this and that and every damn thing he could think of, and I guess the only parts of that car he didn't replace were ones he didn't have replacement parts for.

Through it all, Newt and I sat in a patch of shade and sipped Cokes out of the bottle. Every now and then, that bird would come over and tell us what else he found that he ought to be doing and we'd look at each other and shrug our shoulders and say for him to go ahead and do what had to be done.

"Amazing what was wrong with that car of ours," Newt said to me. "Here I thought it rode pretty good."

"Hell, I pulled in here wanting nothing in the world but a tank of gas. Maybe a quart of oil, and oil was the one thing in the world we didn't need, or it looks like."

"Should ride a whole lot better once he's done with it."

"Well, I guess it should. Man's building a whole new car around the cigarette lighter."

"And the clock. Nothing wrong with that clock, outside of it loses a few minutes a day."

"Lord," I said, "don't you be telling him about those few minutes the clock loses. We won't never get out of here."

That dude took the two hours we gave him and about twelve minutes besides, and then he came on over into the shade and presented us with his bill. It was all neatly itemized, everything listed in the right place. All of it added up and the figure in the bottom right-hand corner with the circle around it read $277.45.

"That there is quite a number," I said.

He put the big hat on the back of his head and ran his hand over his forehead. "Whole lot of work involved," he said. "When you take into account all of those parts and all that labor."

"Oh, that's for certain," Newt said. "And I can see they all been taken into account, all right."

"That's clear as black and white," I said. "One thing, you couldn't call this a nickel-and-dime figure."

"That you couldn't," Newton said. "Well, sir, let me just go and get some money from the car. Vern?"

We walked over to the car together. "Funny how things work out," Newt said. "I swear people get forced into things, I just swear to hell and gone they do. What did either of us want beside a tank of gas?"

"Just a tank of gas is all."

"And here we are," he said. He opened the door on the passenger side, waited for a pickup truck to pass going west to east, then popped the glove compartment. He took the .38 for himself and gave me the .32 revolver. "I'll just settle up with our good buddy here," he said, loud enough for the good buddy in question to hear him. "Meanwhile, why don't you just step across the street and pick us up something to drink later on this evening? You never know, might turn out to be a long ways between liquor stores."

I went and gave him a little punch in the upper arm. He laughed the way he does, and I put the .32 in my pocket and trotted on across the road to the cafe. Turnabout's fair play, they say.

PETER LOVESEY

A MAN WITH A FORTUNE

Most of the passengers were looking to the right, treating themselves to the breath-catching view of San Francisco Bay the captain of the 747 had invited them to enjoy. Not Eva. Her eyes were locked on the lighted No Smoking sign and the order to fasten seatbelts. Until that was switched off, she could not think of relaxing. She knew the takeoff was the most dangerous part of the flight, and it was a delusion to think you were safe the moment the plane was airborne. She refused to be distracted. She would wait for the proof that the takeoff had been safely accomplished: the switching off of that small, lighted sign.

"Your first time?" The man on her left spoke with a West Coast accent. She had sensed that he had been waiting to speak since they took their seats, darting glances her way. Probably he was just friendly, like most San Franciscans she had met on the trip, but she couldn't possibly start a conversation now.

Without turning, she mouthed a negative.

"I mean your first time to England," he went on. "Anyone can see you've flown before, the way you put your hand luggage under the seat before they even asked us, and fixed your belt. I just wondered if this is your first trip to England."

She didn't want to seem ungracious. He was obviously trying to put her at ease. She smiled at the No Smoking sign and nodded. It was, after all, her first flight in this direction. The fact that she was English and had just been on a business trip to California was too much to explain.

"Mine, too," he said. "I've promised myself this for years. My people came from England, you see, forty, fifty years back. All dead now, the old folk. I'm the only one of my family left, and I ain't so fit myself." He planted his hand on his chest. "Heart condition."

Eva gave a slight start as an electronic signal sounded and the light went off on the panel she was watching. A stewardess's voice announced that seatbelts could be unfastened and it was now permissible to smoke in the seats reserved for smoking, to the right of the cabin. Eva closed her eyes a moment and felt the tension ease.

"The doctor says I could go any time," her companion continued. "I could have six months or six years. You know how old I am? Forty-two. When you hear something like that at my age it kind of changes your priorities. I figured I should do what I always promised myself—go to England and see if I had any people left over there. So here I am, and I feel like a kid again. Terrific."

She smiled, mainly from the sense of release from her anxiety at the takeoff, but also at the discovery that the man she was seated beside was as generous and open in expression as he was in conversation. In no way was he a predatory male. She warmed to him—his shining blue eyes in a round, tanned face topped with a patch of hair like cropped corn, his small hands holding tight to the armrests, his Levi shirt bulging over the seatbelt he had not troubled to unclasp. "Are you on a vacation, too?" he asked.

She felt able to respond now. "Actually, I live in England."

"You're English? How about that!" He made it sound like one of the more momentous discoveries of his life, oblivious that there must have been at least a hundred Britons on the flight. "You've been on vacation in California, and now you're traveling home?"

There was a ten-hour flight ahead of them, and Eva's innately shy personality flinched at the prospect of an extended conversation, but the man's candor deserved an honest reply. "Not exactly a vacation. I work in the electronics industry. My company wants to make a big push in the production of microcomputers. They sent me to see the latest developments in your country."

"Around Santa Clara?"

"That's right," said Eva, surprised that he should know. "Are you by any chance in electronics?"

He laughed. "No, I'm just one of the locals. The place is known as Silicone Valley, did you know that? I'm in farming, and I take an interest in the way the land is used. Excuse me for saying this: you're pretty young to be representing your company on a trip like this."

"Not so young, really. I'm twenty-eight." But she understood his reaction. She herself had been amazed when the Director of Research had called her into his office and asked her to make the trip. Some of her colleagues were equally astonished. The most incredulous was her flat-mate, Janet—suave, sophisticated Janet, who was on the editorial side of the *Sunday Telegraph* and had been on assignments to Dublin, Paris, and Geneva, and was always telling Eva how deadly dull it was to be confined to an electronics lab.

"I wish I were twenty-eight," said her fellow traveler. "That was the year I was married. Patty was a wonderful wife to me. We had some great times."

He paused in a way that begged Eva's next question. "Something went wrong?"

"She went missing three years back. Just disappeared. No note, nothing, I came home one night and she was gone."

"That's terrible."

"It broke me up. There was no accounting for it. We were very happily married."

"Did you tell the police?"

"Yes, but they have hundreds of missing persons in their files. They got nowhere. I have to presume she's dead. Patty was happy with me. We had a beautiful home and more money than we could spend. I own two vineyards—big ones. We had grapes in California before silicone chips, you know."

She smiled, and as it seemed that he didn't want to speak any more about his wife she said, "People try to grow grapes in England, but you wouldn't think much of them. When I left London the temperature was in the low fifties, and that's our so-called summer."

"I'm not that interested in the weather. I just want to find the place where all the records of births, marriages, and deaths are stored, so I can find if I have any family left."

Eva understood now. This was not just the trip to England to acquire a few generations of ancestors and a family coat-of-arms. Here was a desperately lonely man. He had lost his wife and abandoned hope of finding her. But he was still searching for someone he could call his own.

"Would that be Somerset House?"

His question broke through her thoughts.

"Yes. That is to say, I think the records are kept now in a building in Kingsway, just a few minutes' walk from there. If you asked at Somerset House, they'd tell you."

"And is it easy to look someone up?"

"It should be, if you have names and dates."

"I figured I'd start with my grandfather. He was born in a village called Edgecombe in Dorset in 1868, and he had three older brothers. Their names were Matthew, Mark, and Luke, and I'm offering no prize for guessing what Grandfather was called. My pa was given the same name and so was I. Each of us was an only child. I'd like to find out if any of Grandfather's brothers got married and had families. If they did, it's possible that I have some second cousins alive somewhere. Do you think I could get that information?"

"Well, it should be there somewhere," said Eva.

"Does it take long?"

"That's up to you. You have to find the names in the index first. That can take some time, depending how common the name is. Unfortunately, they're not computerized. You just have to work through the lists."

"You're serious?"

"Absolutely. There are hundreds of enormous bound books full of names."

For the first time in the flight, his brow creased into a frown.

"Is something wrong?" asked Eva.

"Just that my name happens to be Smith."

Janet thought it was hilarious when Eva told her. "All those Smiths! How long has he got, for heaven's sake?"

"Here in England? Three weeks, I think."

"He could spend the whole time working through the index and still get nowhere. Darling, have you ever been there? The scale of the thing beggars description. I bet he gives up on the first day."

"Oh, I don't think he will. This is very important to him."

"Whatever for? Does he hope to get a title out of it? Lord Smith of San Francisco?"

"I told you. He's alone in the world. His wife disappeared. And he has a weak heart. He expects to die soon."

"Probably when he tries to lift one of those index volumes off the shelf," said Janet. "He must be out of his mind." She could never fathom why other people didn't conform to her ideas of the way life should be conducted.

"He's no fool," said Eva. "He owns two vineyards, and in California that's big business."

"A rich man?" There was a note of respect in Janet's voice.

"Very."

"That begins to make sense. He wants his fortune to stay in the family—if he has one."

"He didn't say that, exactly."

"Darling, it's obvious. He's over here to find his people and see if he likes them enough to make them his beneficiaries." Her lower lip pouted in a way that was meant to be amusing but might have been involuntary. "Two vineyards in California! Someone stands to inherit all that and doesn't know a thing about it!"

"If he finds them," said Eva. "From what you say, the chance is quite remote."

"Just about impossible, the way he's going about it. You say he's starting with the grandfather and his three brothers, and hoping to draw up a family tree. It sounds beautiful in theory, but it's a lost cause. I happen to know a little about this sort of thing. When I was at Oxford I got involved in organizing an exhibition to commemorate Thomas Hughes—*Tom Brown's Schooldays,* right? I volunteered to try to find his descendants, just to see if they had any unpublished correspondence or photographs in the family. It seemed a marvelous idea at the time, but it was hopeless. I did the General Register Office bit, just like your American, and discovered you simply cannot trace people that way. You can work backwards if you know the names and ages of the present generation, but it's practically impossible to do it in reverse. That was with a name like Hughes. Imagine the problems with the name Smith!"

Eva could see Janet was right. She pictured John Smith III at his impossible task and was touched with pity. "There must be some other way he could do it."

Janet grinned. "Like working through the phonebook, ringing up all the Smiths?"

"I feel really bad about this. I encouraged him."

"Darling, you couldn't have done anything else. If this was the guy's only reason for making the trip, you couldn't tell him to abandon it before the plane touched down at Heathrow. Who knows—he might have incredible luck and actually chance on the right name."

"That *would* be incredible."

Janet took a sip of the California wine Eva had brought back as Duty Free. "Actually, there is another way."

"What's that?"

"Through parish records. He told you his grandfather was born somewhere in Dorset?"

"Edgecombe."

"And the four brothers were named after the gospel writers, so it's a good bet they were Church of England. Did all the brothers live in Edgecombe?"

"I think so."

"Then it's easy! Start with the baptisms. When was the grandfather born?"

"Eighteen sixty-eight."

"Right. Look up the Edgecombe baptisms for 1868. There can't be so many John Smiths in a small Dorset village. You'll get the father's name in the register—he signs it, you see—and then you can start looking through other years for the brothers' entries. That's only the beginning. There are the marriage registers and the banns. If the Edgecombe register doesn't have them, they could be in an adjoining parish."

"Hold on, Janet. You're talking as if I'm going off to Dorset myself."

Janet's eyes shone. "Eva, you don't need to go there. The Society of Genealogists in Kensington has copies of thousands of parish registers. Anyone can go there and pay a fee for a few hours in the library. I've got the address somewhere." She got up and went to her bookshelf.

"Don't bother," said Eva. "It's John Smith who needs the

information, not me, and I wouldn't know how to find him now. He didn't tell me where he's staying. Even if I knew, I'd feel embarrassed getting in contact again. It was just a conversation on a plane."

"Eva, I despair of you. When it comes to the point, you're so deplorably shy. I can tell you exactly where to find him: in the General Register Office in Kingsway, working through the Smiths. He'll be there for the next three weeks if someone doesn't help him out."

"Meaning me?"

"No, I can see it's not your scene. Let's handle this another way. Tomorrow I'll take a long lunch break and pop along to the Society of Genealogists to see if they have a copy of the parish registers for Edgecombe. If they haven't, or there's no mention of the Smith family, we'll forget the whole thing."

"And if you *do* find something?"

"Then we'll consider what to do next." Casually, Janet added, "You know, I wouldn't mind telling him myself."

"But you don't know him."

"You could tell me what he looks like."

"How would you introduce yourself?"

"Eva, you're so stuffy! It's easy in a place like that where everyone is shoulder to shoulder at the indexes."

"You make it sound like a cocktail bar."

"Better."

Eva couldn't help smiling.

"Besides," said Janet. "I do have something in common with him. My mother's maiden name was Smith."

The search rooms of the General Register Office were filled with the steady sound of index volumes being lifted from the shelves, deposited on the reading tables, and then returned. There was an intense air of industry as the searchers worked up and down the columns of names, stopping only to note some discovery that usually was marked by a moment of reflection, followed by redoubled activity.

Janet had no trouble recognizing John Smith. He was where she expected to find him: at the indexes of birth for 1868. He was the reader with one volume open in front of him that he had not exchanged in ten minutes. Probably not all morning. His stumpy right hand, wearing three gold rings, checked the rows of Victorian copperplate at a rate appropriate to a marathon effort. But when he turned a page, he shook his head and sighed.

Eva had described him accurately enough without really conveying the total impression he made on Janet. Yes, he was short and slightly overweight and his hair was cut to within a half inch of his scalp, yet he had a teddy-bear quality that would definitely help Janet to be warm towards him. Her worry had been that he would be too pitiable.

She waited for the person next to him to return a volume, then moved to his side, put down the notebook she had brought, and asked him, "Would you be so kind as to keep my place while I look for a missing volume? I think someone must have put it back in the wrong place."

He looked up, quite startled to be addressed. "Why, sure."

Janet thanked him and walked round to the next row of shelves.

In a few minutes she was back. "I can't find it. I must have spent twenty minutes looking for it, and my lunch hour will be over soon."

He kept his finger against the place of birth he had reached and said, "Maybe I could help. Which one are you looking for, Miss?"

"Could you? It's P-to-S for the second quarter of 1868."

"Really? I happen to have it right here."

"Oh, I didn't realize—" Janet managed to blush a little.

"Please." He slid the book in front of her. "Go ahead—I have all day for this. Your time is more valuable than mine."

"Well, thank you." She turned a couple of pages. "Oh dear, this is going to be much more difficult than I imagined. Why did my mother have to be born with a name as common as Smith?"

"Your name is Smith?" He beamed at the discovery, then nodded. "I guess it's not such a coincidence."

"My mother's name actually. I'm Janet Murdoch."

"John Smith." He held out his hand. "I'm a stranger here myself, but if I can help in any way—"

Janet said, "I'm interested in tracing my ancestors, but looking at this I think I'd better give up. My great-grandfather's name was Matthew Smith, and there are pages and pages of them. I'm not even sure of the year he was born. It was either 1868 or 1869."

"Do you know the place he was born?"

"Somewhere in Dorset. Wait, I've got it written here." She opened the notebook to the page where she had made her notes at the Society of Genealogists. "Edgecombe."

"May I see that?" John Smith held it and his hand shook. "Janet, I'm going to tell you something that you'll find hard to believe."

He took her to lunch at the Wig and Pen. It tested her nerve as he questioned her about Matthew Smith of Edgecombe, but she was well prepared. She said she knew there had been four brothers, but she was deliberately vague about their names. Two, she said, had married, and she was the solitary survivor of Matthew's line.

John Smith ate very little lunch. Most of the time, he sat staring at Janet and grinning. He was very like a teddy bear. She found it pleasing at first, because it seemed to show he was a little lightheaded at the surprise she had served him, but as the meal went on it made her feel slightly uneasy, as if he had something in mind that she hadn't foreseen.

"I have an idea," he said just before they got up to leave, "only I hope you won't get me wrong, Janet. What I would like is to go out to Dorset at the weekend and find Edgecombe, and have you come with me. Maybe we could locate the church and see if they still have a record of our people. *Would* you come with me?"

It suited her perfectly. The parish registers would confirm everything she had copied at the Society of Genealogists. Any doubts John Smith might have of her integrity would be removed. And if her information on the Smiths of Edgecombe was shown to be correct, no suspicion need arise that she was not related to them at all. John Smith would accept her as his sole surviving relative. He would return to California in three weeks with his quest accomplished. And sooner or later Janet would inherit two vineyards and a fortune.

"It's a.wonderful idea!" she said. "I'll be delighted to come."

Nearly a fortnight passed before Eva started to be anxious about Janet's absence. Once or twice before she had gone away on assignments for the newspaper without saying she was going. Eva suspected she did it to make her work seem more glamorous—the sudden flight to an undisclosed destination on a mission so delicate it could not be whispered to a friend—but this time the *Sunday Telegraph* called to ask why Janet had not been seen at the office for over a week.

When they called again a day or two later, and Eva still had no news, she decided she had no choice but to make a search of Janet's room for some clue as to her whereabouts. At least she'd see which clothes Janet had taken—whether she had packed for a fortnight's absence. With luck she might find a note of the flight number.

The room was in its usual disorder, as if Janet had just gone for a shower and would sweep in at any moment in her white Dior bathrobe. By the phone, Eva found the calendar Janet used to jot down appointments. There was no entry for the last fortnight. On the dressing-table was her passport. The suitcase she always took on trips of a week or more was still on top of the wardrobe.

Janet was not the sort of person you worried over, but this was becoming a worry. Eva systematically searched the room and found no clue. She phoned the *Sunday Telegraph* and told them she was sorry she couldn't help. As she put down the phone, her attention was taken by the letters beside it. She had put them there herself, the dozen or so items of mail that had arrived for Janet.

Opening someone else's private correspondence was a step on from searching their room, and she hesitated. What right had she to do such a thing? She could tell by the envelopes that two were from the Inland Revenue and she put them back by the phone. Then she noticed one addressed by hand. It was postmarked Edgecombe, Dorset.

Her meeting with the friendly Californian named John Smith

had been pushed to the edge of her memory by more immediate matters, and it took a few moments' thought to recall the significance of Edgecombe. Even then, she was baffled. Janet had told her that Edgecombe was a dead end. She had checked it at the Society of Genealogists. It had no parish register because there was no church there. They had agreed to drop their plan to help John Smith trace his ancestors.

But why should Janet receive a letter from Edgecombe?

Eva decided to open it.

The address on the headed notepaper was The Vicarage, Edgecombe, Dorset.

> Dear Miss Murdoch,
>
> I must apologize for the delay in replying to your letter. I fear that this may arrive after you have left for Dorset. However, it is only to confirm that I shall be pleased to show you the entries in our register pertaining to your family, although I doubt if we have anything you have not seen at the Society of Genealogists.
>
> Yours sincerely,
> Denis Harcourt, Vicar

A dead end? No church in Edgecombe?

Eva decided to go there herself.

The Vicar of Edgecombe had no difficulty in remembering Janet's visit. "Yes, Miss Murdoch called on a Saturday afternoon. At the time I was conducting a baptism, but they waited until it was over and I took them to the vicarage for a cup of tea."

"She had someone with her?"

"Her cousin."

"Cousin?"

"Well, I gather he was not a first cousin, but they were related in some way. He was from America, and his name was John Smith. He was very appreciative of everything I showed him. You see, his father and his grandfather were born here, so I was able to look up their baptisms and their marriages in the register. It goes back to the sixteenth century. We're very proud of our register."

"I'm sure you must be. Tell me, did Janet—Miss Murdoch—claim to be related to the Smiths of Edgecombe?"

"Certainly. Her great-grandfather, Matthew Smith, is buried in the churchyard. He was the brother of the American gentleman's grandfather, if I have it right."

Eva felt the anger like a kick in the stomach. Not only had Janet deceived her, she had committed an appalling fraud on a sweet-natured man. And Eva herself had passed on the information that enabled her to do it. She would never forgive her for this.

"That's the only Smith grave we have in the churchyard," the Vicar continued. "When I first got Miss Murdoch's letter, I had hopes of locating the stones of the two John Smiths, the father and grandfather of our American visitor, but it was not to be. They were buried elsewhere."

Something in the Vicar's tone made Eva ask, "Do you know where they were buried?"

"Yes, indeed. I got it from Mr. Harper, the sexton. He's been here much longer than I."

There was a pause.

"Is it confidential?" Eva asked.

"Not really." The Vicar eased a finger round his collar, as if it were uncomfortable. "It was information that I decided in the circumstances not to volunteer to Miss Murdoch and Mr. Smith. You are not one of the family yourself?"

"Absolutely not."

"Then I might as well tell you. It appears that the first John Smith developed some form of insanity. He was given to fits of violence and became quite dangerous. He was committed to a private asylum in London and died there a year or two later. His only son, the second John Smith, also ended his life in distressing circumstances. He was convicted of murdering two local girls by strangulation, and there was believed to have been a third, but the charge was never brought. He was found guilty but insane and sent to Broadmoor. To compound the tragedy, he had a wife and baby son. They went to America after the trial." The Vicar gave a shrug. "Who knows whether the child was ever told the truth about his father—or his grandfather, for that matter? Perhaps you can understand why I was silent on the matter when Mr. Smith and Miss Murdoch were here. I may be old-fashioned, but I think the psychiatrists make too much of heredity, don't you? If you took it seriously, you'd think no woman was safe with Mr. Smith."

From the vicarage, Eva went straight to the house of the Edgecombe police constable and told her story.

The officer listened patiently. When Eva had finished, he said, "Right, Miss. I'll certainly look into it. Just for the record, this American—what did he say his name was?"

EDWARD D. HOCH

THE THEFT FROM THE ONYX POOL

"You steal things, don't you?"

Nick Velvet regarded the girl with a slight smile. "Only the hearts of beautiful maidens."

"No, seriously. I can pay."

"Seriously, what do you want stolen?"

"The water from a swimming pool."

He continued smiling at her, but a portion of Nick's mind wished he were back on the front porch with Gloria and a cold beer. The habits of the very rich had never been for him. "I could always pull the plug," he suggested, still smiling.

The girl, whose name was Asher Dumont, ground out her cigarette with a gesture of angry irritation. "Look, Mr. Velvet, I didn't arrange to have you invited here so we could trade small talk. I happen to know that you steal unusual things, unique things, and that your fee is twenty thousand dollars. Correct?"

"All right," he told her, playing along. "I don't know exactly how you came upon that information in your circle, but I'll admit it's reasonably accurate, Miss Dumont."

"Then will you?"

"Will I what?"

"Steal the water from Samuel Fitzpatrick's pool?"

Nick Velvet had been approached by many people during his career, and as his peculiar reputation had grown he'd been hired to steal many curious things. He'd once stolen a tiger from a zoo, and a stained-glass window from a museum. His fee for such odd thefts was a flat $20,000, with an extra $10,000 for especially hazardous tasks. He never stole money, or the obvious valuables that other thieves went after. He dealt only in the unusual, often in the bizarre—but in his field he was the best in the business.

"That's a peculiar assignment even for me," he told the girl. She was blonde, with shoulder-length straight hair in the tradition of girl folksingers. He wouldn't have been surprised to see her back in his old Greenwich Village neighborhood—somehow she seemed out of place at a society reception in Westchester. It was only her dress, a gleaming satin sheath, that belonged at the party—not the girl.

"I understood you specialize in the peculiar."

"I do. When do you want it done, and where is it?"

She sipped her cocktail and glanced around to make certain they weren't overheard. "Samuel Fitzpatrick has an estate twenty miles from here in Connecticut. I'll find an excuse to take you over there. After that you're on your own. Only one stipulation—it must be done before next weekend's holiday. Before the Fourth of July."

"I suggested pulling the plug. That would be the easiest way. It would save you twenty thousand."

"You don't seem to understand, Mr. Velvet—I *want* the water from that pool. I want you to steal the water, all of it, and deliver it to me."

"Is this some sort of wild bet?" he asked. He could imagine nothing else.

Asher Dumont stretched her long tanned legs under the table and drew on her cigarette. "I thought you were a businessman, Mr. Velvet. The reason shouldn't be important to you."

"It's not. I was only being inquisitive."

"Can you come with me to the Fitzpatrick estate in the morning?" she asked.

"Who is this Samuel Fitzpatrick? The name is vaguely familiar."

"He's a writer and producer of mysteries. Two hits on Broadway and he's had a very successful series on television. Remember *The Dear Slayer*?"

"I don't follow the theater as closely as I should," Nick admitted, "but I've heard of Fitzpatrick. That's all I need to know about him. It gives me a talking point."

"Then I'll see you in the morning, Mr. Velvet?"

"Since it's business, Miss Dumont, I usually receive a five-thousand-dollar retainer in advance and the balance when I complete the assignment."

She didn't blink. "Very well, I'll have it for you."

Nick left her at the table and threaded his way through the reception crowd. In the outer hall he found a phone booth and dialed Gloria's number.

"Hi, how're things?"

"Great, Nicky. You coming home?"

"I'll be a while. Maybe a week. We're checking out some new plant sites in Connecticut."

"Oh, Nicky! You'll be away over the Fourth!"

"Maybe not. I'll try to be home by then. Maybe we can have a picnic or something."

After he hung up, he thought how often on summer nights, sitting on the porch with Gloria, he'd be tempted to give it all up and take a job as a salesman or a bookkeeper. But always there was the odd invitation from somebody like Asher Dumont to get him back to work. The money was good, and he liked his specialty. He was a thief, and he knew he'd never change.

Asher picked him up in a little white sportscar that seemed hardly big enough for her lanky frame and long legs. The top was down and her long hair spun out behind her like a banner as she wheeled the car onto the parkway and headed for Connecticut.

"You didn't tell me to dress casually," he said, commenting on her shorts and blouse.

"Sam would be suspicious right away if he saw me in a dress." She steered the car around a truck and shot the speed up to seventy. "There's a check for five thousand in my purse. Take it out."

"A check?"

"Go on, I'm not trying to get evidence against you. I don't carry that much around in cash."

"I'll have to cash this before I finish the job."

"Sure. Right now, though, tell me what kind of cover story you'll use with Fitzpatrick. I'm introducing you as someone interested in his plays."

"Better fill me in on the sort of thing he likes to produce."

As she talked, he had the distinct impression she was merely a rich girl indulging in a game. His business associates were more often shady gang figures or nervous diplomats who could afford to hire Nick Velvet. He didn't know if he liked it, but she was nice to look at and, besides, he'd never been commissioned to steal the water from a swimming pool.

Samuel Fitzpatrick's estate was actually a generous-sized house with a double garage, situated at the edge of a gently rolling field of scrub brush and young trees. Nick looked out across the low stone walls and open fields and wondered if people still went fox-hunting in country like this.

Asher didn't bother with the doorbell but took Nick around the back to a flagstone patio which led to a fenced-in swimming pool. A middle-aged man with thinning hair and a tanned, weathered face opened the gate to meet them. "Well, Asher! You're more lovely every day."

"Thanks, Sam," she said, bestowing a quick kiss on his cheek. "This is the man I told you about on the phone—Nick Velvet."

"Velvet?" Fitzpatrick extended his freckled hand. "Glad to meet you."

He led them through the wooden gate to the pool. It was medium-sized, with a shallow end for wading and a deep end with a diving board. There was a woman in the pool, swimming with a powerful breast stroke, but Nick couldn't see her face at the moment. She seemed to have taken no notice of their arrival.

"Nice place you have here," Nick observed.

"I like privacy. Nearest neighbor's more than a mile down the road."

"This is quite a pool." Nick had been drawn to the edge, noticing the way the smooth edge glistened in layers of multiple colors. It was like marble or quartz, but cut through to show the layers of black and white, with sometimes just a hint of red or brown. "What's this edge made of?"

"Onyx. My first big play on Broadway was *The Onyx Ring.* The pool is one of my few luxuries."

Nick was beginning to understand. With the water out of the pool, something might be done to remove these onyx layers from the edge. He wondered if Asher Dumont had a poor boyfriend lurking somewhere offstage.

The woman climbed out of the water, reaching for an oversized bath towel. Her figure was still good, but Nick figured she'd never see forty again. Asher made the introductions. "Nick, this is Sam's wife, Lydia. This is a friend, Nick Velvet, Lydia."

The woman squinted and groped on the poolside table for her glasses. "I'm blind without them," she explained. "Pleased to meet you, Mr. Velvet. Lovely weather, isn't it?"

"Certainly is," Nick agreed, sinking into the red-and-green chair that Fitzpatrick had indicated. He was studying the rear of the house and the street beyond, where no traffic seemed to pass. An idea was beginning to shape itself in his mind.

"Let me get drinks for us," Lydia Fitzpatrick offered, blinking from behind her thick glasses.

"Fine idea," her husband said and asked Nick and Asher what they would have. Then: "Now, what did you want to see me about, Mr. Velvet?"

"I admire your plays," Nick said, running his hand along the plastic webbing of his chair. "Especially *The Dear Slayer.* Quite a tricky ending."

Fitzpatrick leaned back in his own chair and stroked his thinning hair. "That's what you need for Broadway, a trick ending."

"I have a plot that might interest you," Nick told him. "It's never been done before."

"You're a writer?"

"No, that's why Asher suggested I come to you."

The producer smiled slightly, as if he'd heard it all before. Lydia returned, distributed the drinks, and settled to the ground at her husband's side. "I get a lot of people with ideas," Fitzpatrick said. "Usually I don't even like to listen to them. But I'll make an exception since you're a friend of Asher's. This girl is like a daughter to me." He reached out to take her hand and she smiled as if on cue.

Nick sipped his drink. "Well, it's a locked-room sort of thing."

"Locked rooms are a bit old-fashioned for Broadway."

"Not *this* one." Nick hoped he was conveying the proper

enthusiasm. "A man is murdered in a completely locked room. The doors and windows are all sealed and there's no secret passage."

"A locked room is difficult to bring off on the stage, when one whole wall is always open to the audience. But go on—how's it done?"

Nick leaned back and grinned. "There's a type of laser beam that can pass through a transparent surface without damaging it. The killer fires the beam through the closed and sealed window, murders the man inside, and yet the room remains completely locked."

Fitzpatrick nodded. "Not bad. Not bad at all, but I think it would be more effective in print than on the stage. If I were still doing the television series, I might give it a try—I've always liked wild things like that, the wilder the better."

Nick stood up and strolled slowly along the edge of the pool as he talked, and once he managed to intrude a question about the pool's depth. The slanting bottom made it difficult to figure exactly, but he thought the pool probably held close to 19,000 gallons of water. A big job for any thief. It would take days to empty it by ordinary means.

It was nearly four when they finally left the Fitzpatricks, with Nick shaking hands and promising to keep Sam informed of his progress with the idea. Then he was back in the sportscar with Asher, racing through the quiet countryside.

"What do you think?" she asked.

"It can be done," he told her.

"By the weekend?"

"By the weekend. I just have to check on one piece of equipment and find a few people to help me. Do you need *all* the water?"

She thought about it. "Not every drop, naturally, but most of it. Enough to empty the pool."

"I'm interested in why you want it, why it's so valuable to you."

"You're getting twenty thousand dollars," she reminded him. "For that much, you can stay curious."

"I have a couple of ideas," he went on. "Once the pool is empty, perhaps those onyx slabs could be pried up and stolen."

She glanced at him sideways. "You really think I'm a criminal, don't you? Those slabs aren't even real onyx—just a good imitation."

"You can't want the water for itself. It must be the emptiness of the pool that you really want."

"I hired you to be a thief, not a detective."

"Sometimes the logic demanded by the two professions isn't that different," he told her. "What's your connection with Fitzpatrick and his wife, anyway?"

"You mean the bit about my being like a daughter to him? I suppose it's true in a way. His first wife was Mary Dumont, my aunt. I spent most of my childhood with them, and they really did treat me like a daughter. My parents both died early, but there was a great deal of money in both branches of the family. I think, really, that Sam resented my aunt's money. Anyway, a month or so after his first play was a hit, he asserted his independence one night and Aunt Mary left him. That was ten years ago and nobody's seen her since—though she occasionally sends me money through a lawyer in California."

"Fitzpatrick divorced her?"

The girl nodded. "On the grounds of desertion. He married Lydia three years ago."

"You resent Lydia, don't you?"

"Because she took my aunt's place? Oh, I suppose so."

Nick was thinking of Lydia Fitzpatrick's poor eyesight, and her swimming habits. Would she come running out to dive into the pool one morning and find only hard concrete waiting for her?

"One thing," he said. "Of course, Fitzpatrick's going to know the water's being taken. There's no way of stealing nineteen thousand gallons of water without his knowing about it."

"I want him to know," she told Nick. "As long as it's before the holiday weekend." She steered the sportscar like an expert, maneuvering it through the beginnings of the rush-hour traffic. "I still can't imagine how you're going to do it, though. If he knows you're taking it, how are you going to have the time to empty the entire pool?"

"Leave that to me," Nick said with a smile. "That's what you're paying me for."

Friday afternoon was calm and clear, with a musty heaviness about the air that hinted at a change in weather before the long weekend really got underway. Sam Fitzpatrick and his wife were at the pool—she was sunning herself while he was typing a reply to a letter in the morning's mail.

It was midafternoon when he first smelled the smoke and glanced over the fence at the nearby field. "Lydia! There's a grass fire here! Come look!"

"Hadn't we better call the Fire Department, Sam?" The fire already had a good start, spreading in a ring that reached from the distant woods almost to Fitzpatrick's line.

"Damn! I suppose I'd better." But then they heard the rising wail of the schoolhouse siren, and the answering call from the firehouse. The volunteers had been summoned and were on their way.

Within ten minutes the flaming field had been converged upon by two pumpers and a pair of auxiliary water trucks. There were no hydrants out this far, and the volunteers had to bring their own water supply. Fitzpatrick knew most of the volunteer firemen by name, but a stranger in a rubber coat and leather helmet came running up to the fence.

"Mr. Fitzpatrick?"

"Yes. That's quite a blaze you've got there."

"Sure is." He glanced over Fitzpatrick's shoulder. "We need more water than our trucks can supply. Could we throw a hose into your pool and pump out the water?"

"What? Say, don't I know you from somewhere?"

"Better hurry," the fireman warned him, "a shift in the wind could endanger your house!"

"Well—all right, I suppose so!"

Within moments the heavy canvas hose was over the fence, splashing into the deep end of the pool. The fireman gave a signal to the nearest pumper and they started to drain Fitzpatrick's water. Off in the distance, two firemen played a smaller hose on the leading edge of the fire.

The familiar-looking fireman was everywhere, directing activities, shouting orders. After a half hour, when the pool was already half empty, one of the auxiliary water trucks pulled out through the high grass to get a refill at the town tank.

Finally, when another truckload of water and the remainder of the pool's supply had been used up, the fire began to retreat and die. Sam Fitzpatrick watched it with relief, and he called out to the familiar-looking fireman, "You fellows want a drink?"

"No time now, sir. Thanks anyway."

"What about my pool?"

"The trucks will be out tomorrow to refill it. Thanks for your help."

Fitzpatrick watched them pull away and then walked over to stare into the empty swimming pool. At the deepest end, a few inches of water remained, but otherwise there was only the damp concrete below.

He started to light a cigarette, then stopped suddenly with the lighted match in mid-air. He'd just remembered where he had seen the fireman before.

Asher Dumont was waiting in her sportscar a few miles down the road. Nick hopped off one of the pumpers and tossed his helmet and rubber coat onto the seat. Then he ran over to the car. "Where do you want it? Nineteen thousand gallons of Sam Fitzpatrick's swimming-pool water, as ordered."

"You're mad," she said with a laugh. "I never thought you'd be able to do it!"

"I've had harder assignments than this."

"But I still don't understand. The firemen—"

"While we were pumping out his pool with a big hose and filling up one of the auxiliary water trucks, we were fighting the fire with a small hose from the other truck. With the high grass, he couldn't see which hoses went where. And when the first truck was full, we took it out and brought in another empty one. Each of the pumpers has a thousand-gallon tank of its own, so we had plenty of water for the fire without using the water from the pool."

"But these are real firemen and real trucks!"

Nick nodded. "I gave them a hundred each and told them we

wanted to shoot a film for television. They know Fitzpatrick's in the business, so they believed it."

"Where were your cameras, Mr. Television Producer?" she asked with an impish grin.

"I told them this was the dress rehearsal." He opened the door and slid in beside her. "How about the rest of my money now?"

"Just one more thing," she said, suddenly serious.

"What's that?"

"I want you to come back to Sam's house with me and tell him exactly what you did."

"Now we're getting to the root of it, aren't we?"

"Maybe." She gunned the motor into life.

"We're going there now?"

"Tomorrow, when the weekend's started. Then you'll get your money. And it's worth every cent of it to me."

"What about the water?"

"There's a dry creek behind my place. We can dam it up and keep it there."

He shook his head. "You're some girl."

The following morning, Lydia Fitzpatrick led them out to the pool. Asher wore a pale summer dress with a full skirt, and seemed somehow overdressed to Nick after her brief costumes of the past few days. There was something else different about her, too—the spark was gone from her eyes, replaced by something cold and hard.

"Asher! How are you?" Sam asked, rising from his deck chair to greet them.

"I'm fine, Sam." Quietly, tight-lipped.

"And you've brought Mr. Velvet again!" The cheer rang not quite true to Nick's ears.

A garden hose was hanging over the side of the swimming pool, feeding a trickle of water into the puddle at the bottom. "We can't get any pressure out of this thing," Lydia explained. "It'll take us a week to fill it again. Firemen needed the water yesterday for—"

Fitzpatrick had resumed his seat, but Asher remained standing. "I know," she said. "Tell them, Nick."

"I don't think you have to tell me anything," Fitzpatrick said. "I finally recognized Mr. Velvet in his fireman's gear—but not in time to keep him from taking the water. And I suppose you set the fire yourself?"

Nick nodded. "I was paid twenty thousand dollars by this young lady to steal the water from your pool."

"Twenty—! Asher, have you gone completely mad?"

"The money came from my family. I think they would have wanted it spent this way."

"But why?"

"I've taken samples from that water—a hundred samples already, with more to come. They're all being analyzed, Sam."

"Analyzed?"

"There's chlorine in your pool water. Apparently you're not familiar with the effects of chlorine on calcified cement. There'll be traces of calcium in that water, Sam, especially after ten years."

"I don't know what you're talking about."

"I think you do, Sam. I'll be back on Tuesday with the results of the analyses." She turned away.

Nick hesitated a moment, then followed her out, leaving Fitzpatrick and his wife staring after them.

Back in the car, heading away from the house, Nick leaned back in the seat. "I had a question to ask you last night. I'll ask it now. Was Fitzpatrick installing his pool the night your aunt disappeared?"

She drove without answering for a long time, bathing in a morning sun already high in the sky. "How did you know?" she asked finally.

"He built the pool in honor of his first hit play, and you told me your aunt vanished a month or so after it opened. It seems logical that the two events came at about the same time."

She nodded. "The divorce papers were never served on Aunt Mary. That's what first made me suspicious. Last winter I hired a private detective to check on this lawyer who's been sending me the money in my aunt's name. He reported that the money was actually coming from Sam. That's when I really became suspicious that something had happened to her ten years ago."

"And you remembered the pool."

"I remembered. I was only fourteen at the time, but I remember that last day with my aunt. We'd watched them pouring the concrete for the bottom of the pool. Aunt Mary said it wouldn't be hard till morning."

Nick lit a cigarette. "There's no such thing as a chlorine effect on calcified cement. You made that up, and you wasted your twenty thousand."

"I didn't waste the twenty thousand. It had to be a big lie if he was to believe it at all. He'd have laughed in my face if I took a single test-tube sample from the pool. But he's written this sort of thing, remember—wild, way-out stuff. I know him—this is just bizarre enough for him to believe. The calcium from her bones, being drawn out of the cement bottom."

"What do you do now?"

"Wait."

They didn't have long to wait. She came to Nick's hotel room the following morning with his check.

"You're up early," he said. It was the Fourth of July—outside someone was setting off illegal fireworks. The Fire Department would have a busy day.

"Lydia phoned me. He killed himself during the night. Out by the pool."

Nick turned away. "Just one thing," he said. "Why did it have to be over the long weekend?"

"He was a writer, remember?" She was staring out the window at something far away. "I didn't want him calling the library or some science editor in New York to check on my chlorine-on-cement effect. This way he couldn't find out till Tuesday, and I hoped he wouldn't last that long."

Nick thought about Gloria and the picnic he'd promised her. It was time to be going.

PATRICIA HIGHSMITH

SAUCE FOR THE GOOSE

The incident in the garage was the third near-catastrophe in the Amory household, and it put a horrible thought into Loren Amory's head: his darling wife Olivia was trying to kill herself.

Loren had pulled at a plastic clothesline dangling from a high shelf in the garage—his idea had been to tidy up, to coil the clothesline properly—and at the first tug, an avalanche of suitcases, an old lawnmower, and a sewing machine weighing God-knows-how-much crashed down on the spot that he barely had time to leap from.

Loren walked slowly back to the house, his heart pounding at his awful discovery. He entered the kitchen and made his way to the stairs. Olivia was in bed, propped against pillows, a magazine in her lap. "What was that terrible noise, dear?"

Loren cleared his throat and settled his black-rimmed glasses more firmly on his nose. "A lot of stuff in the garage. I pulled just a little bit on a clothesline—" He explained what had happened.

She blinked calmly as if to say, Well, so what? Things like that do happen.

"Have you been up to that shelf for anything lately?"

"Why, no. Why?"

"Because—well, everything was just poised to fall, darling."

"Are you blaming me?" she asked in a small voice.

"Blaming your carelessness, yes. I arranged those suitcases up there and I'd never have put them so they'd fall at a mere touch. And I didn't put the sewing machine on top of the heap. Now, I'm not saying—"

"Blaming my carelessness," she repeated, affronted.

He knelt quickly beside the bed. "Darling, let's not hide things any more. Last week there was the carpet sweeper on the cellar stairs. And that ladder! You were going to climb it to knock down that wasps' nest!—What I'm getting at, darling, is that you *want* something to happen to you, whether you realize it or not. You've got to be more careful, Olivia.—Oh, darling, please don't cry. I'm trying to help you. I'm not criticizing."

"I know, Loren. You're good. But my life—it doesn't seem worth living any more, I suppose. I don't mean I'm *trying* to end my life, but—"

"You're still thinking—of Stephen?" Loren hated the name and hated saying it.

She took her hands down from her pinkened eyes. "You made me promise you not to think of him, so I haven't. I swear it, Loren."

"Good, darling. That's my little girl." He took her hands in his. "What do you say to a cruise soon? Maybe in February? Myers is coming back from the coast and he can take over for me for a couple of weeks. What about Haiti or Bermuda?"

She seemed to think about it for a moment, but at last shook her head and said she knew he was only doing it for her, not because he really wanted to go. Loren remonstrated briefly, then gave it up. If Olivia didn't take to an idea at once, she never took to it. There had been one triumph—his convincing her that it made sense not to see Stephen Castle for a period of three months.

Olivia had met Stephen Castle at a party given by one of Loren's colleagues on the Stock Exchange. Stephen was thirty-five, which was ten years younger than Loren and one year older than Olivia, and Stephen was an actor. Loren had no idea how Toohey, their host that evening, had met him, or why he had invited him to a party at which every other man was either in banking or on the Exchange. But there he'd been, like an evil alien spirit, and he'd concentrated on Olivia the entire evening—and she'd responded with her charming smiles that had captured Loren in a single evening eight years ago.

Afterward, when they were driving back to Old Greenwich, Olivia had said, "It's such fun to talk to somebody who's not in the stock market for a change. He told me he's rehearsing in a play now—*The Frequent Guest.* We've got to see it, Loren."

They saw it. Stephen Castle was on for perhaps five minutes in Act One. They visited Stephen backstage, and Olivia invited him to a cocktail party they were giving the following weekend. He came, and spent that night in their guest room. In the next weeks Olivia drove her car into New York at least twice a week on shopping expeditions, but she made no secret of the fact she saw Stephen for lunch on those days and sometimes for cocktails, too. At last she told Loren she was in love with Stephen and wanted a divorce.

Loren was speechless at first, even inclined to grant her a divorce by way of being sportsmanlike, but forty-eight hours after her announcement he came to what he considered his senses. By the time he had measured himself against his rival—not merely physically (Loren did not come off so well there, being no taller than Olivia, with a receding hairline and a small paunch) but morally and financially as well. In the last two categories, he had it all over Stephen Castle, and he modestly pointed this out to Olivia.

"I'd never marry a man for his money," she retorted.

"I didn't mean you married me for my money, dear, I just happened to have it. But what's Stephen Castle ever going to have? Nothing much, from what I can see of his acting. You're used to more than he can give you. And you've known him only six weeks. How can you be sure his love for you is going to last?"

That last thought made Olivia pause. She said she would see Stephen just once more—"to talk it over." She drove to New York one morning and did not return until midnight. It was a Sunday, when Stephen had no performance. Loren sat up waiting for her.

In tears, Olivia told him that she and Stephen had come to an understanding. They would not see each other for a month, and if at the end of that time they did not feel the same way about each other they would agree to forget the whole thing.

"But of course you'll feel the same," Loren said. "What's a month in the life of an adult? If you'd try it for *three* months—"

She looked at him through tears. "Three months?"

"Against the eight years we've been married? Is that unfair? Our marriage deserves at least a three-month chance, too, doesn't it?"

"All right, it's a bargain. Three months. I'll call Stephen tomorrow and tell him. We won't see each other or telephone for three months."

From that day, Olivia had gone into a decline. She lost interest in gardening, in her bridge club, even in clothes. Her appetite fell off, though she did not lose much weight—perhaps because she was proportionately inactive. They had never had a servant. Olivia took pride in the fact that she had been a working girl—a saleswoman in the gift department of a large store in Manhattan—when Loren met her. She liked to say that she knew how to do things for herself. The big house in Old Greenwich was enough to keep any woman busy, though Loren had bought every conceivable labor-saving device. They also had a walk-in deep freeze, the size of a large closet, in the basement, so that their marketing was done less often than usual, and all food was delivered, anyway. Now that Olivia seemed low in energy, Loren suggested getting a maid, but Olivia refused.

Seven weeks went by, and Olivia kept her word about not seeing Stephen. But she was obviously so depressed, so ready to burst into tears, that Loren lived constantly on the brink of weakening and telling her that if she loved Stephen that much, she had a right to see him. Perhaps, Loren thought, Stephen Castle was feeling the same way, also counting off the weeks until he could see Olivia again. If so, Loren had already lost.

But it was hard for Loren to give Stephen credit for feeling anything. He was a lanky, rather stupid chap with oat-colored hair, and Loren had never seen him without a sickly smile on his mouth—as if he were a human billboard of himself, perpetually displaying what he must have thought was his most flattering expression.

Loren, a bachelor until at thirty-seven he married Olivia, often sighed in dismay at the ways of women. For instance, Olivia. If he had felt so strongly about another woman, he would have set about promptly to extricate himself from his marriage. But here was Olivia hanging on, in a way. What did she expect to gain from it, he wondered. Did she think, or hope, that her infatuation for Stephen might disappear? Or did she want to spite Loren and prove that it wouldn't? Or did she know unconsciously that her love for Stephen was all fantasy and that her present depression represented to her and to Loren a fitting period of mourning for a love she didn't have the courage to go out and take?

But the Saturday of the garage incident made Loren doubt that Olivia was indulging in fantasy. He didn't want to admit that Olivia was attempting to take her own life, but logic compelled him to. He had read about such people. They were different from the accident-prone, who might live to die a natural death, whatever that was. The others were the suicide-prone, and into this category he was sure Olivia fell.

A perfect example was the ladder episode. Olivia had been on the fourth or fifth rung when Loren noticed the crack in the left side of the ladder, and she had been quite unconcerned, even when he pointed it out to her. If it hadn't been for her saying she suddenly felt a little dizzy looking up at the wasps' nest, he never would have started to do the chore himself, and therefore wouldn't have seen the crack.

Loren noticed in the newspaper that Stephen's play was closing, and it seemed to him that Olivia's gloom deepened. Now there were dark circles under her eyes. She claimed she couldn't fall asleep before dawn.

"Call him if you want to, darling," Loren finally said. "See him once again and find out if you both—"

"No, I made a promise to you. Three months, Loren. I'll keep my promise," she said with a trembling lip.

Loren turned away from her, wretched and hating himself.

Olivia grew physically weaker. Once she stumbled coming down the stairs and barely caught herself on the banister. Loren suggested, not for the first time, that she see a doctor, but she refused to.

"The three months are nearly up, dear. I'll survive them," she said, smiling sadly.

It was true. Only two more weeks remained until March fifteenth, the three months' deadline. The Ides of March, Loren realized for the first time. A most ominous coincidence.

On Sunday afternoon, he was looking over some office reports in his study when he heard a long scream, followed by a clattering crash. In an instant he was on his feet and running. It had come from the cellar, he thought, and, if so, he knew what had happened. That damned carpet sweeper again!

"Olivia?"

From the dark cellar he heard a groan. Loren plunged down the steps. There was a little whirr of wheels, his feet flew up in front of him, and in the few seconds before his head smashed against the cement floor he understood everything: Olivia had not fallen down the cellar steps, she had only lured him here. All this time she had been trying to kill *him*—and all for Stephen Castle.

"I was upstairs in bed reading," Olivia told the police, her hands shaking as she clutched her dressing gown around her. "I heard a terrible crash and then—I came down." She gestured helplessly toward Loren's dead body.

The police took down what she told them and commiserated with her. People ought to be more careful, they said, about things like carpet sweepers on dark stairways. There were fatalities like this every day in the United States. Then the body was taken away, and on Tuesday Loren Amory was buried.

Olivia rang Stephen on Wednesday. She had been telephoning him every day except Saturdays and Sundays, but she had not rung him since the previous Friday. They had agreed that any weekday she did not call him at his apartment at 11:00 A.M. would be a signal that their mission had been accomplished. Also, Loren Amory had got quite a lot of space on the obituary page Monday. He had left nearly a million dollars to his widow, and houses in Florida, Connecticut, Maine.

"Dearest! You look so tired!" were Stephen's first words to her when they met in an out-of-the-way bar in New York on Wednesday.

"Nonsense—it's all makeup," Olivia said gaily. "And you an actor!" She laughed. "I have to look properly gloomy for my neighbors, you know. And I'm never sure when I'll run into someone I know in New York."

Stephen looked around him nervously, then said with his habitual smile, "Darling Olivia, how soon can we be together?"

"Very soon," she said promptly. "Not up at the house, of

course, but remember we talked about a cruise? Maybe Trinidad? I've got the money with me. I want you to buy the tickets."

They took separate staterooms, and the local Connecticut paper, without a hint of suspicion, reported that Mrs. Amory's voyage was for reasons of health.

Back in the United States in April, suntanned and looking much improved, Olivia confessed to her friends that she had met someone she was "interested in." Her friends assured her that was normal, and that she shouldn't be alone for the rest of her life. The curious thing was that when Olivia invited Stephen to a dinner party at her house, none of her friends remembered him, though several had met him at that cocktail party a few months before. Stephen was much more sure of himself now, and he behaved like an angel, Olivia thought.

In August they were married. Stephen had been getting nibbles in the way of work, but nothing materialized. Olivia told him not to worry, that things would surely pick up after the summer. Stephen did not seem to worry very much, though he protested he ought to work, and said if necessary he would try for some television parts. He developed an interest in gardening, planted some young blue spruces, and generally made the place look alive again.

Olivia was delighted that Stephen liked the house, because she did. Neither of them ever referred to the cellar stairs, but they had a light-switch put at the top landing so that a similar thing could not occur again. Also, the carpet sweeper was kept in its proper place, in the broom closet in the kitchen.

They entertained more often than Olivia and Loren had done. Stephen had many friends in New York, and Olivia found them amusing. But Stephen, Olivia thought, was drinking just a little too much. At one party, when they were all out on the terrace, Stephen nearly fell over the parapet. Two of the guests had to grab him.

"Better watch out for yourself in this house, Steve," said Parker Barnes, an actor friend of Stephen's. "It just might be jinxed."

"What d'ya mean?" Stephen asked. "I don't believe that for a minute. I may be an actor, but I haven't got a single superstition."

"Oh, so you're an actor, Mr. Castle!" a woman's voice said out of the darkness.

After the guests had gone, Stephen asked Olivia to come out again on the terrace.

"Maybe the air'll clear my head," Stephen said, smiling. "Sorry I was tipsy tonight. Hey, there's old Orion. See him?" He put his arm around Olivia and drew her close. "Brightest constellation in the heavens."

"You're hurting me, Stephen! Not so—" Then she screamed and squirmed, fighting for her life.

"Damn you!" Stephen gasped, astounded at her strength.

She had twisted away from him and was standing near the bedroom door, facing him now. "You were going to push me over, weren't you?"

"No! Good God, Olivia—I lost my balance, that's all! I thought I was going over myself!"

"That's a fine thing to do, then hold onto a woman and pull her over, too."

"I didn't realize. I'm drunk, darling. And I'm sorry."

They lay as usual in the same bed that night, but both of them were only pretending sleep. Until, for Olivia at least, just as she had used to tell Loren, sleep came around dawn.

The next day, casually and surreptitiously, each of them looked over the house from attic to cellar—Olivia with a view to protecting herself from possible death traps, Stephen with a view to setting them. He had already decided that the cellar steps offered the best possibility, in spite of the duplication, because he thought no one would believe anyone would dare to use the same means—if the intention was murder.

Olivia happened to be thinking the same thing.

The cellar steps had never before been so free of impediments or so well lighted. Neither of them took the initiative to turn the light out at night. Outwardly each professed love and faith in the other.

"I'm sorry I ever said such a thing to you, Stephen," she

whispered in his ear as she embraced him. "I was afraid on the terrace that night, that's all. When you said, 'Damn you—' "

"I know, angel. But you *couldn't* have thought I meant to hurt you. I said 'Damn you' because you were there, and I thought I might be pulling you over."

They talked about another cruise. They wanted to go to Europe next spring. But at meals they cautiously tasted every item of food before beginning to eat.

How could *I* have done anything to the food, Stephen thought to himself, since you never leave the kitchen while you're cooking it.

And Olivia: I don't put anything past you. There's only one direction you seem to be bright in, Stephen.

Her humiliation in having lost a lover was hidden by a dark resentment. She realized she had been victimized. The last bit of Stephen's charm had vanished. Yet now, Olivia thought, he was doing the best job of acting in his life—and a twenty-four-hour-a-day acting job at that. She congratulated herself that it did not fool her, and she weighed one plan against another, knowing that this "accident" had to be even more convincing than the one that had freed her from Loren.

Stephen realized he was not in quite so awkward a position. Everyone who knew him and Olivia even slightly thought he adored her. An accident would be assumed to be just that—an accident—if he said so. He was now toying with the idea of the closet-sized deep freeze in the cellar. There was no inside handle on the door, and once in a while Olivia went into the farthest corner of the deep freeze to get steaks or frozen asparagus. But would she dare to go into it, now that her suspicions were aroused, if he happened to be in the cellar at the same time? He doubted it.

While Olivia was breakfasting in bed one morning—she had taken to her own bedroom again, and Stephen brought her breakfast as Loren had always done—Stephen experimented with the door of the deep freeze. If it so much as touched a solid object in swinging open, he discovered, it would slowly but surely swing shut on its rebound. There was no solid object near the door now, and on the contrary the door was intended to be swung fully open so that a catch on the outside of the door would lock in a grip set in the wall for just that purpose, and thus keep the door open. Olivia, he had noticed, always swung the door wide when she went in and it latched onto the wall automatically. But if he put something in its way, even the corner of the box of kindling wood, the door would strike it and swing shut again before Olivia had time to realize what had happened.

However, that particular moment did not seem right to put the kindling box in position, so Stephen did not set his trap. Olivia had said something about their going out to a restaurant tonight. She wouldn't be taking anything out to thaw today.

They took a little walk at three in the afternoon—through the woods behind the house, then back home again—and they almost started holding hands, in a mutually distasteful and insulting pretense of affection, but their fingers only brushed and separated.

"A cup of tea would taste good, wouldn't it, darling?" said Olivia.

"Um." He smiled. Poison in the tea? Poison in the cookies? She'd made them herself that morning.

He remembered how they had plotted Loren's sad demise—her tender whispers of murder over their luncheons, her infinite patience as the weeks went by and plan after plan failed. It was he who had suggested the carpet sweeper on the cellar steps and the lure of a scream from her. What could *her* bird-brain ever plan?

Shortly after their tea—everything had tasted fine—Stephen strolled out of the living room as if with no special purpose. He felt compelled to try out the kindling box again to see if it could really be depended on. He felt inspired, too, to set the trap now and leave it. The light at the head of the cellar stairs was on. He went carefully down the steps.

He listened for a moment to see if Olivia was possibly following him. Then he pulled the kindling box into position, not parallel to the front of the deep freeze, of course, but a little to one side, as if someone had dragged it out of the shadow to see into it better and left it there. He opened the deep-freeze door with exactly the speed and force Olivia might use, flinging the door from him as he stepped in with one foot, his right hand outstretched to catch the door on the rebound. But the foot that bore his weight slid several inches forward just as the door bumped against the kindling box.

Stephen was down on his right knee, his left leg straight out in front of him, and behind him the door shut. He got to his feet instantly and faced the closed door, wide-eyed. It was dark, and he groped for the auxiliary switch to the left of the door, which put a light on at the back of the deep freeze.

How had it happened? The damned glaze of frost on the floor? But it wasn't only the frost, he saw. What he had slipped on was a little piece of suet that he now saw in the middle of the floor, at the end of the greasy streak his slide had made.

Stephen stared at the suet neutrally, blankly, for an instant, then faced the door again, pushed it, felt along its firm, rubber-sealed crack. He could call Olivia, of course. Eventually she'd hear him, or at least *miss* him, before he had time to freeze. She'd come down to the cellar, and she'd be able to hear him there even if she couldn't hear him in the living room. Then she'd open the door, of course.

He smiled weakly and tried to convince himself she *would* open the door.

"Olivia?—Olivia! I'm down in the *cellar!*"

It was nearly a half hour later when Olivia called to Stephen to ask him which restaurant he preferred, a matter that would influence what she wore. She looked for him in his bedroom, in the library, on the terrace, and finally called out the front door, thinking he might be somewhere on the lawn.

At last she tried the cellar.

By this time, hunched in his tweed jacket, his arms crossed, Stephen was walking up and down in the deep freeze, giving out distress signals at intervals of thirty seconds and using the rest of his breath to blow into his shirt in an effort to warm himself. Olivia was just about to leave the cellar when she heard her name called faintly.

"Stephen?—Stephen, where are you?"

"In the deep freeze!" he called as loudly as he could.

Olivia looked at the deep freeze with an incredulous smile.

"Open it, can't you? I'm in the *deep freeze!*" came his muffled voice.

Olivia threw her head back and laughed, not even caring if Stephen heard her. Then, still laughing so hard that she had to bend over, she climbed the cellar stairs.

What amused her was that she had thought of the deep freeze as a fine place to dispose of Stephen, but she hadn't worked out how to get him into it. His being there now, she realized, was owing to some funny accident—maybe he'd been trying to set a trap for her. It was all too comical. And lucky!

Or maybe, she thought cagily, his intention even now was to trick her into opening the deep-freeze door, then to yank her inside and close the door on her. She was certainly not going to let *that* happen!

Olivia took her car and drove nearly twenty miles northward, had a sandwich at a roadside cafe, then went to a movie. When she got home at midnight, she found she hadn't the courage to call Stephen's name at the deep freeze, or even to go down to the cellar. She wasn't sure he'd be dead by now, and even if he were silent it might mean he was only pretending to be dead or unconscious.

But tomorrow, she thought, there wouldn't be any doubt he'd be dead. The very lack of air, for one thing, ought to finish him by that time.

She went to bed and assured herself a night's sleep with a light sedative. She would have a strenuous day tomorrow. Her story of the mild quarrel with Stephen—over which restaurant they'd go to, nothing more—and his storming out of the living room to take a walk, she thought, would have to be very convincing.

At ten the next morning, after orange juice and coffee, Olivia felt ready for her role of the horrified, grief-stricken widow. After all, she told herself, she had practiced the role—it would be the second time she had played the part. She decided to face the police in her dressing gown, as before.

To be quite natural about the whole thing, she went down to the cellar to make the "discovery" before she called the police.

"Stephen? Stephen?" she called out with confidence.

No answer.

She opened the deep freeze with apprehension, gasped at the curled-up, frost-covered figure on the floor, then walked the few feet toward him—aware that her footprints on the floor would be visible to corroborate her story that she had come in to try to revive Stephen.

Kabloom went the door—as if someone standing outside had given it a good hard push.

Now Olivia gasped in earnest, and her mouth stayed open. She'd flung the door wide. It should have latched onto the outside wall. "Hello! Is anybody out there? Open this door, please! At once!"

But she knew there was no one out there. It was just some damnable accident. Maybe an accident that Stephen had arranged.

She looked at his face. His eyes were open, and on his white lips was his familiar little smile, triumphant now, and utterly nasty. Olivia did not look at him again. She drew her flimsy dressing gown as closely about her as she could and began to yell.

"Help! Someone!—*Police!*"

She kept it up for what seemed like hours, until she grew hoarse and until she did not really feel very cold any more, only a little sleepy.

ELLERY QUEEN

THE ADVENTURE OF THE GOOD SAMARITAN

The Characters

ELLERY QUEEN
NIKKI PORTER
INSPECTOR QUEEN
SERGEANT VELIE
MRS. DILL
CHARLEY MORSE
MRS. PISANO
A DOCTOR
PATRICK O'BRIEN
JOHANN SCHMIDT
OLAF NANSEN
HELGA NANSEN
A POSTMAN

SCENE I: *A tenement in a New York slum—the Morse flat*

(MRS. DILL, *a fat and wheezy woman, is climbing a creaky flight of stairs and mumbling to herself.*)

MRS. DILL: And how they expect a propitty owner t'pay taxes an' int'rest on mortgages when they don't pay their rent beats me. Ooomp! (*As* MRS. PISANO *bumps into her*) Whyn't ye look where ye're goin', Mrs. Pisano? Near knocked me down the hull flight o' stairs!

MRS. PISANO: (*She is an excitable, emotional woman.*) 'Scusa me, Mrs. Dill. I looka for my boy, Salvatore. Alla time that keeda he's in trouble.

MRS. DILL: (*Shrilly*) You stop that young hoodlum from swipin' the covers o' the garbage pails, Mrs. Pisano! My other tenants are complainin'.

MRS. PISANO: (*Breathlessly*) Sure, Mrs. Dill—I feex him. (*She clatters downstairs.*) Salvatore! Salva*tooooo*ore?

MRS. DILL: (*To herself*) Prob'ly grow up to be a first-class gangster. (*She resumes her climb.*) Fyoo! That Mrs. O'Brien an' her cabbage! (*Pants*) Whoo. So why d'ye stand it, Martha Dill? Wasn't ye better off when ye was livin' on West End Avenoo, like a lady? Ye was! (*She walks on in an upper hall.*) Martha, you was a fool to invest Mr. Dill's money—rest his soul—in East Side real estate. (MRS. DILL *raps sharply on the door to the Morse flat.*) Mr. Morse, open up! (*Pause*) You don't fool me one bit, Charley Morse—open up! (MORSE *suddenly unlocks and opens his door.*)

MORSE: (*He is a plain American working man, at the moment very nervous.*) Uh, come in, Mrs. Dill. I didn't hear you knock.

MRS. DILL: (*Sniffing*) Now didn't ye? Mr. Morse, I want my rent.

MORSE: Rent. Gimme a little more time, Mrs. Dill—

MRS. DILL: More time! I've given ye four months—ain't that time enough? Four months' rent, twenty-five dollars a month—that's a hundred dollars y'owe me, Charley Morse!

MORSE: But, Mrs. Dill, you know I been outta work—

MRS. DILL: I know! (*Softly*) I know. (*Harshly*) But I can't help it. You got my rent or ain't ye?

MORSE: (*Despairing*) Where would *I* get a hundred dollars?

MRS. DILL: (*Sullenly*) Then I'm servin' you with a dispossess tonight. Tomorra—out ye go!

MORSE: Mrs. Dill, I got a wife an' four kids. We ain't got a cent in the house. Ya can't throw us out on the street this way. (*He begins to cry with rage and defeat.*)

MRS. DILL: (*Passionately*) Whadda you people want from me? Everybody calls me an ol' witch—but I gotta live, too, don't I? I'm a widda—all I got in the world's this piece o' propitty. I'm so poor I gotta live in this flea-trap meself. Stop cryin', Mr. Morse!

MORSE: (*Gulping, angry*) Who's cryin'? (*Earnestly*) Mrs. Dill, you know I'm an auto mechanic by trade, an' a good one if I say so myself. But there just ain't no jobs! If you'll gimme a little more time, I got a prospect—

MRS. DILL: No! (*Then—grudgingly*) What kinda prospect?

MORSE: (*Eagerly*) One o' the taxi companies promised to gimme a chance to drive a cab soon's I can show 'em a hack-driver's license, an' I'm comin' up for a driver's test next week. Wait till next week—huh?

MRS. DILL: No. You gotta git out. I got a new tenant ready to pay two months' rent in advance.

MORSE: (*Hard*) Okay, Mrs. Dill. We'll be outta here tomorra.

MRS. DILL: (*Softly*) I'm sorry, Mr. Morse. But I can't help it. I'm in hard luck, too. I'm awful sorry—

MORSE: (*Bitterly*) Thanks! I can feed my family on sympathy! Go on—get out, you fat ol' miser! "Sorry!" (*There is a knock at the door.*) Whoever you are, beat it!

POSTMAN: (*From the hall*) Special delivery for Charles Morse!

MORSE: Huh? (*He opens the door.*) For me? (*He signs for the letter as* MRS. DILL *speaks.*)

MRS. DILL: (*Eagerly*) You ain't expectin' any money, are ye, Mr. Morse? 'Cause if that's money in that letter, I'd be willin' to let ye stay rather than put ye out in the gutter. Anythin', Mr. Morse—say, one month on account.

(*The* POSTMAN *leaves.*)

MORSE: (*Muttering*) Who'd send *me* dough? (*He rips open the envelope.*) Prob'ly a bill or somepin'. (*Calling*) Annie! (*Lower*) Naw, she's feedin' the baby. Look, Mrs. Dill, ya wanna read this letter for me? I broke my glasses a couple o' minutes ago—I can't see a thing.

MRS. DILL: (*Eagerly*) Sure, Mr. Morse! (*She reads with difficulty.*) "Dear Charles—Morse. Please—accept the en-*enclosed* in—gra-gratitude for—the help you've—given me—in the past. Signed, Your Grate-ful Friend."

MORSE: (*Excited*) Enclosed? See if there's somepin' in the envelope, Mrs. Dill!

MRS. DILL: Yes, Mr. Morse—oh, it's butterfingers I've got— (*She gasps.*) Mr. Morse!

MORSE: (*Very excited*) Money! It's money! How much? Gimme that! (*Disappointed*) Just one bill? (*Gasps*) But it's a—a hundred-dollar bill! (*Dazed*) A *hundred!*

MRS. DILL: (*Ecstatic*) Oh, Mr. Morse, it's wonderful to have such rich, rememberin' friends! Who sent it?

MORSE: (*Dazed*) I dunno. I never done nothin' like what the letter says. (*Happily*) I gotta show Annie. She'll die. Annie! No, wait. (*With stern dignity*) Mrs. Dill, you been belly-achin' about not gettin' your back rent—here's the whole hundred dollars! Charley Morse *pays* his debts.

MRS. DILL: (*In a small voice*) Yes, sir. I mean, thank ye, Mr. Morse. A hundred dollars! 'Tis like money from heaven. (*She exits.*)

MORSE: Annie! Our rent's paid—we got a roof over our heads again! (*He fades, shouting, laughing.*) Annie, the most won'erful thing's happened!

SCENE II: *Mrs. Pisano's flat*

(MRS. PISANO *is crying bitterly in her kitchen as she faces a physician.*)

DOCTOR: But this morning, right after the boy's accident, I told you to notify your husband, Mrs. Pisano.

MRS. PISANO: Luigi's on WPA job, *Doctore*—I don' know how calla him. *Mio bambino,* alla time he run in da street! I tell him, "Salvatore, don' run in da street." (*She sobs.*)

DOCTOR: (*Savagely*) These hit-and-run drivers! (*Gently*) Mrs. Pisano, unless your little boy is operated on within forty-eight hours, I'm afraid he'll be a cripple for the rest of his life.

MRS. PISANO: *Madre mia!*

DOCTOR: I'm sorry, Mrs. Pisano, I had to tell you the truth. Have you any money?

MRS. PISANO: Money? Where we get money? We poor people. My Luigi, he don't make enough for operation, *Doctore.*

DOCTOR: (*Fretfully*) This operation demands exceptional skill. Unless we can get a specialist—

MRS. PISANO: An' he's gonna need a special nurse, huh, *Doctore?* Day nurse? Nighta nurse? Datsa cost mucha mon'.

DOCTOR: Yes, Mrs. Pisano. Are you sure you can't borrow a couple of hundred dollars somewhere?

MRS. PISANO: Coupla hunder' dollar! (*She laughs hysterically.*) You can getta blooda from a stone? (*She weeps again.*)

DOCTOR: Don't cry, Mrs. Pisano. I'll do my best. We'll find some way. (*There is a knock at the door.*) No, don't get up, Mrs. Pisano. I'll answer the door.

MRS. PISANO: *Grazia, Doctore.* (*The* DOCTOR *opens the door.*)

DOCTOR: Yes? What is it, please?

POSTMAN: Special delivery for Luigi Pisano.

DOCTOR: I'll sign for Mr. Pisano—he isn't home. (*The* DOCTOR *signs and returns with a letter.*) Here's a special delivery for your husband, Mrs. Pisano.

MRS. PISANO: (*Scared*) Special deliv'? Whatsa dat, *Doctore?*

DOCTOR: A—er—a quick letter, Mrs. Pisano. Would you like me to open it for you?

MRS. PISANO: Pleasa. (*The* DOCTOR *opens the letter, glances over it quickly.*)

DOCTOR: (*Excited*) Mrs. Pisano! Read this!

MRS. PISANO: Whatsa matter? More troub'? (*She reads slowly.*) "Dear—Luigi—Pisano. Please accept da en-en—" Whatsa dat word, *Doctore?*

DOCTOR: "Enclosed."

MRS. PISANO: "Da enclosed in gra-grati-tude for da—help you givea me in da—past. Your Grate-ful Frien'." (*Dazed*) My Luigi help someone? I no rememb'.

DOCTOR: But you don't understand, Mrs. Pisano. There's money in this envelope. (*She gasps.*) Look! Three one-hundred-dollar bills!

MRS. PISANO: (*Dazed*) T'ree hunder' dollar! (*Laughs hysterically*) Now my Salvatore, he get operation! Getta nurses—getta well! (*Laughing and crying*) Savea my bambino's life! T'ree hunder' dollar—*grazia, grazia, grazia!*

SCENE III: *The Queen apartment*

(*In the apartment are* ELLERY, NIKKI, O'BRIEN, SCHMIDT, *and the* INSPECTOR. O'BRIEN *has a slight Irish brogue,* SCHMIDT *a German accent.* SERGEANT VELIE *enters.*)

NIKKI: Here's Sergeant Velie.

ELLERY: Hullo, Sergeant.

VELIE: Hullohullohullo. Gosh, I'm all in. Say, I'm sorry. Did I bust in on somepin'?

INSPECTOR: Course not, Velie. Shake hands with Patrick O'Brien and Johann Schmidt. Sergeant Velie of my staff. (*They exchange greetings.*)

ELLERY: You're just in time to hear an amazing story, Sergeant.

NIKKI: Mr. O'Brien and Mr. Schmidt came to see us about a sort of divine monkeyshines going on in the East Side tenement where they live.

O'BRIEN: 'Tis on Garrett Street, Sergeant Velie.

SCHMIDT: Number thirteen.

VELIE: Thirteen Garrett Street? Say, Inspector, ain't that the tenement where—

INSPECTOR: (*Quickly*) Take a load off your feet, Velie, and listen in. And what happened after that, Mr. Schmidt?

SCHMIDT: Ach, such eggcitement! The house buzzes from day until nighdt! Who would be neggst, everybody ask. It iss like Bank Nighdt in the movies.

O'BRIEN: So then me friend Schmidt here, *he's* elected! (*Chuckles*) Git on wid ye, Schmiddy—tell 'em what happened.

SCHMIDT: I, I am a butcher. I work in a chain store. We are poor people, the family iss growing—

O'BRIEN: Schmiddy's got six kids. (*Laughs*) An' I think maybe the stork's got 'is beady eye on Mrs. Schmidt again.

SCHMIDT: Shud up, O'Brien. Who iss telling my story? So I haf a life-insurance policy—an old one, I pay for years. It comes time to pay again—no money. A hard year it hass been, we cannodt save—

ELLERY: Couldn't you borrow against your policy, Mr. Schmidt?

SCHMIDT: Ach, I have borrowed already the maximum. So if I cannodt pay the premium, the policy lapses—I cannodt take out anodder. (*Coughs exaggeratedly*) My heart nodt so goodt—they will nodt pass me now. So what am I to do? *Verflucht!* I am left withoudt protection!

NIKKI: That's a shame, Mr. Schmidt.

SCHMIDT: (*Dramatically*) But waidt! All iss not lost! The Good Samaritan! (ELLERY *and the* INSPECTOR *chuckle.*) A special-delivery ledder comes—it iss just like the ledders Charley Morse undt Luigi Pisano receive—and in idt iss a one-hundred-dollar bill! *Wunderbar!* My premium paid! We can sleep again! *Hein?* (*Laughs with joy*) Ach, America iss a wonderful country!

VELIE: (*Tense*) Say, Inspector, I'd like to see ya a minute.

INSPECTOR: (*Smoothly*) You're seeing me, aren't you? Mr. O'Brien, what are you grinning about?

O'BRIEN: 'Tis out of the fullness of me heart, Inspector.

NIKKI: The Good Samaritan visited you, too, Mr. O'Brien?

O'BRIEN: An' how! I was outta work for a long time, we'd et up all our savin's, an' then I get me a job workin' as a trolley conductor. I'm just gettin' back on me feet, mind ye, when, zingo, the finance company cracks down!

ELLERY: You'd borrowed money, Mr. O'Brien?

O'BRIEN: Mr. Queen, I did that. An' they're just goin' to move out all me furniture when a blessed special-delivery letter comes with a nice, cracklin' hundred-dollar bill insoide! (*Chuckles*) So why shouldn't I laugh? Saints be praised—I paid off the finance comp'ny an' saved me furniture!

SCHMIDT: America iss a wonderful country.

VELIE: (*Plaintively*) Inspector—could I see ya a minute? Just one minute, Inspector?

INSPECTOR: (*In an undertone*) No, you cluck, not now.

ELLERY: (*Chuckling*) Almost too good to be true, Mr. O'Brien. But I can't imagine why you two men have called on *me*. There's been no crime.

O'BRIEN: Crime! Ye don't get it, Mr. Queen. We come here t'ask ye to find the daycent, helpful man or woman who's been sendin' us all that money just when we need it most.

SCHMIDT: We wandt to show how we are grateful. We wandt to thank him.

VELIE: (*Low*) Inspector—

INSPECTOR: (*Through his teeth*) You flatfooted small-brain!

NIKKI: Oh, Ellery, I think it's wonderful! You're always being asked to look for a murderer or a thief or a blackmailer, someone who's done wrong—isn't it much more fun looking for someone *good?*

ELLERY: (*Drily*) I'll confess I'm a little dazed, Nikki.

VELIE: If ya'd only gimme a chance to shove my two cents in—

O'BRIEN: No, sor. Six fam'lies live in the house—Pisanos, Morses, Schmidts, an' us, that's four—we were helped. But Mrs. Dill, the owner—she lives there, too—she didn't get no letter or money.

SCHMIDT: *Naturlich!* Mrs. Dill needts no money. She owns the house, no?

ELLERY: That makes five families. Who's the sixth?

O'BRIEN: A Swedish carpenter, Nansen. Wife an' one kid.

VELIE: (*Chuckling*) Slacker! Now if ya'd only—Okay, okay, Inspector, you don't have to draw me no diagrams.

ELLERY: (*Thoughtfully*) So Nansen got no letter, eh? What happened to the letters and envelopes you gentlemen received? And Mr. Morse and Mrs. Pisano?

SCHMIDT: (*Triumphantly*) Whadt didt I tell you, O'Brien?

O'BRIEN: (*Ashamed*) We none of us kept the letters or envelopes, Mr. Queen. Schmiddy here said that was a boner.

NIKKI: Too bad. They might have revealed a clue to the identity of the sender.

ELLERY: Well, gentlemen, that's all for the moment. Thanks for calling me in on this. Strangest assignment I've ever had. Nikki, would you see Mr. O'Brien and Mr. Schmidt to the door?

NIKKI: Of course, Ellery. (*Ad libs of departure*)

ELLERY: (*Calling as they open the door*) I'll investigate and let you know!

VELIE: *Now* can I talk? I'm practically stranglin' to death.

INSPECTOR: (*Low*) Hold it, you eighteen-carat—(*Calling*) Bye, boys! Goodbye! (*Door closes off.*)

ELLERY: Now what's all this about?

NIKKI: (*Running back*) Wait for me! Sergeant, you *know* something about this case!

VELIE: Know somethin'! I should kiss a pig I know somethin'.

INSPECTOR: What do I have to do—break a bat over your head to keep you quiet, Velie? I didn't want those two men to know we knew anything.

NIKKI: Know *what,* for heaven's sake? I'm simply perishing.

ELLERY: Apparently there's a connection in Dad's mind—and Velie's—between Number Thirteen Garrett Street and those rather monotonous hundred-dollar bills. Eh, Dad?

INSPECTOR: Yes. A year ago, a bank messenger was held up and robbed of a hundred thousand dollars in hundred-dollar bills. We caught the thief, all right—

VELIE: An' he camped out at *Number Thirteen Garrett Street!*

ELLERY: (*Thoughtfully*) I see.

NIKKI: But you didn't find the stolen money, is that it?

INSPECTOR: That's it, Nikki. We almost tore the thief's flat apart, but the money wasn't there. He was convicted on the messenger's identification and he's in Sing Sing serving his time right now.

VELIE: We been hammerin' away at him ever since his conviction to tell where he hid the hundred grand, but he's not talkin'.

ELLERY: Which of the six apartments in the tenement did this thief live in at the time you caught him, Dad?

INSPECTOR: The one now occupied by the landlady, Mrs. Dill.

ELLERY: Was he ever known to work with an accomplice?

VELIE: That hatchet-faced lone wolf? He wouldn't cut his own mother in on the California gold rush.

ELLERY: Then I believe I know what happened. Instead of hiding the hundred thousand dollars in his *own* flat, the thief hid it in one of the other flats.

NIKKI: He was *afraid* he'd be caught.

ELLERY: Yes, and he expects to serve out his sentence, return to the tenement, and take back his hidden treasure. (*Chuckles*) But apparently someone's beaten him to it.

NIKKI: Ellery! You think one of the present tenants has found that hundred thousand dollars?

ELLERY: No question about it, Nikki, Probably found it by accident and is playing the Caliph of Bagdad to his fellow unfortunates in the tenement, distributing one-hundred-dollar bills to help them out of their troubles.

VELIE: Question is, in whose apartment was the dough hid?

INSPECTOR: Might be anyone's except Mrs. Dill's. We searched that one a year ago when we collared the thief.

ELLERY: Get your best bib-and-tucker on, Nikki. We march!

NIKKI: Ellery! You've got a clue?

ELLERY: No, but I want to talk with the only tenant in the house who *didn't* receive a letter containing money.

NIKKI: The Swedish carpenter, Nansen.

ELLERY: Yes, my turtle dove. (*Chuckles*) So let's play Diogenes and start looking for an honest man.

SCENE IV: *The Nansen flat*

HELGA: (*She is a frightened Swedish housewife.*) Police? We have done nothing—

NANSEN: (*He has a slight Swedish accent and speaks sternly.*) Helga, go. Go in to the children. I handle this.

HELGA: But, Olaf—

NANSEN: Helga! (HELGA *leaves submissively.*)

ELLERY: (*Smoothly*) But I assure you, Mr. Nansen, you've nothing to fear. I'm *not* a policeman.

NIKKI: It's just that we're trying to find out who's been so generous to your neighbors in this house.

NANSEN: The others—they get money—good. I am happy. They need it. But me, I mind my own business.

ELLERY: You've no idea who's sending that money, Mr. Nansen?

NANSEN: No.

NIKKI: Aren't you a wee bit jealous at being left out, Mr. Nansen? I'm sure you could use one or two of those hundred-dollar bills.

NANSEN: I work. I make living for my family. I need no hundred dollar from who knows who.

ELLERY: Then let's say it would be neighborly of you to assist my investigation, Mr. Nansen.

NANSEN: I am good neighbor. But how? I know nothing.

ELLERY: (*Eagerly*) I have a plan, Mr. Nansen. Apparently our Good Samaritan knows instantly when something goes wrong with a tenant in this house. And four times now within a short period he's managed to send a special-delivery letter with money just in time to avert a catastrophe.

NANSEN: Ya. I hear that. That is so. A good man.

ELLERY: Now suppose you and your wife start complaining in the neighborhood about *yourselves,* Mr. Nansen. *Make believe the Nansen family is in trouble, too.*

NIKKI: Ellery! That's a terribly clever idea.

ELLERY: Tell everyone in the house your doctor's ordered you to go to Arizona for your lungs—life and death—a matter of days.

NANSEN: But I am healthy like a horse.

ELLERY: I know, Mr. Nansen, but say it just the same. Don't you see? I want the Good Samaritan to come to *your* rescue, too.

NIKKI: (*Eagerly*) Then we'll have the letter he sends. It may tell us who he is, Mr. Nansen. Please.

NANSEN: (*Slowly*) I do not like a lie. But—I do it. But if he send money, I don't take it. I mind—

NIKKI: We know—you mind your own business. (*She laughs.*)

ELLERY: Thanks very much, Mr. Nansen. Remember—the instant you receive a special-delivery letter, phone me. *And save the letter.*

SCENE V: *Number Thirteen Garrett Street*

POSTMAN: Special delivery for Olaf Nansen. Sign here.

NANSEN: It comes! I call Mr. Queen! (*Sound effect of coin in payphone. Sound of car in traffic. Sound of steps on creaky tenement stairs.*)

NIKKI: Whew! These *stairs*—

VELIE: An' that aroma. (*Chuckles*) Sweet essence o' corned beef an' cabbage.

INSPECTOR: (*Chuckling*) Deduction: it's from the O'Brien flat. (*Panting*) Where does Nansen live—on the roof?

ELLERY: (*Cheerfully*) One flight more, Dad. I could have kissed that Swede when he rang up just now to say he'd received one of those special-delivery letters.

INSPECTOR: Let's hope it tells us who found that stolen bank money.

NIKKI: Here's the top, thank goodness.

VELIE: (*They walk along the hall.*) Whoever in this rathole is sendin' the hundred-buck bills is the guy who found the hundred grand that crook in stir hid away last year. But what *I* don't savvy is—

INSPECTOR: How about savvying in silence, Velie? Here we are. (*He knocks on the Nansens' door.*)

NIKKI: Oh, if Mr. Nansen's letter only has a clue! (NANSEN *opens the door.*)

ELLERY: Hello, Mr. Nansen.

NANSEN: Come in, Mr. Queen. (*They enter.*) Helga, go to the children.

HELGA: (*She flees.*) Ya, Olaf.

ELLERY: Now, Mr. Nansen, let's have that special delivery.

NANSEN: Here, I don't even open it. (*They chatter excitedly as

ELLERY *opens the envelope: "Hurry, Ellery!" "Let's see that!" etc.*)

ELLERY: "To Olaf Nansen." Same message as to the others—signed "Your Grateful Friend."

NIKKI: Grateful for what? They all say they never did anything important for anybody.

VELIE: Got a sense of humor, whoever he is. Say!

INSPECTOR: *Four* one-hundred-dollar bills enclosed!

NIKKI: It worked.

VELIE: Postmarked the neighborhood post-office station.

ELLERY: Cheap paper, message in block capitals in pencil, address on envelope ditto. Blast it!

NIKKI: That's mean! You'd think he was a criminal, he's been so careful not to be found out.

INSPECTOR: Unless there are fingerprints on this letter or envelope, son, I'm afraid it's a washout.

ELLERY: (*Softly*) Not quite, Dad. Look at the back of this note-paper.

NIKKI: (*Puzzled*) But it's just a jumble of capital letters.

VELIE: (*Disgusted*) A gageroo. Wise guy.

INSPECTOR: Hold on, you two. Ellery, read those letters off aloud.

ELLERY: Written in pencil, too (*Reading*) E—F, P—T, O, Z—L, P, E, D—P, E, C, F, D—E, D, F, C, Z, P. Hmm. The writer of the letter had jotted these capitals down on this sheet of paper at some previous time, then forgot he'd written them and used the reverse side of the same sheet to write to Nansen. We're in luck!

VELIE: What kind? This slumgullion don't mean nothin' to *me.*

NIKKI: I know what it is—it's a code. A cipher.

INSPECTOR: No, Nikki. Notice the capitals aren't all the same size. The first one—E—is the largest. The others get smaller and smaller as you read along.

ELLERY: Yes, and they grow smaller with a definite regularity. Notice the pattern—the letters come in groups. The first capital—the E—stands by itself. Then come F and P, both the same size but slightly smaller than the E. Then the next three—T, O, and Z—are smaller still. The next four are still smaller, the next five smaller than that, and the last six are the smallest of all.

NIKKI: Capital letters in groups of diminishing size—what on earth can it mean?

VELIE: It means some kid was doin' his homework.

INSPECTOR: No, these letters were drawn by an adult, Velie. But I'll admit they're just a meaningless hodgepodge to me.

ELLERY: Meaningless? (*Chuckles*) Quite the contrary, Dad. They tell us the identity of our Good Samaritan.

But do you know the identity of the Good Samaritan of 13 Garrett Street? You can gain additional enjoyment from these unusual little radio plays by playing the same game with each problem that has been played by so many armchair detectives who have listened to The Adventures of Ellery Queen. *And that is—stop reading at this point and try to figure out the identity of the criminal—in this case, the Good Samaritan—before Ellery returns to give you the correct answer and the logical reasoning that led up to that answer.*

And now, if you think you've figured it out, go ahead and read Ellery Queen's own solution to "The Adventure of the Good Samaritan."

SCENE VI: *The same, immediately after*

ELLERY: Before I tell you the name of our Good Samaritan, I'd like you to promise me something, Dad.

INSPECTOR: Sure, son. What?

ELLERY: Well, usually when we solve a crime it's your duty to arrest the criminal and see that he's punished. But in this case I want your word you'll not only let the malefactor go, but give him a helping hand, too.

VELIE: *He* should need a helpin' hand with a hundred grand!

INSPECTOR: (*Chuckling*) I'm way ahead of you, son. I've talked with the bank people. They're willing to give a reward of five thousand dollars to the person or persons instrumental in recovering the money.

ELLERY: (*Laughing*) It's a deal, you old mind-reader! Well, then, I'll tell you who's got that hundred thousand. This long line of capital letters on Nansen's note is the clue—the letters fall into groups, groups diminishing in size. What does this peculiar arrangement of letters suggest? (*Pause*) Where have you seen such capital letters?

VELIE: I'm thinkin', but it ain't doin' me any good.

INSPECTOR: (*Musing*) One large capital, two smaller ones, then three still smaller, and so on—

NIKKI: I can't guess beans. Ellery, don't be mean.

ELLERY: Forget that the letters are strung out in a long line. Visualize them in their diminishing-size groups but one group under another. (*Gasp from* NIKKI) See it? One large E, smaller F and P centered directly under the E, still smaller T, O, and Z centered directly under the F and P. Yes, Nikki?

NIKKI: I know! (*Ruefully*) But I can't imagine how it tells you who the sender of the money is.

INSPECTOR: Never mind that, Nikki. What does it mean?

NIKKI: Well, when you have your eyes tested, the doctor always shows you a sort of poster-card with capital letters on it. There's always just one capital at the top, the largest of all the letters on the chart—generally a big E, too. Then underneath are two smaller capitals, and so on. Right, Ellery?

ELLERY: Of course. Capitals in such groups can mean only one thing—an eye-testing chart.

INSPECTOR: But no one in this house has anything to do with an optometrist or oculist, Ellery.

ELLERY: Ah, then the capitals weren't jotted down on the paper in line with anyone's work or profession. Then why did the sender of the money list them? Obviously, to become familiar with the order and size of the letters used on an eye-chart. Why should anyone do that? *In order to memorize them*—to learn by rote the exact order of the letters. But why should anyone want to memorize them?

NIKKI: Because he can't see.

VELIE: Huh? We gotta look for a blind man now?

ELLERY: No blind person we know of in the house. Who else would want to commit the letters on an eye-chart to memory?

INSPECTOR: *Somebody expecting to take an eye test who can't trust his vision but wants to pass the test!*

ELLERY: Yes, Dad. And that deduction gives us our benevolent criminal. (*Chuckles. They urge him: "Who?"*) Charles Morse. (*They repeat the name.*) Morse, the first recipient of a letter with money—which he sent to himself as a cover-up.

NIKKI: The one who was behind in his rent? But, Ellery—how do you *know* Morse is the Good Samaritan?

ELLERY: Remember that when Morse received the first anonymous letter, he asked Mrs. Dill to read it for him? He told her he'd just broken his eyeglasses. So obviously he couldn't see well without glasses. But he told Mrs. Dill he had a chance to become a cab driver and was to take a driver's-license examination the following week. Well, one part of a driver's exam, as everyone knows, is a simple eye test. So Morse's glasses being broken, unable to see well, anxious to get the job, afraid to use one of the stolen hundred-dollar bills to fix his glasses—the bills would be traced to him—Morse would have perfect reason to copy down and memorize the capital letters of an eye-chart so that he could fake the eye test and get his license. He's the only one in the house who had such a reason.

INSPECTOR: Now I see what happened. The original thief hid the hijacked hundred grand in the flat now occupied by the Morses. Morse just found the hiding place by accident and realized it was stolen money. He's an honest man, but he didn't dare tell the police what he'd found—he'd naturally think we might accuse him of being connected with the year-old holdup. So he just held onto it—worrying his head off.

NIKKI: Till his family was in danger of being thrown into the street for nonpayment of rent.

ELLERY: Yes, then Morse risked using one bill by sending it to himself anonymously—and he only did that to keep a roof over his family's head.

VELIE: Say, this Morse must be a right guy. Used only one bill for himself for back rent, then helped out his neighbors when they were up against it!

ELLERY: Yes, Charley Morse saved the Pisano boy from being a cripple, the O'Briens from losing their household furniture, the Schmidts from being left without life-insurance protection—and he tried to help send Nansen to Arizona for lung trouble.

INSPECTOR: (*Chuckling*) The Santa Claus of crime, by thunder.

NIKKI: *I* move we go right downstairs to Charley Morse's flat and tell him to stop worrying—that he'll get a five-thousand-dollar reward for returning the bank's money.

ELLERY: The best criminal we ever caught. (*Laughing*) Come on, you three—this is going to be a pleasure.

(The music comes up.)

DOROTHY SALISBURY DAVIS

BACKWARD, TURN BACKWARD

Sheriff Andrew Willets stood at the living-room window and watched his deputies herd back from the lawn another surge of the curious, restive people of Pottersville. Some had started out from their houses, shops, or gardens at the first sound of his siren, and throughout the long morning the crowd had swelled, winnowed out, and then swelled again.

Behind him in the kitchen, from which the body of Matt Thompson had been recently removed, the technical crew of the State Police were at work with microscope and camera, ultraviolet lamp and vacuum cleaner. He had full confidence in them but grave doubts that their findings would add much weight to, or counterbalance by much, the spoken testimony against Phil Canby. They had not waited, some of those outside, to give it to police or state's attorney; they passed it one to another, neighbor to stranger, stranger sometimes back again to neighbor.

It was possible to disperse them, the sheriff thought, just as a swarm of flies might be waved from carrion; but they would as quickly collect again, unless it were possible to undo murder—unless it were possible to go out and say to them: "It's all a mistake. Matt Thompson fell and hit his head. His daughter Sue got hysterical when she found him."

Idle conjecture. Even had he been able to say that to the crowd, they would not have dispersed. They would not have believed it. Too many among them were now convinced that they had been expecting something like this to happen.

There was one person in their midst responsible in large measure for this consensus—a lifetime neighbor of both families, Mrs. Mary Lyons—and she was prepared also to give evidence that Phil Canby was not at home with the grandson the night before at the hour he swore he was at home and asleep.

Sheriff Willets went outdoors, collected Mrs. Lyons, and led her across the yard between the Thompson house and the house where Phil Canby lived with his daughter and son-in-law, and up her own back steps. From the flounce of her skirts and the clack of her heels, he could tell she didn't want to come. She smiled when she looked up at him, a quick smile in which her eyes had no part.

"I hope this won't take long, Andy," she said when he deliberately sat down, forcing her hospitality. "I should give the poor girl a hand."

"In what way, Mrs. Lyons?"

"With the house," she said, as though there would be nothing unusual in her helping Sue Thompson with the house. "It must be a terrible mess."

"You've lots of time," he said. "There's nobody going to be in that house for quite a while except the police."

Mrs. Lyons made a noise in her throat, a sort of moan, to indicate how pained she was at what had happened across her back yard.

"You were saying over there," Willets went on, "that you knew something terrible was going to happen."

"Something terrible did happen, even before this," she said. "Phil Canby taking after that girl. Sue Thompson's younger than his own daughter."

"Just what do you mean, taking after her?"

"I saw him kiss her," she said. Then, as though it had hurt her to say it in the first place, she forced herself to be explicit. "A week ago last night I saw Phil Canby take Sue in his arms and kiss her. He's over sixty, Andy."

"He's fifty-nine," the sheriff said, wondering immediately what difference a year or two made, and why he felt it necessary to defend the man in the presence of this woman. It was not that he was defending Canby, he realized; he was defending himself against the influence of a prejudiced witness. "And he gave it out the next day that he was going to marry her, and she gave it out she was going to marry him. At least, that's the way I heard it."

"Oh, you heard it right," Mrs. Lyons said airily, folding her hands in her lap.

If it had been of her doing, he should not have heard it right, the sheriff thought. But Phil Canby had passed the age in life, and had lived too much of that life across the hedge from Mary Lyons, to be either precipitated into something or forestalled from it by her opinions. Had he looked up on the night he proposed to Sue Thompson and seen her staring in the window at them, likely the most he would have done would be to pull the windowshade in her face.

"Would you like your daughter to marry a man of fifty-nine, Andy?"

"My daughter's only fifteen," the sheriff said, knowing the answer to be stupid as soon as he had made it. He was no match for her, and what he feared was that he would be no match for the town, with her sentiments carrying through it as they now were carrying through the crowd across the way. They would want Phil Canby punished for courting a young girl, whatever Canby's involvement in her father's murder. "How old is Sue Thompson, Mrs. Lyons?"

"Nineteen, she must be. Her mother died giving birth to her the year after I lost Jimmie."

"I remember about Jimmie," the sheriff said, with relief. Remembering that Mary Lyons had lost a boy of four made her more tolerable. He wondered now how close she had got to Matt Thompson when his wife died. Nobody had been close to him from then on that Willets could remember. He had been as sour a man as ever gave the devil credence. A gardener by trade, Thompson had worked for the town of Pottersville, tending its landscape. A lot of people said that whatever tenderness he had went into the care of his flowers. One thing was agreed upon by all of them, it didn't go into the care of his daughter.

As he thought about it now, Willets caught a forlorn picture from memory: Sue as a child of five or six trotting to church at her father's side, stopping when he stopped, going on when he went on, catching at his coattail when she needed balance but never at his hand, because it was not offered to her. Would no one but himself remember these things now?

"How long has it been since you were in the Thompson house, Mrs. Lyons?"

Her eyes narrowed while she weighed his purpose in asking it. "I haven't been in the house in fifteen years," she said finally.

He believed her. It accounted in part for her eagerness to get into it now. "She isn't much of a housekeeper, Sue," he said, to whet her curiosity further and to satisfy his own on what she knew of her neighbors. "Or maybe that's the way Matt Thompson wanted it."

She leaned forward. "What way?"

"It has a funny, dead look about it," he said. "It's not dirty, but it just looks like nothing has been put in or taken out in fifteen years."

"He never got over his wife's death," Mrs. Lyons said, "and he never looked at another woman."

Her kind had no higher praise for any man, he thought. "Who took care of Sue when she was a baby?"

"Her father."

"And when he was working?"

"I don't know."

"From what I've heard," he lied, for he had not yet had the opportunity to inquire elsewhere, "you were very good to them, and so was Phil Canby's wife in those days."

"Mrs. Canby was already ailing then," she snapped. "I was good to both families, if I say it myself."

"And if you don't," the sheriff murmured, "nobody else will."

"What?"

"People have a way of being ungrateful," he explained.

"Indeed they do."

"You know, Mrs. Lyons, thinking about it now, I wonder why Matt didn't offer Sue for adoption."

"You might say he did to me once." A bit of color tinged her bleached face after the quick, proud answer. She had probably been at the Thompson house night and day then with solicitudes and soups, when Matt was home and when he wasn't home.

Assuming Thompson to have been sarcastic with her—and

he had had a reputation for sarcasm even that far back—the sheriff said: "Would you have taken the child? You must've been lonesome—after Jimmie."

For once she was candid with him, and soft as he had not known her to be since her youth. "I'd have thought a good deal about it. I had a feeling there was something wrong with her. She was like a little old maid, all to herself. She's been like that all her life—even in school, they say."

"It makes you understand why she was willing to marry Phil Canby," the sheriff said quietly. "Don't it?"

"Oh, I don't blame her," Mrs. Lyons said. "This is one case where I don't blame the woman."

Willets sighed. Nothing would shake her belief that there was something immoral in Phil Canby's having proposed marriage to a girl younger than his own daughter. "Last night," he said, "your husband was away from home?"

"He was at the Elks' meeting. I was over at my sister's and then I came home about ten-thirty. I looked at the clock. I always do. It takes me longer to walk home than it used to."

"And that was when you heard the baby crying?"

"It was crying when I came up the back steps."

Phil Canby had been baby-sitting with his grandson while his daughter, Betty, and his son-in-law, John Murray, were at the movies. It was his custom to stay with young Philip every Thursday night, and sometimes oftener, because he lived with them; but on Thursdays Betty and her husband usually went to the movies.

"And you're sure it was the Murray baby?"

"Who else's would it be over that way? I couldn't hear the Brady child from here. They're five houses down."

The sheriff nodded. Phil Canby swore that he was in bed and asleep by that time, and he swore that the baby had not cried. He was a light sleeper, in the habit of waking up if little Philip so much as whimpered. The neighbors to the south of the Murray house had not heard the crying, nor for that matter the radio in the Murray house, which Canby said he had turned on at ten o'clock for the news. But they had been watching television steadily until eleven-thirty. By that time the Murrays had come home and found Phil and the baby Philip each asleep in his own bed.

But to the north of the Murrays, in the corner house where Sue Thompson claimed she was asleep upstairs, her father Matt had been bludgeoned to death sometime between ten o'clock and midnight.

"And you didn't hear anything else?" the sheriff asked.

"No, but I didn't listen. I thought maybe the baby was sick and I was on the point of going down. Then I remembered it was Thursday night and Mr. Canby would be sitting with him. He wouldn't take the time of day from me."

Not now he wouldn't, the sheriff thought. "Have you any idea how long the baby was crying, Mrs. Lyons?"

"I was getting into bed when he stopped. That was fifteen minutes later maybe. I never heard him like that before, rasping like for breath. I don't know how long the poor thing was crying before I got home."

If Phil Canby had murdered Matt Thompson and then reached home by a quarter to eleven, he would have had time to quiet baby Philip and to make at least a pretense of sleep himself before his family came home. Betty Murray admitted that her father was in the habit of feigning sleep a good deal these days, his waking presence was so much of an embarrassment to all of them. Scarcely relevant except as a practiced art.

Willets took his leave of Mrs. Lyons. What seemed too relevant to be true, he thought, striding over the hedge which separated her yard from the Thompsons, was that Phil Canby admitted quarreling with Thompson at nine o'clock that night, and in the Thompson kitchen.

After the first exchange of violent words between the two households, when Phil Canby and Sue Thompson made known their intentions of marriage, an uneasy, watchful quiet had fallen between them. Sue Thompson had not been out of the house except with her father, and then Sunday prayer meeting. Matt Thompson had started his vacation the morning his daughter told him. Vacation or retirement: he had put the hasty choice up to the town supervisor. Thompson then had gone across to Betty Murray. He had never been in Betty's house before, not once during her mother's long illness or at her funeral; and if he had spoken to Betty as a child, she could not remember it. But that morning he spoke to her as a woman, and in such a manner and with such words that she had screamed at him: "My father is not a lecher!"

To which he had said: "And my daughter is not a whore. Before she takes to the bed of an old man, I'll shackle her!" When John Murray came home from the office that night and heard of it, he swore that he would kill Matt Thompson if ever again he loosed his foul tongue in Betty's presence.

But Matt Thompson had gone into his house and pulled down all the shades on the Murray side, and Phil Canby had gone about the trade he had pursued in Pottersville since boyhood. He was a plumber, and busier that week for all the talk about him in the town. All this the sheriff got in bits and pieces, mostly from Betty Murray. When Thursday night had come around again, she told him, she felt that she wanted to get out of the house. Also, she had begun to feel that if they all ignored the matter, the substance of it might die away.

So she and John had gone to the movies, leaving her father to sit with the baby. About eight-thirty, Sue Thompson had come into the yard and called to Phil. He went out to her. She had asked him to come over and fix the drain to the kitchen sink. Her father was sleeping, she told him, but he had said it would be all right to ask him. Canby had gone back into the house for his tools and then followed her into the Thompson house, carrying a large plumber's wrench in his hand. When Phil Canby had told this to the sheriff that morning—as frankly, openly, as he spoke of the quarrel between himself and Thompson, a quarrel so violent that Sue hid in the pantry through it—Willets got the uncanny feeling that he had heard it all before and that he might expect at the end of the recitation as candid and calm a confession of murder.

But Canby had not confessed to the murder. He had taken alarm, he said, when Matt Thompson swore by his dead wife to have him apprehended by the state and examined as a mental case. He knew the man to do it, Thompson had said, and Canby knew the man of whom he spoke: Alvin Rhodes, the retired head of the state hospital for the insane. Thompson had landscaped Rhodes's place on his own time when Rhodes retired, borrowing a few shrubs from the Pottersville nursery to do it. This the sheriff knew. And he could understand the extent of Canby's alarm when Canby told about the confinement of a friend on the certification of his children, and on no more grounds apparent to Canby than that the man had become cantankerous, and jealous of the house which he had built himself and in which he was becoming, as he grew older, more and more of an unwelcome guest. Phil Canby had bought the house in which he now lived with his daughter. He had paid for it over thirty years, having had to add another mortgage during his wife's invalidism. Unlike his friend, he did not feel a stranger in it. The baby had even been named after him, but he was well aware the tax his wooing of Sue Thompson put upon his daughter and her husband.

All this the sheriff could understand very well. The difficulty was to reconcile it with the facts of the crime. For example, when Canby left the Thompson house, he took with him all his tools save the large wrench with which Thompson was murdered. Why leave it then—or later—except that to have taken it from beside the murdered man and to have had it found in his possession (or without it when its ownership was known) was to leave no doubt at all as to the murderer? All Canby would say was that he had forgotten it.

Willets went to the back door of Canby's house. He knocked, and Betty Murray called out to him to come in. Little Philip was in his high chair, resisting the applesauce his mother was trying to spoon into him.

The sheriff stood a moment watching the child, marveling at the normalcy which persists through any crisis when there is a baby about. Every blob of sauce spilled on the tray Philip tried to shove to the floor. What he couldn't get off the tray with his hands he went after with his tongue.

The sheriff grinned. "That's one way to get it into him."

"He's at that age now," his mother said, cleaning up the floor. She looked at Willets. "But I'm very grateful for him, especially now."

The sheriff nodded. "I know," he said. "Where's your father?"

"Up in his room."

"And the Thompson girl?"

"In the living room. Sheriff, you're not going to take them—"

"Not yet," he said, saving her the pain of finishing the sentence. He started for the inside door and paused. "I think Mrs. Lyons would be willing to have her there for a bit."

"I'll bet she would," Betty said. "I had to close the front windows, with people gaping in to see her. Some of them, and they weren't strangers either, kept asking—where her boyfriend was."

"It won't be for long," Willets said; and then because he had not quite meant that, he added: "It won't be this way for long."

"Then let her stay. I think she feels better here, poor thing, just knowing Papa's in the house." She got up then and came to him. She was a pretty girl and, like her father's, her eyes seemed darker when they were troubled.

"Mr. Willets, I was talking to Papa a while ago. He was trying to tell me about—him and Sue. He told her when he asked her to marry him that he was going to be as much a father to her as a husband." Betty colored a bit. "As a lover," she corrected. "That's what he really said."

"And did he tell you what she had to say to that?"

"She said that's what she wanted because she'd never had either one."

The sheriff nodded at the obvious truth in that.

"I thought I'd tell you," Betty went on, "because I know what everybody says about Papa and her. They think he's peculiar. Almost like what I told you Matt Thompson said. And he's not. All the time mother was sick, until she died, he took care of her himself. He even sent me away to school. Most men would have said that was my job, and maybe it was, but I was terribly glad to go. Then when mother died and I got married, it must have seemed as though something ended for him. And fifty-nine isn't really very old."

"Not very," Willets said, being so much closer to it than she was.

"I'm beginning to understand what happened to him," Betty said. "I wish I'd thought about it sooner. There might have been something—somebody else."

The sheriff shook his head. "That's a man's own problem till he's dead."

"You're right," she said after a moment. "That's what really would have been indecent."

The sheriff nodded.

"I wish it was possible to separate the two things," Betty said as he was leaving, "him and Sue—and Mr. Thompson's murder. I wish to God it was."

"So do I," the sheriff said, thinking again of the pressures that would be put upon him because it was not possible to separate them, not only by the townspeople but by the state's attorney, who would find it so much more favorable to prosecute a murderer in a climate of moral indignation.

On the stairway, with its clear view of the living room, he paused to watch Sue Thompson for a moment, unobserved. She was sitting with a piece of crochet work in her lap at which she stitched with scarcely a glance. Whatever her feelings, the sheriff thought, she was not grieving. She had the attitude of waiting. All her life she had probably waited—but for what? Her father's death? A dream lover? A rescuer? Surely her girlish dreams had not conjured up Phil Canby in that role. The strange part of it was that it seemed unlikely to the sheriff she had dreamed of rescue at all. However she felt about her father, she did not fear him. Had she been afraid of him, she could not have announced to him that she intended to marry Phil Canby. And because she was not afraid of him, Willets decided, it was difficult to imagine that she might have killed him. She was a soft, plump girl, docile-eyed, and no match for her father physically. Yet she was the one alternate to Phil Canby in the deed, and he was the only one who knew her well enough to say if she was capable of it.

The sheriff went on and knocked at Canby's door. "I've got to talk to you some more, Phil."

Canby was lying on the bed staring at the ceiling. "I've told you all I know," he said without moving.

The sheriff sat down in the rocker by the open window. The radio, which Canby claimed to have been listening to at ten o'clock the night before, was on a table closer to the window, and across the way, no more than fifteen yards, the neighbors had not heard it.

"Mrs. Lyons says that little Philip was crying at ten-thirty last night, Phil."

"Mrs. Lyons is a liar," Canby said, still without rising. His thin grey hair was plastered to his head with sweat and yet he lay on his back where no breeze could reach him. A pulse began to throb at his temple. The skin over it was tight and pale—it reminded Willets of a frog's throat.

"Betty admits you didn't change the baby. That wasn't like you, Phil, neglecting him."

"He was sleeping. I didn't want him to wake up. I had to think of my plans."

"What plans?"

"My marriage plans."

"What were they?"

Finally Canby rose and swung his slippered feet over the side of the bed. He looked at Willets. "We're going to be married in Beachwood." It was a village a few miles away. "I've got a house picked out on the highway and I'll open a shop in the front of it."

It was fantastic, Willets thought: both Canby and the girl behaved as though they were not in any way suspected of Matt Thompson's death—as though nothing in the past should interfere with the future. This angered Willets as nothing save Mrs. Lyons's judgments had. "You're in trouble, Phil, and you're going to hang higher than your fancy plans if you don't get out of it. The whole damn town's against you."

"I know that," Canby said. "That's why I'm not afraid."

Ther sheriff looked at him.

"If I didn't know what everybody was saying," Canby went on, "I wouldn't of run off home last night when Matt Thompson said he was going to get me certified."

"Phil," the sheriff said with great deliberateness, "the state's attorney will maintain that's why you *didn't* run home, why you *weren't* in this house to hear the baby crying, why you *weren't* home in time to change him, why you *can't* admit Mrs. Lyons heard Philip crying! Because, he'll say, you were over in the Thompson kitchen, doing murder and cleaning up after murder."

Canby was shaking his head. "That baby don't cry. He don't ever cry with me around."

The sheriff got up and walked the length of the room and back, noting that Phil Canby was careful in his things, their arrangements, their repair. He was a tidy man. "You're still planning to marry her, then?" he said.

"Of course. Why shouldn't I?"

The sheriff leaned down until he was face to face with the man. "Phil, who do *you* think killed her father?"

Canby drew back from him, his eyes darkening. "I don't know," he said, "and I guess I never rightly cared—till now."

Willets returned to the rocker and took a pipe from his shirt pocket. He didn't light it; he merely held it in his hand as though he might light it if they could talk together. "When did you fall in love with Sue Thompson?"

Canby smoothed the crumpled spread. "Sounds funny, saying that about somebody my age, don't it?"

Willets didn't answer and Canby went on: "I don't know. Whatever it was, it happened last spring. She used to stop by ever since she was a little girl, when I was out working in the yard, and watch me. Never said much. Just watched. Then when little Philip came, she used to like to see him. Sometimes I'd invite her in. If I was alone she'd come. Kind of shy of Betty, and whenever John'd speak to her she'd blush. John don't have a good opinion of her. He's like all the young fellows nowadays. They look at a girl's ankles, how she dances, what clothes she puts on. It's pure luck if they get a decent wife, what they look for in a girl."

"You and Sue," the sheriff prompted, when Canby paused.

"Well, I was holding Philip one night and she was watching. He was puckering up to cry, so I rocked him to and fro and he just went off to sleep in my arms. I remember her saying, 'I wish I could do that,' so I offered her the baby. She was kind of scared of it." The man sank back on his elbows and squinted a bit, remembering. "It struck me then all of a sudden how doggone rotten a life Matt had give her as a kid."

"How rotten?" the sheriff said.

"Nothing. No affection, no love at all. He bought her what she needed, but that was all. She was in high school before she knew people was different, what it was like to—to hold hands even."

"I wonder what got into him," Willets said. "Most men, losing a wife like he did, would put everything into the kid till they got another woman."

"He didn't want another woman. He liked his hurt till it got to mean more to him than anything else."

The sheriff shook his head. It might be so, although he could not understand it. "Go on about you and Sue," he said.

Canby took a moment to bring himself back to the contemplation of it. He sat up so that he could illustrate with his strong, calloused, black-nailed hands. "I put Philip into his cradle and she was standing there. I just sort of put out my arms to her like she was maybe a little girl which'd lost something or was hurt, and she came to me." He paused, moistened his lips, and then plunged on. "While I was holding her—Oh, Jesus, what was it happened then?"

He sprang up from the bed and walked, his hands behind his back. "I thought that was all over for me. I hadn't felt nothing like it, not for years." He turned and looked down at Willets. "I was young again, that's all, and she wasn't a little girl. I was ashamed at first, and then I thought—what am I ashamed of? Being a man? I waited all summer, thinking maybe it'd go away. But it didn't. It just got inside me deeper and quieter so's I wasn't afraid of it, and I wasn't ashamed. And when I asked her and she was willing to marry me, I explained to her that it couldn't be for long because I'm fifty-nine, but she didn't care." He opened his hands as if to show they were empty. "That's how it was, Andy. I can't explain it any more than that."

"That's how it was," the sheriff repeated, getting up, "but look how it is right now."

Willets went downstairs to Sue Thompson, where she still sat, crochet work in hand, a bit back from the window yet with the people outside within her view.

"Know any of those folks, Miss Thompson?"

"No," she said, "I don't think I do."

He could believe that, although some of them had lived in the neighborhood all her lifetime. He sat down opposite her so that the light would be in her face. "Last night, Miss Thompson, why did you tell Mr. Canby your father said it would be all right to ask him to fix the drain?"

"Because I wanted him to come over. It was the only excuse I could think of."

"Your father didn't say it would be all right?"

"No."

"Didn't you expect trouble between them?"

"I didn't think my father would wake up."

"I see," the sheriff said. A pair, the two of them, he thought—unless their guilt was black as night, one as naive as the other. The marks of Canby's wrench were on the drainpipe where he had actually commenced to work. "When did you and Mr. Canby expect to be married?"

"Soon. Whenever he said."

"Were you making plans?"

"Oh, yes," she said, smiling. "I've been doing a lot of work." She held up the crocheting by way of illustration.

"Didn't you expect your father to interfere—in fact, to prevent it?"

"No," she said.

The sheriff rested his chin on his hand and looked at her. "Miss Thompson, I'm the sheriff of this county. Your father was murdered last night and I'm going to find out why, and who murdered him. You'd better tell me the truth."

"I'm telling you the truth, Mr. Willets. I know who you are."

"And you didn't expect your father to interfere with your marriage."

"He never interfered with anything I did," she said.

"Did you know he told Betty Murray that he would chain you up rather than see you marry her father?"

"I didn't know that. He never said it to me."

"Just what did he say when you told him?"

"He laughed. I think he said something like, 'Well, doesn't that beat everything.' "

The sheriff sat up. "He was treating you like a halfwit. You're an intelligent girl. Didn't you resent it?"

"Of course," she said, as though surprised that he should ask. "That's one reason why I'm so fond of Phil—Mr. Canby."

"You resented it," Willets repeated, "and you did nothing about it?"

"I was waiting," she said.

"For what? For him to die? To be murdered?"

"No," she said, "just waiting."

"Have you always got everything you wanted by waiting, Miss Thompson?"

She thought about that for a moment. "Yes, I think I have—or else I didn't want it any more."

Passive resistance, that's what it amounted to, the sheriff thought. If nations could be worn down by it, Matt Thompson was not invulnerable. But his murder was not passive resistance. "Last night you hid in the pantry during the quarrel?"

"Yes. Phil told me to go away, so I hid there."

"Did you hear what they were saying?"

"Not much. I put my fingers in my ears."

"What did you hear exactly?"

She looked at him and then away. "I heard my father say 'insane asylum.' That's when I put my fingers to my ears."

"Why?"

"I was there once with him when I was a little girl."

"Can you tell me about it?" the sheriff said.

"Yes," she said thoughtfully. "There was a man working for him in the garden. I liked him, I remember. He would tickle me and laugh just wonderful. When I told my father that I liked him, he took me inside to see the other people. Some of them screamed at us and I was frightened."

"I see," the sheriff said, seeing something of Matt Thompson and his use of the afflicted to alarm the timid. "Last night, when did you come out of the pantry?"

"When my father told me to. He said it was all over and I could go up to bed."

"And you did? No words with him about the quarrel?"

"I went upstairs and went to bed, like I told you this morning."

"And you went to sleep right away because you felt so badly," he said, repeating her earlier account of it. He could see how sleep must have been her salvation many times. She had slept soundly through the night, by her account, and had wakened only to the persistent knocking of Phil Canby—who, when he was about to start his day's work, had remembered, so he said, the plumber's wrench. Going downstairs to answer Canby's knocking, she had discovered her father's body.

The sheriff took his hat. "You can have the funeral tomorrow, Miss Thompson," he said. "I'd arrange it quickly if I were you, and see to it there's a notice of it in the paper."

He went out the front door and across the yard, ignoring the questions pelted at him from the crowd. The technician in charge of the state crew was waiting. "I don't have much for you, Willets. Whoever did the job scrubbed up that kitchen afterward. But good."

"Canby's clothes?"

"Nothing from that job on them. We'll run some more tests to be dead sure if you want us to."

"I want you to. What about hers?"

"Not even a spot to test. I put them back in her room, night clothes and day clothes."

The sheriff thought for a moment. "What was the kitchen cleaned up with?"

"A bundle of rags. Left in the sink. They came out of a bag hanging beside the stove."

"Handy," the sheriff said, and went upstairs.

After the male sparsity and drabness in the rest of the house—and that was how Willets thought of it, as though a woman's hand had not touched it in years—Sue's room screamed with color. Her whole life in the house was in this one room. There was crochet work and needlework of multi- and clashing colors, laces and linens, stacked piece on piece. She had fashioned herself a fancy lampshade that almost dripped with lace.

At some time not too long before, she had tried her hand at painting, too. It was crude, primitive, and might very well be art for all he knew, but in his reckoning it was in contrast to the exact work of her needle. In a small rocker, left over from her childhood—perhaps even from her mother's childhood, by its shape and age—sat two dolls, faded and matted, and one with an eye that would never close again. The dust of years was ground into them and he wondered if they had been sitting there while she grew into womanhood, or if upon her recent courtship—if Phil Canby's attentions could be called that—she, a timid girl, and likely aware of her own ignorance, had taken them out to help her bridge the thoughts of marriage.

The bed was still unmade, Sue's pajamas lying on it. Not a button on the top, he noticed, and the cloth torn out. The technician had put them back where he had found them. Her dress lay with its sleeves over the back of the chair, just as she had flung it on retiring. She had, no doubt, put on a fresh dress to go out to the fence and call Phil Canby. There was scarcely a crease in it. The sheriff trod upon her slippers, a button, a comb. The rug, as he looked at it, was dappled with colored thread from her sewing. Not the best of housekeepers, Sue Thompson, he thought, going downstairs and locking up the house—but small wonder, keeping house only for herself in one room.

George Harris, the state's attorney, was in the sheriff's office when he returned to the county building. He didn't want to seem too eager, Willets thought, since obviously the sheriff had not yet made an arrest. He spoke of the murder as a tragedy and not a case, and thus no doubt he had spoken of it in town.

"I've had a lot of calls, Andy," he said, "a lot of calls."

The sheriff grunted. "Did you answer them?"

Harris ignored the flippancy. "Not enough evidence yet, eh?"

"I'm going to put it all together now," Willets said. "When I get it in a package I'll show it to you. Maybe in the morning."

"That's fine by me," Harris said. He started for the door and then turned back. "Andy, I'm not trying to tell you how to run your office, but if I were you I'd call the local radio station and give them a nice handout on it—something good for the nerves."

"Like what?"

"Oh, something to the effect that any suspect in the matter is under police surveillance."

He was right, of course, Willets thought. The very mention of such surveillance could temper would-be vigilantes. He called the radio station and then worked through most of the night.

His last tour of duty took him past the two darkened houses where his deputies kept sullen vigil.

Fifty or so people attended the funeral service and as many more were outside the chapel. Among them were faces he had seen about the town most of his life. With the murder they seemed to have become disembodied from the people who clerked, drove delivery trucks, or kept house. They watched him with the eyes of ghouls to see how long it would take him to devour his prey.

The minister spoke more kindly of Matt Thompson than his life deserved, but the clergyman had the whole orbit of righteousness, frugality, and justice to explore and, under the circumstances and in the presence of those attending, the word "love" to avoid.

Phil Canby stood beside the girl as tall as he could, with the hard stoop of his trade upon his back. His head was high, his face grim. Sue wept as did the other women, one prompted by another's tears. Behind Canby stood his daughter and his son-in-law, John Murray—who, when the sheriff spoke to him at the chapel door, said he had taken the day off to "see this thing finished." It would be nice, Willets thought, if it could be finished by John Murray's taking the day off.

When the final words were said, people shuffled about uneasily. It was customary to take a last look at the deceased, but Matt Thompson's coffin remained unopened. Then his daughter leaned forward and fumbled at a floral wreath. Everyone watched. She caught one flower in her hand and pulled it from the rest, nearly upsetting the piece. She opened her hand and looked at the bloom. Willets glanced at Mrs. Lyons, who was on tiptoe watching the girl. She, too, was moved to tears by that. Then the girl looked up at the man beside her. If she did not smile, there was the promise of it in her round, blithe face. She offered him the flower. Phil Canby took it, but his face went as grey as the tie he wore. Mrs. Lyons let escape a hissing sound, as sure a condemnation as any words she might have cried aloud, and a murmur of wrathful shock went through the congregation. Willets stepped quickly to Canby's side and stayed beside him until they returned to the Murray house, outside which he then doubled the guard.

He went directly to the state's attorney's office, for George Harris had had the report on his investigation since nine o'clock that morning.

"Everything go off all right?" Harris offered Willets a cigarette, shaking four or five out on the desk from the package. He was feeling expansive, the sheriff thought.

"Fine," he said, refusing the cigarette.

The attorney stacked the loose cigarettes. "I'll tell you the truth, Andy, I'm damned if I can see why you didn't bring him in last night." He patted the folder closest to him. It chanced to be the coroner's report. "You've done a fine job all the way. It's tight, neat."

"Maybe that's why I didn't bring him in," Willets said.

Harris cocked his head and smiled his inquisitiveness. At forty-five, he was still boyish, and he had the manner of always seeming to want to understand fully the other man's point of view. He would listen to it, weigh it, and change his tactics—but not his mind.

"Because," the sheriff said, "I haven't really gone outside their houses to look for a motive."

The attorney drummed his fingers on the file. "Tell me the God's truth, Andy, don't you think it's here?"

"Not all of it," the sheriff said doggedly.

"But the heart of it?"

"The heart of it's there," he admitted.

" 'All of it' to you means a confession. Some policemen might have got it. I don't blame you for that."

"Thanks," Willets said drily. "I take it, Mr. Harris, you feel the case is strong against him?"

"I don't predict the outcome," the attorney said, his patience strained. "I prosecute and I take the verdict in good grace. I believe the state has a strong case, yes." He shrugged off his irritation. "Much hinges, I think, on whether Canby could feel secure from interruption while he did the job—and afterward, while he cleaned up."

Willets nodded.

Harris fingered through the folder and brought out a paper.

"Here. The girl hid in the pantry when he told her to leave. She went upstairs to bed when her father told her to. Now, I say that if she came downstairs again, all Canby had to do was tell her to go up again. She's the amenable type. Not bright, not stupid, just willing and obedient."

That from his documentation, Willets thought. If ever Harris had seen the girl, it was by accident. "Then you think she was an accessory?" Certainly most people did now, having seen or heard of her conduct at the funeral.

The attorney pursed his lips. "I wouldn't pursue that right now. You haven't turned up anything to prove it. But he could feel secure about being able to send her upstairs again before she saw anything. That's what was important: that he could feel secure. That's how I'd use it. Put that together with the Lyons woman's testimony and his own daughter's. No jury will take his word that he was home with his grandson between ten and eleven."

"Did he strip naked to do the job?" said Willets. "His clothes went through the lab."

"Old work clothes." The attorney looked him in the eyes. "There's been cleaner jobs than this before and I'll prove it. I don't expect to go in with the perfect case. There's no such thing."

"Then all I have to do," Willets said, "is get the warrant and bring him in."

"That's all. The rest is up to me." The sheriff had reached the door when Harris called after him. "Andy—I'm not the s.o.b. you seem to think I am. It's all in here." He indicated the file. "You'll see it yourself when you get to where you can have some perspective."

Harris might very well be right, the sheriff thought as he walked through the county court building. He had to accept it. Either Harris was right and he had done his job as sheriff to the best of his ability and without prejudice, making the facts stand out from sentiments, or he had to accept something that logic would not sanction: Sue Thompson as the murderer of her own father.

That this amenable girl, as Harris called her, who by the very imperturbability of her disposition had managed a life for herself in the house of her father—that she, soft and slovenly, could do a neat and terrible job of murder, he could not believe. But even granting that she could have done it, could someone as emotionally untried as she withstand the strain of guilt? He doubted it. Such a strain would crack her, he thought, much as an overripe plum bursts while yet hanging on the tree.

But the motive, Canby's motive: it was there and it was not there, he thought. It was the thing which so far had restrained him from making the arrest—that, and his own stubborn refusal to be pressured by the followers of Mary Lyons.

The sheriff sat for some time at his desk, and then he telephoned Matt Thompson's friend, Alvin Rhodes. The appointment made, he drove out to see the former superintendent of the state hospital for the insane.

Rhodes, as affable as Thompson had been dour, told of Matt Thompson's visiting him the previous Wednesday, the day before his death.

"We were not friends, Willets," the older man said, "although his visit implies that we were. He was seeking advice on his daughter's infatuation with a man three times her age."

As Thompson had grown more sullen with the years, the sheriff thought, Rhodes had mellowed into affability upon retirement. Such advice was not sought of someone uncongenial to the seeker. "And did you advise him, Mr. Rhodes?"

"I advised him to do nothing about it. I recounted my experience with men of Canby's age who were similarly afflicted. The closer they came to consummation, shall we say, the more they feared it. That's why the May and December affairs are rare indeed. I advised him to keep close watch on the girl, to forestall an elopement, and leave the rest to nature. In truth, Willets, although I did not say it to him, I felt that if they were determined he could not prevent it."

"He cared so little for the girl," Willets said, "I wonder why he interfered at all. Why not let her go and good riddance?"

Rhodes drew his white brows together while he phrased the words carefully. "Because as long as he kept her in the house, he could atone for having begot her, and in those terms for having caused his wife's death." Willets shook his head. Rhodes added then: "I told him frankly that if anyone in the family should be examined, it was he and not the girl."

Willets felt the shock like a blow. "The girl?"

Rhodes nodded. "That's why he came to me, to explore the possibility of confining her—temporarily. In his distorted mind, he calculated the stigma of such proceedings to be sufficient to discourage Canby."

And the threat of such proceedings, Willets thought, was sufficient to drive Canby to murder—as such threats against his own person were not. "I should think," he said, preparing to depart, "you might have taken steps against Matt Thompson yourself."

Rhodes rose with him. "I intended to," he said coldly. "If you consult the state's attorney, you will discover that I made an appointment with him for two o'clock yesterday afternoon. By then Thompson was dead. I shall give evidence when I am called upon."

The sheriff returned to the courthouse and swore out the warrant before the county judge. At peace with his conscience at last, he drove again to the Murray house. Betty Murray was staring out boldly at the watchers who had reconvened—as boldly as they were again staring in at her.

There would be a time now, Willets thought, when they could stare their fill and feel righteous in their prejudgment of the man. Only then would they be willing to judge the full story, only then would they be merciful, vindicating their vindictiveness. He ordered his deputies to clear the street. John Murray opened the door when the sheriff reached the steps.

"Better take Betty upstairs," Willets said to her husband. He could see the others in the living room, Sue and Phil Canby sitting at either end of the couch, their hands touching as he came.

"The old man?" John whispered. Willets nodded and Murray called to his wife. Betty looked at him over her shoulder but did not move from the window.

"You, too, Miss Thompson," Willets said quietly. "You both better go upstairs with John."

Betty lifted her chin. "I shall stay," she said. "This is my father's house and I'll stay where I want to in it."

Nor did Sue Thompson make any move to rise. Willets strode across to Canby. "Get up," he said. "I'm arresting you, Phil Canby, for the willful murder of Matt Thompson."

"I don't believe it," Betty said from behind them, her voice high, tremulous. "If God's own angel stood here now and said it, I still wouldn't believe it."

"Betty, Betty," her husband soothed, murmuring something about good lawyers.

Canby's eyes were cold and dark upon the sheriff. "What's to become of her?" he said, with a slight indication of his head toward Sue.

"I don't know," Willets said. No one did, he thought, for she looked completely bemused, her eyes wide upon him as she tried to understand.

"You're taking him away?" she said as Canby rose. Willets nodded.

"It won't be for long," John Murray said in hollow comfort, and more to his wife than to the girl.

"Don't lie to her," Canby said. "If they can arrest me for something I didn't do, they can hang me for it." He turned to Willets. "If you're taking me, do it now."

"You can get some things if you want."

"I don't want no things."

Willets started to the door with him. Betty looked to her husband. He shook his head. She whirled around then on Sue Thmpson. "Don't you understand? They're taking him to jail. Because of you, Sue Thompson!"

Canby stiffened at the door. "You leave her alone, Betty. Just leave her alone."

"I won't leave her alone and I won't leave Sheriff Willets alone. What's the matter with everyone? My father's not a murderer." Again she turned on Sue. "He's not! He's a good man. You've got to say it, too. We've got to shout it out at everybody, do you hear me?"

"Betty, leave her alone," her father repeated.

"Then get her out of here," John Murray said, his own fury

rising with his helplessness. "She sits like a bloody cat and you don't know what's going on in her mind—"

The sheriff cut him off. "That's enough, John. It's no good." He looked at the girl. Her face was puckered up almost like an infant's about to cry. "You can go over home now, Miss Thompson. I'll send a deputy in to help you."

She did not answer. Instead she seemed convulsed with the effort to cry, although there was no sound to her apparent agony. Little choking noises came then. She made no move to cover her face and, as Willets watched, the face purpled in its distortion. All of them stared at her, themselves feeling straitened with the ache of tears they could not shed. Sue's body quivered and her face crinkled up still more.

Then the sound of crying came—a high, gurgling noise—and it carried with the very timbre and rasp of a baby's. Willets felt Phil Canby clutch his arm and he felt terror icing its way up his own spine. He heard a sick, fainting moan from Betty Murray between the girl's spasms, but he couldn't take his eyes from the sight. Nor could he move to help her. Sue hammered her clenched fists on her knees helplessly. Then she tried to get up, rocking from side to side. Finally she rolled over on the couch and, her backside in the air, pushed herself up as a very small child must. Her first steps were like a toddle when she turned and tried to balance herself. Then, catching up an ashstand which chanced to stand in her way, she ran headlong at Willets with it, the infantile screams tearing from her throat.

In time it would be told that Sue Thompson reverted to the infancy she coveted at least once before her attack on Willets, rising from sleep as a child on the night of her father's quarrel with Canby, ripping off her night clothes when she could not manage the buttons, and in a rage with her father—when, perhaps, he berated her for nudity, immodesty, or some such thing a child's mind cannot comprehend—attacking him with a child's fury and an adult's frenzied strength, using the weapon at hand—Phil's wrench.

Sheriff Willets could document much of it when the sad horror had been manifest before him: the crying Mrs. Lyons heard, even the cleaning up after the murder, for he had watched Canby's grandson clean off the tray of his highchair. And he could believe she had then gone upstairs to fall asleep again and wake in the morning as Sue Thompson, nineteen years old and the happy betrothed of Phil Canby.

HENRY SLESAR

THE MEMORY EXPERT

Olin Mearns sat alone in the makeshift classroom above the El Greco Restaurant and buried his face in his hands. He knew he would never forget this day. But that wasn't unusual. Olin's profession was remembering things and instructing others in that serviceable art. He was a memory teacher, and in good times his class in the Britt Building on Forty-second Street numbered between twenty and thirty students a semester. He could put a name to every face in less than ten minutes after the course began, a feat which never failed to impress his pupils.

Of course, the trick was much easier to perform these days, since Olin's classes never boasted more than five or six students, a practical reality that had forced him to abandon his Forty-second Street address for smaller quarters above the Greek restaurant downtown. (The most memorable thing about his course was the smell of burning olive oil.) One of those few students had been Penelope Walz, the cause of his current misery. She had just turned twenty-four (today) and had a face that Olin couldn't forget even if he tried. She had an hourglass figure, although perhaps a little plump around the six o'clock mark. She also had a mind like a sieve.

It was this latter feature that had attracted Penelope to the small advertisement Olin ran regularly in the *Daily News:*

> "Never forget another face! Never forget another name! Never forget another fact that may be vital to your business or social success! In just four short weeks Olin Mearns, Ph.D., will help you develop a perfect memory!"

Only that morning, Penelope's imperfect memory had cost her the fourth secretarial job that year. She worked for a lawyer named Nerdlinger, but rarely remembered his name. That day

Mr. Nerdlinger himself had walked into the office and Penelope had said, "May I help you?" She had been there four months. When she left, she even forgot to take her salary check.

The truth is, Olin had failed to do much for Penelope's mnemonic powers. Their encounter was memorable for a different reason. Olin had fallen passionately, hopelessly in love for the first time in his forty-nine years. Penelope was flattered enough to respond, despite the difference in their ages, the spareness of Olin's physique, and the fact that his hair was only a memory. It was his brain that impressed her—that vast storehouse of facts that reposed inside his naked dome.

But there was something very different about Penelope's attitude when he arrived with her birthday gift that afternoon.

"What's wrong, sweetness?" Olin said. "Don't you like the roses?"

"Half a dozen," Penelope said sourly. "Imagine bringing anybody half a dozen roses!"

"Sugar, I told you that I have to cut expenses."

"You have to cut!" Penelope cried. "What about me? Do you know they're raising the rent on this apartment by thirty dollars a month? Do you know how much money I owe the grocery store? What about that loan you were going to make me?"

Olin swallowed hard, wishing there were things Penelope *didn't* remember. "Honey, sweetheart, you know how rough business has been lately. I haven't enrolled *one* student yet this term—"

"And the ring you were going to buy me?" she accused. "Whatever happened to *that?* Honestly, Olin, for a memory teacher you have a very short memory sometimes!"

"Sweetness, I'm waiting until things pick up. It's the economy—people think education is a luxury these days."

"I don't know about luxuries," Penelope said icily. "All I know is that I'm not getting any younger. And that's why I've decided to take that job whosit offered me, with the whatsit company."

Olin gasped. "Honey, baby, you don't mean that job in Alaska? What do you want to freeze up there for?"

"Whosit said it isn't really cold, not in you-know—"

"Juneau," Olin said. He tried to put his arm around the middle of the hourglass and winced when she pushed him away.

"I'm sorry," Penelope said firmly. "A girl has to think of her future, Olin, and you don't seem to have any."

Sitting alone now in the empty classroom, Olin heard an echo of that statement in his head. It became part of his memory bank, along with the capitals of the world, the Hall of Fame pitching and batting records, and all the other facts that now seemed useless and trivial to him.

When the doorbell sounded, he wasn't stirred into action until the third ring. But habit was stronger than sorrow, and when he opened the door and saw the face of the man outside he took a mental photograph of his features—the beetling brows, the square chin cleft unnaturally by a scar, the thin lips, the yellowish eyes shifty with suspicion. And with the same sense of triumph he always felt on these occasions, Olin Mearns realized he could actually put a name to this stranger's face. He wasn't quite sure why, but he knew his name was Morgan Krebs.

"Mike Kingston," the man said, baffling Olin. "I called you this morning, Mr. Mearns, remember?"

"Oh," Olin said. "Oh, yes, of course, Mr.—Kingston. Please come in."

The man entered and seemed relieved to have the door shut behind him. "I read your ad," he said. "About the memory course?"

"Ah," Olin answered vaguely, still puzzled by the mystery. He never forgot a face, or the name that went with it. Was he losing his grip, in addition to his girl and his career? But then, as Kingston refused the chair he was offered and wandered toward the window, Olin had the answer. Kingston was using an alias, and no wonder. The name Morgan Krebs had appeared under a picture of his face (two views) on Wanted posters and in newspaper stories.

"The thing is," Kingston was saying, "I don't want to take the whole course. I don't have the time, you know?"

"Well—er, what did you have in mind then?" Olin asked.

"What I really need to remember is just one thing," Kingston said. He glanced sideways out of the window toward the street.

Whether he thought he was being followed or if it was simply force of habit, Olin couldn't tell.

"Just one thing," Olin repeated. "I'm afraid I don't understand."

"Understand? I forgot something and I haven't been able to remember it since, and it bothers me. I mean like it bothers me a lot. I figured a guy who knows about memory, he ought to know how to make me remember. Am I wrong or what?"

The man made Olin nervous, but he was the closest thing to a live pupil he had seen in weeks. "Well," he said carefully, "I'm not sure you understand my course, Mr. Krebston."

"Kingston."

"Kingston, yes. You see, what I do is teach people how to develop their memories, how to use the processes of association, correlation, assimilation." The man's face was like a blank white sheet. Olin finished lamely, "Maybe if you told me more about this—"

"All right," Krebs said. "You see, a couple of days ago I stored some, er, personal belongings in one of them new lockers in the railway station, you know? One of the lockers that works without a key. It's one of them combination-lock lockers, you know?"

Olin nodded, fascinated by the man's nervous manner and his shifting eyes.

"Well, that was a dumb thing, you know, on account of I went and forgot the number. I mean, I had a ticket with the locker number and the combination, but I lost it when things got hot. —The weather, I mean," he said quickly. "I mean, changing into a summer suit, you know?" Olin was still nodding. "I keep trying to remember them numbers—I'm going crazy trying to remember them. It's important!"

Olin said, "Well, perhaps if you spoke to someone—an official of the railroad, or the company that makes the lockers?"

"Forget it," Kingston said flatly, ignoring Olin's profession. "That's one thing I can't do, never mind why. I got to remember them numbers, and I got to get them, er, personal belongings out of the locker. So what I want you to do, Professor, is help me remember it—dig?"

Olin dug only too well. Obviously Mr. Morgan Krebs placed

quite a value on the, er, personal belongings. "Well, it's unusual," he said. "I mean, I'm not sure that my particular techniques can *prod* memory as well as improve it."

Krebs, who had his hand on the window shade, flapped it with an impatient gesture.

"Can you help me or not?"

"I might, I might," Olin said hastily. "I mean, the basic principles should be the same. But I'm not sure I can succeed."

"I'll pay you whether it works or not," Krebs said. "Either way, I'll pay you the full price of your course. That's a hundred and fifty bucks, right?"

"Yes."

"Okay, I'll pay you a big one and a half just for trying. And if you make me remember them numbers, Professor, there'll be a bonus in it for you. I mean, a real nice bonus."

Olin seemed to be considering the proposition. Actually, he had already agreed to say yes.

"Yes," he said finally. "All I can do is try."

He told Krebs to return the next morning, when the private tutoring would begin.

The moment his new pupil left, Olin dived for the telephone.

"Penelope?" he said. "I've got to see you! There's something I have to tell you!"

"The names of all the Presidents and Vice Presidents? I'm not interested, thank you."

"You don't understand! Something has happened that may be very important—"

"I'm going to bed," Penelope told him. "I've got to get up early. I'm meeting Mr. Whosit about the whatchamacallit. The job. In Alaska."

"Just give me a little time," he pleaded. "Just a few more days."

"Forget about me," she said. "I've already forgotten about you, Harlan."

"Olin," he said miserably, and heard the hanging-up click in the receiver.

When Krebs arrived the next morning, promptly at the appointed time, he didn't seem aware of the fact that his instructor had slept only two hours the night before, spending the rest of his normal sleeping time scanning books, most of which he had already committed to memory. But Olin had failed to find any foolproof system for dredging up already forgotten facts.

He'd just have to wing it.

"We'll try the technique called association," he told his pupil. "Every memory has association with other memories, and if we can put one together with the other—"

"Whatever you say, Professor."

"Try to tell me what you were doing on the day you put this, er, personal property into the locker."

"I don't remember."

"Do you recall what you were *thinking* when you put this, er, property away?"

"Never mind what I was thinking," Krebs said coldly. "Just tell me how to remember them numbers."

"All right. Shut your eyes and visualize yourself placing the, er, property in the locker." Kingston closed his eyes. "What do you see?"

"Nothing. It's too dark."

"Can you see the shape of the, er, thing you're placing in the locker?"

"Yeah, I remember the shape of it. It's a little black suitc—" His eyes flew open. "Never mind the shape of it, Professor. I know the shape of it. What I want to know is, *where is it?"*

"Can you recall even *one* of the digits?"

"What's a digit?"

"Can you remember even *one* of the numbers? A zero, one, two, three, or four?"

"Yeah," Kingston said.

"Which one, which one?" Olin said excitedly. "Can you remember which of those it was?"

"It was either a zero, a one, a two, a three, or a four. Only I don't remember whether it came first, second, third, or last."

Olin leaned back with a sigh.

That night he telephoned Penelope again.

She said, "Whom did you say is calling?"

* * *

The next day Olin told his pupil, "Today we're going to try a word-association test. Although I guess I mean a number-association test."

Without much hope for success, he began reading off a long list of four-digit combinations. To each of them Kingston either grunted no or merely shrugged. Eventually, after two hours of this, the student grew so tried he stretched out on Olin's sofa and shut his eyes.

"Nine nine one eight," Olin said, his voice hoarse.

Kingston didn't reply. He was asleep.

That night, instead of phoning Penelope, Olin went to her apartment. He found her in the midst of packing.

"Go away, Nolan," she said. "I'm leaving this weekend. Mr. Hammerschmidt is picking me up Saturday morning."

"Who?" Olin said, feeling a pang of jealousy at hearing the name of her new employer for the first time.

"Mr. Hammerschmidt," Penelope said. "He's in the pharmaceutical business."

"A druggist?"

"He's not a druggist. He's opening a whole chain of drugstores in Alaska and I'm going to be his personal secretary." She softened when she saw Olin's mournful reaction. "I'm sorry, I really am. But I told you I had to think of my future, remember?"

"I remember," Olin said, without pride.

The next day he took Krebs on a field trip. They went to the railway terminal together and tried to recreate the circumstances. Krebs warned Olin that he had attempted the same procedure on his own, wandering past the banks of lockers for hours on end, always to no avail.

Olin's encouragement didn't help. Krebs simply couldn't remember.

It began to look hopeless.

That night, skimming through treatises on memory that he'd previously thought worthless or impractical, Olin felt the greatest sense of discouragement he had ever known.

Then Sigmund Freud helped him out.

He had never attempted to analyze the *reasons* behind Krebs's forgetfulness. But rereading Freud and his works on the theory of the unconscious, he suddenly became aware that

Morgan Krebs felt *guilty* about whatever it was he had hidden away. That was it! He didn't *want* to remember the number.

But how was he to break the barrier Krebs had erected? Olin wasn't an analyst. He couldn't hypnotize Krebs into loosening his hold on the truth. What would make him cooperate?

Then it dawned on him.

Drugs!

When Penelope heard what he had in mind, she gasped.

"Olin, I couldn't do such a thing!"

"You could do anything if you tried," Olin said, stroking her arm. "All you have to do is remember the name. Sodium pentathol. You don't even have to remember it—I'll write it down for you, honey sweetheart. And you can tell your nice friend Mr. Hammerschmidt that you absolutely *have* to have some of it or you can't possibly go to Alaska with him."

"But what are you going to *do* with it?"

"I'm going to *help* Mr. Krebs, sugar, I'm going to help my patient—I mean my pupil—remember something very, very important. And when he does, it's going to make all the difference in the world to you and me."

"I don't see how," Penelope said. But he could see she was wavering.

Penelope had surprisingly little trouble obtaining the drug from Mr. Hammerschmidt. Obviously, the threat of going to cold Alaska without her warm hourglass body was enough to make him produce the drug without asking too many questions.

On Friday morning, the day before her scheduled flight to Juneau, Olin called her from his office and told her to stand by for exciting developments.

When Krebs entered his office and learned what the professor had in mind, he blanched. "I don't like needles!" he said bluntly.

"You needn't worry," Olin said. "I was a medical corpsman in the Army. I gave thousands of shots, and I never lost a patient." He gave Krebs a toothy smile meant to be reassuring.

Krebs resisted for another fifteen minutes, but then, spurred on by Olin's promises of immediate results, finally relented.

Olin gave him the injection.

He had never administered a "truth serum" before, but he had seen enough movies to know that he was supposed to ask his subject to start counting backward from one hundred. Krebs scowled and said, "Nah," and promptly fell asleep.

For a moment Olin thought his plan had failed, but then Krebs stirred and said, "I didn't do it, Officer."

Olin leaned over the sofa and said, "Mr. Kingston, listen to me." He got a snore for a response. "Morgan!" he said loudly. "Morgan Krebs! Listen to me!"

"Yeah, what is it?" his pupil said testily. "What do you want?"

"I want you to remember something, Morgan! I want you to remember the day you walked into the railroad station carrying a small black suitcase! Do you remember it?"

"So what?" Krebs said with hostility, his eyes still closed.

"You *do* remember it, don't you, Morgan?"

"Yeah, I remember."

"You knew you had to get rid of that suitcase, didn't you, Morgan? You knew the police were closing in on you!"

"Dirty stoolie pigs!" Morgan shouted, kicking his legs against the arm of the sofa.

"You went to the lockers, didn't you, Morgan? You picked out a locker, and you put the money into the slot, and you placed the little suitcase inside, is that right?"

"Yeah. I had to get rid of it. They were after me!"

"You took the ticket, didn't you, Morgan? What did you do with the ticket? Did you throw it away so the cops couldn't ever find it?"

"Yeah!"

"That means you committed the ticket numbers to memory, is that right? You thought you could remember those numbers without any trouble, didn't you?"

"Yeah! Anybody can remember a few numbers!"

"Of course you can, Morgan! In fact, you can remember it right now!"

"No—I can't!"

"You *can,*" Olin said, licking his dry lips. "All you have to do is look at the ticket—look at the ticket in your mind—and you can see those numbers plain as day! Can't you, Morgan? Plain as day!"

"Krebs's face was getting wet. There were beads of sweat in the scar on his chin.

"Yeah," he said. "Yeah. Plain as day!"

Olin began sweating himself. "You see them, Morgan? You *see* the numbers?"

"Yeah, I see them!"

"What are they? What are the numbers?"

A smile was softening Krebs's thin lips.

"Five, zero, one, one," he said dreamily. His whole body seemed to relax. "Locker number five zero one one, combination number two two five."

A great sense of peace seemed to descend over the man on the sofa. He was so content he drifted off to sleep again. But his contentment couldn't match Olin Mearns's sense of triumph. In fact, Olin was so elated he decided to telephone Penelope Walz then and there, with Kingston snoring smilingly on his sofa.

"You're not going to Alaska, sugar baby," he said. "You're going to Palm Beach, Florida, where it's nice and warm. You're going to lie in the sun with your Olin and turn brown as a little berry."

"Florida!" Penelope said. "Oh, Marlon, wouldn't that be wonderful! But how can you afford it?"

"Pack your bags again," he chuckled. "Only this time pack for warm weather, sweetness."

An hour later Krebs woke and sat up.

"What happened?" he said groggily. "What happened, Professor?"

Olin looked at him sadly and shook his head. "I'm sorry, Mr. Kingston. The sodium pentathol was my last resort and I'm afraid it failed."

"You couldn't make me remember them numbers?"

"No," Olin said. "It just didn't work. But I have one good piece of news for you."

"What's that?"

"I'm only charging you half the fee," Olin said smugly. "I feel it's only right."

Krebs's burly shoulders slumped so far down he looked almost puny.

Olin waited for an hour after Krebs left the office. He was in no hurry. He didn't even bother to write the numbers down. He knew he could trust his memory. He always had. Once again he felt pride in his ability, confidence in the future.

The police found Penelope's name and address in Olin Mearns's pocket notebook, which explained why they called on her that night.

"But I don't understand," she whimpered. "How could anything like that happened to Olin?"

"We thought maybe you could explain it, Miss Walz. What made him open that locker? And when he did, why did he take that bag out of it? Do you know?"

"It wasn't *his* locker," Penelope sobbed. "It belonged to a pupil of his—a man name Tibbs. No, sounded more like Crabs."

"Krebs? Morgan Krebs?"

"That was the name! What was in that suitcase, anyway?"

"Something Krebs didn't want any inspector to find when he opened the locker. Usually he left those little beauties in telephone-company offices, after hours. He's got a hate on the telephone company, but he never wanted to *kill* anyone."

"Kill anyone? You mean he was a *killer?"*

"Too bad your friend didn't remember who Krebs really was. If he had, he wouldn't be pasted all over the terminal now. He should have remembered what the newspapers called Morgan Krebs."

"What was that?"

"The Mad Bomber of the Bronx."

ARTHUR CONAN DOYLE

THE RED-HEADED LEAGUE

I had called upon my friend, Mr. Sherlock Holmes, one day in the autumn of last year, and found him in deep conversation with a very stout, florid-faced elderly gentleman with fiery red hair. With an apology for my intrusion I was about to withdraw, when Holmes pulled me abruptly into the room and closed the door behind me.

"You could not possibly have come at a better time, my dear Watson," he said cordially.

"I was afraid that you were engaged."

"So I am. Very much so."

"Then I can wait in the next room."

"Not at all. This gentleman, Mr. Wilson, has been my partner and helper in many of my most successful cases, and I have no doubt that he will be of the utmost use to me in yours also."

The stout gentleman half rose from his chair and gave a bob of greeting, with a quick little questioning glance from his small, fat-encircled eyes.

"Try the settee," said Holmes, relapsing into his armchair and putting his fingertips together, as was his custom when in judicial moods. "I know, my dear Watson, that you share my love of all that is bizarre and outside the conventions and humdrum routine of everyday life. You have shown your relish for it by the enthusiasm which has prompted you to chronicle, and, if you will excuse my saying so, somewhat to embellish so many of my own little adventures."

"Your cases have indeed been of the greatest interest to me," I observed.

"You will remember that I remarked the other day, just before we went into the very simple problem presented by Miss Mary Sutherland, that for strange effects and extraordinary combinations we must go to life itself, which is always far more daring than any effort of the imagination."

"A proposition which I took the liberty of doubting."

"You did, Doctor, but nonetheless you must come round to my view, for otherwise I shall keep on piling fact upon fact on you, until your reason breaks down under them and acknowledges me to be right. Now, Mr. Jabez Wilson here has been good enough to call upon me this morning, and to begin a narrative which promises to be one of the most singular which I have listened to for some time. You have heard me remark that the strangest and most unique things are very often connected not with the larger but with the smaller crimes, and occasionally, indeed, where there is room for doubt whether any positive crime has been committed. As far as I have heard, it is impossible for me to say whether the present case is an instance of crime or not, but the course of events is certainly among the most singular that I have ever listened to.

"Perhaps, Mr. Wilson, you would have the great kindness to recommence your narrative. I ask you not merely because my friend, Dr. Watson, has not heard the opening part, but also because the peculiar nature of the story makes me anxious to have every possible detail from your lips. As a rule, when I have heard some slight indication of the course of events I am able to guide myself by the thousands of other similar cases which occur to my memory. In the present instance, I am forced to admit that the facts are, to the best of my belief, unique."

The portly client puffed out his chest with an appearance of some little pride, and pulled a dirty and wrinkled newspaper from the inside pocket of his greatcoat. As he glanced down the advertisement column, with his head thrust forward and the paper flattened out upon his knee, I took a good look at the man and endeavored, after the fashion of my companion, to read the indications which might be presented by his dress or appearance.

I did not gain very much, however, by my inspection. Our visitor bore every mark of being an average, commonplace British tradesman, obese, pompous, and slow. He wore rather baggy, gray, shepherd's-check trousers, a not over-clean black frock-coat, unbuttoned in the front, and a drab waistcoat with a heavy, brassy Albert chain and a square, pierced bit of metal dangling down as an ornament. A frayed top hat and a faded brown overcoat with a wrinkled velvet collar lay upon a chair beside him. Altogether, look as I would, there was nothing remarkable about the man save his blazing red head and the expression of extreme chagrin and discontent upon his features.

Sherlock Holmes's quick eye took in my occupation, and he shook his head with a smile as he noticed my questioning glances. "Beyond the obvious facts that he has at some time done manual labor, that he takes snuff, that he is a Freemason, that he has been in China, and that he has done a considerable amount of writing lately, I can deduce nothing else."

Mr. Jabez Wilson started up in his chair, with his forefinger upon the paper but his eyes upon my companion.

"How, in the name of good fortune, did you know all that, Mr. Holmes?" he asked. "How did you know, for example, that I did manual labor? It's as true as gospel, for I began as a ship's carpenter."

"Your hands, my dear sir. Your right hand is quite a size larger than your left. You have worked with it and the muscles are more developed."

"Well, the snuff, then, and the Freemasonry?"

"I won't insult your intelligence by telling you how I read that, especially as, rather against the strict rules of your order, you use an arc-and-compass breastpin."

"Ah, of course, I forgot that. But the writing?"

"What else can be indicated by that right cuff so very shiny for five inches, and the left one with the smooth patch near the elbow where you rest it upon the desk."

"Well, but China?"

"The fish which you have tattooed immediately above your wrist could only have been done in China. I have made a small study of tattoo marks, and have even contributed to the literature of the subject. That trick of staining the fishes' scales a delicate pink is quite peculiar to China. When, in addition, I see a Chinese coin hanging from your watch-chain, the matter becomes even more simple."

Mr. Jabez Wilson laughed heavily. "Well, I never!" said he. "I thought at first that you had done something clever, but I see that there was nothing in it after all."

"I begin to think, Watson," said Holmes, "that I make a mistake in explaining. *'Omne ignotum pro magnifico,'* you know, and my poor little reputation, such as it is, will suffer shipwreck if I am so candid. Can you not find the advertisement, Mr. Wilson?"

"Yes, I have got it now," he answered, with his thick red finger planted halfway down the column. "Here it is. This is what began it all."

I took the paper from him and read as follows:

> "To the Red-Headed League: On account of the bequest of the late Ezekiah Hopkins, of Lebanon, Pa., U.S.A., there is now another vacancy open which entitles a member of the League to a salary of four pounds a week for purely nominal services. All red-headed men who are sound in body and mind and above the age of twenty-one years are eligible. Apply in person on Monday, at eleven o'clock, to Duncan Ross, at the offices of the League, 7 Pope's Court, Fleet Street."

"What on earth does this mean?" I ejaculated after I had twice read over the extraordinary announcement.

Holmes chuckled and wriggled in his chair, as was his habit when in high spirits. "It is a little off the beaten track, isn't it?" said he. "And now, Mr. Wilson, off you go at scratch, and tell us all about yourself, your household, and the effect which this advertisement had upon your fortunes. You will first make a note, Doctor, of the paper and the date."

"It is *The Morning Chronicle* of April 27, 1890. Just two months ago."

"Very good. Now, Mr. Wilson."

"Well, it is just as I have been telling you, Mr. Sherlock Holmes," said Jabez Wilson, mopping his forehead, "I have a small pawnbroker's business at Coburg Square, near the City. It's not a very large affair, and of late years it has not done more than just give me a living. I used to be able to keep two assistants, but now I only keep one, and I would have a job to pay him but that he is willing to come for half wages to learn the business."

"What is the name of this obliging youth?" asked Sherlock Holmes.

"His name is Vincent Spaulding, and he's not such a youth, either. It's hard to say his age. I should not wish a smarter assistant, Mr. Holmes, and I know very well that he could better himself, and earn twice what I am able to give him. But, after all, if he is satisfied, why should I put ideas in his head?"

"Why, indeed? You seem most fortunate in having an employee who comes under the full market price. It is not a common experience among employers in this age. I don't know that your assistant is not as remarkable as your advertisement."

"Oh, he has his faults, too," said Mr. Wilson. "Never was such a fellow for photography. Snapping away with a camera when he ought to be improving his mind, and then diving down into the cellar like a rabbit into its hole to develop his pictures. That is his main fault; but, on the whole, he's a good worker. There's no vice in him."

"He is still with you, I presume?"

"Yes, sir. He and a girl of fourteen, who does a bit of simple cooking and keeps the place clean—that's all I have in the house, for I am a widower and never had any family. We live very quietly, sir, the three of us; and we keep a roof over our heads and we pay our debts, if we do nothing more.

"The first thing that put us out was that advertisement. Spaulding, he came down into the office just this day eight weeks, with this very paper in his hand, and he says:

" 'I wish to the Lord, Mr. Wilson, that I was a red-headed man.'

" 'Why that?' I asks.

" 'Why,' says he, 'here's another vacancy in the League of the Red-Headed Men. It's worth quite a little fortune to any man who gets it, and I understand that there are more vacancies than there are men, so that the trustees are at their wits' end what to do with the money. If my hair would only change color here's a nice little crib all ready for me.'

" 'Why, what is it, then?' I asked. You see, Mr. Holmes, I am a very stay-at-home man, and, as my business came to me instead of my having to go to it, I was often weeks on end without putting my foot over the doormat. In that way I didn't know much of what was going on outside, and I was always glad of a bit of news.

" 'Have you never heard of the League of the Red-Headed Men?' he asked, with his eyes open.

" 'Never.'

" 'Why, I wonder at that, for you are eligible yourself for one of the vacancies.'

" 'And what are they worth?'

" 'Oh, merely a couple of hundred a year, but the work is slight, and it need not interfere very much with one's other occupations.'

"Well, you can easily think that that made me prick up my ears, for the business has not been over good for some years, and an extra couple of hundred would have been very handy.

" 'Tell me all about it,' said I.

" 'Well,' said he, showing me the advertisement, 'you can see for yourself that the League has a vacancy, and there is the address where you should apply for particulars. As far as I can make out, the League was founded by an American millionaire, Ezekiah Hopkins, who was very peculiar in his ways. He was himself red-headed, and he had a great sympathy for all red-headed men; so, when he died, it was found that he had left his enormous fortune in the hands of trustees, with instructions to apply the interest to the providing of easy berths to men whose hair is of that color. From all I hear, it is splendid pay, and very little to do.'

" 'But,' said I, 'there would be millions of red-headed men who would apply.'

" 'Not so many as you might think,' he answered. 'You see, it is really confined to Londoners, and to grown men. This American had started from London where he was young, and he wanted to do the old town a good turn. Then again, I have heard it is no use applying if your hair is light red, or dark red, or anything but real, bright, blazing, fiery red. Now, if you cared to apply, Mr. Wilson, you would just walk in, but perhaps it would hardly be worth your while to put yourself out of the way for the sake of a few hundred pounds.'

"Now it is a fact, gentlemen, as you may see for yourselves, that my hair is of a very full and rich tint, so that it seemed to me that if there was to be any competition in the matter, I stood as good a chance as any man that I had ever met. Vincent Spaulding seemed to know so much about it that I thought he might prove useful, so I just ordered him to put up the shutters for the day and to come right away with me. He was very willing to have a holiday, so we shut the business up and started off for the address that was given us in the advertisement.

"I never hope to see such a sight as that again, Mr. Holmes. From north, south, east, and west every man who had a shade of red in his hair had trampled into the City to answer the advertisement. Fleet Street was choked with red-headed folk, and Pope's Court looked like a coster's orange barrow. I should not have thought there were so many in the whole country as were brought together by that single advertisement. Every shade of color they were—straw, lemon, orange, brick, Irish-setter, liver, clay; but, as Spaulding said, there were not many who had the real vivid flame-colored tint. When I saw how many were waiting, I would have given it up in despair, but Spaulding would not hear of it. How he did it I could not imagine, but he pushed and pulled and butted until he got me through the crowd, and right up to the steps which led to the office. There was a double stream upon the stair, some going up in hope, and some coming back dejected, but we wedged in as well as we could, and soon found ourselves in the office."

"Your experience has been a most entertaining one," remarked Holmes, as his client paused and refreshed his memory with a huge pinch of snuff. "Pray continue your very interesting statement."

"There was nothing in the office but a couple of wooden chairs and a deal table, behind which sat a small man, with a head that was even redder than mine. He said a few words to each candidate as he came up, and then he always managed to find some fault in them which would disqualify them. Getting a vacancy did not seem to be such a very easy matter after all. However, when our turn came, the little man was much more favorable to me than to any of the others, and he closed the door as we entered so that he might have a private word with us.

" 'This is Mr. Jabez Wilson,' said my assistant, 'and he is willing to fill a vacancy in the League.'

" 'And he is admirably suited for it,' the other answered. 'He has every requirement. I cannot recall when I have seen anything so fine.' He took a step backward, cocked his head on one side, and gazed at my hair until I felt quite bashful. Then suddenly he plunged forward, wrung my hand, and congratulated me warmly.

" 'It would be injustice to hesitate,' said he. 'You will, however, I am sure, excuse me for taking an obvious precaution.' With that he seized my hair in both his hands and tugged until I yelled with the pain. 'There is water in your eyes,' said he as he released me. 'I perceive that all is as it should be. But we have to be careful, for we have twice been deceived by wigs and once by paint. I could tell you tales of cobbler's wax which would disgust you with human nature.' He stepped over to the window and shouted through it at the top of his voice that the vacancy was filled. A groan of disappointment came up from below, and the folk all trooped away in different directions, until there was not a red head to be seen except my own and that of the manager.

" 'My name,' said he, 'is Mr. Duncan Ross, and I am myself one of the pensioners upon the fund left by our noble benefactor. Are you a married man, Mr. Wilson? Have you a family?'

"I answered that I had not.

"His face fell immediately.

" 'Dear me!' he said gravely, 'that is very serious indeed. I am sorry to hear you say that. The fund was, of course, for the propagation and spread of the redheads as well as for their maintenance. It is exceedingly unfortunate that you should be a bachelor.'

"My face lengthened at this, Mr. Holmes, for I thought that I was not to have the vacancy after all; but, after thinking it over for a few minutes, he said that it would be all right.

" 'In the case of another,' said he, 'the objection might be fatal, but we must stretch a point in favor of a man with such a head of hair as yours. When shall you be able to enter upon your new duties?'

" 'Well, It is a little awkward, for I do have a business already,' said I.

" 'Oh, never mind about that, Mr. Wilson!' said Vincent Spaulding. 'I shall be able to look after that.'

" 'What would be the hours?' I asked.

" 'Ten to two.'

"Now a pawnbroker's business is mostly done of an evening, Mr. Holmes, especially Thursday and Friday evenings, which is just before payday, so it would suit me very well to earn a little in the mornings. Besides, I knew that my assistant was a good man, and that he would see to anything that turned up.

" 'That would suit me very well,' said I. 'And the pay?'

" 'Is four pounds a week.'

" 'And the work?'

" 'Is purely nominal.'

" 'What do you call purely nominal?'

" 'Well, you have to be in the office, or at least in the building, the whole time. If you leave, you forfeit your whole position forever. The will is very clear upon that point. You don't comply with the conditions if you budge from the office during that time.'

" 'It's only four hours a day, and I should not think of leaving,' said I.

" 'No excuse will avail,' said Mr. Duncan Ross. 'Neither sickness, nor business, nor anything else. There you must stay, or you lose your billet.'

" 'And the work?'

" 'Is to copy out the *Encyclopedia Britannica.* There is the first volume of it in that press. You must find your own ink, pens, and blotting-paper, but we provide this table and chair. Will you be ready tomorrow?'

" 'Certainly,' I answered.

" 'Then goodbye, Mr. Jabez Wilson, and let me congratulate you once more on the important position which you have been fortunate enough to gain.' He bowed me out of the room, and I went home with my assistant, hardly knowing what to say or do, I was so pleased at my own good fortunte.

"Well, I thought over the matter all day, and by evening I was in low spirits again, for I had quite persuaded myself that the whole affair must be some great hoax or fraud, though what its object might be I could not imagine. It seemed altogether past belief that anyone could make such a will, or that they would pay such a sum for doing anything so simple as copying out the *Encyclopedia Britannica.* Vincent Spaulding did what he could to cheer me up, but by bedtime I had reasoned myself out of the whole thing. However, in the morning I determined to have a look at it anyhow, so I bought a penny bottle of ink, and with a quill pen and seven sheets of foolscap paper I started off for Pope's Court.

"Well, to my surprise and delight everything was as right as possible. The table was set out ready for me, and Mr. Duncan Ross was there to see that I got fairly to work. He started me off upon the letter A, and then he left me; but he would drop in from time to time to see that all was right with me. At two o'clock, he bade me good-day, complimented me upon the amount that I had written, and then locked the door of the office after me.

"This went on day after day, Mr. Holmes, and on Saturday the manager came in and planked down four golden sovereigns for my week's work. It was the same next week, and the same the week after. Every morning I was there at ten, and every afternoon I left at two. By degrees, Mr. Duncan Ross took to coming in only once of a morning, and then, after a time, he did not come in at all. Still, or course, I never dared to leave the room for an instant, for I was not sure when he might come, and the billet was such a good one, and suited me so well, that I would not risk the loss of it.

"Eight weeks passed away like this, and I had written about Abbots, and Archery, and Armor, and Architecture, and Attica, and hoped with diligence that I might get on to the B's before very long. It cost me something in foolscap, and I had pretty nearly filled a shelf with my writings, and then suddenly the whole business came to an end."

"To an end?"

"Yes, sir. And no later than this morning. I went to my work as usual at ten o'clock, but the door was shut and locked, with a little square of cardboard hammered onto the middle of the panel with a tack. Here it is, and you can read what it says for yourself."

He held up a piece of white cardboard, about the size of a sheet of note-paper. It read in this fashion:

"THE RED-HEADED LEAGUE DISSOLVED.
Oct. 9, 1890."

Sherlock Holmes and I surveyed this curt announcement and the rueful face behind it, until the comical side of the affair so completely overtopped every consideration that we both burst out into a roar of laughter.

"I cannot see that there is anything very funny," cried our client, flushing up to the roots of his flaming hair. "If you can do nothing better than laugh at me, I can go elsewhere."

"No, no," cried Holmes, shoving him back into the chair from which he had half risen. "I really wouldn't miss your case for the world. It is most refreshingly unusual. But there is, if you will excuse my saying so, something just a little funny about it. Pray what steps did you take when you found the card upon the door?"

"I was staggered, sir. I did not know what to do. Then I called at the offices round, but none of them seemed to know anything about it. Finally, I went to the landlord, who is an accountant living on the ground floor, and I asked him if he could tell me what had become of the Red-Headed League. He said that he had never heard of any such body. Then I asked him who Mr. Duncan Ross was. He said that the name was new to him.

" 'Well,' said I, 'the gentleman at Number Four.'

" 'What, the red-headed man?'

" 'Yes.'

" 'Oh,' said he, 'his name was William Morris. He was a solicitor and was using my room as a temporary convenience until his new premises were ready. He moved out yesterday.'

" 'Where could I find him?'

" 'Oh, at his new offices. He did tell me the address. Yes, 17 King Edward Street, near St. Paul's.'

"I started off, Mr. Holmes, but when I got to that address it was a manufactory of artificial knee-caps, and no one in it had ever heard of either Mr. William Morris or Mr. Duncan Ross."

"I went home to Saxe-Coburg Square, and I asked the advice of my assistant. But he could not help me in any way. He could only say that if I waited I should hear by post. But that was not quite good enough, Mr. Holmes. I did not wish to lose such a place without a struggle, so, as I had heard that you were good enough to give advice to poor folk who were in need of it, I came right away to you."

"And you did very wisely," said Holmes. "Your case is an exceedingly remarkable one, and I shall be happy to look into it. From what you have told me, I think that it is possible that graver issues hang from it than might at first sight appear."

"Grave enough!" said Mr. Jabez Wilson. "Why, I have lost four pound a week."

"As far as you are personally concerned," remarked Holmes, "I do not see that you have any grievance against this extraordinary league. On the contrary, you are, as I understand, richer by some thirty pounds, to say nothing of the minute knowledge which you have gained on every subject which comes under the letter A. You have lost nothing by them."

"No, sir. But I want to find out about them, and who they are, and what their object was in playing this prank—if it was a prank—upon me. It was a pretty expensive joke for them, for it cost them two-and-thirty pounds."

"We shall endeavor to clear up these points for you. And, first, one or two questions, Mr. Wilson. This assistant of yours who first called your attention to the advertisement—how long had he been with you?"

"About a month then."

"How did he come?"

"In answer to an advertisement."

"Was he the only applicant?"

"No, I had a dozen."

"Why did you pick him?"

"Because he was handy and would come cheap."

"At half wages, in fact."

"Yes."

"What is he like, this Vincent Spaulding?"

"Small, stout-built, very quick in his ways, no hair on his face, though he's not short of thirty. Has a white splash of acid upon his forehead."

Holmes sat up in his chair, in considerable excitement. "I thought as much," said he. "have you ever observed that his ears are pierced for earrings?"

"Yes, sir. He told me that a gypsy had done it for him when he was a lad."

"Hum!" said Holmes, sinking back in deep thought. "He is still with you?"

"Oh, yes, sir; I have only just left him."

"And has your business been attended to in your absence?"

"Nothing to complain of, sir. There's never very much to do of a morning."

"That will do, Mr. Wilson. I shall be happy to give you an opinion upon the subject in the course of a day or two. Today is Saturday, and I hope that by Monday we may come to a conclusion."

"Well, Watson," said Holmes when our visitor had left us, "what do you make of it all?"

"I make nothing of it," I answered frankly. "It is a most mysterious business."

"As a rule," said Holmes, "the more bizarre a thing is, the less mysterious it proves to be. It is your commonplace, featureless crimes which are really puzzling, just as a commonplace face is the most difficult to identify. But I must be prompt over this matter."

"What are you going to do, then?"

"To smoke," he answered. "It is quite a three-pipe problem, and I beg that you won't speak to me for fifty minutes." He curled himself up in his chair, with his thin knees drawn up to his hawklike nose, and there he sat with his eyes closed and his black clay pipe thrusting out like the bill of some strange bird. I had come to the conclusion that he had dropped asleep, and indeed was nodding myself, when he suddenly sprang out of his chair, with the gesture of a man who has made up his mind, and put his pipe down upon the mantelpiece.

"Sarasate plays at St. James's Hall this afternoon," he remarked. "What do you think, Watson? Could your patients spare you for a few hours?"

"I have nothing to do today. My practice is never very absorbing."

"Then put on your hat and come. I am going through the City first, and we can have some lunch on the way. I observe, that there is a good deal of German music on the program, which is rather more to my taste than Italian or French. It is introspective, and I want to introspect. Come along!"

We traveled by the Underground as far as Aldersgate, and a short walk took us to Saxe-Coburg Square, the scene of the singular story we had listened to in the morning. It was a poky, little, shabby-genteel place, where four lines of dingy, two-storied brick houses looked out into a small railed-in enclosure, where a lawn of weedy grass and a few clumps of faded laurel bushes made a hard fight against a smoke-laden and uncongenial atmosphere. Three gilt balls and a brown board with JABEZ WILSON in white letters upon a corner house announced the place where our red-headed client carried on his business. Sherlock Holmes stopped in front of it with his head on one side, and looked it all over, with his eyes shining brightly between puckered lids. Then he walked slowly up the street, and then down again to the corner, still looking keenly at the houses. Finally he returned to the pawnbroker's and, having thumped vigorously upon the pavement with his stick two or three times, he went up to the door and knocked. It was instantly opened by a bright-looking, clean-shaven young fellow, who asked him to step in.

"Thank you," said Holmes, "I only wished to ask you how you would go from here to the Strand."

"Third right, four left," answered the assistant promptly, closing the door.

"Smart fellow, that," observed Holmes as we walked away. "He is, in my judgment, the fourth smartest man in London, and for daring I am not sure that he has not a claim to be third. I have known something of him before."

"Evidently," said I, "Mr. Wilson's assistant counts for a good deal in this mystery of the Red-Headed League. I am sure that you inquired your way merely in order that you might see him."

"Not him."

"What then?"

"The knees of his trousers."

"And what did you see?"

"What I expected to see."

"Why did you beat the pavement?"

"My dear Doctor, this is a time for observation, not for talk. We are spies in an enemy's country. We know something of Saxe-Coburg Square. Let us now explore the parts which lie behind it."

The road in which we found ourselves as we turned round the corner from the retired Saxe-Coburg Square presented as great a contrast to it as the front of a picture does to the back. It was one of the main arteries which convey the traffic of the City to the north and west. The roadway was blocked with the immense stream of commerce flowing in a double tide inward and outward, while the footpaths were black with the hurrying swarm of pedestrians. It was difficult to realize, as we looked at the line of fine shops and stately business premises, that they really abutted on the other side upon the faded and stagnant square which we had just quitted.

"Let me see," said Holmes, standing at the corner and glancing along the line, "I should like just to remember the order of the houses here. It is a hobby of mine to have an exact knowledge of London. There is Mortimer's, the tobacconist; the little newspaper shop; the Coburg branch of the City and Suburban Bank; the vegetarian restaurant; and McFarlane's carriage-building depot. That carries us right on to the other block. And now, Doctor, we've done our work, so it's time we had some play. A sandwich and a cup of coffee, and then off to violin-land, where all is sweetness and delicacy and harmony, and there are no red-headed clients to vex us with their conundrums."

My friend was an enthusiastic musician, being himself not only a very capable performer but a composer of no ordinary merit. All the afternoon he sat in the stalls wrapped in the most perfect happiness, gently waving his long thin fingers in time to the music, while his gently smiling face and his languid, dreamy eyes were as unlike those of Holmes the sleuth-hound, Holmes the relentless, keen-witted, ready-handed criminal agent, as it was possible to conceive.

In his singular character, the dual nature alternately asserted itself, and his extreme exactness and astuteness represented, as I have often thought, the reaction against the poetic and contemplative mood which occasionally predominated in him. The swing of his nature took him from extreme languor to devouring energy, and, as I knew well, he was never so truly formidable as when, for days on end, he had been lounging in his armchair amid his improvisations and his black-letter editions. Then it was that the lust of the chase would suddenly come upon him, and that his brilliant reasoning power would rise to the level of intuition, until those who were unacquainted with his methods would look askance at him as on a man whose knowledge was not that of other mortals. When I saw him that afternoon so enwrapped in the music of St. James's Hall, I felt that an evil time might be coming upon those whom he had set himself to hunt down.

"You want to go home, no doubt, Doctor," he remarked as we emerged.

"Yes, it would be as well."

"And I have some business to do which will take some hours. This business at Coburg Square is serious."

"Why serious?"

"A considerable crime is in contemplation. I have every reason to believe that we shall be in time to stop it. But today being Saturday rather complicates matters. I shall want your help tonight."

"At what time?"

"Ten will be early enough."

"I shall be at Baker Street at ten."

"Very well. And I say, Doctor! There may be some little danger, so kindly put your army revolver in your pocket." He waved his hand, turned on his heel, and disappeared in an instant among the crowd.

I trust that I am not more dense than my neighbors, but I was always oppressed with a sense of my own stupidity in my dealings with Sherlock Holmes. Here I had heard what he had heard, I had seen what he had seen, and yet from his words it was evident that he saw clearly not only what had happened, but what was about to happen, while to me the whole business was still confused and grotesque. As I drove home to my house in Kensington, I thought over it all, from the extraordinary story of the red-headed copier of the *Encyclopedia* down to the visit to Saxe-Coburg Square, and the ominous words with which he had parted from me. What was this nocturnal expedition, and why should I go armed? Where were we going, and what were we to do? I had the hint from Holmes that this smooth-faced pawnbroker's assistant was a formidable man—a man who might play a deep game. I tried to puzzle it out, but gave it up in despair, and set the matter aside until night should bring an explanation.

It was a quarter-past nine when I started from home and made my way across the Park, and so through Oxford Street to Baker Street. Two hansoms were standing at the door, and as I entered the passage I heard the sound of voices from above. On entering his room, I found Holmes in animated conversation with two men, one of whom I recognized as Peter Jones, the official police agent, while the other was a long, thin, sad-faced man, with a very shiny hat and oppressively respectable frock-coat.

"Ha! Our party is complete," said Holmes, buttoning up his pea-jacket and taking his heavy hunting crop from the rack. "Watson, I think you know Mr. Jones of Scotland Yard? Let me introduce you to Mr. Merryweather, who is to be our companion in tonight's adventure."

"We're hunting in couples again, Doctor, you see," said Jones, in his consequential way. "Our friend here is a wonderful man for starting a chase. All he wants is an old dog to help him do the running down."

"I hope a wild goose may not prove to be the end of our chase," observed Mr. Merryweather gloomily.

"You may place considerable confidence in Mr. Holmes, sir," said the police agent loftily. "He has his own little methods, which are, if he won't mind my saying so, just a little too theoretical and fantastic, but he has the makings of a detective in him. It is not too much to say that once or twice, as in that business of the Sholto murder and the Agra treasure, he has been more nearly correct than the official force."

"Oh, if you say so, Mr. Jones, it is all right," said the stranger with deference. "Still, I confess that I miss my rubber. It is the first Saturday night for seven-and-twenty years that I have not had my rubber."

"I think you will find," said Sherlock Holmes, "that you will play for a higher stake tonight than you have ever done yet, and that the play will be more exciting. For you, Mr. Merryweather, the stake will be some thirty thousand pounds, and for you, Jones, it will be the man upon whom you wish to lay your hands."

"John Clay, the murderer, thief, smasher, and forger. He's a young man, Mr. Merryweather, but he is at the head of his profession and I would rather have my bracelets on him than on any criminal in London. He's a remarkable man, is young John Clay. His grandfather was a royal duke, and he himself has been to Eton and Oxford. His brain is as cunning as his fingers, and though we meet signs of him at every turn, we never know where to find the man himself. He'll crack a crib in Scotland one week and be raising money to build an orphanage in Cornwall the next. I've been on his track for years and have never set eyes on him yet."

"I hope that I may have the pleasure of introducing you tonight. I've had one or two little turns also with Mr. John Clay and I agree with you that he is at the head of his profession. It is past ten, however, and quite time that we started. If you two will take the first hansom, Watson and I will follow in the second."

Sherlock Holmes was not very communicative during the long drive, and lay back in the cab humming the tunes which he had heard in the afternoon. We rattled through an endless labyrinth of gas-lit streets until we emerged into Farringdon Street.

"We are close there now," my friend remarked. "This fellow Merryweather is a bank director and personally interested in the matter. I thought it as well to have Jones with us also. He is not a bad fellow, though an absolute imbecile in his profession. He has one positive virtue. He is as brave as a bulldog, and as tenacious as a lobster if he gets his claws upon anyone. Here we are, and they are waiting for us."

We had reached the same crowded thoroughfare in which we had found ourselves in the morning. Our cabs were dismissed and, following the guidance of Mr. Merryweather, we passed down a narrow passage and through a side door which he opened for us. Within, there was a small corridor, which ended in a very massive iron gate. This also was opened, and led down a flight of winding stone steps which terminated at another formidable gate. Mr. Merryweather stopped to light a lantern and then conducted us down a dark, earth-smelling passage, and so, after opening a third door, into a huge vault or cellar, which was piled all round with crates and massive boxes.

"You are not very vulnerable from above," Holmes remarked as he held up the lantern and gazed about him.

"Nor from below," said Mr. Merryweather, striking his stick upon the flags which lined the floor. "Why, dear me, it sounds quite hollow!" he remarked, looking up in surprise.

"I must really ask you to be a little more quiet," said Holmes severely. "You have already imperiled the whole success of our expedition. Might I beg that you would have the goodness to sit down upon one of those boxes and not to interfere?"

The solemn Mr. Merryweather perched himself upon a crate with a very injured expression upon his face while Holmes fell on his knees upon the floor and, with the lantern and a magnifying lens, began to examine minutely the cracks between the stones. A few seconds sufficed to satisfy him, for he sprang to his feet again and put his glass in his pocket.

"We have at least an hour before us," he remarked, "for they can hardly take any steps until the good pawnbroker is safely in bed. Then they will not lose a minute, for the sooner they do their work the longer time they will have for their escape. We are at present, Doctor—as no doubt you have divined—in the cellar of the City branch of one of the principal London banks. Mr. Merryweather is the chairman of directors, and he will explain to you that there are reasons why the more daring criminals of London should take a considerable interest in this cellar at present."

"It is our French gold," whispered the director. "We have had several warnings that an attempt might be made upon it."

"Your French gold?"

"Yes. We had occasion some months ago to strengthen our resources, and borrowed, for that purpose, thirty thousand napoleons from the Bank of France. It has become known that we have never had occasion to unpack the money and that it is still lying in our cellar. The crate upon which I sit contains two thousand napoleons packed between layers of lead foil. Our reserve of bullion is much larger at present than is usually kept in a single branch office and the directors have had misgivings upon the subject."

"Which were very well justified," observed Holmes. "And now it is time that we arranged our little plans. I expect that within an hour matters will come to a head. In the meantime, Mr. Merryweather, we must put the screen over that dark lantern."

"And sit in the dark?"

"I am afraid so. I had brought a pack of cards in my pocket and I thought that, as we were a *partie carrée,* you might have your rubber after all. But I see that the enemy's preparations have gone so far that we cannot risk the presence of a light. And, first of all, we must choose our positions. These are daring men, and, though we shall take them at a disadvantage, they may do us some harm unless we are careful. I shall stand behind this crate and you conceal yourself behind those. Then, when I flash a light upon them, close in swiftly. If they fire, Watson, have no compunction about shooting them down."

I placed my revolver, cocked, upon the top of the wooden case behind which I crouched. Holmes shot the slide across the front of his lantern, and left us in pitch darkness—such an absolute darkness as I have never before experienced. The smell of hot metal remained to assure us that the light was still there, ready to flash out at a moment's notice. To me, with my nerves worked up to a pitch of expectancy, there was something depressing and subduing in the sudden gloom, and in the dank air of the vault.

"They have but one retreat," whispered Holmes. "That is back through the house into Saxe-Coburg Square. I hope that you have done what I asked you, Jones?"

"I have an inspector and two offices waiting at the front door."

"Then we have stopped all the holes. And now we must be silent and wait."

What a time it seemed! From comparing notes afterwards, it was but an hour and a quarter, yet it appeared to me that the night must have almost gone and the dawn be breaking above us. My limbs were weary and stiff, for I feared to change my position, yet my nerves were worked up to the highest pitch of tension and my hearing was so acute that I could not only hear the gentle breathing of my companions but I could distinguish the deeper, heavier inbreath of the bulky Jones from the thin, sighing note of the bank director.

From my position, I could look over the case in the direction of the floor. Suddenly my eyes caught a glint of light.

At first it was but a lurid spark upon the stone pavement. Then it lengthened out until it became a yellow line, and then, without any warning or sound, a gash seemed to open and a hand appeared—a white, almost womanly hand, which felt about in the center of the little area of light. For a minute or more the hand, with its writhing fingers, protruded out of the floor. Then it was withdrawn as suddenly as it appeared, and all was dark again save the single lurid spark which marked a chink between the stones.

Its disappearance, however, was but momentary. With a rending, tearing sound, one of the broad white stones turned over upon its side, and left a square, gaping hole, through which streamed the light of a lantern. Over the edge there peeped a clean-cut, boyish face, which looked keenly about it, and then, with a hand on either side of the aperture, drew itself shoulder-high and waist-high, until one knee rested upon the edge. In another instant he stood at the side of the hole, and was hauling after him a companion, lithe and small like himself, with a pale face and a shock of very red hair.

"It's all clear," he whispered. "Have you the chisel and the bags? Great Scott! Jump, Archie, jump, and I'll swing for it!"

Sherlock Holmes had sprung out and seized the intruder by the collar. The other dived down the hole and I heard the sound of rending cloth as Jones clutched at his skirts. The light flashed upon the barrel of a revolver, but Holmes's hunting crop came down on the man's wrist and the pistol clinked upon the stone floor.

"It's no use, John Clay," said Holmes blandly, "you have no chance at all."

"So I see," the other answered with the utmost coolness. "I fancy that my pal is all right, though I see you have got his coattails."

"There are three men waiting for him at the door," said Holmes.

"Oh, indeed. You seem to have done the thing very completely. I must compliment you."

"And I you," Holmes answerd. "Your red-headed idea was very new and effective."

"You'll see your pal again presently," said Jones. "He's quicker at climbing down holes than I am. Just hold out while I fix the derbies."

"I beg that you will not touch me with your filthy hands," remarked our prisoner, as the handcuffs clattered upon his wrists. "You may not be aware that I have royal blood in my veins. Have the goodness also, when you address me, always to say 'sir' and 'please.' "

"All right," said Jones, with a stare and a snigger. "Well, would you please, sir, march upstairs where we can get a cab to carry your highness to the police station."

"That is better," said John Clay serenely. He made a sweeping bow to the three of us and walked quietly off.

"Really, Mr. Holmes," said Mr. Merryweather as we followed them from the cellar, "I do not know how the bank can thank you or repay you. There is no doubt that you have detected and defeated in the most complete manner one of the most determined attempts at bank robbery that has ever come within my experience."

"I have had one or two little scores of my own to settle with

Mr. John Clay," said Holmes. "I have been at some small expense over this matter, which I shall expect the bank to refund, but beyond that I am amply repaid by having had an experience which is in many ways unique, and by hearing the very remarkable narrative of the Red-Headed League."

"You see, Watson," he explained in the early hours of the morning, as we sat over a glass of whisky and soda in Baker Street, "it was perfectly obvious from the first that the only possible object of this rather fantastic business of the advertisement of the League, and the copying of the *Encyclopedia*, must be to get this not overbright pawnbroker out of the way for a number of hours every day. It was a curious way of managing it, but really it would be difficult to suggest a better. The method was no doubt suggested to Clay's ingenious mind by the color of his accomplice's hair. The four pounds a week was a lure which must draw him, and what was it to them, who were playing for thousands? They put in the advertisement, one rogue has the temporary office, the other rogue incites the man to apply for it, and together they manage to secure his absence every morning in the week. From the time that I heard of the assistant having come for half wages, it was obvious to me that he had some strong motive for securing the situation."

"But how could you guess what the motive was?"

"Had there been women in the house, I should have suspected a mere vulgar intrigue. That, however, was out of the question. The man's business was a small one, and there was nothing in his house which could account for such, elaborate preparations and such an expenditure as they were at. It must then be something *out* of the house. What could it be? I thought of the assistant's fondness for photography and his trick of vanishing into the cellar. The cellar! There was the end of this tangled clue. Then I made inquiries as to this mysterious assistant, and found that I had to deal with one of the coolest and most daring criminals in London. He was doing something in the cellar—something which took many hours a day for months on end. What could it be, once more? I could think of nothing save that he was running a tunnel to some other building.

"So far I had got when we went to visit the scene of action. I surprised you by beating upon the pavement with my stick. I was ascertaining whether the cellar stretched out in front or behind. It was not in front. Then I rang the bell, and, as I hoped, the assistant answered it. We have had some skirmishes, but we had never set eyes upon each other before. I hardly looked at his face. His knees were what I wished to see. You must yourself have remarked how worn, wrinkled, and stained they were. They spoke of those hours of burrowing. The only remaining point was what they were burrowing for. I walked round the corner, saw that the City and Suburban Bank abutted on our friend's premises, and felt that I had solved my problem. When you drove home after the concert, I called upon Scotland Yard and upon the chairman of the bank directors, with the result that you have seen."

"And how could you tell that they would make their attempt tonight?"

"Well, when they closed their League offices, that was a sign that they cared no longer about Mr. Jabez Wilson's presence—in other words, that they had completed their tunnel. But it was essential that they should use it soon, as it might be discovered, or the bullion might be removed. Saturday would suit them better than any other day, as it would give them two days for their escape. For all these reasons I expected them tonight."

"You reasoned it out beautifully," I exclaimed, in unfeigned admiration. "It is so long a chain, and yet every link rings true."

"It saved me from ennui," he answered, yawning. "Alas! I already feel it closing in upon me. My life is spent in one long effort to escape from the commonplaces of existence. These little problems help me to do so."

"And you are a benefactor of the race," said I.

He shrugged his shoulders. "Well, perhaps, after all, it is of some little use," he remarked. "*'L'homme c'est rien—l'œuvre c'est tout,'* as Gustave Flaubert wrote to George Sand."

GEORGE BAXT

WHAT YOU BEEN UP TO LATELY?

Richard Weiler carefully maneuvered his wife's Mercedes Benz along Sunset Boulevard. The traffic wasn't particularly heavy in the early afternoon, but he was anxious to avoid any dents or scrapes. It was known to his friends that he respected the car more than he did the woman. Elissa had been a beautiful bride, her family's wealth easily enhancing her attractiveness, but twenty years ago when he watched her coming slowly down the aisle on her father's arm, he was very much in love with her. Today he loved nothing, just the feel of the magnificent vehicle as he idled along and the exhilarating sense of a newly discovered freedom that had blossomed a few hours earlier.

Elissa was gone, leaving behind the Mercedes, a bored husband, and, somewhere out there in the world, a ninteen-year-old son and an eighteen-year-old daughter who had flown the nest with what Richard considered unbecoming alacrity. He repositioned the mirror for a good look at himself. After a moment's careful consideration, he decided he looked better than he had in months. The face familiar from numerous television commercials ("Diabolica will kill your crab grass!"—"Ahhhh, the smooth, easy taste of decaffeinated Boluta!" etc.) now reflected a somewhat sheepish grin, revealing magnificent white teeth against a background of carefully shaded tanned skin. Oh, yes, thought Richard, I feel like a new man.

I feel like a new life. I need a new world. I could use a drink. He kept his eye out for a bar. He couldn't decide which was shabbier, the few pedestrians or the palm trees. He remembered a charming bar he used to frequent years ago when he was a struggling young actor. Come to think of it, that's where he was first introduced to Elissa, in that charming bar across from the bus terminal. Behind the building that housed that bar had been a small theater where a German refugee held acting classes. Richard didn't learn much about acting, but he perfected a superb German accent. And he made friends. And he met Elissa and they married and now they were parted and there straight ahead was the bus terminal.

So shabby—Los Angeles is so shabby, he thought. The bus terminal looked filthy and unloved and there was no bar across the street. There was a bench in front of the bus terminal with a solitary occupant, a man who appeared to be Richard's age. Memory of an earlier friendship began to nag. There was something familiar about this man sitting on the bench. He was hatless and the shock of hair hanging over his ears reminded Richard of the one good friend he had made in acting class, Augustus Locke. The cavalier and devil-may-care Augustus who aspired to Shakespeare and Ibsen and all things esthetic and beautiful, all things alien to Hollywood. Augie the original, the madman who once climbed the old Hollywood sign and then hung by his knees from the H.

"Now, *that's* macho," Richard remembered saying to Elissa.

And Elissa said with a sniff of disinterest, "Macho do about nothing."

My God. Oh, my God. Richard remembered. Elissa had been Augie's girl!

He pulled over to the curb for a better look at the man on the bench. It was at least ten years since he had last seen Augie, but he could never forget that face, those beautiful classical features that cried for matinee-idol acclaim but were in the wrong city. Richard rolled down the window and shouted, "Augie?"

The man leaped to his feet. His right hand went to his inside jacket pocket.

"Hey, Augie, it's me! Richard! Richard Weiler!"

Slowly Augustus Locke lowered his right hand. He moved toward the Mercedes with caution, as though he distrusted even the sound of a familiar voice. He squinted against the glare of the hard, harsh sun.

Richard conjured up the ugly guttural German accent from the bowels of memory. "Iss nod enuff to be secksy, Herr Locke, muss also sprechen zer dialock zo awdience hunderstands, fahrshtay?"

"Fahrshtay," said Augustus softly and now approached the automobile with confidence. He stuck his hand through the window, meeting Richard's and shaking it with vigor. "Of all the people I never expected to run into today."

"You looked as though you didn't want to run into *any* people. I thought for a minute there you were going to pull a gun on me."

Augustus said nothing but found a smile.

Richard continued, "What you been up to lately?"

"Well, right now I'm waiting for a bus to San Diego."

"Where's your car?"

Augustus looked sheepish. "I totaled it yesterday. It's a miracle I'm alive."

"I'm glad you are. I've thought a lot about you lately. If I'd known where to reach you—" He heard himself sounding like almost everyone else in his profession. *"We must get in touch sometime." "I've been meaning to call you." "I swear I never got your message."*

Augustus roared with laughter. "That old Hollywood jazz! Well, I see you're doing great! A Mercedes yet! You seem to be in every commercial on the tube." His voice softened. "How's Elissa?"

"How's about a drink?"

Augustus thought for a moment. "I really have to make that bus."

"What's so urgent?"

"Well—" he seemed to be fumbling for an explanation "—you see, there's this guy I need to connect with in San Diego and then we're driving into Mexico. I got this deal going."

"Come on, there are lots of buses to San Diego but not enough old friends. Come on, Augie, let's go talk awhile. Let's indulge, get corny over the old days."

Augie thought a moment, looked warily over his shoulder to the bus terminal, and got into the car.

Ten minutes later, they sat at a bar Richard found at the foot of Fairfax Avenue. Maggie, the barperson, brought them two beers, set a plate of peanuts between them, and crossed to the kitchen.

"Had I known you and Elissa were finished," said Augustus as he scooped up some peanuts, "I'd have shown up sooner. That's the girl I should have married, but you beat me to it."

Richard chuckled and sipped his beer. "Say, what happened to that dreary dame who used to make up our foursome? You know, the one who was all art but no craft. I can see her like she's standing in front of us. Blazing red hair pulled back and tied in a tight bun. A big pearl earring attached to each lobe. Sweater and skirt—always a sweater and skirt. Nice hips but no bosom to speak of. God, how I disliked her. What was her name again?"

"Madeline. Madeline Longley."

"Madeline! That's it, Madeline. I wonder what became of her."

"I married her."

Richard's face reddened as he stared at Augustus. "Hell, I'm sorry. I mean I—"

Augustus was laughing uncontrollably. His head was flung back and his chest was heaving. Maggie, returning from the kitchen and carrying a tray of clean glasses, wondered if he was having a fit.

"Oh," gasped Augie, "oh, my God, that was funny." He wiped the tears from his eyes with a paper napkin. "How I wish I'd heard that description eighteen years ago, before I decided to marry her."

Richard stared hard at Augustus. He sensed there was something wrong with the man. He kept looking over his shoulder and every so often he patted his jacket where the inside breast pocket would be, as though seeking reassurance from something the pocket contained. His laughter was almost maniacal. And from the ferocity with which he chomped on the peanuts, Richard expected to see blood come trickling from his mouth.

"That last time we met—in Grauman's lobby, remember?"

"Sure. It was at least ten years ago, but I remember."

"That wasn't Madeline you were with."

"No. Can't remember that one's name. Some bimbo I picked up somewhere." Augie's face hardened as he stared into his beer. "Madeline and I weren't much of a marriage. I didn't make it as an actor. That was her first disappointment. Then we couldn't have any children—that was her second disappointment. Then she found out I was steadily unfaithful. So she turned to religion and illness. When she wasn't in church, she was in the hospital."

"You still married?"

Augie was watching Maggie carefully giving the glasses a second polish. She was fastidious. He liked that in people. She took pride in her bar—he could see by the way it was all so neatly laid out. She was what his father would have called a fine figure of a woman, for sure. Her eyes caught his. He felt something stirring and was astonished. She was not his type at all. He winked, she smiled, and he turned to Richard.

"Funny us running into each other like this today. I wish it had been last week."

"Oh, yeah? Why?"

"It would have been different, that's all." There was an awkward silence, and then Augie asked, "Where are your kids?"

"Gone. Flown. My son's in New York, or at least he was when he last sent a postcard. He was in some drug-rehabilitation program. I hope he stuck it out."

"And the girl?"

"I don't know. I'm not sure. She always liked kids. Maybe she's working with kids somewhere." Richard was sounding morose, and that was not what he had in mind for himself. He was free of Elissa and he'd been driving around trying to find a new avenue for himself. He tried to explain this to Augustus, who kept nodding his head but was actually retaining little of what he heard, his mind now containing an olio of his next sip of beer, Maggie behind the bar, and getting to San Diego.

"Augie?" asked Richard.

"What?" What is it?" His eyes were wide and he was sneaking a quick look over his shoulder.

"You're not listening to me."

"Sure I am! Anyway, listen old buddy, I got to get back to the bus terminal." He was toying with Richard's car keys. Richard had placed them on the bar between their drinks.

"I'll drive you back as soon as we finish our drinks. Unless you're in that big a hurry—"

"Oh, no, no. It's great running into each other like this again."

"When do you get back from Mexico?"

"I'm not sure."

"I just thought we could get together again."

"That would be great. Believe me, I really have missed seeing you, shooting the breeze the way we used to, rehearsing our scenes together—and those times we'd do nothing but compare poverty."

They both laughed and Maggie smiled. She liked the actor she recognized from the television commercials. He was suave and smooth and obviously a gentleman. And she'd been very impressed by the Mercedes when she noticed Richard pulling into the adjoining parking lot. But his companion made her nervous and uneasy. His eyes had what she would later describe as "a very haunted look, like the banshees were after him." And there was something unsettling about the way he kept looking over his shoulder and patting his jacket as though maybe there was some weapon hidden there.

Richard was staring at the ceiling. "Old Meyerbeer?" Augustus had asked him if he knew what had become of their German drama instructor. "Well, I'll tell you. Last I heard, he went back to Germany where he directed a new translation of *King Lear* in which Lear not only does not go mad but throws those rotten daughters of his into exile."

"You're putting me on."

"I kid you not. Elissa saw the production in Munich. She was traveling with her mother. She couldn't wait to get home to tell me about it." His voice softened. "That was back in the days when she couldn't wait to get home to me."

Maggie had turned on the radio on a shelf above the glasses and was worrying the tuner.

Augustus said, "I'd love to see Elissa again. That beautiful blonde hair, that white, white skin, that gash of red mouth. By God, she was a looker! Has she changed much?"

"Elissa was rich enough to afford not to change much. Still blonde, skin still white, still the red gash of mouth. But the eyes got steely."

"I'd sure love to see her." Augustus sounded as wistful as a small penniless child with its nose pressed against the window of a candy store.

"Well, if I thought she was back at the house, I'd drive you there. But I don't think she's there."

Augustus clapped a hand on Richard's shoulder. "Well, man, I think it's time we started making tracks."

Richard raised his stein to drink up.

Maggie found the news on the radio and was listening intently. The announcer was reading carefully and without emotional commitment. Richard and Augustus stared at the radio. They had heard a familiar name. "The brutally battered body of Madeline Locke was found in the bedroom of her Topanga Canyon home this morning by a neighbor who said she had seen the victim's husband drive away early yesterday morning. Augustus Locke is wanted for questioning in his wife's murder. Late yesterday morning, a wrecked car found near Mr. Locke's home was identified as belonging to the suspect—"

Richard was staring at the snub-nosed revolver Augustus had taken from his inside jacket pocket and was pointing at Richard's chest. "Augie," whispered Richard.

Augustus got to his feet and with his free hand took the keys to the Mercedes. Maggie held her breath and silently prayed to the Jesus she loved to deliver both herself and the handsome actor.

"I'll try not to total the Mercedes." Augie was backing away to the door. "Don't follow me out."

For reasons he would never be able to explain to himself, Richard restrained a wild urge to burst out laughing. *What you been up to lately?* he had asked Augie earlier. Well, he certainly found out.

Augustus was smiling as he ran out the door.

"Jesus, Mary, and Joseph!" cried Maggie as she rushed to the phone.

"Wait!" The mixture of harshness and urgency in Richard's voice stopped her. 'Not yet," said Richard. "Let's give him a head start."

"But—but he's a murderer."

"They'll catch him. He won't get away. But let's give him this break. He's never really had a decent break in his life."

* * *

What a magnificent car, thought Augustus, what a truly magnificent car. Now if *I* had married Elissa, this would have been *my* car. And the marriage would have worked. That's what was wrong. Elissa and I were meant for each other until Richard came along. Beautiful, beautiful Elissa of the blonde hair, white skin, and red gash of a mouth. Ugly, whining, sickly Madeline. How did I put up with her under the same roof all these years?

The Mercedes was headed south for the San Diego freeway when the patrol car spied it and gave chase, siren screaming. But Augie's mind was elsewhere. It was dwelling on the unfairness and inequity of life and what a rotten shuffle he himself had got. His foot pressed the accelerator and the Mercedes seemed to be fighting him. He began losing control of the steering wheel and soon he was in the wrong lane with a truck bearing down on him. He swerved to avoid the collision, and instead sent the car plummeting over the edge of the road into a ravine that lay hundreds of feet beneath.

The Mercedes rolled over and over. First, the roof was torn away, then both right fenders wrenched free with sickening groans. Augie's door sprang open and he tried desperately to hold onto the wheel, but blood was streaming down his face, his right arm was broken, he knew both his legs were shattered and he was nearing the end of the tragi-comedy known as the life of Augustus Locke.

When the Mercedes hit the bottom of the ravine, the door to the trunk was flung open and Augustus, thrown from the car and just a few moments away from death, stared with pleasure at the person he had so longed to see once more. She had fallen out of the trunk, her head hanging loosely, the neck broken. But the blonde hair and the white skin were still beautiful, though the red gash of lips was now a large ugly stain caked with blood. Elissa, my beloved, my beautiful Elissa!

What you been up to lately?

EDGAR WALLACE

THE GHOST OF JOHN HOLLING

"There are things about the sea that never alter," said Felix Jenks, the steward. "I had a writing gentleman in one of my suites last voyage who said the same thing, and when writing people say anything original, it's worth jotting down. Not that if often happens.

" 'Felix,' he said, 'the sea has got a mystery that can never be solved—a magic that has never been and never will be something-or-other to the tests of science.' (I'm sure it was 'tests of science,' though the other word has slipped overboard.)

"Magic—that's the word. Something we don't understand, like the mirror in the bridal suit of the *Canothic*. Two men cut their throats before that mirror. One of 'em died right off, and one lived long enough to tell the steward who found him that he'd seen a shadowy sort of face looking over his shoulder and heard a voice telling him that death was only another word for sleep.

"That last fellow was Holling—the coolest cabin thief that ever traveled the Western Ocean. And what Holling did to us when he was alive was nothing to what he's done since, according to certain stories I've heard.

"Spooky told me that when the mirror was taken out of the ship and put in the stores at Liverpool, first the storekeeper and then a clerk in his office were found dead in the storeroom. After that it was carried out to sea and dropped into fifty fathoms of water. But that didn't get rid of Holling's ghost.

"The principal authority on Holling was the steward who worked with me. Spooky Simms his name was, and Spooky was so called because he believed in ghosts. There wasn't anything in the supernatural line that he didn't keep tag on, and when he wasn't making tables rap he was casting horror-scopes—is that the way you pronounce it?

" 'I certainly believe in Holling's ghost,' said Spooky on this voyage I'm talking about now, 'and if he's not on this packet at this minute, I'm no clairvoyager. We passed right over the spot where he died at three-seven this morning, and I woke up with the creeps. He's come aboard—he always does when we go near the place he committed suicide.'

"There was no doubt that Spooky believed this, and he was a man with only one delusion: that he'd die in the poorhouse and his children would sell matches on the street. That accounts for the fact that he hoarded every cent he made.

"Personally, I don't believe in spooks, but I do admit that there is one magical thing about the sea—the way it affects men and women. Take any girl and any man, perfect strangers and not wanting to be anything else, put them on the same ship and give them a chance of talking to one another, and before you know where you are his wastepaper basket is full of poetry that he's torn up because he can't find a rhyme for 'love,' and her wastepaper basket's top-high with bits of letters she's written to the man she was going to marry, explaining that they are unsuitable for one another and that now she sees in a great white light the path that love has opened for her.

"I know, because I've read 'em. And the man hasn't got to be handsome or the girl a doll for this to happen.

"There was a gang working the *Mesopotamia* when I served in her a few years ago that was no better and no worse than any other crowd that travels for business. They used to call this crowd 'Charley's,' Charley Pole being the leader. He was a nice young fellow with fair, curly hair, and he spoke London English, wore London clothes, and had a London eyeglass in his left eye.

"Charley had to work very carefully, and he was handicapped, just as all the other gangs were handicapped, by the Pure Ocean Movement, which our company started. Known cardsharps were stopped at the quayside by the company police and sent back home again—to America if they were American, to England if they were English. About thirty of our stewards were suspended, and almost every bar steward in the line, and it looked as if the Western Ocean was going to be a dull place. Some of the crowds worked the French ships—and nearly starved to death, for though the French are, by all accounts, a romantic race, they're very practical when it comes to money.

"So the boys began to drift back to the English and American lines, but they had to watch out, and it was as much as a steward's place was worth to tip them off. Charley was luckier than most people, for he hadn't got the name that others had got, and though the company officials looked down their noses every time he went ashore at Southampton, they let him through.

"Now the Barons of the Pack (as our old skipper used to call them) are plain businessmen. They go traveling to earn a living, and have the same responsibilities as other people. They've got wives and families and girls at high school and boys at college, and when they're not cutting up human lamb they're discussing the high cost of living and the speculation in the stock market and how something ought to be done about it.

"But on one point they're inhuman: they have no shipboard friendships that can't pay dividends. Women—young, old, beautiful, or just women—mean nothing in their lives. So far as they are concerned, women passengers are in the same category as table decorations—they look nice, but they mean nothing. Naturally, they meet them, but beyond a 'Glad to meet you, Mrs. So-and-so,' the big men never bother with women.

"That was why I was surprised when I saw Charley Pole walking the boat deck with Miss Lydia Penn for two nights in succession. I wasn't surprised at her, because I've given up being surprised at women.

"She had Suite 107 on C deck, and Spooky Simms and I were her room stewards—we shared that series—so that I knew as much about her as anybody. She was a gold-and-tortoiseshell lady and had more junk on her dressing-table than anybody I've known. Silver and glass and framed photographs and manicure sets, and all her things were in silk, embroidered with rosebuds. A real lady.

"From what she told me, she was traveling for a big women's outfitters in Chicago. She had to go backward and forward to London and Paris to see new designs, and by the way she traveled it looked as if no expenses were spared.

"As a looker, Miss Lydia Penn was in the deluxe class. She had golden hair, just dull enough to be genuine, and a complexion like a baby's. Her eyebrows were dark and so were her eyelashes.

"I admire pretty girls. I don't mean that I fall in love with them. Stewards don't fall in love—they get married between trips and better acquainted when the ship's in dry dock. But if I was a young man with plenty of money and enough education to pass across the line of talk she'd require, I shouldn't have gone further than Miss Penn.

"But she wasn't everybody's woman—being a little too clever to suit the average young businessman.

"The day before we made Nantucket Lightship, Spooky Simms came to me as I was going off watch. 'Remember me telling you about Holling?' he said.

"As a matter of fact, I'd forgotten all about the matter.

" 'He's on board—saw him last night as plain as you—if it's possible, plainer. He was leaning up against Number Seven boat, looking white and ill. Plain! Why, I can see him now. There will be trouble!"

"And he was right. Mr. Alex McLeod of Los Angeles took his bag from the purser's safe that night to save himself trouble first thing in the morning. He locked the bag in a big trunk and locked the door of his cabin, and wanted to give the key to Spooky, who was his steward. But Spooky was dead-scared.

" 'No, sir, you'd better keep it. And if you'll allow me to say so, sir, I shouldn't leave any valuables lying about tonight if I was you.'

"When Mr. McLeod went to his bag the next morning, three thousand dollars and a gold watch and chain were gone.

" 'Holling,' said Spooky, and you couldn't budge him. He was one of those thin, bald men that never change their opinions.

"The Central Office people investigated the case, but that's where it ended.

"It wasn't much of a coincidence that Miss Penn and Charley were on the ship when it turned round. Charley was on business, and so was she. I saw them together lots of times, and once he came down with her and stood outside her cabin while she dug up some photographs of the South Sea Islands.

"Charley's partner was a fellow named Cowan, a little fellow with the biggest hands I've ever seen. They say he could palm a whole pack and light a cigarette with the same hand without the sharpest pair of eyes spotting it.

"One morning I took Cowan in his coffee and fruit, and I thought he was sleeping, but just as I was going away he turned round.

" 'Felix,' he said, 'who is that dame in the private suite?'

"I told him about Miss Penn.

" 'She's got Charley going down for the third time,' he said, worried, 'and he's sidestepping business. We're eight hundred dollars bad this trip unless somebody comes and pushes it into my hand—and that only happens in dreams.'

" 'Well, it's your funeral, Mr. Cowan,' I said.

" 'And I'll be buried at sea,' he groaned.

"Cowan must have talked straight to Charley, because that same night the smoke-room waiter told me that Charley had caught an English Member of Parliament for a thousand dollars over a two-handed game this bird was trying to teach him.

"We got to Cherbourg that trip early in the morning, and I had to go down to lock up the lady's baggage, because she was bound for Paris. She was kneeling on the sofa looking out of the porthole at Cherbourg, which is about the same thing as saying she was looking at nothing, for Cherbourg is just a place where the sea stops and land begins.

" 'Oh, steward,' she said, turning round, 'do you know if Mr. Pole is going ashore?'

" 'No, Miss,' I said, 'not unless he's going ashore in his pajamas. The tender is coming alongside, and when I went into his cabin just now he was still asleep.'

" 'Thank you,' she said, and that was all.

"She went off in the tender and left me the usual souvenir. She was the only woman I've met that tipped honest.

"There was some delay after the tender left, and I wondered why, till I heard that a certain English marquis who was traveling with us discovered that his wife's jewel-case had been lifted in the night, and about twenty thousand pounds' worth of pearls had been taken.

"It is very unpleasant for everybody when a thing like that happens, because the first person to be suspected is the bedroom steward. After that, suspicion goes over to the deck hands, and works its way round to the passengers.

"The chief steward sent for all the room-men, and he talked straight.

" 'What's all this talk of Holling's ghost?' he said, extremely unpleasant. 'I am here to tell you that the place where Holling's gone, money—especially paper money—would be no sort of use at all, so we can rule spirits out entirely. Now, Spooky, let's hear what you saw.'

" 'I saw a man go down the alleyway toward Lord Crethborough's suite,' he said, 'and I turned back and followed him. When I got into the alleyway, there was nobody there. I tried the door of his cabin and it was locked. So I knocked, and his lordship opened the door and asked me what I wanted. This was at two o'clock this morning—and his lordship will bear me out.'

" 'What made you think it was a ghost?' asked the chief steward.

" 'Because I saw his face—it was Holling.'

"The chief steward thought for a long time.

" 'There's one thing you can bet on—he's gone ashore at Cherbourg. That town was certainly made for ghosts. Go to your stations and give the police all the information you can when they arrive.'

"On the trip out, Miss Penn was not on the passenger list, and the only person who was really glad was Cowan. When he wasn't working, I used to see Charley moping about the alleyway where her cabin had been, looking sort of miserable, and I guessed that she'd made a hit. We had no robberies, either; in fact, what with the weather being calm and the passengers generous, it was one of the best trips I've ever had.

"We were in dock for a fortnight replacing a propeller, and just before we sailed I had a look at the chief steward's list and found I'd got Miss Penn again, and to tell you the truth I wasn't sorry, although she was really Spooky's passenger.

"I don't think I've ever seen a man who looked happier than Charley Pole when she came on board. He sort of fussed round her like a pet dog, and for the rest of the voyage he went out of business. Cowan felt it terribly.

" 'I've never seen anything more unprofessional in my life, Felix,' he said bitterly to me one day. 'I'm going to quit at the end of this trip and take up scientific farming.'

"He was playing patience in his room—the kind of patience that gentlemen of Mr. Cowan's profession play when they want to get the cards in a certain order.

" 'What poor old Holling said about Charley is right—a college education is always liable to break through the skin.'

" 'Did you know Holling?' I asked.

" 'Did I know him? I was the second man in the cabin after Spooky found him. In fact, I helped Spooky get together his belongings to send to his widow.' He sighed heavily. 'Holling did some foolish things in his time, but he never fell in love except with his wife.'

" 'Have you heard about his ghost?' I asked.

"Cowan smiled.

" 'Let us be intelligent,' he said. "Though I admit that the way Charley goes on is enough to make any self-respecting cardman turn in his watery tomb.'

"Two days out of New York we struck a real ripsnorting southwester—the last weather in the world you'd expect Holling to choose for a visit. At about four o'clock in the morning, Spooky, who slept in the next bunk to me, woke up with a yell and tumbled out onto the deck.

" 'He's aboard!' he gasped.

"There were thirty stewards in our quarters, and the things they said to Spooky about Holling and him were shocking to hear.

" 'He's come on board,' said Spooky, very solemn.

"He sat on the edge of his bunk, his bald head shining in the bulkhead light, his hands trembling.

" 'You fellows don't think as I think,' he said. 'You haven't got my spiritual eyesight. You laugh at me when I tell you that I shall end my days in the poorhouse and my children will be selling matches, and you laugh at me when I tell you that Holling's come aboard—but I know. I *absolutely* know!' "

"When we got to New York, the ship was held up for two hours while the police were at work, for a lady passenger's diamond sunburst had disappeared between seven o'clock in the evening and five o'clock in the morning, and it was not discovered.

"Miss Penn was a passenger on the home trip, and this time Charley wasn't as attentive. He didn't work, either, and Cowan, who was giving him his last chance, threw in his hand and spent his days counting the bits of gulf weed we passed.

"As I've said before, there's one place on a ship for getting information and that's the boat deck after dark. Not that I ever spy on passengers—I'd scorn the action. But when a man's having a smoke between the boats, information naturally comes to him.

"It was the night we sighted England, and the Start Light was winking and blinking on the port bow, and I was up there having a few short pulls at a pipe, when I heard Charley's voice. It wasn't a pleasant kind of night—it was cold and drizzling—and they had the deck to themselves, he and Miss Penn.

" 'You're landing at Cherbourg?' said Charley.

" 'Yes,' said Miss Penn, and then: 'What has been the matter with you all this voyage?'

"He didn't answer at once. I could smell the scent of his Havana. He was thinking things over before he spoke.

" 'You generally get off a boat pretty quick, don't you?' he asked in his drawling voice.

" 'Why, yes,' she said. 'I'm naturally in a hurry to get ashore. Why do you say that?'

" 'I hope Holling's ghost isn't walking this trip,' he said.

" 'What do you mean?' she asked.

"And then he said in a low voice, 'I hope there'll be no sunbursts missing tomorrow. If there are, there's a tugful of police meeting us twenty miles out of Cherbourg. I heard it coming through on the wireless tonight—I can read Morse code—and you'll have to be pretty quick to jump the boat this time.'

"It was such a long while before she answered that I wondered what had happened, and then I heard her say, 'I think we'll go down, shall we?' "

"It was six o'clock the next morning and I was taking round the early coffee when I heard the squeal. There was a Russian count, or prince or something, traveling on C deck, and he was one of the clever people who never put their valuables in the purser's safe. Under his pillow he had a packet of loose diamonds that he'd been trying to sell in New York. I believe that he couldn't comply with some Customs regulations and had to bring them back. At any rate, the pocketbook that held them was found empty in the alleyway, and the diamonds were gone. I had to go to the purser's office for something and I saw him writing out a radiogram, and I knew that this time nothing was being left to chance and that the ship would be searched from the keel upwards.

" 'They can search it from the keel downwards,' said Spooky gloomily when I told him. 'You don't believe in Holling, Felix, but I do. Those diamonds are gone.'

"And then what I expected happened. The ship's police took charge of the firemen's and stewards' quarters; nobody was allowed in or out and we were ordered to get ready to make a complete search of passengers' baggage. The tug came up about nine o'clock and it was crowded, not with French police but with Scotland Yard men who had been waiting at Cherbourg.

"The police interviewed the Russian and got all they could out of him, which was very little, and then the passengers were called to the main saloon and the purser said a few words to them. He apologized for giving them trouble, but pointed out that it was in the interests of the company that the thief should be discovered.

" 'We shan't keep you long, ladies and gentlemen,' he said. 'There is an adequate force of detectives on board to make the search a rapid one, but I want every trunk and every bag opened.'

"The ship slowed down to half speed, and then began the biggest and most thorough search I've ever seen in all my experience of seagoing. Naturally, some of the passengers kicked, but the majority of them behaved sensibly and helped the police all they knew how. And the end of it was—not a loose diamond was brought to light.

"There was only one person who was really upset by the search, and that was Charley. He was as pale as death and could hardly keep still for a second. I watched him, and I watched

Miss Penn, who was the coolest person on board. He kept as close to the girl as he could, his eyes never leaving her, and when the search of the baggage was finished and the passengers were brought to the main saloon again, he was close behind her. This time the purser was accompanied by a dozen men from headquarters, and it was the Inspector in Charge who addressed the crowd.

" 'I want, first of all, to search all the ladies' handbags, and then I wish the passengers to file out—the ladies to the left, the gentlemen to the right—for a personal search.'

"There was a growl or two at this, but most of the people took it as a joke. The ladies were lined up and a detective went along, opened each handbag, examined it quickly, and passed on to the next. When they got to Miss Penn, I saw friend Charley leave the men's side and, crossing the saloon, stand behind the detective as he took the girl's bag in his hand and opened it. I was close enough to see the officer's changed expression.

" 'Hullo, what's this?' he said, and took out a paper package.

"He put it on the table and unrolled it. First there was a lot of cotton wool, and then row upon row of sparkling stones. You could have heard a pin drop.

" 'How do you account for having these in your possession, Madam?' asked the detective.

"Before she could reply, Charley spoke.

" 'I put them there,' he said. 'I took them last night and placed them in Miss Penn's handbag in the hope that her handbag would not be searched.'

"I never saw anybody more surprised than Miss Penn.

" 'You're mad,' she said. 'Of course you did nothing of the sort.'

"She looked round the saloon. The stewards were standing in a line to cover the doors, and after a while she saw Spooky.

" 'Simms,' she called.

"Spooky came forward. As he came, Miss Penn spoke in a low voice to the detective.

" 'Simms, do you remember that I sent you down to my cabin for my bag?'

" 'No, Miss,' he said, 'you never asked me for a bag.'

"She nodded. 'I didn't think you'd remember.' And then: 'That is your man, Inspector.'

"Before Spooky could turn, the police had him, and then Miss Penn spoke.

" 'I am a detective in the employment of the company, engaged in marketing down cardsharpers, but more especially on the Holling case. I charge this man with the willful murder of John Holling on the high seas, and with a number of thefts, particulars of which you have.'

"Yes, it was Spooky who killed Holling—Spooky, half mad with the lunatic idea he'd die in the poorhouse, who had robbed and robbed and robbed, and when he was detected by Holling, who woke up and found Spooky going through his pocketbook, had slashed him with a razor and invented the story of the face in the mirror. Whether he killed the other man I don't know—it is very likely. One murder more or less wouldn't worry Spooky, when he thought of his children selling matches on the streets. Was he mad? I should say he was. You see, *he had no children!*

"I didn't see Miss Penn again until she came out on her honeymoon trip. There was a new gang working on the ship—a crowd that had been pushed off the China route and weren't very well acquainted with the regulars that worked the Western Ocean. One of them tried to get Miss Penn's husband into a little game.

" 'No, thank you,' said Charley. 'I never play cards these days.' "

CLARK HOWARD

ONE WAY OUT

Despite his loss of blood, first from the wound in his side and then from the emergency operation to get the bullet out, Gerald Walsh's face, instead of being pale, was flushed with hot, dry fever. His body was limp, still painless from the anesthetic. Although his mental capacities felt tired and somewhat fuzzy, he was still aware of what was going on around him, and he was still certain he could handle himself all right.

"Who was with you on the holdup, Gerry?" a voice asked from somewhere above his bed. Walsh forced a grin without opening his eyes. He had his answer ready.

"Jesse James," he replied as lightly as his dry mouth would permit.

"We want your partner, Gerry," another voice said. "Tell us where he went."

Walsh did not answer. He forced his heavy eyelids half open and looked up at the ring of faces peering down at him. The two cops had on hats and overcoats. One of them had a fat face. Walsh had seen him around but could not recall his name. The other he knew—Tevell, a captain from downtown. The rest of the people were strangers—doctors and nurses, he guessed—all wearing white. One of the nurses was a redhead with nice eyes, nice lips, nice everything, at least from the waist up. The other was plain-faced, doughy-looking, homely. Walsh closed his eyes again and concentrated on a picture of the redhead.

"We'll want to move him to the jail hospital right away," he heard Tevell say.

"Can't be done," a voice told the captain.

"Doctor," Tevell's voice was flat, firm, "this man killed a policeman a few hours ago. I want him behind bars."

"You move him now," the doctor said, "and the only place you'll be able to put him will be in a coffin. He'll hemorrhage and die."

Walsh's mind fought through the haze around it to listen more closely. So I'm in a private hospital, he thought. Very interesting. He forced himself to stay awake but did not open his eyes. After a moment he heard Tevell sigh heavily.

"How long before he can be moved without it killing him?"

"That's hard to say. The danger of internal disorder usually passes as the post-surgery fever drops back to normal. He's running a hundred and two right now. It'll have to come down gradually; his system won't take fever depressants for a while. It might be a week, might be ten days."

"Aside from the fever," Tevell wanted to know, "what's his physical condition?"

"Pretty good. Very good, in fact. The bullet went in above the hipbone and below the lower rib ridge. It couldn't have been more perfectly placed—from a medical standpoint, that is. Didn't even disturb the appendix. Came out the back well clear of the pelvic girdle and spine. Minimum tissue damage all the way around. Repair will be good, recovery quick. He should even be able to walk a little by next week. The only thing we have to wait out is that fever."

Walsh smiled inwardly. Walk in one week, that's good. That's nice. Because if I can walk, it won't be long before I can run.

"All right, Doctor," Tevell said grudgingly. "We'll leave him here until you say move him. His staying, however, is going to entail our taking some necessary security precautions. We'll want to put steel grilles on the insides of both windows, and there will have to be two guards here around the clock. In addition, we're going to have to request that one of the nurses be assigned exclusively to this room and that all other hospital people—excluding yourself, of course—be kept out."

"I can understand the guards and the special nurse, Captain," the doctor said. "But are the steel grilles really necessary? Surely you don't expect him to jump out a fifth-story window?"

"No more than we expect his partner to come through the window after him," Tevell admitted, "but anything is possible when you deal with people like this. I can get a court order, if it'll make you feel any better about it."

The doctor sighed wearily. "No, don't trouble. Go ahead with whatever you think necessary."

Walsh heard footsteps as the people around his bed moved slowly away. He strained to hear as their voices grew fainter.

"What about the private nurse?" Tevell asked.

"Miss Hatch here is a resident," the doctor said. "I can assign her to the room."

Walsh smiled inwardly, wondering if Miss Hatch was the well-built one with the red hair. The voices in the room dissolved completely then and silence settled heavily over Walsh. He opened his eyes once, looked at everything he could see without moving his head, then closed them again. A warmth began to creep upward into his head and a few moments later he was floating off into the void of drugged sleep.

A cool hand was holding his wrist the next time Walsh awoke. Opening his eyes a crack, he saw the homely nurse who had been in the room the night before. She was taking his pulse, studying her wristwatch as she mentally recorded each beat. An identification badge pinned to her uniform read, ALMA HATCH, R.N.

Just my lousy luck, Walsh cursed to himself. He wouldn't be getting the redhead, after all.

"Well, I see you're awake," Alma said before Walsh could close his eyes again. "Good, I want to take your temperature."

She put a thermometer under his tongue and began writing on a medical chart while she waited. Walsh studied her closely. She was, as he had noticed the first time, an extremely plain girl. Her complexion was pasty, like stale dough on a baker's table, and her lips were too large for her face. There was no life in either her eyes or her hair, the former being dull, the latter thin and colorless. She looked to be about twenty-seven. Walsh noticed that she wore no wedding ring.

"All right," she said, taking the thermometer from his mouth, "let's see." She held the instrument at eye level, turning it slowly to find the mercury. "Hundred and one point four," she announced. "Not bad—down more than half a degree. How do you feel?"

"Sick," Walsh said thickly. "Sick and hot and hungry."

"Does your side hurt where the wound is?"

Walsh shook his head slightly. "No."

"All right, the doctor left some medication for your nausea. I'll give you that, and in a little while I'll feed you some broth." She turned and started away.

"Wait," Walsh said softly. Alma paused and turned back.

"Yes?"

"Hold my hand for a minute."

"What?" She frowned, looking incredulous.

"Please," Walsh said, "just for a minute. Please."

Alma blushed slightly. She parted her lips, about to refuse, then glanced across the room at the uniformed police guard. He was reading the paper, paying no attention to them. Hesitantly, still blushing, she reached out and took Walsh's hand. He gripped her fingers gently and forced a weak smile.

"Thanks," he said after a moment. Then he closed his eyes.

Alma Hatch did not reply. She turned away to go for his medicine.

The next morning, while his head was propped up and she was feeding him cream-of-rice cereal, Walsh apologized.

"I didn't mean to seem fresh," he said sheepishly. "It's just that you remind me of a girl I used to know."

His face took on a sad expression. "She was kind of special to me," he added quietly.

Alma studied him curiously for a moment, looking at his dark, wavy hair, his finely cut, handsome face. Her too-large lips parted slightly in obvious disbelief at what he had just told her.

"What's the matter?" Walsh asked her.

"Nothing," she answered in a cool voice. "It just seems a little far-fetched that you would have been—well, attracted to a girl who resembles me."

"Why do you say that?" Walsh asked in mild astonishment.

"Well, I'm not blind, you know." Her voice grew cooler with every word. "I'm fully aware of how I look."

"What's the matter with the way you look?" Walsh made his tone slightly indignant, but kept his voice down so the guard would not hear. "Listen," he went on, "don't think you're not pretty just because you don't wear a lot of lipstick and paint your eyes blue and dye your hair six different colors. A lot of guys like girls that keep their natural beauty, and I happen to be one of them. Not everybody goes for flashy dames, you know."

"Well, I certainly never thought of myself as having 'natural beauty' before," Alma said. Her voice was still not friendly but some of its coolness had disappeared.

"Stop feeling sorry for yourself, then," Walsh told her flatly. "I'll admit you're no Miss America, but you're still a very pretty girl." He put his head down abruptly. "I don't want any more," he said impatiently, closing his eyes.

Alma stood for a moment holding a spoonful of cereal she had been about to put to his lips. When she saw that he didn't intend to eat any more, and apparently didn't want to talk any further, she put the spoon back in the bowl and silently went away.

Walsh smiled after she had gone. Two points, he thought. Now she owes me an apology . . .

"I was rude to you yesterday," Alma said quietly the next morning, as Walsh lay with the thermometer in his mouth. "You were trying to be nice to me and I was very impolite. I'm sorry." She took the thermometer from his mouth and held it up to read.

"Forget it," Walsh said easily. "I wasn't exactly trying to be nice to you—I mean, not like I was forcing myself to be nice. I was just paying you a compliment is all. Sometimes I'm a little clumsy with words."

"Oh, I don't think you are at all," she said quickly. "I think you speak very well."

"Now who's trying to be nice?" he chided gently. He watched her record her temperature on the chart. "What is it today?" he asked casually.

"One hundred point two," she told him. They both felt drawn at that moment to look across the room at the silent, ever-present guard, who, as usual, was paying no attention to them. Then Alma turned back to look at Walsh.

She stared intently at him for what seemed like a long time. Walsh returned her fixed stare, seeing in her eyes now the sympathy he had been hoping for, working toward, counting on. She's falling for it, the wounded man thought. She's buying it.

"It'll still be a few days," she told him quietly, "maybe another week. When it gets below a hundred, it will drop very slowly."

"Sure," Walsh said, making his voice sound very flat and hopeless.

Alma bit her lower lip in a brief moment of frustration and uncertainty, then took the medical chart and left the room. Walsh grinned.

A while later the guard got up from his chair just inside the door and stepped out into the hall. Raising himself on one elbow, Walsh could see him talking to a second uniformed officer who was stationed outside. Walsh wet his dry lips and looked around the room. Both windows had heavy steel grilles locked into place on the inside. One way out, Walsh thought. The door. Then the hallway. Elevator next, or stairs. Then the street. One way, just the one way out.

So that's how it'll have to be, he decided.

He was able to sit up the next evening and partially feed himself supper, with Alma's help. When he had finished, Alma gave him a cigarette and lighted it for him.

"Thanks," he said, smiling. "That sure tastes good." She gave him a half smile in return and began stacking the few dishes on a tray. Walsh glanced over at the door and saw that the guard was out in the hall again. He reached out and took Alma's hand.

"I want to tell you something," he said urgently. "I want you to know that I didn't kill that policeman. How can I convince you?"

"I don't want to talk about that," Alma said quickly. She pulled her hand away, but Walsh instantly grabbed it again.

"Alma, please," he pleaded, "you've got to listen! It's very important to me that you understand. I don't care what anybody else thinks, but with you it's different."

"Different?" She stared at him for a moment, no longer trying to pull away. "What do you mean, different? I'm nobody to you."

"You are, Alma, you are," Walsh insisted. "Listen, I don't expect you to feel the same way about me, I know you couldn't—"

Alma's hand suddenly tightened in his until it was she who

was doing the holding. "Feel how?" she almost whispered. "Tell me what you mean."

Walsh lowered his eyes to avoid looking at her. "I—I think I've fallen in love with you."

Alma parted her lips to speak but no words came. She put the back of one hand to her mouth for a moment, then squeezed Walsh's hand briefly and turned quickly away from his bed. Picking up the tray of dishes, she hurried from the room.

Walsh sighed heavily and took a final drag on his cigarette. So far, so good, he thought. Glancing at the door, he saw that the two guards were still idly talking in the corridor. Quickly he flipped back the sheet and sat up straight. Carefully moving his legs over the side of the bed, he held one hand over his bandaged wound and slowly stood up. His body was stiff and weak, and a wave of nausea flooded over him for a few seconds, but he braced himself with his free hand and held on until the feeling passed. Then he was able to take a few short steps to the end of the bed and back.

In bed again, he was sweaty and out of breath, but now he had found out just how much strength he had, and now he knew just how much work he had to do. He decided to start exercising his legs and arms that night as soon as the lights went out.

Tevell came to see him the next afternoon.

"How are you, killer?" the police captain asked in a level, professional voice.

"I'll live," Walsh said.

Tevell grunted loudly. "Not for long you won't. A year from now, after a trial and an appeal and all the rest of the rigmarole, they'll be strapping you in the electric chair. Unless you're smart, that is."

Here it comes, Walsh thought knowingly. The old you-help-us-and-we'll-help-you bit. "Well, tell me, Captain," Walsh said with mock interest, "what do I have to do to be smart?"

"Just give us an address. The address where Cappo is hiding out."

Walsh knit his brow in feigned bewilderment. "Who?"

"Cappo," the policeman repeated, "George Cappo. You remember him. He was your partner on the stickup, the one who put three of those five bullets into the officer you two murdered."

"I don't know what you're talking about," Walsh said tightly.

"We already checked," Tevell said, "so save your lies. You and Cappo have been thick for two or three months. You've been going to the races together, shooting pool together, nightclubbing all over town together. Then you and another guy pull a loan company heist, and now all of a sudden Cappo has dropped out of sight. We can put two and two together, kid."

"Three cheers for you," said Walsh.

"The way it stands now," Tevell continued, "you can clam up and go straight to the chair. We'll still catch Cappo sooner or later. Or you can play it smart, tell us where he is, turn state's evidence at the trial, and come out of it with a life sentence that will get you a parole in fifteen or twenty years. You're still young yet, kid. Staying alive is something to think about."

Tevell leaned back in his chair and took a cigar from his breast pocket. He slipped off the cellophane wrapper, put the cigar in the middle of his mouth, and lighted it. After several preliminary puffs, he shifted it over to one corner of his mouth and talked around it. "Come on, Gerry," he prodded, "tell me where Cappo is."

"He took a slow boat to China," Walsh said, curling his lips into a sneer. Tevell sighed heavily and shrugged his shoulders.

"Some people," he observed patiently, "just have to do it the hard way. Okay, kid." He got up to leave. "See you in the death house."

After the policeman left, Gerry lay back in bed, pale and cold in spite of his fever, thinking thoughts of the electric chair.

"What can I do to help you?" Alma whispered to him that night as he ate supper. Walsh's heart skipped a beat at the sound of the words he had been waiting to hear. This is the beginning of it, he thought. My one way out.

"What do you mean?" he asked her in a controlled voice.

"I can't let them take you to jail," she said, "now that we feel the way we do about each other." She slipped her hand over his and held it firmly and reassuringly.

"I don't want you to get involved, Alma," Walsh said with forced sincerity.

"But I am involved. I became involved the moment you said you loved me. You've got to let me help you. There must be something I can do."

"I—I don't know," he said hesitantly, "I haven't thought about you helping me. If I had a few more days here, maybe I could figure out something."

"I can have you kept here," she told him quickly. "I can indicate on your chart that your fever is still high. The doctor never checks it himself. And I know he won't give permission for you to be moved until your temperature is normal again."

"I never thought of that," Walsh lied. "Are you sure you can get away with it?"

She nodded enthusiastically. "I'm sure. Maybe in those few days we can think of a way for you to get out."

"Alma," Walsh said, looking at her balefully, "if we do find a way, will you come with me? We could go away somewhere, make a new start—"

"Are you sure you'd want me to?" she asked, her voice almost pathetic in tone. "I know I'm not pretty, no matter what you told me, and I'm not very smart, except about nursing."

"I want you to, Alma," he assured her. "I wouldn't go without you."

Alma gave his hand a final squeeze and smiled. "I'll go," she said happily.

During the next four days, Walsh laid the mental and physical groundwork of his escape plan. Giving Alma a list of sizes, he instructed her to buy him a complete set of clothing. She was to keep the things in her car on the staff parking lot and smuggle them into her hospital locker, one article at a time. He also told her to get a small supply of whatever medicines he would need once he was out of the hospital. These she was to keep in a kit in her glove compartment.

At night when the lights were out, while the two police guards passed their monotonous watches talking in the corridor, Walsh would be awake, exercising his legs, flexing his arm muscles, standing next to the bed for long periods of time in order to regain his equilibrium. In addition to building up his strength in this fashion, Alma was secretly giving him daily injections of high-potency vitamins.

Folded in a newspaper, Alma slipped him a typewritten schedule of all hospital personnel on duty on the fifth floor between 10:00 P.M., when the lights were turned off, and six o'clock the next morning when the day shift came on.

And, most important of all, he had Alma start bringing each of the two night guards a cup of coffee around midnight.

On the fifth day, Alma put a fresh dressing on his wound. "How does it look?" he asked her.

"Good," she said. "All the secondary tissue has closed and the epidermis, the upper layer, is already forming."

"Can I walk all right?"

Alma nodded. "As long as you move slowly and don't bump anything, or slip. Do you think you're strong enough?"

"I'm strong enough," he assured her. "We'll go tonight if you can manage to serve our friends in blue some special coffee. What are you going to give them, anyway?"

"Cobazine. It's tasteless and dissolves completely in liquid. I'll give them enough for about five hours."

"Good. No one else will be on duty tonight?"

She shook her head. "Not in this corridor."

"Okay. You're sure everything else is set? My clothes all in your locker? The car got plenty of gas?"

"Yes, everything just like you said." Alma bit her lower lip and stared at Walsh for a long moment. "I haven't asked before," she said quietly, "but what's going to happen to us after tonight? Where will we go? What will we do?"

Walsh spread his lips into a personable smile and reached out for her hand. "We'll hide out for a while until I get good and well, then we'll go away together. We'll move somewhere far away, where nobody will know us. We'll make a new start together, just you and me."

"Do you really mean it, Gerry?" she asked. "You wouldn't just say those things, would you, just so I'd help you?"

"Alma, honey"—Walsh spoke softly, squeezing her hand—"I love you, please believe me. All I want is to be with you." He put a pained expression on his face. "Why, you don't think I could lie about a thing like that?"

"All right, Gerry," she interrupted. "All right. I believe you."

"Tonight, then?"

She nodded. "Tonight."

Walsh winked at her, grinning. "That's my girl."

Thirty minutes after midnight, Alma came into the room, past the two heavily sleeping guards, and gave Walsh his new clothes.

"Are you sure they're both out good?" he asked anxiously as she helped him into a shirt.

"Yes, I'm sure. They won't wake up until four or five o'clock."

"Okay. Come on—hurry."

When he was dressed, he put one arm around Alma's shoulder and they started out into the hall. As they passed the inside guard, slumped down low in his chair, arms hanging limply to the floor, Walsh stopped. "Just a second—"

He flipped open the grip strap of the guard's holster and removed the heavy regulation revolver from its leather nest. "Just in case," he said easily, shoving the weapon under his belt. Alma looked at the gun a little fearfully but said nothing. Slipping her arm around his waist again, she helped him out into the corridor.

They used the food-service elevator to go down to the deserted hospital kitchen, and from there Alma guided him out the receiving entrance to a small loading dock at the rear of the building. They moved quickly at first, then slowed down as Walsh tired and began to sweat from the now unfamiliar exertion of walking. Luckily, they met no one in the quiet night recesses of the sleeping hospital and, after several pauses to let Walsh rest, they finally negotiated the loading dock steps, and the personnel parking lot, and reached Alma's car.

"You're shivering," Alma said. "I've got a blanket in the back seat."

"Forget it," he snapped. "Come on, drive." He slumped in the seat, leaning against the passenger door. Alma saw that he had one hand on the gun in his belt. She bit her lip nervously and started the car.

Walsh showed her the way to go, directing her first down one street, then another, almost snarling his instructions, using a threatening voice and tone she had not before heard from him. Still she said nothing.

They drove miles across the night city, using side streets, changing routes often, avoiding the boulevards and shopping districts where encounter with police patrols was likely. They drove for nearly an hour, the neighborhoods around them gradually deteriorating into a shabby tenement district that looked almost dead in the grey moonlight.

"Pull over in the middle of this block," Walsh said finally, "the third building past that streetlight." They were on a narrow street of ancient brownstones, five-story walkups with skeletons of iron railings along their flat cement porches, drawn shades in curtainless windows, gnarled, lidless garbage cans lining the sidewalk—a bleak, spiritless street, where the past, present, and future are all one, and better days never come.

"Right there," Walsh said crisply. Alma parked at the curb and helped him out. "Get the medicine from the glove compartment," he ordered.

She helped him into one of the tombstonelike buildings and they took the bare wooden stairs quietly and slowly, very slowly, up to the third floor. Walsh began sweating again and leaned heavily on Alma as they shuffled down a dark hall to the rear apartment. He knocked softly on the door.

"Who is it?" a muffled voice asked from inside.

"Open up, Cappo," Walsh said quietly. "It's Gerry."

The door opened at once, exposing a shabby, cheaply furnished living room filled with the thick air of stale smoke and warm whisky. A thick-shouldered, unshaved man in an undershirt stared incredulously at Walsh and Alma, and behind him, her mouth agape in like surprise, stood a red-lipped, voluptuous woman with hair bleached almost yellow. The eyes of both of them—the man's bloodshot and darkly ringed, the woman's heavy with makeup—were wide in wonder at the sight of Walsh. Neither of them moved.

"Ain't nobody gonna asked me in?" Walsh inquired flatly, pushing past the man. "Get that stuff," he ordered Cappo, indicating the packet of medicine Alma held.

"Gerry!" The blonde woman finally found her voice and

hurried over to Walsh, throwing her arms around him. "Gerry, honey, are you all right?"

"Yeah; swell." Walsh hugged the woman as she deluged him with wet, lipstick-smeared kisses. "Help me to the couch, doll," he told her, "before I drop."

From the couch, with his arm around the blonde, Walsh looked up at Alma, who stood silently with her back to the closed door. Her face was flushed and she stood very still, with her eyes downcast.

"Okay, nursie," Walsh said levelly, "you can go now."

Alma raised her eyes and looked at him steadily, saying nothing.

"Wait a minute," said Cappo. "You can't let her out of here! She'll run straight to the cops."

"Relax," Walsh told him. "She ain't going to do nothing stupid. Are you, nursie?" He turned to Alma. "You don't want to go to jail, do you? As an accessory after the fact to murder? That's what they'll get you for, you know. They're never lenient with people who aid and abet cop killers."

"You said you didn't do it," Alma reminded him. "You said he did it—" She looked at Cappo.

"Well," Walsh grinned, "it was only half a lie. Actually, we both blasted him." He picked up a cigarette from the coffee table and lighted it, leaning his head back as the blonde stroked his forehead. "If you're smart, sister," he said, "you'll hustle back to the hospital and drink some of that spiked coffee yourself. That way it'll look like an outside job and you won't get caught. It's better than spending the next ten years in a women's prison."

"You said you loved me—" Alma accused quietly.

"Look," Walsh snapped, his grin fading, "I said a lot of things—so what? You didn't really think I'd fall for a dame with a face like yours, did you?"

Alma stared at him for a moment, then slowly shook her head. "I suppose not," she said heavily. She turned to leave.

"So long, dearie," the blonde woman said smugly.

Alma went out and closed the door behind her. She heard Walsh and Cappo chuckle softly beyond the door. The narrow, dark hallway stretched out before her like infinity. She walked mechanically.

That's always the way, Alma thought. She slowly descended the stairs. A girl that was homely—how she hated that word!—but a girl like her, a plain girl, just didn't have a chance with men. Not men like Gerry Walsh, anyway. Not the sharp, good-looking men, the ones who appealed, the operators.

How many times now had she been taken in? There was that intern a few years back, the one with the nice smile. She didn't even remember his name now. And the ambulance driver with the curly black hair. And the one she met on a blind date who was such a good dancer. And the one with the build who picked her up (she might as well admit it) at the beach. And the one—

She paused on the second-floor landing and shook them all out of her mind. Too many to count, she thought. Besides, it hurt to remember them. They had all treated her the same way, all made her think she meant something to them, then all dropped her when they were finished with her. Nice guys, these sharp operators with their good looks, their grooming, their easy smiles and practiced lines.

Well, it's your own fault, homely, she said bitterly to herself. Dull face, dull mind. It figured. She walked on down the stairs.

There were a dozen men waiting in the first-floor foyer when she stepped off the last step. One of them moved quietly out of the shadows and came over to her. When he stepped into the dim hall light, Alma saw that it was Tevell, the police captain.

"Are you all right?" he asked.

"Yes."

"Where is he?"

"Third floor," Alma told him, "rear apartment."

"Is Cappo there, too?"

"Yes. And a woman."

Tevell nodded and turned to one of his officers. "Third-floor rear—get six men around back, we'll go up this way in five minutes."

"May I leave?" Alma asked.

"Yes." The policeman took her arm. "I'll see you to your car."

They walked down the outside steps and over to her car. Tevell opened the car door for her.

"Miss Hatch," he said, "I want you to know how much we appreciate your help. You did a good job."

Alma smiled, a tight, almost cruel smile. She thought about Walsh upstairs with his blonde.

"Don't mention it, Captain," she said evenly. "It was a pleasure."

She started her car and drove off down the bleak, deserted street.

HENRY JAMES

OWEN WINGRAVE

"Upon my honor you must be off your head!" cried Spencer Coyle as the young man, with a white face, stood there panting a little and repeating "Really, I've quite decided," and "I assure you I've thought it all out." They were both pale, but Owen Wingrave smiled in a manner exasperating to his supervisor, who, however, still discriminated sufficently to feel his grimace—it was like an irrelevant leer—the result of extreme and conceivable nervousness.

"It was certainly a mistake to have gone so far, but that's exactly why it strikes me I mustn't go further," poor Owen said, waiting mechanically, almost humbly—he wished not to swagger, and indeed had nothing to swagger about—and carrying through the window to the stupid opposite houses the dry glitter of his eyes.

"I'm unspeakably disgusted. You've made me dreadfully ill"—and Mr. Coyle looked in truth thoroughly upset.

"I'm very sorry. It was the fear of the effect on you that kept me from speaking sooner."

"You should have spoken three months ago. Don't you know your mind from one day to the other?" the elder of the pair demanded.

The young man for a moment held himself—then he quavered his plea. "You're very angry with me and I expected it. I'm awfully obliged to you for all you've done for me. I'll do anything else for you in return, but I can't do that. Everyone else will let me have it, of course. I'm prepared for that—I'm prepared for everything. It's what has taken the time: to be sure I was prepared. I think it's your displeasure I feel most and regret most. But little by little you'll get over it," Owen wound up.

"*You'll* get over it rather fast, I suppose!" the other satirically exclaimed. He was quite as agitated as his young friend, and they were evidently in no condition to prolong an encounter in which each drew blood. Mr. Coyle was a professional "coach"—he prepared aspirants for the Army, taking only three or four at a time, to whom he applied the irresistible stimulus, the possession of which was both his secret and his fortune. He hadn't a great establishment; he would have said himself that it was not a wholesale business. Neither his system, his health, nor his temper could have concorded with numbers, so he weighed and measured his pupils and turned away more applicants than he passed.

He was an artist in his line, caring only for picked subjects and capable of sacrifices almost passionate for the individual. He liked ardent young men—there were types of facility and kinds of capacity to which he was indifferent—and he had taken a particular fancy to Owen Wingrave. This young man's particular shade of ability, to say nothing of his whole personality, almost cast a spell and at any rate worked a charm. Mr. Coyle's candidates usually did wonders, and he might have sent up a multitude. He was a person exactly of the stature of the great Napoleon, with a certain flicker of genius in his light-blue eye—it had been said of him that he looked like a concert-giving pianist. The tone of his favorite pupil now expressed, without intention indeed, a superior wisdom that irritated him. He hadn't at all suffered before from Wingrave's high opinion of himself, which had seemed justified by remarkable parts, but today, of a sudden, it struck him as intolerable. He cut short the discussion, declining absolutely to regard their relations as terminated, and remarked to his pupil that he had better go off somewhere—down to Eastbourne, say: the sea would bring him round—and take a few days to find his feet and come to his senses. He could afford the time, he was so well up. When Spencer Coyle remembered how well up he was he could have boxed his ears.

The tall athletic young man wasn't physically a subject for simplified reasoning, but a troubled gentleness in his handsome face—the index of compunction mixed with resolution—virtually signified that if it could have done any good he would have turned both cheeks. He evidently didn't pretend that his wisdom was superior; he only presented it as his own. It was his own career, after all, that was in question. He couldn't refuse to go through the form of trying Eastbourne, or at least of holding his tongue, though there was that in his manner which implied that if he should do so it would be really to give Mr. Coyle a chance to recuperate. He didn't feel a bit overworked, but there was nothing more natural than that, with their tremendous pressure, Mr. Coyle should be. Mr. Coyle's own intellect would derive an advantage from his pupil's holiday.

Mr. Coyle saw what he meant, but controlled himself; he only demanded, as his right, a truce of three days. Owen granted it, though as fostering sad illusions this went visibly against his conscience. But before they separated, the famous crammer remarked: "All the same, I feel I ought to see someone. I think you mentioned to me that your aunt had come to town?"

"Oh, yes—she's in Baker Street. Do go and see her," the boy said for comfort.

His tutor sharply eyed him. "Have you broached this folly to her?"

"Not yet—to no one. I thought it right to speak to you first."

"Oh, what you 'think right'!" cried Spencer Coyle, outraged by his young friend's standards. He added that he would probably call on Miss Wingrave—after which the recreant youth got out of the house.

The latter didn't, none the less, start at once for Eastbourne; he only directed his steps to Kensington Gardens, from which Mr. Coyle's desirable residence—he was terribly expensive and had a big house—was not far removed. The famous coach "put up" his pupils, and Owen had mentioned to the butler that he would be back to dinner.

The spring day was warm to his young blood, and he had a book in his pocket which, when he had passed into the Gardens and, after a short stroll, dropped into a chair, he took out with the slow soft sigh that finally ushers in a pleasure postponed. He stretched his long legs and began to read it. It was a volume of Goethe's poems. He had been for days in a state of the highest tension, and now that the cord had snapped the relief was proportionate—only it was characteristic of him that this deliverance should take the form of an intellectual pleasure. If he had thrown up the probability of a magnificent career, it wasn't to dawdle along Bond Street nor parade his indifference in the window of a club. At any rate, he had in a few moments forgotten everything—the tremendous pressure, Mr. Coyle's disappointment, and even his formidable aunt in Baker Street. If these watchers had overtaken him, there would surely have been some excuse for their exasperation. There was no doubt he was perverse, for his very choice of a pastime only showed how he had got up his German.

"What the devil's the matter with him, do *you* know?" Spencer Coyle asked that afternoon of young Lechmere, who had never before observed the head of the establishment to set a fellow such an example of bad language. Young Lechmere was not only Wingrave's fellow pupil, he was supposed to be his intimate—indeed quite his best friend—and he had unconsciously performed for Mr. Coyle the office of making the promise of his great gifts more vivid by contrast. He was short and sturdy and as a general thing uninspired, and Mr. Coyle, who found no amusement in believing in him, had never thought him less exciting than as he stared now out of a face from which you could no more guess whether he had caught an idea than you could judge of your dinner by looking at a dish-cover.

Young Lechmere concealed such achievements as if they had been youthful indiscretions. At any rate, he could evidently conceive no reason why it should be thought there was anything more than usual the matter with the companion of his studies, so Mr. Coyle had to continue: "He declines to go up. He chucks the whole shop!"

The first thing that struck young Lechmere in the case was the freshness, as of a forgotten vernacular, it had imparted to the governor's vocabulary. "He doesn't want to go to Sandhurst?"

"He doesn't want to go anywhere. He gives up the Army altogether. He objects," said Mr. Coyle in a tone that made young Lechmere almost hold his breath, "to the military profession."

"Why, it has been the profession of all his family!"

"Their profession? It has been their religion! Do you know Miss Wingrave?"

"Oh, yes. Isn't she awful?" young Lechmere candidly ejaculated.

His instructor demurred. "She formidable, if you mean that, and it's right she should be; because somehow in her very person, good maiden lady as she is, she represents the might, she represents the traditions and the exploits, of the British Army. She represents the expansive property of the English name. I think his family can be trusted to come down on him, but every influence should be set in motion. I want to know what yours is. Can *you* do anything in the matter?"

"I can try a couple of rounds with him," said young Lechmere reflectively. "But he knows a fearful lot. He has the most extraordinary ideas."

"Then he has told you some of them—he has taken you into his confidence?"

"I've heard him jaw by the yard," smiled the honest youth. "He has told me he despises it."

"What *is* it he despises? I can't make out."

The most consecutive of Mr. Coyle's nurslings considered a moment, as if he were conscious of a responsibility. "Why, I think just soldiering, don't you know? He says we take the wrong view of it."

"He oughtn't to talk to *you* that way. It's corrupting the youth of Athens. It's sowing sedition."

"Oh, I'm all right!" said young Lechmere. "And he never told me he meant to chuck it. I always thought he meant to see it through, simply because he had to. He'll argue on any side you like. He can talk your head off—I will say *that* for him. But it's a tremendous pity—I'm sure he'd have a big career."

"Tell him so, then. Plead with him, struggle with him—for God's sake."

"I'll do what I can—I'll tell him it's a regular shame."

"Yes, strike *that* note—insist on the disgrace of it."

The young man gave Mr. Coyle a queer look. "I'm sure he wouldn't do anything dishonorable."

"Well—it won't look right. He must be made to feel *that*. Work it up. Give him a comrade's point of view—that of a brother-in-arms."

"That's what I thought we were going to be!" young Lechmere mused romantically, much uplifted by the nature of the mission imposed on him. "He's an awfully good sort."

"No one will think so if he backs out!" said Spencer Coyle.

"Well, they mustn't say it to *me!*" his pupil rejoined with a flush.

Mr. Coyle debated, noting his tone and aware that in the perversity of things, though this young man was a born soldier, no excitement would ever attach to *his* alternatives, save perhaps on the part of the nice girl to whom at an early day he was sure to be placidly united. "Do you like him very much—do you believe in him?"

Young Lechmere's life in these days was spent in answering terrible questions, but he had never been put through so straight a lot as these. "Believe in him? Rather!"

"Then *save* him!"

The poor boy was puzzled, as if it were forced upon him by this intensity that there was more in such an appeal than could appear on the surface—and he doubtless felt that he was but apprehending a complex situation when after another moment, with his hands in his pockets, he replied hopefully but not pompously: "I daresay I can bring him round!"

Before seeing young Lechmere, Mr. Coyle had determined to telegraph an inquiry to Miss Wingrave. He had prepaid the answer, which, being promptly put into his hand, brought the interview we have just related to a close. He immediately drove off to Baker Street, where the lady had said she awaited him, and five minutes after he got there, as he sat with Owen Wingrave's remarkable aunt, he repeated several times over, in his angry sadness and with the infallibility of his experience: "He's so intelligent—he's so intelligent!" He had declared it had been a luxury to put such a fellow through.

"Of course he's intelligent—what else could he be? We've never, that I know of, had but *one* idiot in the family!" said Jane Wingrave. This was an allusion that Mr. Coyle could understand, and it brought home to him another of the reasons for the disappointment, the humiliation as it were, of the good people at Paramore, at the same time that it gave an example of the conscientious coarseness he had on former occasions observed in his hostess.

Poor Philip Wingrave, her late brother's eldest son, was literally imbecile and banished from view—deformed, unsocial, irretrievable, he had been relegated to a private asylum and had become among the friends of the family only a little hushed lugubrious legend. All the hopes of the house, picturesque Paramore, now unintermittently old Sir Philip's rather melancholy home—his infirmities would keep him there to the last—were therefore gathered on the second boy's head, which nature, as if in compunction for her previous botch, had, in addition to making it strikingly handsome, filled with a marked and general readiness. These two had been the only children of the old man's only son, who, like so many of his ancestors, had given up a gallant young life to the service of his country. Owen Wingrave the elder had received his death-cut, in close quarters, from an Afghan saber. The blow had come crashing across his skull. His wife, at that time in India, was about to give birth to her third child, and when the event took place, in darkness and anguish, the baby came lifeless into the world and the mother sank under the multiplication of her woes.

The second of the little boys in England, who was at Paramore with his grandfather, became the peculiar charge of his aunt, the only unmarried one, and during the interesting Sunday that, by urgent invitation, Spencer Coyle, busy as he was, had, after consenting to put Owen through, spent under that roof, the celebrated crammer received a vivid impression of the influence exerted, at least in intention, by Miss Wingrave. Indeed the picture of this short visit remained with the observant little man a curious one—the vision of an impoverished Jacobean house, shabby and remarkably "creepy," but full of character still, and full of felicity as a setting for the distinguished figure of the peaceful old soldier. Sir Philip Wingrave, a relic rather than a celebrity, was a small, brown, erect octogenerian, with smoldering eyes and a studied courtesy. He liked to do the diminished honors of his house, but even when with a shaky hand he lighted a bedroom candle for a deprecating guest it was impossible not to feel him, beneath the surface, a merciless old man of blood. The eye of the imagination could glance back into his crowded Eastern past—back at episodes in which his scrupulous forms would only have made him more terrible. He had his legend—and, oh, there were stories about him!

Mr. Coyle remembered also two other figures—a faded, inoffensive Mrs. Julian, domesticated there by a system of frequent visits as the widow of an officer and a particular friend of Miss Wingrave, and a remarkably clever little girl of eighteen, who was this lady's daughter and who struck the speculative visitor as already formed for other relations. She was very impertinent to Owen, and in the course of a long walk that he had taken with the young man, the effect of which, in much talk, had been to clinch his high opinion of him, he had learned—for Owen chattered confidentially—that Mrs. Julian was the sister of a very gallant gentleman, Captain Hume-Walker of the Artillery, who had fallen in the Indian Mutiny and between whom and Miss Wingrave (it had been that lady's one known concession) a passage of some delicacy, taking a tragic turn, was believed to have been enacted. They had been engaged to be married, but she had given way to the jealousy of her nature—had broken with him and sent him off to his fate, which had been horrible. A passionate sense of having wronged him, a hard eternal remorse had thereupon taken possession of her, and when his poor sister, linked also to a soldier, had by a still heavier blow been left almost without resources, she had devoted herself grimly to a long expiation. She had sought comfort in taking Mrs. Julian to live much of the time at Paramore, where she became an unremunerated though not uncriticized housekeeper, and Spencer Coyle rather fancied it a part of this comfort that she could at leisure trample on her.

The impression of Jane Wingrave was not the faintest he had gathered on that intensifying Sunday—an occasion singularly tinged for him with the sense of bereavement and mourning and memory, of names never mentioned, of the faraway plaint of widows and the echoes of battles and bad news. It was all military indeed, and Mr. Coyle was made to shudder a little at the profession of which he helped to open the door to otherwise harmless young men. Miss Wingrave might, moreover, have made such a bad conscience worse—so cold and clear a good one looked at him out of her hard fine eyes and trumpeted in her sonorous voice.

She was a high, distinguished person, angular but not awkward, with a large forehead and abundant black hair arranged like that of a woman conceiving, perhaps excusably, of her head as "noble," and today irregularly streaked with white. If, however, she represented for our troubled friend the genius of a military race, it was not that she had the step of a grenadier or the vocabulary of a camp-follower—it was only that such sympathies were vividly implied in the general fact to which her very presence and each of her actions and glances and tones were a constant and direct allusion—the paramount valor of her family. If she was military, it was because she sprang from a military house and because she wouldn't for the world have been anything but what the Wingraves had been. She was almost vulgar about her ancestors, and if one had been tempted to quarrel with her one would have found a fair pretext in her defective sense of proportion.

This temptation, however, said nothing to Spencer Coyle, for whom, as a strong character revealing itself in color and sound, she was almost a "treat" and who was glad to regard her as a force exerted on his own side. He wished her nephew had more of her narrowness, instead of being almost cursed with the tendency to look at things in their relations. He wondered why when she came up to town she always resorted to Baker Street for lodgings. He had never known or heard of Baker Street as a residence—he associated it only with bazaars and photographers. He divined in her a rigid indifference to everything that was not the passion of her life. Nothing really mattered to her but that, and she would have occupied apartments in Whitechapel if they had been an item in her tactics. She had received her visitor in a large, cold, faded room, furnished with slipper seats and decorated with alabaster vases and wax flowers. The only little personal comfort for which she appeared to have looked out was a fat catalogue of the Army and Navy Stores, which reposed on a vast, desolate table-cover of false blue.

Her clear forehead—it was like a porcelain slate, a receptable for addresses and sums—had flushed when her nephew's crammer told her the extraordinary news, but he saw she was fortunately more angry than frightened. She had essentially, she would always have, too little imagination for fear, and the healthy habit moreover of facing everything had taught her that the occasion usually found her a quantity to reckon with. He saw that her only present fear could have been that of the failure to prevent her nephew's showing publicly for an ass, or for worse, and that to such an apprehension as this she was in fact inaccessible. Practically, too, she was not troubled by surprise—she recognized none of the futile, none of the subtle sentiments. If Owen had for an hour made a fool of himself, she was angry—disconcerted as she would have been on learning that he had confessed to debts or fallen in love with a low girl. But there remained in any annoyance the saving fact that no one could make a fool of *her*.

"I don't know when I've taken such an interest in a young man—I think I've never done it since I began to handle them," Mr. Coyle said. "I like him, I believe in him. It's been a delight to see how he was going."

"Oh, I know how they go!" Miss Wingrave threw back her head with an air as acquainted as if a headlong array of the generations had flashed before her with a rattle of their scabbards and spurs. Spencer Coyle recognized the intimation that she had nothing to learn from anybody about the natural carriage of a Wingrave, and he even felt convicted by her next words of being, in her eyes, with the troubled story of his check, his weak complaint of his pupil, rather a poor creature. "If you like him," she exclaimed, "for mercy's sake keep him quiet!"

Mr. Coyle began to explain to her that this was less easy than she appeared to imagine; but it came home to him that she really grasped little of what he said. The more he insisted that the boy had a kind of intellectual independence, the more this struck her as a conclusive proof that her nephew was a Wingrave and a soldier. It was not till he mentioned to her that Owen had spoken of the profession of arms as of something that would be "beneath" him, it was not till her attention was arrested by this intenser light on the complexity of the problem, that she broke out after a moment's stupefied reflexion: "Send him to see me at once!"

"That's exactly what I wanted to ask your leave to do. But I've wanted also to prepare you for the worst, to make you understand that he strikes me as really obstinate, and to suggest to you that the most powerful arguments at your command—especially if you should be able to put your hand on some intensely practical one—will be none too effective."

"I think I've got a powerful argument"—and Miss Wingrave looked hard at her visitor. He didn't know in the least what this engine might be, but he begged her to drag it without delay into the field. He promised their young man should come to Baker Street that evening, mentioned however that he had already urged him to spend a couple of the very next days at Eastbourne. This led Jane Wingrave to inquire with surprise what virtue there might be in *that* expensive remedy, and to reply with decision when he had said "The virtue of a little rest, a little change, a little relief to overwrought nerves": "Ah don't coddle him—he's costing us a great deal of money! I'll talk to him and I'll take him down to Paramore. He'll be dealt with there and I'll send him back to you straightened out."

Spencer Coyle hailed this pledge superficially with satisfaction, but before he quitted the strenuous lady he knew he had really taken on a new anxiety—a restlessness that made him say to himself, groaning inwardly: Oh she *is* a grenadier at bottom, and she'll have no tact. I don't know what her powerful argument is, I'm only afraid she'll be stupid and make him worse. The old man's better—*he's* capable of tact, though he's not quite an extinct volcano. Owen will probably put him in a rage. In short, it's a difficulty that the boy's the best of them.

He felt afresh that evening at dinner that the boy was the best of them. Young Wingrave—who, he was pleased to observe, had not yet proceeded to the seaside—appeared at the repast as usual, looking inevitably a little self-conscious, but not too original for Bayswater. He talked very naturally to Mrs. Coyle, who had thought him from the first the most beautiful young man they had ever received. So that the person most ill at ease was poor Lechmere, who took great trouble, as if from the deepest delicacy, not to meet the eye of his misguided mate.

Spencer Coyle, however, paid the price of his own profundity in feeling more and more worried—he could so easily see that there were all sorts of things in his young friend that the people of Paramore wouldn't understand. He began even already to react against the notion of his being harassed—to reflect that, after all, he had a right to his ideas—to remember that he was of a substance too fine to be handled with blunt fingers. It was in this way that the ardent little crammer, with his whimsical perceptions and complicated sympathies, was generally condemned not to settle down comfortably either to his displeasures or to his enthusiasms. His love of the real truth never gave him a chance to enjoy them. He mentioned to Wingrave after dinner the propriety of an immediate visit to Baker Street, and the young man, looking "queer," as he thought—that is, smiling again with the perverse high spirit in a wrong cause that he had shown in their recent interview—went off to face the ordeal. Spencer Coyle was sure he was scared—he was afraid of his aunt—but somehow this didn't strike him as a sign of pusillanimity. *He* should have been scared, he was well aware, in the poor boy's place, and the sight of his pupil marching up to the battery in spite of his terrors was a positive suggestion of the temperament of the soldier. Many a plucky youth would have funked this special exposure.

"He *has* got ideas!" young Lechmere broke out to his instructor after his comrade had quitted the house. He was bewildered and rather rueful—he had an emotion to work off. He had before dinner gone straight at his friend, as Mr. Coyle had requested, and had elicited from him that his scruples were founded on an overwhelming conviction of the stupidity—the "crass barbarism" he called it—of war. His great complaint was that people hadn't invented anything cleverer, and he was determined to show, the only way he could, that *he* wasn't so dull a brute.

"And he thinks all the great generals ought to have been shot, and that Napoleon Bonaparte in particular, the greatest, was a scoundrel, a criminal, a monster for whom language has no adequate name!"

Mr. Coyle rejoined, completing young Lechmere's picture,

"He favored you, I see, with exactly the same pearls of wisdom that he produced for me. But I want to know what *you* said."

"I said they were awful rot!" Young Lechmere spoke with emphasis and was slightly surprised to hear Mr. Coyle laugh, out of tune, at this just declaration, and then after a moment continue:

"It's all very curious—I daresay there's something in it. But it's a pity!"

"He told me when it was that the question began to strike him in that light. Four or five years ago, when he did a lot of reading about all the great swells and their campaigns—Hannibal and Julius Caesar, Marlborough and Frederick and Bonaparte. He *has* done a lot of reading, and he says it opened his eyes. He says that a wave of disgust rolled over him. He talked about the 'immeasurable misery' of wars, and asked me why nations don't tear to pieces the governments, the rulers that go in for them. He hates poor old Bonaparte worst of all."

"Well, poor old Bonaparte *was* a scoundrel. He was a frightful ruffian," Mr. Coyle unexpectedly declared. "But I suppose you didn't admit that."

"Oh, I daresay he was objectionable, and I'm very glad we laid him on his back. But the point I made to Wingrave was that his own behavior would excite no end of remark." And young Lechmere hung back but an instant before adding: "I told him he must be prepared for the worst."

"Of course he asked you what you meant by the worst," said Spencer Coyle.

"Yes, he asked me that, and do you know what I said? I said people would call his conscientious scruples and his wave of disgust a mere pretext. Then he asked, 'A pretext for what?' "

"Ah, he rather had you there!" Mr. Coyle returned with a small laugh that was mystifying to his pupil.

"Not a bit—for I told him."

"What did you tell him?"

Once more, for a few seconds, with his conscious eyes in his instructor's, the young man delayed. "Why, what we spoke of a few hours ago. The appearance he'd present of not having—" The honest youth faltered afresh, but brought it out: "The military temperament, don't you know? But do you know how he cheeked us on that?" young Lechmere went on.

"Damn the military temperament!" the crammer promptly replied.

Young Lechmere stared. Mr. Coyle's tone left him uncertain if he were attributing the phrase to Wingrave or uttering his own opinion, but he exclaimed: "Those were exactly his words!"

"He doesn't care," said Mr. Coyle.

"Perhaps not. But it isn't fair for him to abuse *us* fellows. I told him it's the finest temperament in the world, and that there's nothing so splendid as pluck and heroism."

"Ah, there you had *him!*"

"I told him it was unworthy of him to abuse a gallant, a magnificent profession. I told him there's no type so fine as that of the soldier doing his duty."

"That's esssentially *your* type, my dear boy."

Young Lechmere blushed. He couldn't make out—and the danger was naturally unexpected to him—whether at that moment he didn't exist mainly for the recreation of his friend. But he was partly reassured by the genial way this friend continued, laying a hand on his shoulder: "Keep *at* him that way! We may do something. I'm in any case extremely obliged to you."

Another doubt, however, remained unassuaged—a doubt which led him to overflow yet again before they dropped the painful subject: "He *doesn't* care! But it's awfully odd he shouldn't!"

"So it is, but remember what you said this afternoon—I mean about your not advising people to make insinuations to *you.*"

"I believe I should knock the beggar down!" said young Lechmere. Mr. Coyle had got up—the conversation had taken place while they sat together after Mrs. Coyle's withdrawal from the dinner-table—and the head of the establishment administered to his candid charge, on principles that were a part of his thoroughness, a glass of excellent claret. The disciple in question, also on his feet, lingered an instant, not for another "go," as he would have called it, at the decanter, but to wipe his microscopic moustache with prolonged and unusual care. His companion saw he had something to bring out which required a final effort, and waited for him an instant with a hand on the knob of the door. Then, as young Lechmere drew nearer, Spencer Coyle grew conscious of an unwonted intensity in the round and ingenuous face. The boy was nervous, but tried to behave like a man of the world. "Of course, it's between ourselves," he stammered, "and I wouldn't breathe such a word to anyone who wasn't interested in poor Wingrave as you are. But do you think he funks it?"

Mr. Coyle looked at him so hard an instant that he was visibly frightened at what he had said. "Funks it! Funks what?"

"Why, what we're talking about—the service." Young Lechmere gave a little gulp and added with a want of active wit almost pathetic to Spencer Coyle: "The dangers, you know."

"Do you mean he's thinking of his skin?"

Young Lechmere's eyes expanded appealingly, and what his instructor saw in his pink face—even thinking he saw a tear—was the dread of a disappointment shocking in the degree in which the loyalty of admiration had been great.

"Is he—is he beastly *afraid?"* repeated the honest lad with a quaver of suspense.

"Dear no!" said Spencer Coyle, turning his back.

On which young Lechmere felt a little snubbed and even a little ashamed. But still more, he felt relieved.

Less than a week after this, the elder man received a note from Miss Wingrave, who had immediately quitted London with her nephew. She proposed he should come down to Paramore for the following Sunday—Owen was really so tiresome. On the spot, in that house of examples and memories and in combination with her poor dear father, who was "dreadfully annoyed," it might be worth their while to make a last stand. Mr. Coyle read between the lines of this letter that the party at Paramore had got over a good deal of ground since Miss Wingrave, in Baker Street, had treated his despair as superficial. She wasn't an insinuating woman, but she went so far as to put the question on the ground of his conferring a particular favor on an afflicted family, and she expressed the pleasure it would give them should he be accompanied by Mrs. Coyle, for whom she enclosed a separate invitation. She mentioned that she was also writing, subject to Mr. Coyle's approval, to young Lechmere. She thought such a nice, manly boy might do her wretched nephew some good.

The celebrated crammer decided to embrace this occasion, and now it was the case not so much that he was angry as that he was anxious. As he directed his answer to Miss Wingrave's letter, he caught himself smiling at the thought that at bottom he was going to defend his ex-pupil rather than to give him away. He said to his wife, who was a fair, fresh, slow woman—a person of much more presence than himself—that she had better take Miss Wingrave at her word: it was such an extraordinary, such a fascinating specimen of an old English home. This last allusion was softly sarcastic—he had accused the good lady more than once of being in love with Owen Wingrave. She admitted that she was, she even gloried in her passion—which shows that the subject, between them, was treated in a liberal spirit. She carried out the joke by accepting the invitation with eagerness.

Young Lechmere was delighted to do the same. His instructor had good-naturedly taken the view that the little break would freshen him up for his last spurt.

It was the fact that the occupants of Paramore did indeed take their trouble hard that struck our friend after he had been an hour or two in that fine old house. This very short second visit, beginning on the Saturday evening, was to constitute the strangest episode of his life. As soon as he found himself in private with his wife—they had retired to dress for dinner—they called each other's attention with effusion and almost with alarm to the sinister gloom diffused through the place. The house was admirable from its old grey front, which came forward in wings so as to form three sides of a square, but Mrs. Coyle made no scruple to declare that if she had known in advance the sort of impression she was going to receive she would never have put her foot in it. She characterized it as "uncanny" and as looking wicked and weird, and she accused her husband of not having warned her properly. He had named to her in advance some of the appearances she was to expect, but while she almost feverishly dressed she had innumerable questions to ask. He hadn't told her about the girl, the extraordinary girl, Miss Julian—that is, he hadn't told her that this young lady, who in plain terms was a mere dependent, would be in effect, and as a consequence of the way she carried herself, the most important person in the house. Mrs. Coyle was already prepared to announce that she hated Miss Julian's affectations. Her husband, above all, hadn't told her that they should find their young charge looking five years older.

"I couldn't imagine that," Spencer said, "nor that the character of the crisis here would be quite so perceptible. But I suggested to Miss Wingrave the other day that they should press her nephew in real earnest, and she has taken me at my word. They've cut off his supplies—they're trying to starve him out. That's not what I meant—but indeed I don't quite *know* today what I meant. Owen feels the pressure, but he won't yield."

The strange thing was that, now he was there, the brooding little coach knew still better, even while half closing his eyes to it, that his own spirit had been caught up by a wave of reaction. If he was there, it was because he was on poor Owen's side. His whole impression, his whole apprehension, had on the spot become much deeper. There was something in the young fanatic's very resistance that began to charm him. When his wife, in the intimacy of the conference I have mentioned, threw off the mask and commended even with extravagance the stand his pupil had taken (he was too good to be a horrid soldier and it was noble of him to suffer for his convictions—wasn't he as upright as a young hero, even though as pale as a Christian martyr?), the good lady only expressed the sympathy which, under cover of regarding his late inmate as a rare exception, he had already recognized in his own soul.

For, half an hour ago, after they had had superficial tea in the brown old hall of the house, that searcher into the reasons of things had proposed to him, before going to dress, a short turn outside, and had even, on the terrace, as they walked together to one of the far ends, passed his hand entreatingly into his companion's arm, permitting himself thus a familiarity unusual between pupil and master and calculated to show he had guessed whom he could most depend on to be kind to him.

Spencer Coyle had on his own side guessed something, so

that he wasn't surprised at the boy's having a particular confidence to make. He had felt on arriving that each member of the party would want to get hold of him first, and he knew that at that moment Jane Wingrave was peering through the ancient blur of one of the windows—the house had been modernized so little that the thick dim panes were three centuries old—to see whether her nephew looked as if he were poisoning the visitor's mind. Mr. Coyle lost no time, therefore, in reminding the youth—though careful to turn it to a laugh as he did so—that he hadn't come down to Paramore to be corrupted. He had come down to make, face to face, a last appeal, which he hoped wouldn't be utterly vain. Owen smiled sadly as they went, asking him if he thought he had the general air of a fellow who was going to knock under.

"I think you look odd—I think you look ill," Spencer Coyle said very honestly. They had paused at the end of the terrace.

"I've had to exercise a great power of resistance, and it rather takes it out of one."

"Ah, my dear boy, I wish your great power—for you evidently possess it—were exerted in a better cause!"

Owen Wingrave smiled down at his small but erect instructor. "I don't believe that!" Then he added, to explain why: "Isn't what you want (if you're so good as to think well of my character) to see me exert *most* power, in whatever direction? Well, this is the way I exert most." He allowed he had had some terrible hours with his grandfather, who had denounced him in a way to make his hair stand up on his head. He had expected them not to like it, not a bit, but had had no idea they would make such a row. His aunt was different, but she was equally insulting.

Oh, they had made him feel they were ashamed of him—they accused him of putting a public dishonor on their name. He was the only one who had ever backed out—he was the first for three hundred years. Everyone had known he was to go up, and now everyone would know him for a young hypocrite who suddenly pretended to have scruples. They talked of his scruples as you wouldn't talk of a cannibal's god. His grandfather had called him outrageous names. "He called me—he called me—" Here Owen faltered and his voice failed him. He looked as haggard as was possible to a young man in such splendid health.

"I probably know!" said Spencer Coyle with a nervous laugh.

His companion's clouded eyes, as if following the last strange consequences of things, rested for an instant on a distant object. Then they met his own and for another moment sounded them deeply. "It isn't true. No, it isn't. It's not *that!*"

"I don't suppose it is! But what *do* you propose instead of it?"

"Instead of what?"

"Instead of the stupid solution of war. If you take that away, you should suggest at least a substitute."

"That's for the people in charge, for governments and cabinets," said Owen. *"They'll* arrive soon enough at a substitute, in the particular case, if they're made to understand that they'll be hanged—and also drawn and quartered—if they don't find one. Make it a capital crime—*that* will quicken the wits of ministers!"

His eyes brightened as he spoke, and he looked assured and exalted. Mr. Coyle gave a sigh of sad surrender—it was really a stiff obsession. He saw the moment after this when Owen was on the point of asking if he, too, thought him a coward, but he was relieved to be able to judge that he either didn't suspect him of it or shrank uncomfortably from putting the question to the test. Spencer Coyle wished to show confidence, but somehow a direct assurance that he didn't doubt of his courage was too gross a compliment—it would be like saying he didn't doubt of his honesty.

The difficulty was presently averted by Owen's continuing: "My grandfather can't break the entail, but I shall have nothing but this place, which, as you know, is small and, with the way rents are going, has quite ceased to yield an income. He has some money—not much, but such as it is he cuts me off. My aunt does the same—she has let me know her intentions. She was to have left me her six hundred a year. It was all settled, but now what's definite is that I don't get a penny of it if I give up the Army. I must add in fairness that I have from my mother three hundred a year of my own. And I tell you the simple truth when I say I don't care a rap for the loss of the money." The young man drew the long slow breath of a creature in pain, then he added: *"That's* not what worries me!"

"What are you going to do instead, then?" his friend asked without other comment.

"I don't know—perhaps nothing. Nothing great, at all events. Only something peaceful!"

Owen gave a weary smile, as if, worried as he was, he could yet appreciate the humorous effect of such a declaration from a Wingrave, but what it suggested to his guest, who looked up at him with a sense that he was, after all, not a Wingrave for nothing and had a military steadiness under fire, was the exasperation that such a profession, made in such a way and striking them as the last word of the inglorious, might well have produced on the part of his grandfather and his aunt. "Perhaps nothing"—when he might carry on the great tradition! Yes, he wasn't weak, and he was interesting; but there was clearly a point of view from which he was provoking. "What *is* it, then, that worries you?" Mr. Coyle demanded.

"Oh, the house—the very air and feeling of it. There are strange voices in it that seem to mutter at me—to say dreadful things as I pass. I mean, the general consciousness and responsibility of what I was doing. Of course it hasn't been easy for me—anything rather! I assure you I don't enjoy it." With a light in them that was like a longing for justice, Owen again bent his eyes on those of the little coach—then he pursued: "I've started up all the old ghosts. The very portraits glower at me on the walls. There's one of my great-great-grandfather (the one the extraordinary story you know is about—the old fellow who hangs on the second landing of the big staircase) that fairly stirs on the canvas, just heaves a little, when I come near it. I have to go up and down stairs—it's rather awkward! It's what my aunt calls the family circle, and they sit, ever so grimly, in judgment. The circle's all constituted here, it's a kind of awful encompassing presence, it stretches away into the past, and when I came back with her the other day Miss Wingrave told me I wouldn't have the impudence to stand in the midst of it and say such things. I *had* to say them to my grandfather, but now that I've said them it seems to me the question's ended. I want to go away—I don't care if I never come back again."

"Oh you *are* a soldier—you must fight it out!" Mr. Coyle laughed.

The young man seemed discouraged at his levity, but as they turned round, strolling back in the direction from which they had come, he himself smiled faintly after an instant and replied: "Ah, we're tainted all!"

They walked in silence part of the way to the old portico, then the elder of the pair, stopping short after having assured himself he was at a sufficient distance from the house not to be heard, suddenly put the question: "What does Miss Julian say?"

"Miss Julian?" Owen had perceptibly colored.

"I'm sure *she* hasn't concealed her opinion."

"Oh, it's the opinion of the family circle—for she's a member of it, of course. And then she has her own as well."

"Her own opinion?"

"Her own family circle."

"Do you mean her mother—that patient lady?"

"I mean more particularly her father, who fell in battle. And her grandfather, and *his* father, and her uncles and great-uncles—they all fell in battle."

"Mr. Coyle, his face now rather oddly set, took it in. "Hasn't the sacrifice of so many lives been sufficient? Why should she sacrifice *you?"*

"Oh, she *hates* me!" Owen declared as they resumed their walk.

"Ah, the hatred of pretty girls for fine young men!" cried Spencer Coyle.

He didn't believe in it, but his wife did, it appeared perfectly, when he mentioned this conversation while, in the fashion that has been described, the visitors dressed for dinner. Mrs. Coyle had already discovered that nothing could have been nastier than Miss Julian's manner to the disgraced youth during the half hour the party had spent in the hall—and it was this lady's judgment that one must have had no eyes in one's head not to see that she was already trying outrageously to flirt with young Lechmere. It was a pity they had brought that silly boy: he was down in the hall with the creature at that moment.

Spencer Coyle's version was different—he believed finer elements involved. The girl's footing in the house was inexplicable on any ground save that of her being predestined to Miss Wingrave's nephew. As the niece of Miss Wingrave's own unhappy intended, she had been devoted early by this lady to the office of healing by a union with the hope of the race the tragic breach that had separated their elders—and if in reply to this it was to be said that a girl of spirit couldn't enjoy in such a matter having her duty cut out for her, Owen's enlightened friend was ready with the argument that a young person in Miss Julian's position would never be such a fool as really to quarrel with a capital chance. She was familiar at Paramore and she felt safe; therefore she might treat herself to the amusement of pretending she had her option. It was all innocent tricks and airs. She had a curious charm, and it was vain to pretend that the heir of that house wouldn't seem good enough to a girl, clever as she might be, of eighteen. Mrs. Coyle reminded her husband that their late charge was precisely now *not* of that house: this question was among the articles that exercised their wits after the two men had taken the turn on the terrace. Spencer then mentioned to his wife that Owen was afraid of the portrait of his great-great-grandfather. He would show it to her, since she hadn't noticed it on their way downstairs.

"Why of his great-great-grandfather more than of any of the others?"

"Oh, because he's the most formidable. He's the one who's sometimes seen."

"Seen where?" Mrs. Coyle had turned round with a jerk.

"In the room he was found dead in—the White Room, they've always called it."

"Do you mean to say the house has a proved *ghost?"* Mrs. Coyle almost shrieked. "You brought me here without telling me?"

"Didn't I mention it after my other visit?"

"Not a word. You only talked about Miss Wingrave."

"Oh, I was full of the story—you've simply forgotten."

"Then you should have reminded me!"

"If I had thought of it, I'd have held my peace—for you wouldn't have come."

"I wish indeed I hadn't!" cried Mrs. Coyle. "But what," she immediately asked, *"is* the story?"

"Oh, a deed of violence that took place here ages ago. I think it was in George the Second's time that Colonel Wingrave, one of their ancestors, struck in a fit of passion one of his children, a lad just growing up, a blow on the head of which the unhappy child died. The matter was hushed up for the hour and some other explanation put about. The poor boy was laid out in one of those rooms on the other side of the house, and amid strange, smothered rumors the funeral was hurried on. The next morning, when the household assembled, Colonel Wingrave was missing. He was looked for vainly, and at last it occurred to someone that he might perhaps be in the room from which his child had been carried to burial. The seeker knocked without an answer—then opened the door. The poor man lay dead on the floor, in his clothes, as if he had reeled and fallen back, without a wound, without a mark, without anything in his appearance to indicate that he had either struggled or suffered. He was a strong, sound man—there was nothing to account for such a stroke. He's supposed to have gone to the room during the night, just before going to bed, in some fit of compunction or some fascination of dread. It was only after this that the truth about the boy came out. But no one ever sleeps in the room."

Mrs. Coyle had fairly turned pale. "I hope not indeed! Thank heaven they haven't put *us* there!"

"We're at a comfortable distance—I know the scene of the event."

"Do you mean you've been *in—?"*

"For a few moments. They're rather proud of the place, and my young friend showed it me when I was here before."

Mrs. Coyle stared. "And what is it like?"

"Simply an empty, dull, old-fashioned bedroom, rather big, and furnished with the things of the period. It's paneled from floor to ceiling, and the panels evidently, years ago, were painted white. But the paint has darkened with time and there are three or four quaint little ancient 'samplers,' framed and glazed, hung on the walls."

Mrs. Coyle looked round with a shudder. "I'm glad there are no samplers here! I never heard anything so jumpy! Come down to dinner."

On the staircase as they went, her husband showed her the

portrait of Colonel Wingrave—a representation, with some force and style for the place and period, of a gentleman with a hard, handsome face, in a red coat and a peruke. Mrs. Coyle pronounced his descendant, old Sir Philip, wonderfully like him, and her husband could fancy, though he kept it to himself, that if one should have the courage to walk the old corridors of Paramore at night one might meet a figure that resembled him roaming, with the restlessness of a ghost, hand in hand with the figure of a tall boy. As he proceeded to the drawing room with his wife, he found himself suddenly wishing he had made more of a point of his pupil's going to Eastbourne.

The evening, however, seemed to have taken upon itself to dissipate any such whimsical forebodings, for the grimness of the family circle, as he had preconceived its composition, was mitigated by an infusion of the "neighborhood." The company at dinner was recruited by two cheerful couples, one of them the vicar and his wife, and by a silent young man who had come down to fish. This was a relief to Mr. Coyle who had begun to wonder what was after all expected of him and why he had been such a fool as to come, and who now felt that for the first hours, at least, the situation wouldn't have directly to be dealt with. Indeed, he found, as he had found before, sufficient occupation for his ingenuity in reading the various symptoms of which the social scene that spread about him was an expression. He should probably have a trying day on the morrow: he foresaw the difficulty of the long decorous Sunday and how dry Jane Wingrave's ideas, elicited in strenuous conference, would taste. She and her father would make him feel they depended upon him for the impossible, and if they should try to associate him with too tactless a policy he might end by telling them what he thought of it—an accident not required to make his visit a depressed mistake.

The old man's actual design was evidently to let their friends see in it a positive mark of their being all right. The presence of the great London coach was tantamount to a profession of faith in the results of the impending examination. It had clearly been obtained from Owen, rather to the principal visitor's surprise, that he would do nothing to interfere with the apparent concord. He let the allusions to his hard work pass and, holding his tongue about his affairs, talked to the ladies as amicably as if he hadn't been "cut off." When Mr. Coyle looked at him once or twice across the table, catching his eye, which showed an indefinable passion, he found a puzzling pathos in his laughing face: one couldn't resist a pang for a young lamb so visibly marked for sacrifice. Hang him, what a pity he's such a fighter! he privately sighed—and with a want of logic that was only superficial.

This idea, however, would have absorbed him more if so much of his attention hadn't been for Kate Julian, who now that he had her well before him struck him as a remarkable and even as a possibly interesting young woman. The interest resided not in any extraordinary prettiness, for if she was handsome, with her long Eastern eyes, her magnificent hair, and her general unabashed originality, he had seen complexions rosier and features that pleased him more: it dwelt in a strange impression that she gave of being exactly the sort of person whom, in her position, common considerations—those of prudence and perhaps even a little those of decorum—would have enjoined on her not to be.

She was what was vulgarly termed a dependent—penniless, patronized, tolerated—but something in all her air conveyed that if her situation was inferior, her spirit, to make up for it, was above precautions or submissions. It wasn't in the least that she was aggressive—she was too indifferent for that—it was only as if, having nothing either to gain or to lose, she could afford to do as she liked. It occurred to Spencer Coyle that she might really have had more at stake than her imagination appeared to take account of. Whatever this quantity might be, at any rate, he had never seen a young woman at less pains to keep the safe side. He wondered inevitably what terms prevailed between Jane Wingrave and such an inmate as this, but those questions of course were unfathomable deeps. Perhaps keen Kate lorded it even over her protectress. The other time he was at Paramore, he had received an impression that, with Sir Philip beside her, the girl could fight with her back to the wall. She amused Sir Philip, she charmed him, and he liked people who weren't afraid. Between him and his daughter, moreover, there was no doubt which was the higher in command. Miss Wingrave took many things for granted, and most of all the rigor of discipline and the fate of the vanquished and the captive.

But between their clever boy and so original a companion of his childhood what odd relation would have grown up? It couldn't be indifference, and yet on the part of happy, handsome, youthful creatures it was still less likely to be aversion. They weren't Paul and Virginia, but they must have had their common summer and their idyll: no nice girl could have disliked such a nice fellow for anything but not liking *her,* and no nice fellow could have resisted such propinquity. Mr. Coyle remembered indeed that Mrs. Julian had spoken to him as if the propinquity had been by no means constant, owing to her daughter's absences at school, to say nothing of Owen's; her visits to a few friends who were so kind as to take her from time to time; her sojourns in London—so difficult to manage, but still managed by God's help—for "advantages," for drawing and singing, especially drawing, or rather painting in oils, for which she had gained high credit. But the good lady had also mentioned that the young people were quite brother and sister, which *was* a little, after all, like Paul and Virginia. Mrs. Coyle had been right, and it was apparent that Virginia was doing her best to make the time pass agreeably for young Lechmere.

There was no such whirl of conversation as to render it an effort for our critic to reflect on these things: the tone of the occasion, thanks principally to the other guests, was not disposed to stray—it tended to the repetition of anecdote and the discussion of rents, topics that huddled together like uneasy animals. He could judge how intensely his hosts wished the evening to pass off as if nothing had happened, and this gave him the measure of their private resentment. Before dinner was over, he found himself fidgety about his second pupil. Young Lechmere, since he began to cram, had done all that might have been expected of him, but this couldn't blind his instructor to a present perception of his being in moments of relaxation as innocent as a babe. Mr. Coyle had considered that the amusements of Paramore would probably give him a fillip, and the poor youth's manner testified to the soundness of the forecast. The fillip had been unmistakably administered—it had come in the form of a revelation. The light on young Lechmere's brow announced with a candor that was almost an appeal for compassion, or at least a deprecation of ridicule, that he had never seen anything like Miss Julian.

In the drawing room after dinner, the girl found a chance to approach Owen's late preceptor. She stood before him a moment, smiling while she opened and shut her fan, and then said abruptly, raising her strange eyes: "I know what you've come for, but it isn't any use."

"I've come to look after *you* a little. Isn't *that* any use?"

"It's very kind. But I'm not the question of the hour. You won't do anything with Owen."

Spencer Coyle hesitated a moment. "What will *you* do with his young friend?"

She stared, looked round her. "Mr. Lechmere? Oh, poor little lad! We've been talking about Owen. He admires him so."

"So do I. I should tell you that."

"So do we all. That's why we're in such despair."

"Personally, then, you'd *like* him to be a soldier?" the visitor asked.

"I've quite set my heart on it. I adore the Army and I'm awfully fond of my old playmate," said Miss Julian.

Spencer recalled the young man's own different version of her attitude, but he judged it loyal not to challenge her. "It's not conceivable that your old playmate shouldn't be fond of you. He must therefore wish to please you, and I don't see why—between you, such clever young people as you are—you don't set the matter right."

"Wish to please me!" Miss Julian echoed. "I'm sorry to say he shows no such desire. He thinks me an impudent wretch. I've told him what I think of *him*, and he simply hates me."

"But you think so highly! You just told me you admire him."

"His talents, his possibilities, yes—even his personal appearance, if I may allude to such a matter. But I don't admire his present behavior."

"Have you had the question out with him?" Spencer asked.

"Oh, yes, I've ventured to be frank—the occasion seemed to excuse it. He couldn't like what I said."

"What did you say?"

The girl, thinking a moment, opened and shut her fan again. "Why—as we're such good old friends—that such conduct doesn't begin to be that of a gentleman!"

After she had spoken, her eyes met Mr. Coyle's, who looked into their ambiguous depths. "What, then, would you have said without that tie?

"How odd for *you* to ask that—in such a way!" she returned with a laugh. "I don't understand your position: I thought your line was to *make* soldiers!"

"You should take my little joke. But, as regards Owen Wingrave, there's no 'making' needed," he declared. "To my sense"—and the little crammer paused as with a consciousness of responsibility for his paradox—"to my sense, he *is,* in a high sense of the term, a fighting man."

"Ah, let him prove it!" she cried with impatience and turning short off.

Spencer Coyle let her go—something in her tone annoyed and even not a little shocked him. There had evidently been a violent passage between these young persons, and the reflexion that such a matter was, after all, none of his business but troubled him the more. It was indeed a military house, and she was at any rate a damsel who placed her ideal of manhood—damsels doubtless always had their ideals of manhood—in the type of the belted warrior. It was a taste like another, but even a quarter of an hour later, finding himself near young Lechmere, in whom this type was embodied, Spencer Coyle was still so ruffled that he addressed the innocent lad with a certain magisterial dryness. "You're under no pressure to sit up late, you know. That's not what I brought you down for." The dinner guests were taking leave and the bedroom candles twinkled in a monitory row. Young Lechmere, however, was too agreeably agitated to be accessible to a snub; he had a happy preoccupation which almost engendered a grin.

"I'm only too eager for bedtime. Do you know there's an awfully jolly room?"

Coyle debated a moment as to whether he should take the allusion—then spoke from his general tension. "Surely they haven't put you there?"

"No, indeed—no one has passed a night in it for ages. But

that's exactly what I wanted to do—it would be tremendous fun."

"And have you been trying to get Miss Julian's leave?"

"Oh, *she* can't give it, she says. But she believes in it, and she maintains that no man has ever dared."

"No man *shall* ever!" said Spencer with decision. "A fellow in your critical position in particular must have a quiet night."

Young Lechmere gave a disappointed but reasonable sigh. "Oh, all right. But mayn't I sit up for a little go at Wingrave? I haven't had any yet."

Mr. Coyle looked at his watch. "You may smoke *one* cigarette."

He felt a hand on his shoulder and turned round to see his wife tilting candle-grease upon his coat. The ladies were going to bed and it was Sir Philip's inveterate hour, but Mrs. Coyle confided to her husband that after the dreadful things he had told her she positively declined to be left alone, for no matter how short an interval, in any part of the house. He promised to follow her within three minutes, and after the orthodox handshakes the ladies rustled away.

The forms were kept up at Paramore as bravely as if the old house had no present intensity of heartache. The only one of which Coyle noticed the drop was some salutation to himself from Kate Julian. She gave him neither a word nor a glance, but he saw her look hard at Owen. Her mother, timid and pitying, was apparently the only person from whom this young man caught an inclination of the head. Miss Wingrave marshaled the three ladies—her little procession of twinkling tapers—up the wide oaken stairs and past the watching portrait of her ill-fated ancestor.

Sir Philip's servant appeared and offered his arm to the old man, who turned a perpendicular back on poor Owen when the boy made a vague movement to anticipate this office. Mr. Coyle learned later that before Owen had forfeited favor, it had always, when he was at home, been his privilege at bedtime to conduct his grandfather ceremoniously to rest. Sir Philip's habits were contemptuously different now. His apartments were on the lower floor and he shuffled stiffly off to them with his valet's help, after fixing for a moment significantly on the most responsible of his visitors the thick red ray, like the glow of stirred embers, that always made his eyes conflict oddly with his mild manners. They seemed to say to poor Spencer "We'll let the young scoundrel have it tomorrow!" One might have gathered from them that the young scoundrel, who had now strolled to the other end of the hall, had at least forged a check. His friend watched him an instant, saw him drop nervously into a chair, and then with a restless movement get up. The same movement brought him back to where Mr. Coyle stood, addressing a last injunction to young Lechmere.

"I'm going to bed and I should like you particularly to conform to what I said to you a short time ago. Smoke a single cigarette with our host here and then go to your room. You'll have me down on you if I hear of your having, during the night, tried any preposterous games."

Young Lechmere, looking down with his hands in his pockets, said nothing—he only poked at the corner of a rug with his toe, so that his fellow visitor, dissatisfied with so tacit a pledge, presently went on to Owen. "I must request you, Wingrave, not to keep so sensitive a subject sitting up—and indeed to put him to bed and turn his key in the door." As Owen stared an instant, apparently not understanding the motive of so much solicitude, he added: "Lechmere has a morbid curiosity about one of your legends—of your historic rooms. Nip it in the bud."

"Oh, the legend's rather good, but I'm afraid the room's an awful sell!" Owen laughed.

"You know you don't *believe* that, my boy!" young Lechmere returned.

"I don't think he does"—Mr. Coyle noticed Owen's mottled flush.

"He wouldn't try a night there himself!" their companion pursued.

"I know who told you that," said Owen, lighting a cigarette in an embarrassed way at the candle, without offering one to either of his friends.

"Well, what if she did?" asked the younger of these gentlemen, rather red. "Do you want them *all* yourself?" he continued facetiously, fumbling in the cigarette box.

Owen Wingrave only smoked quietly, then he brought out: "Yes—what if she did? But she doesn't know," he added.

"She doesn't know what?"

"She doesn't know anything!—I'll tuck him in!" Owen went on gaily to Mr. Coyle, who saw that his presence, now a certain note had been struck, made the young men uncomfortable. He was curious, but there were discretions and delicacies with his pupils that he had always pretended to practice—scruples which however didn't prevent, as he took his way upstairs, his recommending them not to be donkeys.

At the top of the staircase, to his surprise, he met Miss Julian, who was apparently going down again. She hadn't begun to undress, nor was she perceptibly disconcerted at seeing him. She nevertheless, in a manner slightly at variance with the rigor with which she had overlooked him ten minutes before, dropped the words: "I'm going down to look for something. I've lost a jewel."

"A jewel?"

"A rather good turquoise, out of my locket. As it's the only *real* ornament I've the honor to possess—!" And she began to descend.

"Shall I go with you and help you?" asked Spencer Coyle.

She paused a few steps below him, looking back with her Oriental eyes. "Don't I hear our friends' voices in the hall?"

"Those remarkable young men are there."

"They'll help me." And Kate Julian passed down.

Spencer Coyle was tempted to follow her, but remembering his standard of tact he rejoined his wife in their apartment. He delayed nevertheless to go to bed and, though he looked into his dressing room, couldn't bring himself even to take off his coat. He pretended for half an hour to read a novel—after which, quietly, or perhaps I should say agitatedly, he stepped from the dressing room into the corridor.

He followed this passage to the door of the room he knew to have been assigned to young Lechmere and was comforted to see it closed. Half an hour earlier he had noticed it stand open—therefore he could take for granted the bewildered boy had come to bed. It was of this he had wished to assure himself, and having done so he was on the point of retreating. But at the same instant, he heard a sound in the room—the occupant was doing, at the window, something that showed him he might knock without the reproach of waking his pupil up.

Young Lechmere came, in fact, to the door in his shirt and trousers. He admitted his visitor in some surprise, and when the door was closed again the latter said: "I don't want to make your life a burden, but I had it on my conscience to see for myself that you're not exposed to undue excitement."

"Oh, there's plenty of that!" said the ingenuous youth. "Miss Julian came down again."

"To look for a turquoise?"

"So she said."

"Did she find it?"

"I don't know. I came up. I left her with poor Owens."

"Quite the right thing," said Spencer Coyle.

"I don't know," young Lechmere repeated uneasily. "I left them quarreling."

"What about?"

"I don't understand. They're a quaint pair!"

Spencer turned it over. He had, fundamentally, principles and high decencies, but what he had in particular just now was a curiosity—or rather, to recognize it for what it was, sympathy—which brushed them away. "Does it strike you that *she's* down on him?" he permitted himself to inquire.

"Rather!—when she tells him he lies!"

"What do you mean?"

"Why, before *me.* It made me leave them—it was getting too hot. I stupidly brought up the question of that bad room again, and said how sorry I was I had had to promise you not to try my luck with it."

"You can't pry about in that gross way in other people's houses—you can't take such liberties, you know!" Mr. Coyle interjected.

"I'm all right—see how good I am? I don't want to go *near* the place!" said young Lechmere confidingly. "Miss Julian said to me, 'Oh, I daresay *you'd* risk it, but'—and she turned and laughed at poor Owen—'that's more than we can expect of a gentleman who has taken *his* extraordinary line.' I could see that something had already passed between them on the subject—some teasing or challenging of hers. It may have been only chaff, but his chucking the profession had evidently brought up the question of the white feather—I mean of his pluck."

"And what did Owen say?"

"Nothing at first—but presently he brought out very quietly: 'I spent all last night in the confounded place.' We both stared and cried out at this and I asked him what he had seen there. He said he had seen nothing, and Miss Julian replied that he ought to tell his story better than that—he ought to make something good of it. 'It's not a story—it's a simple fact,' said he; on which she jeered at him and wanted to know why, if he had done it, he hadn't told her in the morning, since he knew what she thought of him. 'I know, my dear, but I don't care,' the poor devil said. This made her angry, and she asked him quite seriously whether he'd care if he should know she believed him to be trying to deceive us."

"Ah what a brute!" cried Spencer Coyle.

"She's a most extraordinary girl—I don't know what she's up to," young Lechmere quite panted.

"Extraordinary, indeed—to be romping and bandying words at that hour of the night with fast young men!"

But young Lechmere made his distinction. "I mean because I think she likes him."

Mr. Coyle was so struck with this unwonted symptom of subtlety that he flashed out: "And do you think he likes *her?"*

It produced on his pupil's part a drop and a plaintive sigh. "I don't know—I give it up! But I'm sure he *did* see something or hear something," the youth added.

"In that ridiculous place? What makes you sure?"

"Well, because he looks as if he had. I've an idea you can tell—in such a case. He behaves as if he had."

"Why then shouldn't he name it?"

Young Lechmere wondered and found. "Perhaps it's too bad to mention."

Spencer Coyle gave a laugh. "Aren't you glad then *you're* not in it?"

"Uncommonly!"

"Go to bed, you goose," Spencer said with renewed nervous

derision. "But before you go, tell me how he met her charge that he was trying to deceive you."

" 'Take me there yourself then and lock me in!' "

"And *did* she take him?"

"I don't know—I came up."

Spencer exchanged a long look with his pupil. "I don't think they're in the hall now. Where's Owen's own room?"

"I haven't the least idea."

Mr. Coyle was at a loss—he was in equal ignorance and he couldn't go about trying doors. He bade young Lechmere sink to slumber, after which he came out into the passage. He asked himself if he should be able to find his way to the room Owen had formerly shown him, remembering that in common with many of the others it had its ancient name painted on it. But the corridors of Paramore were intricate. Moreover, some of the servants would still be up, and he didn't wish to appear unduly to prowl.

He went back to his own quarters, where Mrs. Coyle soon noted the continuance of his inability to rest. As she confessed for her own part, in the dreadful place, to an increased sense of "creepiness," they spent the early part of the night in conversation, so that a portion of their vigil was inevitably beguiled by her husband's account of his colloquy with Lechmere and by their exchange of opinions upon it.

Toward two o'clock, Mrs. Coyle became so nervous about their persecuted young friend, and so possessed by the fear that that wicked girl had availed herself of his invitation to put him to an abominable test, that she begged her husband to go and look into the matter at whatever cost to his own tranquility. But Spencer, perversely, had ended, as the perfect stillness of the night settled upon them, by charming himself into a pale acceptance of Owen's readiness to face God-knew-what unholy strain—an exposure the more trying to excited sensibilities as the poor boy had now learned by the ordeal of the previous night how resolute an effort he should have to make.

"I hope he *is* there," he said to his wife: "it puts them all so hideously in the wrong!" At any rate, he couldn't take on himself to explore a house he knew so little. He was inconsequent—he didn't prepare for bed. He sat in the dressing room with his light and his novel—he waited to find himself nod. At last, however, Mrs. Coyle turned over and ceased to talk, and at last, too, he fell asleep in his chair.

How long he slept he only knew afterward by computation. What he knew to begin with was that he had started up in confusion and under the shock of an appalling sound. His consciousness cleared itself fast, helped doubtless by a confirmatory cry of horror from his wife's room. But he gave no heed to his wife—he had already bounded into the passage. There the sound was repeated—it was the "Help! help!" of a woman in agonized terror. It came from a distant quarter of the house, but the quarter was sufficiently indicated.

He rushed straight before him, the sound of opening doors and alarmed voices in his ears and the faintness of the early dawn in his eyes. At a turn of one of the passages, he came upon the white figure of a girl in a swoon on a bench, and in the vividness of the revelation he read as he went that Kate Julian, stricken in her pride too late with a chill of compunction for what she had mockingly done, had, after coming to release the victim of her derision, reeled away, overwhelmed, from the catastrophe that was her work—the catastrophe that the next moment he found himself aghast at on the threshold of an open door. Owen Wingrave, dressed as he had last seen him, lay dead on the spot on which his ancestor had been found. He was all the young soldier on the gained field.

MARY ORR

THE WISDOM OF EVE

A young girl is on her way to Hollywood with a contract for one thousand dollars a week from a major film company in her pocketbook. I shall call her Eve Harrington because that is not her name, though the Eve part of the alias is not unapt, considering the original's snaky activities in a once-peaceful garden. In a year or two I am sure Miss Harrington will be as much a household word to you as Ingrid Bergman or Joan Fontaine. When she is a star, I am equally positive that the slick publicity agents of Hollywood who surround these celestial beings with glamor will give you their version of her success. But no matter what they concoct, it will not be as interesting or ironic as her real story. It would never occur to them to tell you the truth. Stars must be presented to their public in a warm, sympathetic light, and one could scratch a long time before kindling any such spark from the personality of Eve Harrington.

I first saw her on a cold, snowy night in January. I was sitting snugly under a fur rug in the back seat of Margola Cranston's town car. We were parked at the stage entrance of Margola's theater, waiting for her to come out. By we, I mean her chauffeur Henry and I. Henry sat patiently in front of me, displaying the proper fortitude of one whose chief occupation in life was to wait. But marking time is not my long suit, and my gloved fingers played an irritated tattoo on Margola's polychrome upholstery. I am an actress myself and am able to get in and out of my makeup with the same speed that I duck in and out of a cold shower. Not so Margola. Rarely did she leave the theater before a quarter to twelve. What went on in her dressing room for three quarters of an hour was a mystery known only to her maid, Alice, and herself. Consequently, if one wanted to see Margola after the theater one waited. However, it was not a lone vigil.

There was a crowd at the stage door. They were the usual autograph fans, all with little books open and fountain pens dripping ink. Some appeared to be intelligent theatergoers; they carried programs for Margola to sign and had obviously seen the play that evening. I could hear their enthusiastic comments through the tiny opening where I had lowered the car window to let my cigarette smoke escape. A few were boys in uniform with dreams of dating Margola—dreams that would not come true. There was only one person standing there I could not catalogue. She stood nearest the car, and I could see her face clearly in the light of the streetlamp.

It was a young, unusual face, but not in the least pretty. Because she was rather plain, the amount of makeup she was wearing seemed to me very odd. What I mean is, false eyelashes can look very much at home on Lana Turner, but the same pair could be incongruous on a schoolteacher. This girl had a serious, prim expression. She was dressed in a warm, practical red coat. On her head she wore a small dark tam-o'-shanter which didn't seem to agree with the coat. She also wore high-heeled, open-toed shoes, and standing there in the slush her feet must have been cold. Her hands were thrust into her coat pockets and a shabby purse dangled from her left arm. Her manner was shy and reticent. Under their long lashes, her eyes stared at the ground. She stood first on one foot and then on the other to keep warm, but displayed no fatigue at the long wait.

I continued to wonder who she was and why she was there until Margola finally appeared at the stage entrance. I had seen her come out many times. It was a superb act. I knew perfectly well she was not in the least surprised to see the crowd gathered there, but her expression was one of delighted amazement. So many people gathered there to see her! It could not be! She smiled and signed the autograph books and spoke first to one and then to another. She radiated graciousness. Everyone would go away exclaiming, "What charm!" "So modest!" "How kind!"

Margola would then climb into the car and apologize for keeping me waiting by saying, "Those tiresome people! Such bores! What fools!"

I was one of Margola's few women friends. My husband, Lloyd Richards, had written the play in which she was then appearing with great success. Lloyd had also written another one of her most popular vehicles. No one knew better than he that a large part of their success was due to Margola's performance. Without her, they might have run five, six, or seven weeks. With her, the first play had lasted two years, and the current smash hit showed stubborn signs of outdoing it. For there was no doubt that Margola was a truly great actress.

Watching her sign the autographs, I wondered for the thousandth time what made her so great. Nobody would guess it to see her out of the theater. She was tiny, with the childish figure of a Botticelli angel. On stage, her clothes were done by Carnegie, Valentia, and Mainbocher. Off stage, they were done by Cranston. They consisted generally of old sweaters and tweed skirts. I had once peeked into her closet and discovered a dozen gowns utterly unworn. I have known her six years and seen her twice in a decent dress. Once was at the funeral of a big producer for whom she had no respect and once when she had to receive a Critics Award she didn't want.

Her hair was another cross her friends had to bear. When she was not on stage, it was generally piled on the top of her head as if she had just fallen out of the bath. Even on stage it could sometimes be said to resemble a theater cleaner's mop. That night it was tucked beneath a hand-painted handkerchief which she had tied under her chin, peasant fashion. She wore a mink coat, true enough, but on her it might have been an old muskrat. It was down to her ankles and six years out of style. Nobody but a genius could dress as she did and get away with it.

Lloyd has always said that for him she is utterly devoid of sex appeal. To me she is tremendously attractive. He gives her one asset in the way of beauty—a very obvious one—a pair of enormous eyes, which behind the footlights can betray every thought in a character's mind with crystal clarity. Also, she seems to have the secret of eternal youth. I have seen her in the bright sunshine with no makeup on and she doesn't look a day over twenty-nine or thirty. If Margola ever sees forty-five again, I'll have my eyes lifted.

We got along together from the first day we met. I often

disagreed with her, argued with her, and wisecracked at her expense. Sometimes Lloyd would look worried and tell me not to go too far, to remember that I owed my penthouse and sables largely to her. However, in spite of my acid tongue, to this day she has preferred my company to most other women's.

Being Margola's best friend is in many ways a bit of a bore. I'm the type of female who only feels at home dressed in a Daché hat at the Stork Club or El Morocco. As Margola always looks like a tourist, it is well nigh impossible to persuade her to have supper at any café-society haunt. She favors a bar behind some delicatessen shop, in Sardi's, or her own home.

On the night in question it was home—and home to Margola is a nest of forty rooms at Great Neck, Long Island, called Capulet's Cottage. That meant I had to stay all night, for first there would be a huge supper, and then conversation until three or four in the morning, as Margola loves to talk by the light of the moon. Consequently, my overnight bag rested uncomfortably on my feet. Lloyd had kissed me goodbye when I'd left for the theater and gone off with a gleam in his eye to a stag poker session.

"Have a nice cat party" had been his parting words, and I knew that he was privately relieved we were not having a foursome with Margola's husband, Clement Howell. Clement is a clever enough director and producer but very English and pompous. Lloyd can take only a certain number of broad *A*'s.

Margola was close to the car when the shabby little girl with the red coat suddenly stepped into her line of vision. I saw Margola's eyes cloud up and her expression change to one of annoyance. The girl spoke a few words and looked at her in the most supplicating way, her large eyes filled with tears. But she didn't succeed in melting the star's icy attitude. I couldn't hear what Margola said to her exactly, but I knew it wasn't nice, and I did catch the last phrase, which was, "I don't want you pestering me every night." With that, she climbed into the car and slammed the door. "Get going, Henry," she commanded the chauffeur and sank back into the corner of the seat like a sulky child.

"Well," I said in my most sarcastic tone, "I thought you were always so charming to your public. What's the matter with little Miss Redcoat? Is she selling something?"

Margola glared at me. "You don't know what I've been through with that girl. You can't imagine what she's said and done to me. How she lied to me and made a fool of me."

"Now, Margola," I said, "don't act. Don't be so dramatic. What could a poor girl like that do to you?"

"It's too long a story," she said. "Besides, I get in a rage every time I think about it."

I lighted a cigarette and handed it to her. "Come on," I said. "You'll have to tell me now. We've got a long drive ahead and nothing to do but talk."

She inhaled deeply. "Her name's Eve Harrington," she said. "Translated, it spells—well, she is the most awful girl I've ever met. There are no lengths to which she won't go."

"Start at the beginning," I urged. "Not with the third act. How did you happen to meet this paragon of all the virtues?"

"It was Clement's fault," Margola sighed after a moment's pause. "He first drew my attention to her. He asked me if I'd ever noticed the girl who stood at the stage entrance and simply watched me come out. She didn't ask for an autograph or a picture or try to speak to me—just stood there and looked.

"I said that I hadn't.

"He said she always wore a red coat and to be sure to give a look next time."

"She was wearing a red coat tonight," I interrupted.

"I know." She flicked my remark aside impatiently. "Well, the next time I went into the theater—for a matinee it was—I saw her. She was there when the afternoon performance was over. I saw her again when I came back after dinner, and when the evening performance was over she was still there.

"This time, when I got rid of the crowd. I spoke to her. I asked her if there was anything I could do for her, and she said no. I said I had noticed her at the matinee and that my husband had seen her before. She said she stood there every night. I couldn't believe my ears. I said, 'Well, what do you want?' She said, 'Nothing.' I said, 'There must be something,' and finally she said that she knew if she stood there long enough eventually I would speak to her. I asked if that was all she wanted and she said yes, that she had first seen me in San Francisco when I toured in *Have a Heart.*" That was my husband's first play in which Margola had appeared. "She said she had followed me to Los Angeles and eventually come on to New York."

"Just to stand at your stage door?" I asked, amazed.

"She went to the play," Margola added, "as often as she could afford to."

"What devotion," I said.

"That," said Margola sadly, "is what I assumed. I was most impressed. I thought: This is my most ardent fan. She follows me clear across the Great Divide. She sees my plays constantly when she obviously has very little money. She stands night after night at my stage door just to see me come out and finally have me speak to her. I was moved."

"So what went on?" I urged.

"Well," Margola answered, "I felt that I had to do something to repay this child for her admiration. She was only twenty-two. I thought: I'll give her an evening she'll always remember. So I invited her to come home with me. She acted as if she were in a seventh heaven. She had a slight accent which she told me was Norwegian.

"She said that her people had come over here six or seven years before and had finally left her with an aunt and gone back to Norway on a trip. Of course, because of the war they hadn't been able to return, and she hadn't heard from them in months. In the meantime, she had married a young American flier and had been living in San Francisco because he had gone to the Pacific from there. I asked her how she got along and she said that at first she had had her husband's allotment, but then he had been killed over Bougainville and since then she had lived very meagerly on his insurance."

"How sad."

"Exactly what I thought," Margola said. "She told me that seeing me act and watching my plays had been her only happiness since she had had the wire about her husband. It seemed to me that I must do something for her. I found out that she could type and do shorthand. She'd worked as a secretary in San Francisco. It suddenly came to me that this girl might make just the secretary for me. You know I'm hard to please, but here was someone who adored me, who would be loyal, who was quiet and at the same time well-bred. She spoke English beautifully and seemed intelligent.

"So I asked her if she'd like to work for me. You've never seen such a response. She burst into tears and kissed my hand. I generally hate that sort of thing because I know it's insincere, but this time I was sure it was genuine. She was so naive, so unsubtle."

"The way you read that line suggests she wasn't."

"Don't jump cues," Margola snapped. And for my impatience, I had to wait until she had drawn three or four puffs on her cigarette.

"Well, I gave the wretched girl clothes to wear. I gave her twenty-five dollars a week. All she had to do was tend to my correspondence, send out pictures, and so forth. Some letters she was to answer without bothering me, but anything that she felt needed my particular attention she was to show to me. At first she was ideal. Then after a month or so she began to annoy me."

"How?" I couldn't help asking.

"By staring at me. She stared at me all the time. I would turn around suddenly and catch her eyes on me. It gave me the creeps. Finally, I couldn't stand it any longer. I suddenly realized that she was studying me, imitating my gestures, my ways of speech, almost doing the same things. It was like having a living shadow. At last I told Clement that he should use the girl at the office, that she could attend to my mail there instead of at home. I wanted to get her out of the house, and at the same time I didn't want to fire her. I still felt sorry for her. Besides, her work was very satisfactory.

"Clement was delighted with her," Margola continued, a little thin-lipped. "His own secretary had just left to be married and this girl fitted right into her place. She began to read plays for us and made some quite intelligent observations. Then one day we had a rehearsal— it was when we were putting Miss Caswell into the sister part—and I had a toothache and didn't go.

"My understudy hadn't been called. She was out, and the stage manager wasn't able to get in touch with her. Eve had gone to the rehearsal with Clement to take his notes, and when there wasn't anybody to do my part, she volunteered. Clement told the stage manager to give her the script so that she could read it, and to his amazement she said, 'Oh, I don't need that.' Well, my dear"—Margola leaned closer to me as the car spun around a corner—"would you believe it, she knew every line of my part? Not only every line but every *inflection,* every *gesture.* Clement was there to watch Miss Caswell and he said he forgot all about her, he was so fascinated by Eve's unexpected performance."

"Was she really good?"

"Good?" Margola raised a penciled eyebrow. "Good? She was marvelous! Clement even hinted she was slightly better than I am. He didn't dare say so, of course, but he teased me that she was. He said if he'd closed his eyes he wouldn't have known the difference."

"What about the Norwegian accent?"

"Apparently"—Margola shrugged—"that just went. I understand why now."

"I don't," I said.

"You will," Margola stated bluntly. "Anyway, Clement was so amazed at the girl's exhibition that he took her out to tea afterward. She confessed to him that she had always wanted to be an actress and asked him to help her. Asked *him*—not me! Don't you think that was hatefully deceitful?"

I admitted that it was, but I thought privately that the girl had been rather smart. Great actresses are not noted for encouraging brilliant ingenues.

"She told him that she'd only stood around my stage door because she wanted to meet *him,* that she considered him the most brilliant director and producer in New York. He didn't tell me that. I found it out later. But Clem was very flattered. After all, he's only a man, and I get more than my share of attention. He's always introduced as Miss Cranston's husband—it probably irritates him more than he admits. But here was somebody looking up at him with saucer eyes, telling him he was wonderful, and he fell for it. He told me she was the most talented young girl he had seen in years, that we must help her. I said nothing. I knew I had to handle this very carefully. I asked Eve why she hadn't told *me* she wanted to be an actress and asked *me* to help her. She had the nerve"—Margola paused for effect—"to tell me she knew I wouldn't like the competition."

I laughed out loud. It was so ridiculous. Even the best actors in her supporting casts have a tendency to melt into the scenery when Margola gets into her stride. "She doesn't lack ego," I chuckled.

"Ego!" Margola stubbed out her cigarette in the ashtray. "Wait till I tell you about the letter! It arrived several days after this rehearsal. Eve came to my dressing room before the performance with four or five letters. This particular one was among them. She told me that she thought I ought to give them my personal attention. I put them into my purse, took them home, and forgot about them.

"Several days later, Eve asked me if I had read them, and I said that I hadn't. She particularly urged me to do so. I promised to, but I still put it off. I hate reading mail. In a few days, she was nagging me again to know if I had read the letters. I still hadn't. That night Alice told me that Miss Harrington had come to my dressing room while I was on stage and had gone through my pockets and my purse looking for something.

"I didn't like that, and after the show I called Eve down for it. She said she was looking for those letters, that there was one that, on second thought, she felt I ought not to see. I said that as she had given me the letter in the first place it was a little absurd to decide now that I shouldn't see it. But whether I read the letters or not, she was never again to go through my things.

"She burst into tears and cried that she only wanted to spare me pain. I had been so kind to her, she didn't want my feelings hurt. She had only given me the letter because when she had first read it she had been so thrilled that she wanted me to see it; thinking it over, she realized that it might hurt me.

"I remarked that after the things critics had written about me, nothing in any letter could possibly faze me.

"I realize now that this entire performance was to get me to read that letter without any more delay, and I'm sorry to say it worked. That night when I got home it was the first thing I did. It was very easy to pick out the one she was referring to. It went something like this—

"Dear Miss Cranston,

"Today I was buying a ticket to see a performance of your play. The door to the theater was open, and as I could hear voices and no one was watching the door I wandered inside to see what was going on. It seemed to be a rehearsal. A young girl was playing the part that I recognized, when I saw the actual performance, as your role—I presume she was your understudy. I know that stars of your caliber are always jealous of the ability of young people, but my dear Miss Cranston, I put you above such petty feelings. I am sure that loving the theater as you do, you will wish to enrich it. In your company, hidden backstage, is the most brilliant young performer I have ever seen. I was spellbound. She brought all your ability plus youth to the part. I waited outside for this young girl and asked her name. It was Harrington. Do help her to get the break she so richly deserves.

"It was signed 'One of your devoted followers.' "

"Of course she wrote it herself," I gasped.

"I think so," Margola said. "I was positive, but it was typewritten, so I couldn't prove it. The next day I merely said to Eve that it was quite a coincidence that the theater door was ajar when she happened to be rehearsing my part. We never mentioned it again."

I resisted comment. I could sense Margola was working up to a big scene.

"Not long after this, the John Bishop auditions came up."

I nodded. John Bishop is one of Broadway's better producers. Every season he holds auditions where talented unknowns can come and do a scene of their own choosing on the stage of his theater. The judges are other producers, talent scouts from film companies, and agents. Mr. Bishop's official reason for this competition is his altruistic desire to give embryonic thespians a chance to be seen—the winner often steps right into a Broadway show.

"Well, darling," Margola went on, "Eve was crazy to participate in Johnny's auditions. She went to Clem and pleaded with him to give her an introduction to Johnny. He said it wasn't necessary, that she merely had to fill in the application blank in Johnny's office and when her turn came she would be called.

She found that to be true, and from then on she was no use as a secretary at all. She was in a complete dither about what scene to do and wanted Clement to advise her and coach her. I told her to do a scene from *A Kiss for Cinderella* as I felt she was rather the pathetic, wistful type, but Clem picked out a bit of Ibsen—Hilda in *The Master Builder*—because it would suit her Scandinavian accent.

"She naturally took Clement's advice—not mine. She studied the scene, and when she had memorized it Clement heard her go through it. He came home enthralled. Again, he thought she was marvelous. He insisted that I come down to the theater and give her some suggestions. By this time I was so curious to see this future Jeanne Eagels that I consented. One day before the matinee, I went to the theater early and she did the scene for me."

"Was she really terrific?" I asked.

"I was impressed," Margola admitted reluctantly. "She was talented, there was no question about that. She had a marvelous voice and she read the lines with great sincerity, though this didn't disguise the fact that she was utterly inexperienced and awkward. I suppose that didn't show up when she was copying me in my part because she had me for a model. I did what I could to help her to hide these defects and showed her a few other little tricks, and she picked them up quickly enough. I wasn't as excited as Clement, but I could see that there was something to his statements.

"The auditions took place in a few days. She got down to the finals, and then, on the big day, won them. Everybody was terribly excited about her. Movie scouts knocked themselves out to make tests of her, agents wanted to put her on their files. She thought she was made. She was a star overnight, so now the story could come out."

"What story?"

"Her story. Her true story. Pathetic, wistful, naive Eve Harrington gave out an interview to the newspapers on how she had fooled the finest actress in the theater for several months!"

"Fooled you? How?"

"In every way. Her entire story was a piece of fiction. She'd never been any closer to San Francisco than Milwaukee, where she was born. She was Norwegian by descent, but had picked up her accent from a waitress in her father's restaurant. Her parents were safely in Wisconsin."

"Why did she want an accent?"

"Glamor, my dear. So many foreign actresses are successful here. She thought an accent would make her."

"But the parents being trapped by the war in Norway. What was the point of that?" I asked.

"Sympathy. The husband was a plea in the same direction."

"You mean she wasn't a widow?"

"She'd never been married."

"My God!" I said.

"The entire plot was a masterpiece of detail," Margola went on, enjoying my amazement. "In Milwaukee she had been a secretary with stage ambitions. She saved enough money to come to New York and live for six months. Once here, she laid a careful campaign to get ahead in the theater. She made up her mind to become acquainted with Clem and me. I think her ideas went even further. I believe she planned to break up our marriage.

"Being married to a big producer-director would just suit Eve. She once made a remark to me that every important actress in the theater had a successful man behind her. That part hadn't jelled, but the rest had worked pretty well. As Clem's secretary she had met most of the big agents, playwrights, and important actors. Now, in addition to these contacts, she'd received a chance to show her ability and had come off the winner.

"It looked very amusing in print that director Clement Howell had had a genius right in his own office and that it had remained for another producer to discover her. Poor Clem took a lot of kidding on that score. That interview was the loudest crowing I ever read. The funniest part was how I had fallen for that stuff about her being my great fan. It made her out an even greater actress—that she had played a role in real life so convincingly that we had both been taken completely for a ride. I could have strangled her. Naturally, she didn't wait to be fired. She resigned as Clem's secretary—told him she couldn't be tied down to an office any longer.

"She began to dress in clothes and costumes that would be

noticed. And she began to wear makeup in quantity because the report on most of her screen tests was 'no sex appeal.' "

"Why is she still standing at your stage door?" I asked. "I don't understand."

"That's where we had the last laugh," said Margola brightly. "The only thing happened that she hadn't bargained for. You know what Broadway is like. One day you're the toast of the town and the next you're forgotten. She was too inexperienced to have learned that real and lasting success is built only on a long-term foundation. She thought she was all set, and it went to her head. She took a few more screen tests but didn't photograph well enough to be sensational, and Hollywood doesn't bother to experiment with lights and makeup unless you have a real hit behind you. She was an odd type—certainly not the conventional ingenue—and no part turned up for her. Pretty soon the agents and producers just forgot about her. She couldn't even get in to see John Bishop himself, and she was his official protegee.

"That's when she came crying back to Clem and me. She says she'll stand at the stage door every night until I forgive her, that she was a silly fool when she gave out that interview. That she really did adore me and at first her only thought had been to get to know me. That she'll be everlastingly grateful if we will only help her to get a part. But I don't fall into the same trap twice," said Margola determinedly. "So far as I'm concerned she can stand at that entrance until she turns into a statue. I shan't lift a finger to help her."

"It's rather a pity," I said, "since you say she really is talented."

"So what?" Margola said. "Lots of girls are talented and never get a chance to show it. She had a chance, and she muffed it by her own conceit. She'll never get another opportunity."

"Probably not." I sighed and stared through the car window at the reflected stars twinkling like footlights in Little Neck Bay. No, I thought to myself, the little girl with the red coat will probably spend the rest of her life in obscurity.

But I was wrong. So was Margola. Eve Harrington had that rare second chance. I curse the day that she got it. For Margola was right. Eve was a bitch. I know, for it was through me that opportunity knocked twice on her door.

Several weeks after Margola told me this story, Lloyd finished his new play and a prominent manager made immediate plans to produce it. It was a strange play, different from anything Lloyd had written before and very hard to cast. There was one part which presented a real dilemma. It required a young emotional actress of great strength and power. At the same time, it wasn't large enough for a star, having only three scenes.

Lloyd and the manager tried actress after actress, and no one was right. He wanted a certain timid quality that was apparently unobtainable from the synthetic blondes of Broadway. I knew where he could find it. I knew the perfect girl was standing at Margola's stage door. I had never forgotten the shy expression in Eve Harrington's wide eyes. Finally, when in desperation the manager was about to call the production off, I suggested her to Lloyd.

"Go around there," I suggested. "She always wears a red coat. You can't miss her. If you wash the makeup off her face, you'll have exactly the right type. Furthermore, I hear she really can act."

Lloyd thought I was kidding, but finally he did as I told him. Eve read the part the next day, and they gave it to her. The search was over.

All through rehearsals, Lloyd and the director carefully coached Eve to hide her awkwardness. Lloyd began taking her out to lunch to talk about the part. On the opening night, she walked off with the show. It was a hit, and I had to admit it was partly her performance.

Her notices were amazing. The movies got excited about her all over again. This time, with her success behind her, her tests were a different story. What had once struck Hollywood as a lack of sex appeal now was called a "a rare quality." So Eve is on the train with her contract in her pocket.

I'm going on a trip also. I'm heading for Reno to get a divorce. For in spite of her success, Eve had found the time to get engaged to a famous playwright. She's going to marry my husband, Lloyd Richards.

If you have enjoyed this book and would like to receive details of other Walker Mystery-Suspense Novels or join our *Crime After Crime* Book Club please write to: